Praise for *The Collarbound*

'Zahabi deftly creates a fully-realized and richly described world, providing a quiet yet striking exploration of the way inequality and injustice often serve as the bedrock of systems of power'   M. J. Kuhn, author of *Among Thieves*

'Oh, my heart! What an imaginative plot! What fantastic writing! What awesome characters! And what an incredible world!'   NetGalley Reviewer

'Beautifully wrought dark fantasy'   NetGalley Reviewer

'*The Collarbound* by Rebecca Zahabi is a wonderfully imaginative novel which revels in mystery, intrigue, and dazzling magic, set against the backdrop of a world torn by rebellion. This is a story of closely guarded secrets and of characters who are caught between two warring sides'
fantasy-hive.co.uk

'*The Collarbound* is pure entertainment'   libridraconis.com

THE COLLAR BOUND

Tales of the Edge: volume 1

Rebecca Zahabi

This edition first published in Great Britain in 2023 by Gollancz

First published in Great Britain in 2022 by Gollancz
an imprint of The Orion Publishing Group Ltd
Carmelite House, 50 Victoria Embankment
London EC4Y 0DZ

An Hachette UK Company

3 5 7 9 10 8 6 4 2

Copyright © Rebecca Zahabi 2022

A CIP catalogue record for this book is
available from the British Library.

ISBN (Mass Market Paperback) 978 1 473 23439 0
ISBN (eBook) 978 1 473 23440 6

Typeset at The Spartan Press Ltd,
Lymington, Hants

Printed and bound in Great Britain by Clays Ltd,
Elcograf S.p.A.

www.gollancz.co.uk

Mum,
Happy birthday, today and for the many to come.

Chapter One

Tatters knew the girl was a newcomer by the way she stared at him. City folk didn't stare at collarbounds. But people who didn't know what it was were attracted to the glint of gold, and they didn't know any better, and they looked. Not that Tatters had anything against newcomers. There had been a time when he didn't know what a collarbound was, either.

The tavern was crowded this evening. The wood had soaked up the beer and puke from generations of apprentices, and now, thanks to the heat of too many bodies, the heady aroma was seeping out of the old beams. The owner was pouring foamy drinks into wooden tumblers. He took a copper for the cup, which he kept if you became too drunk to give it back. He was all right. He rented the room upstairs to Tatters and never asked questions. Questions weren't good for trade; besides, Tatters was good at bringing customers in.

At the start of autumn, the young mages who had recently been recruited poured into the high towers of the Nest. The first evening, guided by older apprentices, they left their Nest and flooded the streets. The ones who had been around long enough came to see Tatters.

The girl stood out immediately. She was the only human Tatters had ever seen with a tattoo. It covered the left side of her face, from chin to brow. It was weird, ragged, the black lines smudged as if the ink had spilt. She had dark curly hair, the kind that wouldn't fall down her shoulders and couldn't be brushed. Tatters winked at her and she – at last, but too late – turned away.

He wondered who the girl had come with. The tavern – which locals called the Coop – was crowded, and he soon lost sight of her in the throng. Amongst the apprentices jostling each other for space, Tatters spotted Kilian. She must be with him, judging by the way he tailed her, guided her to the counter, handed her a drink. He was taller than her; older but not that much older. They all looked like children to Tatters, these twenty-something kids who thought the city was theirs. Kilian flounced about as if he owned the place. Of course, he'd been here a year already and was officially a disciple.

Most of the guys who'd been around a year or more were assigned newbies and the task of showing them around, which they did either by flirting with them or teasing them, depending on their mood. Kilian was blond-haired, blue-eyed, and tall-ish, so he was often considered attractive by the female population. But he wasn't charming, and he wasn't much of a magician. She'd grow tired of him soon enough.

Well, it would only be a matter of time before they came to talk to him. Kilian would want to show off. Tatters relaxed against the wall, resting his shoulders against the stones. He liked this part. Meeting people was fun. He wouldn't have chosen a tavern as a refuge if he didn't believe that.

It took fifteen minutes. Kilian joined him with the girl and a mismatched group of apprentices from the first and second years. Soon they were pulling stools across, shouting greetings to Tatters. He touched wrists with a few people before turning to Kilian.

'May you grow tall, young man. Haven't seen you in a while.' Tatters smirked. You had to laugh with these young ones, otherwise they got on your nerves.

Despite his good looks, Kilian didn't know where to put all of himself. He reminded Tatters of a dippy horse that couldn't work out how to use four legs at the same time.

'Good to be back, Tatters,' said Kilian. Before he could do the introductions, Tatters turned to the girl. She was too dark-skinned to be from the city, but her features weren't quite Sunriser. She held his gaze.

'And I'm sure I've never seen you,' said Tatters.

She extended her forearm and they touched wrists. He could feel her eyes sliding down his face to his throat. The circle of gold was so close to his skin that it could have been part of his neck – a metallic deformity.

'Isha,' she said. A Sunriser name, then, probably Wingshade. She didn't hesitate before asking, 'Is Tatters your real name?'

Kilian rolled his eyes at her.

'As real as any name,' said Tatters.

He'd been around long enough to be careful about who he gave his name to. The people who knew the real one were far away; far enough that he would never have to worry about them again, hopefully.

But you're still in hiding, whispered Lal inside his mind.

Nice of you to remind me, he thought back.

To brush away Isha's frown, Tatters said, 'Don't worry. Within the safe community of the Nest, everyone knows everyone's name.'

'And you're not part of the safe community, then?'

'I told you we'd go deep tonight,' whispered Kilian. Tatters tried not to laugh. He hid it as a sort of cough behind his mug of ale.

She crossed her arms. Clearly struggling to get used to the Nest's robes, she tugged at the cloth to make herself comfortable on her stool. Tatters was perched at one end of a bench, the plank nailed into the wall to form a sort of booth, which he shared with Kilian. The thrum of voices echoed across the tavern.

Tatters was curious about the girl, not least because of the tattoo. He could see why Kilian had been drawn to her. Isha had a strange intensity about her. She must be eighteen, nineteen at a stretch. She hadn't quite shaken off the ungainliness of that in-between age, half an adult, half a child.

'I'm not a regular mage, as you might have guessed,' Tatters said. He sipped some beer, considering his options. 'Hey,' he spoke only to her. 'How about I ask you a question you don't want me to ask, and then you ask me a question I don't want you to ask?'

Kilian seemed nonplussed at this. He must have planned to speak about duels and impress Isha with his knowledge of underground mindbrawling. But Tatters wasn't much interested in Kilian or what he believed to be deep. He was curious about this tattoo. He wasn't sure what it represented. It could be an outstretched wing, or a cliff-edge, or a monstrous hand with too many fingers. It was difficult to pin down.

He had the eerie feeling he'd seen the pattern before, but he couldn't place it. Something thrummed at the back of his skull, a half-recalled dream. A hand covered in blood, fingers stained – or maybe it wasn't blood but cloth, red cloth, running down like liquid from the clenched fist. But the moment he tried to remember it, the image faded.

Not wanting to be left out, Kilian chipped in, 'I didn't know Tatters answered questions for anyone. Lucky you!'

'Go paint your face and you might have a chance,' chuckled someone further down their table.

4

Isha's expression didn't change. 'What makes you think I've got a question for you that you don't want me to ask?'

Tatters smiled. Cute, but he'd been playing this game much longer than her.

'You mean you've got nothing to ask the first collarbound you've ever met?'

She bristled, clenching her jaw, which only seemed to emphasise the black lines along her cheek. Body art like that wasn't human. Only khers did it. Tatters would have sworn it was a tribal kher tattoo, if it hadn't been on a human – and on a mage, at that.

'Very well,' said Isha. She cast him glares that would have withered a twenty-year-old hoping to score. Kilian was trying to find a way back into the conversation, but Isha spoke before he could: 'Go on. Ask me. I know what it's going to be, and you won't like the answer anyway.'

'I was going to say ladies first, but if you insist . . .' Tatters wondered if it would be too cheeky to ask her to show him more of the tattoo by pushing the tangled hair out of the way, and decided it would. 'Where does that tattoo come from?'

'My parents did it to me when I was born. That's all there is to know.'

Isha hadn't uncrossed her arms, although she'd rested them on the sticky table. She was hunched there, a dark shape in the flickering light of the tavern. There was clatter and laughter around them, but she stayed in that position, her grey robes creasing around her waist.

Tatters didn't push, but he was puzzled. What had gone through her parents' minds, branding their newborn like a kher?

If it really was her parents who did it, thought Lal.

Not everyone lies as much as we do. Give the girl the benefit of the doubt.

5

Why?

Tatters couldn't argue with Lal. He drank some more beer. He didn't even taste it any more, he was so used to it. It could have been water.

'Where does the collar come from?' Isha asked.

'A collarbound is someone bound by magic to obey his master. This is what the collar is. A bind.' Tatters was used to this. It was like the beer; he couldn't taste it anymore.

'That doesn't answer my question.'

Tatters lifted an eyebrow. Isha hadn't budged. Kilian glanced from her to Tatters, before giving Tatters a grimace behind her back, as if to say, 'terrible manners, I know'.

'I asked where it came from.'

Good for her, laughed Lal inside Tatters' head.

Whose side are you on?

Give the girl that, at least. She's right. And what you've just said, Kilian could've told her.

Someone opened the door of the Coop, and cold night air wafted in. As soon as it shut, the din and smell of sweat closed in on him once more – the heat of people, the shouting across the room, the surfaces glistening with grime.

'Fine,' he said. 'Where it comes from…' How to put it? 'It comes from the other side of the Shadowpass,' he said at last, relieved to have found a way to say it that didn't involve unpacking the past.

'I lived close to the Shadowpass,' she said. 'You crossed?'

'I crossed.' Although not during the light-tide, like you should, like everybody did. But there was no point in admitting he had crossed during the night-tide. For one thing, nobody would believe him.

If she had lived close to the Shadowpass, like she said, then all the more reason *not* to believe him. She must have seen her share of poor fools caught by the night-tide, emerging wrecked on the other side. It messed you up, crossing the Shadowpass, even when it went well. That was one of the reasons there was so little contact between both halves of the country – because the crossing was so tough. Not much was worth the trip.

'Trying to get out of trouble, were you?' said Kilian, giving Tatters a prod with his elbow. He smiled widely, showing too much tooth and lip.

'I'm always trying to get out of trouble.'

'One of the downsides of being too good at mindbrawl, I guess,' said Kilian. 'Speaking of which, will you give us a demonstration?'

Isha's interest perked up; she pulled her stool closer to the table. Tatters stretched, cracking his fingers as he tugged them towards the ceiling.

'We'll see. If someone's up for a fight, I might consider it.' He eyed Kilian, but the boy hated getting messy. If he could watch, he would. If he could avoid getting involved, all the better. Kilian was a sore loser – and of course, Tatters would win a mindbrawl. Plus, no point in losing in front of his maybe-girlfriend on the first night out. No, the lad wouldn't fight tonight.

'What was home like?' Tatters turned towards Isha, trying to change the subject.

'Different,' she said. She glanced around the room, trying to find a way to express the change. 'Going from my village to this is …'

'It's always a shock,' interrupted Kilian. Tatters did wish he would shut up. Isha might have something interesting to say, but Kilian only came out with platitudes and, occasionally, dirty jokes. 'The city is so big, isn't it?'

'Yes,' she agreed.

Tell me something I don't know, thought Tatters. Lal did the mental equivalent of a shrug.

'The village I was sent to this summer was a bore,' said Kilian. Disciples were usually dispatched to different areas during the summer, so they could learn first-hand how a mage ruled over a piece of land. 'Nothing happened. I helped the local mage organise the harvest and decide on the price for brews and flour. I wrote reports that I'm pretty sure nobody at the Nest reads. That's about it.'

He didn't seem to notice the conversation subject was also a bore. Isha turned to Tatters and asked: 'You do fights?'

Tatters nodded. Kilian launched into an enthusiastic explanation of how a mindbrawl went, and how you could duel someone, and how it was forbidden outside the Nest, and how you could do it with Tatters. This, supposedly, would awe Isha. She didn't seem awed so far.

'We did cock fights in the village,' she said.

Tatters burst out laughing. She cracked an inch of a smile when he did, just about visible under the thick black hair.

'This isn't cockerels! It's a clash of minds!' said Kilian. So much for impressing the new girl.

It brought in money, as far as Tatters was concerned, and it meant he could keep informed about the Nest. The apprentices coming to see him for extra training – and drinking afterwards – meant his room was kept at a few silvers a week. He was on the edge of legality, but he suspected the high mages didn't mind. He would know if the Nest disapproved. A bit of fighting cleared the air, the teachers believed, and kept everyone on their toes.

'Could I do it?' Isha's voice snapped Tatters out of his reverie.
'What?'
'Could I duel you?'

8

Kilian's eyes goggled. Someone nearby laughed loudly. The right answer was 'no', but to the underworlds with right answers.

'How often have you used mindlink?' asked Tatters.

Isha shrugged. She pushed up the heavy wool sleeves of her robes, knotting her fingers together, resting her tanned forearms on the table.

'They gave me a talk today.' She held his gaze.

The farm girl who wanted to prove herself. Too young to impress the adults. Too much of a peasant to impress the city-dwellers. Too much of a newcomer to impress the mages. And the tattoo everyone looked at, which meant they only asked about that and never about her. Yes, he could read her without even using mindlink. It had happened to him, too. He'd been sick of people mentioning the collar and forgetting to ask if he was more than what was etched across his skin.

'Why not? Kilian, will you be so good as to be the settler?'

It was difficult to know if Kilian was more shocked by Isha offering the challenge, or Tatters accepting it.

'You won't hurt her, will you?' He gaped.

'If I've never hurt you, I won't hurt her.'

'If you're sure...' Kilian addressed this as much to Isha as Tatters. She shrugged.

'I'm here to learn,' she said.

'That's the spirit.' Tatters smiled. This evening promised to be interesting.

As the settler, Kilian created a space inside his mind, a mental platform where they could meet. He had an imagery that he had built for that purpose. Tatters stepped inside Kilian's mind. It was a theatre of velvet chairs and wrought balconies, with ornate statues at every corner. The stage was the space where the duellists fought. Kilian wanted to impress his guests with complicated, several-storeys-high architecture and detailed decoration.

The problem was, he wasn't a good enough mage. Around the third level the seats disappeared into a black fog, where Kilian was hazy on how the roof linked to the balconies. Some statues started melting if guests focused on them hard enough, like carved chunks of soft cheese. The perspective didn't work; the chairs were mismatched sizes depending on their distance from the stage, and the pillars didn't always reach the ceiling or the floor. The overall effect was an ambitious sketch from someone who had no idea how to draw, and who had grown bored with the exercise halfway through.

Kilian imagined himself in a chair close to the stage. He didn't need to – he *was* the arena, from its floorboards to its columns. But some mages found it easier to visualise a space if they could place themselves inside it.

Isha stumbled inside the arena, struggling to find her footing. Inside Kilian's mind, she was different. She looked the way she believed herself to be, which wasn't flattering. She painted herself plumper, and smudged the tattoo even more, as if the ink had been flung at her face. She appeared younger, too, with less refined features, more of the ruddy peasant girl she must have been told she was.

Tatters knew how to draw himself in someone's mind. He made himself taller – a few extra inches couldn't hurt. He thickened his hair, giving it more shine. He cleaned away some of the freckles that dappled his skin. Most importantly, he didn't try to underplay the collar. If anything, he thickened the rim of gold and made sure it burned with inner light, adding decorations to the plain line of metal cutting across his throat.

'You attack,' said Tatters. 'See what you can do. See what

you can imagine. Trust me, you probably won't hurt me. I'd be surprised if you grazed me.'

Isha gritted her teeth. She lifted both her hands, palms towards Tatters. This kind of gesturing could help you concentrate, but it didn't affect the strength of your mindbrawl. She imagined fire and hurled it at him. He imagined water, crashing down from the pulleys and other special effects gear hanging fuzzily above the stage, dousing the flame before drenching her. She jumped in shock at the cold. First contact with mindlink was always surprising, especially if the imaginings used against you were well-crafted, using all five senses. Tatters was good. He knew she could taste salt on her tongue.

The water dribbled between the stage's wooden floorboards and was gone. She stood, straggled, wet.

'Dry it off,' said Tatters.

'How?'

'Just imagine yourself dry,' he said.

It took her a while. Kilian was sitting on the front row, on a chair of frayed red velvet. 'Should I let anyone else in?' he asked.

'Be a gentleman,' said Tatters. 'The last thing she wants is an audience.'

Isha shook herself dry. She brushed back her black hair, tucking the curls behind her ears.

'You're doing something,' she said.

Tatters shrugged. 'You'll have to be more specific.'

She waved at him. 'You're … manlier.'

'Ouch!' he laughed. She had bite. He couldn't help but enjoy her frankness. He wondered what she saw when she looked at him: the lanky red hair – which usually surprised Sunrisers – the freckles down his arms, the mark of age and weathered skin over his face. The unkempt beard growing in sprouts across his cheeks, which he trimmed only when he remembered to. He was lean, even when he had eaten well, and the rags he was wearing were too large for him, which revealed how gaunt he was. He wondered what she guessed of who he was while she watched him, and whether it was as crude as what he guessed of her.

He drew himself to his full height, which became taller as she watched. He changed the rags he wore into a dyed shirt and matching trousers. 'Why should I let you see me as I am when I can show you what I could be?'

She fumbled around for a while as she tried to grow herself. 'Size isn't everything,' said Kilian.

'Later on, not now, practise thinking about your perfect self. A good shell to visit other people's minds is something you need to work on.'

She nodded. At least she didn't blabber as much as Kilian. During his first fight with Tatters, the boy had barely stopped long enough to breathe.

Isha studied Tatters, then Kilian lounging in his gilded chair.

She wants to impress him as much as he wants to impress her, whispered Lal.

Shouldn't you be making sure no-one gets inside my mind while I'm doing this? Tatters wasn't so much bothered as amused. Lal was showing unusual interest. They were both curious about this tattooed Isha, for whatever reason. It was something about the energy she radiated, he decided. As if she believed she could take over the world.

I was sharing my female insights with you, Lal said.

Noted.

Isha suddenly lifted one hand and did a power grip in front of her.

'Kneel, slave!'

It was a good attempt, but only half-hearted. She didn't expect him to bend the knee; she probably would've felt bad if he had.

The collar glowed, but the pang that squeezed Tatters' heart was only that – a pang.

'Everyone goes for the collar, girl.' But still, she'd gone from physical manifestations, such as fire, to more cerebral attacks. It was an improvement.

'But there must be something there, right?'

'Of course. But it's also where I'm most expecting you. And, to tell you the truth, no-one has ever managed to get the collar to work in a mindbrawl against me. Everyone tries it, but it never works.'

Except for the times it did. But that was a long time ago, and the memory was faded, like an oil painting smudged with a wet sponge. Tatters was careful to keep such recollections as far away as possible, especially during a fight.

'You're not all there,' said Isha.

'Why should I be? You're not enough of a threat.' He knew from her expression that she was stung. Even with a settled mind, it betrayed what she was thinking. That would be something else to work on. But one thing at a time.

They sparred in Kilian's mind for a few more minutes; he stayed defensive for the whole brawl. He didn't want to risk hurting her. It was like fencing – if the opponent had no idea how to fight, and the weapons were sharp, then you didn't hit them, or only lightly, as lightly as you could, to be sure you wouldn't cut them.

Isha tried different tactics, but her imagination wasn't vivid enough. She lacked training, but that would come. Some of her approaches to mindbrawl were original and would prove dangerous to her enemies in the long run, if she ever got the discipline to practise. Some mages never did and remained mediocre their whole lives.

'Enough,' said Tatters, when he decided she was looking tired.

'Why?' asked Isha. 'I haven't even touched you yet.'

The faith she had in her own talent! He'd had that once. Like everyone else, life had kicked him in the teeth until he learnt otherwise. Maybe it was a bit early to start the teeth-kicking on Isha, though.

'No offence, but you won't do that any time soon,' he said. 'Now leave Kilian's mind. If he collapses it, you'll be stuck.'

'Collapses?'

'See what I mean? When you've got the basics of mindbrawl, come back to me, and we'll see if you can land a hit that hurts.'

Tatters left Kilian's mind. He opened his eyes. The sounds and lights of the tavern hit him in waves; voices first, then music from a bard in the corner, then the bangs of chairs being pushed back and the hiss of beer pouring out of kegs. He rubbed his arms and his shoulders, blinking a few times, trying to shake off the after-effects of mindlink. Isha sat very straight on her stool, her eyes vacant. Her lips were parted, a thin line of spittle running down the side of her mouth.

Tatters waved the tavern keeper over for another round of beer. The man picked up their empty tumblers to refill them at the barrels.

'Already starting on the duels?' the keeper asked.

'Nah, this was more like training.' Tatters indicated Isha with his chin. 'New to the game.'

'Good. Start them young.' The innkeeper glanced across the room, shaking his head. He rubbed the back of his hand against his beard to scratch it. 'Lucky sods, training without even getting up from their chairs, while I'm running around refilling cups, me. I'm getting too old for this, you know.'

'Get yourself a servant. Be sure to choose a kher, so they don't get mindlinked when counting the change.'

The innkeeper grunted. 'You think I'm rich or something?

Mages are the worst payers.' He was wearing kher horn himself, as a protection against mindmagic. It coiled around his forearm several times, annulated like a ram's horn, the spiral smaller towards the wrist, growing larger as it reached the elbow. It must have belonged to a small kher. It was tight on the innkeeper's arm; skin and fat bulged between the annulations.

Kilian snapped out of mindlink and gratefully downed the beer. Isha emerged as if from a deep sleep, struggling to place herself. She nearly fell off her stool, but Kilian caught her in time.

'Careful there!'

She rubbed her eyes and forehead. She hated being off-guard, Tatters could tell. At first, she refused the drink, but Kilian insisted. 'Sense of taste helps you come back,' he said. Reluctantly, she sipped the bitter ale.

Tatters gave them time together. He drank slowly and talked to a few other people around the table, or to apprentices who were curious about this closed mindbrawl and wanted to know the outcome. He told them it was only training.

'If you do free training, I'm up for it!' said someone.

'Nothing's free in this world,' Tatters answered.

Kilian couldn't believe his luck – Isha needed him after all, to help her hold onto her stool and to explain the after-effects of mindbrawl. She let him take her hand, and he used this as an excuse to bring her to the bench and hug her close.

She cast Tatters crushing glares, although he didn't see what he'd done wrong. They didn't stay long after that. When they left, Tatters crossed his hands on his lap and closed his eyes. It was getting late, but he couldn't be bothered pushing through the crowd for the relief of a bed. It would be as noisy upstairs as it was here, anyway. And this way, if someone wanted anything from him, they'd tap his shoulder or chat loudly next to him until he woke up.

Now that he didn't need to focus, memories of past training sessions drifted inside his mind. It hadn't always been as controlled as it was today, not when he was the one learning. The shock of the stick across his face. The blue and yellow bruise going from his thumb to his wrist. The first time Passerine introduced himself and told Tatters he would remember his name soon enough. The weight of the shield strapped across his left arm.

You don't want to go there, warned Lal.

The problem with being a mage was that remembering was never as easy as it had been. He was trained to keep an eye on his mind, and so nothing could ever drift, or emerge, or float to the surface. Everything was hand-picked.

'Tatters? You sleeping?'

Maybe it was for the best. Tatters put the memories away and opened his eyes. He knew this disciple – Caitlin. She was beautiful but, compared to Isha, she was bland. Auburn, tall, bristling with the energy of youth but lacking the motivation to do anything with it.

'May you grow tall, Tatters.'

They touched wrists. 'It's nice to see you too,' he said. 'How have you been?'

Caitlin was one of the older disciples. She worked with Tatters on his duels. She wanted to be rich and powerful and, because she had a face that could make boys swoon, she would be. But she didn't want to work too hard for it.

'I've spent the summer doing someone else's accounts and counting coin that wasn't mine. I'm fine.' She had a deadpan, sharp humour. 'Apparently you're doing free training for the puffins? I never got that.'

He rolled his eyes. 'Skies, I gave one free lesson to one cute face! Don't get excited, starting from now everyone is paying.'

She pulled her stool closer to the table, revealing her sleeves, where she had embroidered her grey robes with gold thread.

'As I understood it, it wasn't her pretty face. You were interested in her tattoo.'

'Curious. I wouldn't go as far as interested. But if you've got something to tell me, I might reconsider free training.'

'Well, I thought you might want to know which mage brought her in, for starters,' she said. That was true. Tatters hadn't thought to ask. Depending on who it was, it might have influenced how much training she'd had, or how they'd introduced her to the Nest. Although, she might just as well have been sent by her family after they experienced weird phenomena around her.

'Go on. Surprise me.'

'It wasn't someone sent off to pick up low-talented peasants across the countryside. It was a high mage who happened to meet her during his travels, and who decided she was too good to be left behind.'

Tatters picked up his half-empty cup and lifted it to salute Caitlin's speech.

'There's more,' she said. 'He's not a local mage. He's not from the Nest. He crossed the Shadowpass with news from the Sunrisers.'

'I'm interested now.'

So, someone had waded through the Shadowpass, then found Isha and dragged her all the way to the Nest. He obviously thought she was too important to let out of his sight. 'Who was the high mage?'

'A guy called Sir Passerine.'

A shiver ran down Tatters, starting at the nape of his neck and crawling down his spine. The hairs on the back of his arms rose.

'That's an original story.' He shrugged. 'Not quite good enough for a full training session, but I'll give you thirty minutes free. I'm running a business here.'

She grumbled and teased and grumbled some more, but he didn't yield. For one thing, he didn't want to show her that what she'd said mattered.

But we'll have to look into it, said Lal.

She was right, as always.

Chapter Two

Isha's head spun. She kept misjudging distances. She bumped her toes against the floor. She lurched; she stumbled. It was like being drunk, without the high. She kept trying to do something or say something and failing, as if it was the world that kept pulling itself away at the last minute, rather than her mind that was lagging behind.

'It's normal, mindlink does that to you,' Kilian kept repeating.

'Tatters looked fine,' she grumbled.

Kilian shrugged. 'He's used to it.'

They walked arm in arm. She'd tried to push him off, but without his support she was unbearably slow. It was best to lean on him, just a bit, to avoid the humiliation of falling over. Kilian was taller than her and, despite his slim frame, he was stronger. He didn't hold on hard, but she was sure he would keep her upright if her knees buckled.

They were with other apprentices, breaths stale with alcohol, some laughing, some shouting. It was her first day and she was already staggering back with a group of drunkards, needing help to put one foot in front of the other. What would Passerine think?

As they reached the outskirts of the city, the houses changed from stately stone to wooden shacks, before stopping abruptly, piled up against the city gates. Beyond, the houses were replaced by moorland, with the odd bunch of heather and wildflowers. Acres of untamed grounds surrounded the Nest, which meant the castle stood out on the horizon. Shrubland grew as far as the eye could see, except for a small forest to the right, hiding the lightborn Temple from view. But Isha knew it was there, perched above the Edge, threatening at any time to fall.

Beyond, the world abruptly ended.

Standing on the Edge, you might think you were at the top of a cliff. But this wasn't a cliff down which you could simply climb. It was the rim of the world. Beyond, there was nothing. Below, there were clouds and mist and, further down, the underworlds where the dead flew. Isha had never lived near the Edge. To think that you could drop and fall through all the underworlds made her shiver.

None of the other apprentices seemed to care. They threw their heads back and yelled at the stars to get ready for when they would ascend and join them. Four girls had linked arms, singing and dancing, swaying as they tried to stay together. Kilian joined in, although he was out of tune. The song dwindled when everyone started forgetting the lyrics.

'Are welcome days like this every year?' asked Isha.

Kilian laughed. Someone behind her said, 'You've seen nothing! Wait until the puffins get their act together!'

The puffins were the newbies. Like her. Because puffins are tiny and get bullied by seagulls, just like newcomers got bullied by disciples. And seagulls and puffins nested in the cliff, like the mages did.

'It's a pretty average first night,' said Kilian.

A wonder anyone gets any mindlink done.

Before the Nest, a cleft in the cliff ripped the earth into two jagged pieces. It wasn't so much a gorge as a scar across the countryside; a reminder that they were near the Edge, where pieces of the world sometimes fell into oblivion. It was full of wild, foam-white water, which curved in front of the Nest and then crashed over the Edge.

A bridge arched over the chasm – an impressive, if bleak, stone structure. Beneath it, metal chains were deeply embedded in both sides of the fissure, holding the pieces together. The links were of a thicker iron than men had ever forged, covered in a layer of rust. The legend had it that the same feathered giants who had built the Nest had made the chains to keep this sacred piece of the cliff from breaking off.

When Isha stepped onto the bridge, the rush of water below shook her chest. She clung to Kilian tighter. He rested his cheek playfully against the top of her head.

'Tatters was really into your tattoo,' he said.

'I know,' she muttered. He couldn't hear her above the roar of the river, and she had to repeat herself.

'I think it's awesome,' said Kilian. 'It suits you.'

He was being polite, but Isha appreciated the effort. So far, half the apprentices had pretended not to see the tattoo and the other half had asked nosy questions. One had even asked her if she was a halfbreed. At least Tatters hadn't asked her *that*.

Maybe sensing this was a sensitive topic, Kilian changed the subject. 'What do you think of your new home?'

'I'm not sure I think of it as home, yet,' she answered.

The Nest was a high castle, which went as far above ground as below. Some chambers opened up on the face of the cliff, peering down into the mist. On the left side of the Nest the rift continued, its river spilling over the Edge, a silver moonlit waterfall. The air all around was filled with spray. On the right, woodland separated the Nest from the Temple. Isha was used to hills and mountainsides, but here, where the horizon and the sky met, no land rose to meet the eye. Everything was flat.

And in front of them were the Nest's gates. They were higher than any humans would ever need, too big to be manned by one person, with metal strung across the wooden planks. At this time of night, they were closed. But in order for the apprentices to get back to their dormitories, the mages had built a more manageable, human-size door within them. A kher and a lawmage guarded it.

On either side of the gates sat a bleak blend of beggars. They slept at a distance from each other. A few were awake, and the whites of their eyes caught the light. They stared at the mages, muttering to themselves.

'Ignore the lacunants,' advised Kilian.

Isha nodded. She also forced herself to ignore the shudder that went up her spine and caught in her throat. She wasn't used to the lacunants' presence yet.

When they reached the doors, the girls in front of them squeezed past, teasing the lawmage. But he lifted his hand when he spotted Kilian and Isha.

'None of this, lad,' he told Kilian.

'What?' Kilian looked around, confused. He exchanged a glance with Isha. She didn't know what the lawmage meant, either. Self-conscious, she untangled her arm from Kilian's. Maybe he didn't want them to go through the doors holding hands.

The lawmage sounded bored.

'You want to go out with a mongrel, it's your business,' he said. 'But you don't bring them back to the Nest.'

Isha's stomach lurched. She took a step forward. 'I'm not…'

Before she could even finish her sentence, the lawmage interrupted her. His tone became sharp.

'Shut up, halfcow. You should know better than to try to get into the Nest. And I could get you fined for dressing up like an apprentice. But it's a long night, I'm tired of this shit, and I'm going nice on you. So, you trot home and we can forget about this.'

The kher guard didn't react to any of the insults. Her red tan stood out beside the lawmage's paler skin. She leant against the doorframe, arms crossed, chin pushed low on her chest. She scanned the people walking past and didn't seem to hear her colleague's comments. A torch was planted in the ground beside her. She had black horns, like a gazelle, which glinted in the firelight.

'You're making a mistake,' said Kilian. 'Isha isn't a halfbreed.'

From beyond the doors, a girl turned around and called for Kilian to come over. Childish laughter echoed across the inner courtyard. It rang in Isha's skull like a headache.

'I've heard it before, kid. But look, I'll show you I'm trying.' The lawmage turned to his colleague. 'Whatya think of her tattoo?'

The kher barely glanced at Isha. 'It's a kher tattoo, all right.'

The lawmage nodded and smiled, as if this was new, un-expected information. He gave them a beaming fake smile. 'Now, piss off.'

'I can mindlink,' said Isha. 'Halfbreeds can't do that, can they?'

Kilian stuck by her side. 'I've seen her.'

'You must have a register with all the apprentices,' Isha ploughed on. 'Can you check if my name is on it?'

The lawmage stretched to his full height and took a step towards them. His smile faded. When he crossed his arms in front of him, Isha spotted thick rings across his fingers. Some of the lacunants who had been clustered around the gates scrambled out of the way. One pointed at the rings and shouted some nonsense about lost treasure, before breaking into gasping sobs.

'Look.' The lawmage's voice was low, and Isha had to strain to hear it above the whimpering. 'Maybe you've only got a tiny bit of cowblood in you, and that's why you're all nice and hornless. But you're a kher, so unless you're wearing the uniform, you'll keep out of the Nest. Screw that inside your brain.'

Isha felt sick and tired; she wasn't ready for a fight. She backed down. Much to her relief, Kilian followed her. She had to rest one hand against the heavy oaken door – her eyesight was blurring. She thought she might throw up. The crying lacunant was clutching his chest and moaning like a banshee in the night.

'What are you going to do?' asked Kilian.

Isha swallowed a few times and rubbed her forehead with both hands. She hated herself as she said it: 'I think I need Passerine to let me in.'

I'm going to make a fool of myself in front of him.

'If you tell me where his chambers are, I'll ask him to come to the doors,' said Kilian.

She looked at Kilian's earnest expression. He wasn't charming – his brow was too large, his nose too long. He moved his hands too close to her face when he spoke, and she always felt he was going to land a finger in her eye. But this was a kind offer, from someone who didn't owe her anything, especially not bothering a high mage at night. Apprentices could get into trouble for less.

'That would be wonderful,' she said. 'Please.'

She told him where to find Passerine, in the guest wing of the Nest. Kilian said he would be back soon. When he slipped through the door, the lawmage snickered. The kher didn't. She could have been a statue.

Isha stepped away from the gates so she wouldn't have to hold the lawmage's eye, or see the disciples peeking as they passed through the doors. She stood before the river as it churned underneath her feet and listened to the white sound of swirling water. It crackled and spat like fire. It was so loud, it could have been anything – it could have been wind in the treetops, it could have been rain. She let the noise overpower her; it rushed through her mind, leaving it rinsed and cleared, like a pebble slick and smooth at the bottom of a stream.

She took a deep breath. The air was cold and wet. She touched her cheek where the tattoo was. Spray left damp lines on her fingertips.

The lacunants were returning to their shacks for the night, like birds going to roost. The shacks were flimsy wooden structures packed along the Nest's gates, vile things with rotted straw scattered inside. At least they left her alone.

The river arched, heading towards a sky that was freckled with stars. Beyond the Edge, the stars weren't only above her – they continued along the horizon and down the cliff. Isha had never seen stars below her. It gave her a feeling like vertigo, as if the world were upside-down and she was bound to fall.

At last, she heard Kilian's voice calling her. Part of her was relieved; part of her squirmed. She closed her fists tightly, then forced herself to spread out her fingers before turning around. She walked towards the gates. At least she felt sober now, in control of her senses.

Passerine was waiting for her, looming a head above Kilian. He stood out amongst the Duskdwellers and their pale complexions; his hair, eyes and skin were black.

The lawmage and the kher both straightened their postures at the sight of a high mage.

'Are the kids being too noisy?' asked the lawmage. 'I'll tell them to shut up.'

'No,' said Passerine. 'It's not them I have a problem with.' He was one of these men who, alongside their height and gait, had a very deep voice. It sounded like a long-forgotten instrument.

Passerine was clothed in dark robes, not his travelling outfit. Isha had never seen him in the deep dye of the high mages, with a golden brooch across the front of his cloak and the crest of the Nest sewn on the front fold of his robe. It gave him presence. Although he hadn't wrapped the cloth in the Sunriser style, he did have a long black scarf across his shoulders, a sacred nasivyati. He stood in silence by the gates and everyone, guards and apprentices, wriggled uncomfortably under his gaze. Even Kilian, who was beside him, looked as if he would rather be somewhere else.

He was searching the crowd for her. Isha felt like burying herself underground, but she gave him a wave. He nodded for her to come closer.

The lawmage spotted her and frowned. He mouthed something, probably a swearword or an order to get out of the way. The kher took a step backwards, so she wouldn't brush against the high mage by mistake.

'Let me introduce you to someone you need to know,' said Passerine.

Isha hesitated a short distance from the entrance, not wanting to annoy the lawmage even further. Passerine must have sensed her unease because he crossed the door with one easy stride and placed a hand on her shoulder. Heat seeped from his hand down her arm. He pushed her towards the lawmage as one would guide a dancing partner.

'As you can imagine, I hate having to get up at midnight to teach doormen how to do their work,' Passerine said. 'So, I will say this once.'

The lawmage was the colour of ash. He nodded. Behind him, the kher smiled at Isha. If anything, she seemed faintly amused.

'This young woman is Isha. She is an apprentice. She lives in

26

the Nest at my invitation.' Passerine gave the lawmage a long, hard stare. They said nothing for a few seconds.

Kilian caught Isha's eye from the other side of the door. He shoved his chin towards Passerine and wiggled his eyebrows. At first she couldn't make sense of his contortions. Then she understood what he was trying to tell her – the two men must be mindlinking.

Whatever had been said, the lawmage swallowed and answered, 'Of course, sir. My mistake.'

'It is,' said Passerine dismissively.

'I won't do it again.'

'No, I don't think so.'

The lawmage ushered Isha through the door, giving her a sheepish, we're-good-friends-really sort of smile. All the apprentices were gawking. It wasn't common for a high mage to get up in the middle of the night to protect a puffin. If her guardian had been less concerned about her wellbeing, they would have noticed her absence the next morning. She would have been allowed in – after breakfast for them, after sleeping rough for her.

Passerine didn't take his hand off her shoulder. She was conscious of the weight of it.

'Thank you,' she whispered to Kilian.

'It's the least I could do.' He smiled. 'Want me to walk you to your dorm?'

'Thank you, young man.' Passerine's voice was smooth, but it was the kind of softness that betrayed how hard it could become. Like molten metal, it was liquid for now, but could turn sharp. 'Your help is appreciated. I'll escort Isha.'

They crossed the courtyard together, leaving Kilian stranded behind. It was only when they reached the Nest's main hall that Passerine lowered his hand. Isha kept her face low. She couldn't bear to see his disappointment.

The Nest's front hall was a concave circle, like an upside-down dome. Legends assumed that it was more comfortable for the feathered giants to rest curled up inside the circle. It wasn't deep – only a slight inclination in the floor, not enough to make it awkward to walk. Isha could still hear water whispering through the large hall, despite the thud of their leather soles hitting the sandstone.

'I thought we would have this conversation tomorrow,' said Passerine, 'but in light of what has happened, now seems a good time.'

She sensed him glancing at her. She didn't look up. When she was with Passerine, she always seemed to say the most stupid thing that went through her mind. Whatever she did, she was gauche, and she sounded young and silly, like those cackling girls holding hands and smudging kisses on each other's cheeks, even though they barely knew each other.

'Tomorrow, most apprentices will ask a master to teach them,' Passerine went on, never breaking his stride. 'As you have witnessed tonight, it might be difficult to convince a teacher to take you on. Be sure to stand your ground.'

Isha nodded. The Nest worked through a complicated network of favours offered and returned, and although in theory only the supreme mage could decide where she was sent or which administrative tasks she fulfilled, in practice, it would be her powerful friends and foes who would make those choices.

She struggled to keep up. Passerine was fast, his robes billowing behind him as if he were gliding above the floor. The central hall was circled by balconies, from which announcements could be made to the people below. The balconies had been built to better use the space left by the giants. In the same way, the staircase leading up from the hall was too large for human feet, so mages had added wooden steps between each stone one.

When Isha and Passerine climbed up, the two kinds of steps had a different echo – muted on stone, loud on wood. Clunk, thud, clunk, thud, clunk.

'Won't you teach me how to mindlink?' she asked. She cringed at the shrillness of her voice compared to his.

Passerine shook his head. 'I won't be taking on apprentices.'

His tone was final. They reached the first floor in silence. Ahead, a tapestry hung from the wall, spilling from the ceiling all the way down to the beginning of the stairs. It was the Nest's heraldry: a golden castle with spires on a blue background. In the corridors beyond, Isha spotted draperies of gold, green and red; the silk glimmered in the dim light. Torches and kher guards stood at regular intervals.

They headed down the maze of corridors, each leading to rooms like the honeycombs of a beehive.

'Find people you trust to teach you,' said Passerine.

Isha wanted to blurt out that she trusted him – after all, he had brought her where she needed to be. He had escorted her from her farm all the way to the Nest, only to protect her. She held her tongue.

It was the end of the summer when Passerine had come to visit. He had been wearing a cape, poppy-red, wrapped around him like a sash in the Sunriser style. As the light-tide poured out of the Shadowpass, he'd arrived with a group of travellers, some of them on horseback, some of them on foot. Isha always waited with her foster brother at dawn beside the tunnel, to see who would emerge.

When these men and women surfaced from the pass below the Ridge, Isha had immediately known they weren't the usual wayfarers. They weren't merchants and tradesmen. These looked weary, bleary-eyed, their clothes and hair thick with dust. Whole families were gathered, mothers holding their children's hands, several dogs, some of the animals strapped with bundles of goods, a few lanky donkeys. Amongst them, towering above everyone else, standing straight despite the harrowing journey, was Passerine.

They were refugees.

She snapped out of her reflections as they reached the entrance to the female dormitory. Passerine stopped before the high oaken door. Like the gates, it contained a smaller door.

He untied a leather pouch from his belt and handed it to her. The clink was more subdued than metal coins would be.

'Here's some baina,' he explained. 'You can spend it inside the castle, but not the city.'

Isha opened the purse and counted the little bone coins. They were of various shapes, white with black outlines, each with a hole in the centre. She didn't know how to start thanking him for the help he'd given her. Before she could say anything, Passerine continued: 'The Nest pays its teachers, and you shouldn't spend anything for lessons. But if need be, use these to make sure a good mage takes you on.'

In other words, if they think you are a mixblood, buy them off. Isha's mouth was dry. She nodded.

Slipping through the tiny inset door into the dormitory, she felt like a cat slinking through a cat-flap. The thought made her feel better about the lawmage at the door.

Maybe I don't belong. But in the giants' Nest, no-one does.

***

Early in the morning, Tatters prepared to set off for the Nest. When he stretched, his fists bumped against the kegs of beer piled at the head of his bed. Yawning, he picked up his cloak, which doubled as a pillow when he slept. It wasn't technically a cloak but a stana – an unstitched piece of cloth that one could wear straight off the loom. Sunrisers believed very different things, depending on their ethnicity, but one idea that seemed to cross borders was that sewing was unholy; or, rather, that unsewn clothes – the nasivyati – were holy. Peasants could stitch their tunics, and warriors their armour, but a mage couldn't, not if they intended to ascend.

It had been a black stana originally, now it was the colour of mud. Tatters had owned it before he crossed the Shadowpass. Since, it had served so many purposes it could hardly qualify as a piece of clothing.

He plucked his belt off the broken chair where he'd draped it. The belt was a Duskdweller item. On the belt, he tied his purse, his keys and, after consideration, his knife. He unearthed his sandals from a pile of spare wooden cups. Their soles were so worn he might as well have walked barefoot.

You're taking ages, complained Lal.

It's barely dawn, said Tatters. *What's the rush?*

The fewer people in the Nest, the better.

Tatters stepped around the mess of chairs, stools, spare linen and empty barrels to reach the door of the attic. From there, the staircase brought him behind the counter. The innkeeper, who slept in the back room, wasn't up yet. Tatters let himself out through the front door.

The city was bustling with life – shopkeepers were opening their wooden shutters, placing them horizontally in front of their windows to serve as a counter on which to display their wares. Girls carrying buckets of water from the wells passed him in the street. A few khers milled about, their curved horns as black as onyx, their skin various shades of clay-red.

The mages' influence hung heavy in the air. Tatters could sense it, shifting slightly as he went through quarters belonging to different factions. He was always conscious of crossing a bound-ary, even when there was no-one to guard it. It was one of the downsides of being attuned to mindlink. The city reeked of the stench of the people fighting over it.

Aside from magic, the streets smelt of urine, rotten food and manure. Grooms brushed horses with hay to clean them before the day's work. Tatters stopped to pet a few on his way. The grooms were welcoming enough: it was bad luck to bother a collarbound, just as it was bad luck to shoo off a beggar.

He patted the warm flanks of the animals and, for those he knew best, stroked their soft noses and wished them good luck for the day to come. Most horses were overworked, with sores between their front legs and along their mouths. He touched those delicately, alleviating the pain through fleshbinding when he could.

When Tatters reached the central square, it was already full. Groups of children sat around the statue of the woman who cur-rently ruled the Nest, Lady Siobhan. They perched on her spread marble robes, lounging between the folds of stone. They spat in her upturned hands, to curse the mages and bring themselves some good fortune, which was rare enough amongst humans who weren't magicians. These children were born ungifted, which had condemned them from the start to being servants, farmers and thieves.

There was one girl with tangled red hair who reminded him of Lal. She was busy plucking lice from in between her toes.

In front of the statue there was something that could have been confused with a birdbath. It was a circle of stone on a small stand, filled with mercury. No birds were bathing in the glinting metal; ungifted kept well away from it. Mages used certain metals – mercury, gold – in combination with mindlink, suffusing them with imaginings, warnings, emotions. This wasn't as crude as a cut head stuck on a pole, but it carried the same meaning. Tatters gave it a wide berth.

He headed up a paved street two coaches wide that was already swarming with horses and people on foot. To avoid the bustle, he walked alongside the road, in the churned mud on the side of the track. The path led out of the city and into the moors, set in a straight line towards the Nest.

Tatters walked briskly, breathing in the cold morning air. He enjoyed stretching his legs. Now that the cramped buildings were behind him, Tatters could see the Nest looming on the horizon. A castle built for giants but inhabited by dwarves.

The giants made the collars, thought Lal. *Good thing they're all dead.*

Mist was rising from the rim of the cliff, draping the bottom of the castle in clouds. It gave the impression that the Nest was hanging in mid-air, about to float away. Seagulls mottled the sky with flecks of white. They flew off the Edge to catch fish from the river. Their screams filled the air, piercing above the thunder of the waterfall. Tatters didn't know how mages managed to sleep between the cries of birds and rushing of water.

He crossed the bridge. The great doors of the Nest, which required a crew of human hands and pulleys to manoeuvre, stood open. Merchants were already bringing food to the servants, who would then rush to prepare breakfast. By the time the mages dragged themselves out of bed, the Nest would have been awake and brimming for hours.

Across the threshold were beggars of a different kind – the lacunants. Tatters tried not to look at them nor catch their eye.

Whether the gates were open or closed, the lacunants stayed begging at the entrance. Their welcome didn't extend to the Nest's courtyard. Once Tatters had made his way through, it was a relief to be away from their glazed stares.

The Nest was built out of creamy sandstone, pockmarked by years of wind and rain. Its inner courtyard was large enough to set up a market inside. On the right was the gibbet to hang criminals from, with the prison just behind. On the left were the stables. And in front of Tatters was a series of arches, each one as large as the door of the tavern, all leading into the Nest's main hall. On either side of each arch, a kher stood guard. Only mages or their servants could cross into the Nest itself.

Tatters strolled closer, intending to walk past without asking for permission. That was usually enough to be let through. Nobody impeded a collarbound – at least, most days.

'What do you think you're doing?' A kher guard. Only khers could serve as efficient guardsmen within the Nest, as they were immune to mindlink. She was a woman, of course – most males weren't allowed to work. He spotted the sword at her side and gave her his best smile.

'Errands for my master,' he answered.

This didn't seem to woo her. 'And who would your master be?'

Tatters didn't hesitate. 'That's private information. I'd rather not tell.' He crossed his hands in front of him and brought his feet closer together, trying to display a servant's meekness.

The kher hesitated. This was above her paygrade. If she caused trouble for a high mage's servant, she would be in trouble too. She motioned for Tatters to follow her, and guided him towards the gibbet, where a watchtower had been set up for the guards. There, another female kher was talking to a group of disciples. The guard escorting Tatters waited for their conversation to finish before introducing him. Tatters stifled a sigh. Still, when he was presented to this second kher, he made an effort to smile.

She was smaller than him, with slim annulated horns that grew out of her forehead and curved around her skull to reach the bottom of her ears. Her hair rested in a bun between them. She'd polished the keratin of her horns until they shone ebony, and painted complex drawings across them. The tips were unpolished, a duller shade of black.

She repeated the same questions. He repeated the same answers.

'You are dismissed,' this new kher told the younger guard. The guard nodded and left them to it. 'You will have to answer, you realise,' she said, this time to Tatters.

'I doubt my master will be happy to hear I shared their name and errands with, no offence, simple doormen. Doorkhers.'

The kher pushed up her sleeves, and Tatters spotted tattoos across her scarlet skin, starting at the wrists. Triangles and circles, interlocked patterns like cogs in a wheel, followed the curves of her muscles. She crossed her arms.

'Not good enough, I'm afraid,' she said. 'You want in, you and your master have to be on the register.'

Are we going for the usual gamble? Lady Siobhan?

Yes, said Lal. Tatters sensed her hesitation. *We shouldn't push our luck, though.*

We'll find a way.

Instead of giving Lady Siobhan's name, Tatters held the kher's gaze. 'This is new. Are you sure the head of guards knows about this?'

She flashed a mirthless smile. 'I'm the new head of guards. Rules have always been there; I'm just making sure they're being followed.'

That explained it. Tatters didn't like new recruits – they did twice the work required of them. They always gave him a tougher time.

They were standing in the shade of the tower as young mages flocked by, their grey robes trailing against the ground. 'Are you going to check all these folks are on the register?' asked Tatters. 'That'll take forever.'

'No,' she said. 'I'm going to check you are.'

'Will you let me through if I buy a grey robe?'

She shrugged. Her leather armour, freshly sewn, was tightly fitted around her shoulders. It wasn't yet frayed or soiled. 'If you feel like risking the crime of impersonating a mage, by all means. But you're looking at a prison sentence.'

She won't give in, said Lal.

'My master is Lady Siobhan,' said Tatters. 'But I'm relying on your discretion here.' He might as well have punched her. Lady Siobhan was the supreme mage in charge of the Nest. No-one could afford to disturb her, especially not a recently employed kher.

The guard looked him up and down. Like most khers, she had jet-black eyes and jet-black hair to match her horns. 'I'll check you're on the register,' she decided.

You've pissed her off, said Lal.

No kidding.

The kher brought him inside the watchtower, past a thick door reinforced with iron. In the tower's circular room there was a weapon rack, a round table with a few knucklebones scattered across it, and a ledger. She opened the heavy volume.

'Do you know when Lady Siobhan officially announced you?' she asked. 'It's in chronological order.'

She's not buying it. We'll never get out of here, moaned Lal.

'No idea,' said Tatters. 'Ten years ago?' He hadn't been around the Nest ten years, but realistically, Lady Siobhan could only have obtained a collarbound in her – not youth, exactly – but in her formative years. She wasn't in a state to do anything these days, let alone control a slave.

The kher glared at him, as if he were wasting her time on

purpose. She pulled the only stool of the room towards her to sit down. She rested her horned head in her hands and started scrolling through the ledger, with the grim slowness of someone determined to do this right.

Tatters stood and waited. After a while, he picked up a knucklebone and had fun bouncing it on his fingers, swapping between the back and front of his hand. When she didn't stop him, he took a handful, increasing the difficulty of the juggling. He kept at it until she snapped at him to stop.

'Couldn't you at least try to remember the day you were brought to the Nest?' she grumbled.

They sank into a sulky silence. The only sound was the rasp of vellum pages as she turned them.

'Aren't you a bit old to be doing this?' he asked.

She didn't even glance up from the book.

'Don't pretend you can tell,' she said. Khers' faces were always smooth-skinned, unwrinkled. To humans, they seemed stuck at twenty years old, enjoying the beauty and health of youth. The saying went: *Grow up, not old – no wisdom, but bold.* Khers were supposed to be brave, strong, and as thick as the walls of the Nest.

'I can,' he said. 'I'm not any old flatface.'

The word 'flatface' caught her attention, at least. She stopped turning the pages and looked up.

'The horns are on the inside,' he said, tapping his forehead. He'd heard Mezyan say that often enough. She lifted an eyebrow. Obviously his kherer-than-thou technique wasn't working. He picked up three knucklebones and wedged them between his fingers on his left hand.

'Surprise me,' she said. 'How old am I?'

If she's a longlived, you've had it, said Lal.

Thanks for your support.

He watched the kher. She had an elegant face, with sharp features. She was thin and wiry, but handsome nonetheless, like birds are, despite the jutting bones.

From the horns' curve, she must have lived two-thirds of her life, more or less. Often khers in the last third of their life didn't start anything new, especially not a job. He quietly counted the annulations on the horns. If they were growing at a normal rate, she was probably fifty years or so. Which meant she had another thirty to go before the horns looped back towards the front of her face and started growing through her head, eventually breaking the skull and piercing the brain.

Khers died when their horns killed them. They didn't age from the inside out, but from the outside in.

What if she's tampered with her age by sanding down her horns? asked Lal.

Most khers don't, he argued. *It goes against their traditions.*

But she's a city-kher.

Tatters shook off Lal's thoughts. He threw the knucklebones and caught them, to keep his hands busy. 'I'd say you're fifty, give or take five years.'

He knew he'd got it right when she shrugged and turned back to the book.

'Someone told you,' she said.

She was rather cute when she sulked.

By the underworlds, if you start flirting, I'll puke.

Sometimes sharing thoughts with Lal was wonderful. And sometimes it wasn't. *Give me a break,* he thought. *I'm not flirting. Plus, you can't puke.*

In any case, he wasn't sure the kher would be interested in a human nearly as small as she was, with the tell-tale size and gait of someone who was underfed as a child. Sometimes, to tease him, Hawk would lean against him, putting all her weight on his shoulders, and say he should call himself Gnarled, not Tatters. She would ruffle his red hair – not bright red, murky red – and comment on his eyes – not blue, murky brown.

And yet Hawk liked you well enough, at the start, said Lal.

He turned to the kher. 'Your mother told you how to count people's age too, didn't she? I'm sure you did circles with your friends, trying to guess strangers' ages, betting on who'd get it right.' It was a stretch, but Mezyan had described his childhood in those terms, so Tatters assumed it was true for most khers. Children were the same everywhere, after all. Tatters continued playing with the knucklebones.

She put one hand across the pages of the book, fingers spread out. 'All right,' she said. 'Who taught you how to do it?'

Tatters put the knucklebones down. He pretended to pick at something underneath his nails. 'What does it matter?' It was nice to have her watching him, for a change. Then, to rub it in: 'Have you found me in there yet?'

'No.' She tapped her fingers across the thick page.

On impulse, Tatters said, 'Not a betting man, but I bet you can't get my age right.' It was a little-known fact that khers also found it difficult to work out how old a human was. Wrinkles and small marks on the skin weren't something they were taught to look out for. They could tell very withered and crooked humans were old, and very smooth and smaller humans were young. But they couldn't do much better than that.

She narrowed her eyes at him. 'You're ...' She paused. She studied him more closely.

'If you get it wrong, can I go in?' he asked.

She shook her head. 'I'm not risking my job on a bet.'

'Why? Worried you'll lose?'

She snorted a laugh. She brushed her horn, as humans pass

fingers through their hair. 'You won't get me like this. I'm not a child.'

He gave her time to think about his age. He sensed Lal's shifting moods inside him, impatient and worried, annoyed that he was playing, relieved that the kher wasn't looking too closely at her ledger. He focused on his breathing, keeping his thoughts and hers distinct. He watched the kher's frown, the way she rubbed her eyebrows with her thumb. Now that he had time to admire her tattoos, he saw that the overlapping shapes were mimicking the knots of a tree's bark. Black squares were filled with slim, flesh-coloured curls, to figure shoots and young leaves.

'Sixty?' she said at last.

He couldn't help but laugh. 'That is *not* a compliment. Nope. Half as old as that. Well, more than half, maybe, but close enough.'

She ran her finger down the ledger, not really looking at it. 'How old are you exactly?'

'Who knows?' He smiled. 'I've not been keeping count. And I haven't got a reminder growing out of my head.'

The kher got up from her stool and closed the register.

'If I ever find out that you lied to me,' she said, 'I'll kick you over the Edge.'

He bowed to her. 'Much obliged.'

He was about to head for the watchtower's door when she asked:

'As a slave, do you have spare time?'

It was an unusual question. He glanced from the tower's wooden door to her, the other side of the table. She was standing in front of the weapons rack, where someone had piled shields with the heraldry of the Nest painted on them. It was a reminder that she was a guard. So was her leather armour, and the hand resting casually on her sword.

'Sometimes,' he said cautiously. 'Why?'

'If you're that interested, I could give you a taste of kher food.'

'Erm...' Tatters hadn't been invited to eat by anyone since he'd worn his collar. Apprentices paid him drinks in exchange for lessons, but that was as far as it went. People didn't much care for someone with so little freedom he didn't even belong to himself.

The kher – whose name he didn't even know – walked around the table and up to the door. She opened it for both of them. It was warmer outside the stone tower, and for the first time Tatters became conscious of how cold he'd been. He rubbed his arms as she closed the door behind them.

'So?'

'I mean, I'd be flattered,' he said.

'You don't look flattered.' She stood by the door, arms crossed before her. She was wearing a linen shirt underneath her leather jacket. She wasn't rich – the shirt was undyed, the shoes were worn, the armour was a benefit from the Nest – but she wasn't wearing rags that would mark her out as poor.

'You do realise I'm a slave, right?'

'You do realise I'm a kher, right?'

She didn't smile, but her face softened. She was right, of course. Khers who worked within the Nest weren't considered much better than guard dogs – animals needed for a specific task, but animals still.

And if Passerine is here, we could do with more friends, said Lal.

'All right,' he said. 'I'd love to taste kher food.'

That was how Tatters met Arushi.

Chapter Three

Isha woke up in the dormitory, in a small bed packed with hay and fresh sheets. For a moment, she thought she could hear her foster brother snoring quietly, but of course it was only the girl in the next bed. It was daybreak. In the dimness, Isha could make out shapes; sleeping figures shrouded in shadow. The stained-glass windows cast eerie colours across their closed eyes.

When she got up, the ceiling felt too high, the arches too wide, the stone walls too compact. Every room was a reminder that it hadn't been built for humans. To adapt it to their size, the mages had built wooden lodgings within the stone castle. Inside the dormitory, they had set up a mezzanine across half the room. The disciples slept upstairs, where the wood kept the heat better, and they could stomp their feet to annoy the people below. Apprentices lying under the mezzanine didn't benefit from the high-placed windows; they had to prepare for bed and rise in the gloom.

Isha rubbed some life into her frozen feet before getting dressed for the day, struggling to tie her robes with some hemp rope so they would fall comfortably. Most apprentices had dyed belts; rope was only for newcomers, to indicate they weren't yet fully-fledged members of the Nest. She should have waited for Kilian, her official guide, but he wouldn't be awake yet, so she left the dorm without him. She listened to the hum of life growing inside the Nest: voices, the patter of servants' footsteps, the low rumble of people waking up. The change of guards, with the clang of armour and weaponry as they finished their rounds or started new ones. As she reached the mess, a bell rang loudly, summoning the apprentices from their beds.

In the mess, several fires already blazed, warming the whole room. Porridge bubbled in the soot-black pots hanging above the flames. There was honey and dried fruits, apples and pears, to sweeten the oatmeal. Servants were chatting amongst themselves, bringing more bowls of fruit, stirring the porridge. Long wooden tables and benches were scattered across the room.

The main chimney was built against the furthest wall; the hearth was the size of a pony. It was the only fireplace that wasn't lit.

After Isha had helped herself to some food, she went to sit near the chimney. In front of it stood a metal screen, blackened by time, wrought with the abstract curves the giants loved. The windows were decorated with similar swirling patterns. The hearth was clean. Isha guessed it didn't see many fires. She marvelled at its size, trying to imagine the giants' pots and pans, the size and sound of their flames.

The mess started filling up – apprentices ambled in, yawning and stretching, ladling more than their share of porridge into bowls. A group of five disciples walked up to Isha's table. They were thick-shouldered, grim-faced boys.

'You training with Sir Leofric?' one of them asked.

'No,' she said.

'This is Sir Leofric's table.'

Isha weighed her options. She wondered if she would be able to make a better attempt at mindbrawl than she had at the

Coop. But she didn't want trouble this early in the day, not after yesterday's fiasco.

'Sorry, I didn't know.' She got up. Bowl in hand, she searched for another table.

It proved more difficult than it should have been. A group of girls laughed in her face when she tried to sit beside them, and told her servants weren't supposed to eat in the mess. Another group of disciples politely explained that they were having a private conversation about their teacher and didn't want her to eavesdrop. It seemed that only apprentices with masters were allowed to sit down. She spotted several other puffins wandering helplessly from table to table – they must have lost their guide, like her, and now they couldn't find a seat.

It was the rope around their waist, of course. It screamed out that they didn't belong. In her case it was even worse, because of the tattoo.

Isha was starting to wonder if she would have to eat her porridge standing up when Kilian called her over. She turned to him in relief. He was seated at a table, his hair ruffled, his face still scrunched by sleep.

'What are you doing on your own? Come along!'

His table was a noisy one, where his friends were busy complaining that the servants were cheap with honey, and that the early risers had finished the apples.

'Who do you belong to, then?' Isha asked as she squeezed onto the bench.

'Uh?' Kilian gave her a good-natured, clueless smile.

'Who is your teacher?'

'Oh,' he laughed. 'Sir Daegan. One of the best!'

'The best,' corrected a girl beside him. Around this table, they all wore yellow cloth as belts. Maybe it was supposed to be golden, but the dye had faded.

The conversation turned to choosing a teacher. Kilian's friends were disciples who all studied with Sir Daegan, but they couldn't resist advising Isha on who to train with. Isha listened and ate her porridge. It had turned cold and slimy.

'First year really matters, 'cause if you have your eye on a high mage and train with someone they hate, they'll never have you when you ask them the next year,' said one girl.

'Can't I train with a few different people?' asked Isha.

'As a puffin, yes,' said Kilian. 'The first few months you can swap around, but then you'll have to choose.'

It turned out that picking a teacher meant picking a side. Kilian explained that mages duelled each other for money and control over quarters of the city. Some mages also owned villages and land far from the Edge, all the way up to the Ridge, but those mages didn't live at the Nest. Although they took on disciples during the summer and were accountable to the Nest, they rarely returned. Powerful mages were owed a tithe by city-dwellers and farmers, so their area of influence directly affected their income. They trained followers who were loyal to them: disciples were expected to win their duels, fight their battles, collect money from their serfs.

If you didn't want to serve your master, you could pay them. But Isha didn't have much baina, and Passerine seemed to think she would need it to even be considered by some of the mages.

'Some mages take anyone, they're so desperate for support,' said one guy. 'But the great teachers are a lot more selective.'

'Best bet is to go with someone not too fussy, to get the basics, then get picky once you've improved,' advised Kilian. 'That's what I did.'

Isha wasn't sure she wanted 'someone not too fussy' or even 'the basics'. She wasn't planning on being a bullied puffin amongst other fish-hungry bedraggled birds. Their lives were here; hers wasn't. She was here to learn, and because Passerine had said it was safe. As soon as she was strong enough, she wouldn't stay cowering in the Nest – she'd leave.

'If you decide you don't want to be a mage, you can train until you're deemed safe by a teacher, then go home, as long as you promise never to use mindlink.' This came from a young woman with impossibly long, lush hair. She popped raisins into her mouth as she spoke. 'It's only compulsory to have training so you don't mindscrew someone by mistake. Believe me, the Nest is happy to send you home and not pay for your tutoring.'

Isha gave the young woman a tense smile. *What makes you think I'm not cut out to be a mage?*

'Ah, come on, Caitlin, I think Isha's gonna stick around,' said Kilian.

Caitlin. The name rang a bell. Isha might have seen her at the tavern yesterday. She was what a soon-to-be-ordained mage should look like: tall, with pale Duskdweller skin, glossy hair that looked as if she had just finished brushing it. Grey robes decorated with gold thread along the seams; patterned leaves, flowers and suns running across her sleeves. A jaunty smile.

Caitlin rested her cheek in the palm of her hand, using the other to pick at the dried fruit. She didn't bother with the porridge, which might explain her slim shoulders and waist. She helped herself from the stack of raisins Kilian had placed next to his bowl. He let her do it.

'The other solution is to wait it out,' said another guy. 'After two or three years, you can pass the trial to be an ordained mage. After that, you can ask to be assigned to your hometown. If it's small, no-one will care, and they'll let you go.' He shovelled some porridge down his throat before concluding, his mouth full: 'That's what I'll do.'

In Isha's homeland, in the village below the farm, three mages bickered and ruled over the locals, disagreeing on everything but raising taxes each year. She vaguely remembered that they sometimes hosted feasts for emissaries from the Nest, who were supposed to check they weren't abusing their power. 'Abusing' seemed to be a loose term. Isha's local mages had never been challenged by anyone except each other.

'Or you can join the lawmages,' said Kilian.

Caitlin gave out a crystalline laugh. It wasn't clear if she was laughing at the idea, at Isha, or at something amusing that no-one else had spotted.

'Lawmages only accept ordained mages in their ranks, and only after six years at the Nest,' she clarified.

That didn't surprise Isha. As the Nest's right arm, the lawmages managed law enforcement. It mostly consisted of hunting out people who were using illegal mindlink. Depending on their rank, they filled the duties of guards, judges or soldiers. They would need to ascertain disciples were loyal to the Nest and its ideals before they allowed them to join. They wore undyed belts – cloth, not rope, nothing that would link them to the apprentices – as a sign that they were neutral. And humble. They didn't belong to a faction, but to the Nest itself.

But Isha wasn't waiting that long. The sooner she knew how to defend herself, the better.

She had run to the end of the world, but she wouldn't be able to run any further. Sooner or later, her pursuers would find her. When she faced them again, she would be ready. If they never came, then she would go to them herself. She would confront them and get, if not revenge, then at least answers.

'Can I train with your teacher?' she asked Kilian. After all, he was her formal guide, and she had already been invited to the table. Next to that, being accepted by the teacher himself seemed like a formality.

To her surprise, Kilian shook his head. 'Sir Daegan is out of your league.'

'To be fair, he's out of Kilian's league – not sure what made him so desperate to take you on,' Caitlin teased.

'Get mindscrewed,' Kilian answered with a smirk.

Caitlin finished the last of his dried fruits. She threw them into her mouth from a distance, craning her pretty neck to catch them.

'Seriously,' Kilian added, 'Sir Daegan doesn't take on puffins. He likes meeting the followers who are interested in joining him beforehand, to see what they can do. And you'll need some experience before you get to his class.' He got up to fetch more raisins for Caitlin.

Once he'd returned with a refill of porridge and sweeteners, Kilian was adamant Sir Daegan was brilliant. Out of loyalty or not, Isha couldn't tell. Still, he was a high mage, which meant he was powerful – even if all his power didn't stem from mindlink. Some of it might simply be prestige, status and money.

'There's a few high mages to look out for,' said one girl. 'Lady Mathilda is doing well. Apparently she has secret mindlink techniques that only her followers get to learn.'

The disciples touched on a few other names, which Isha didn't commit to memory. There was too much choice. In order, the hierarchy consisted of the supreme mage, Lady Siobhan; a circle of twenty or so high mages who served as her counsellors; a larger circle of ordained mages prestigious enough to challenge the high mages; then people with less power, and lesser still, until it came down to the apprentices. And to her.

'I think I'll try my luck with Sir Daegan,' she said.

Caitlin chuckled, and the other apprentices, emboldened by her, laughed out loud. Isha couldn't have cared less. She'd had worse.

'I want to see this,' said one of the boys.

'I think you'll be surprised,' said Kilian. 'This puffin duelled Tatters *and* got a high mage out of bed to help her. That was only yesterday. She's just got here and she's already messing people around.'

He smiled at Isha. She wasn't sure if she could trust him yet – maybe he meant it nicely, maybe not. If nothing else, she was providing entertainment. She could see how someone like Kilian might stick around for the show, but leave before the battle. Still, it was support. She smiled back.

***

The guards were happy to show Tatters the way to Passerine's chambers. Although the Nest was well-guarded, it didn't know how to deal with enemies on the inside. The mages could be fooled by cuckoos: they tended chicks inside their Nest whether they were friends or foes.

Except for Goldie, said Lal.

I wonder if he's around.

Tatters had been a regular of the Nest for years, but recently his visits had become less frequent. This was because of a lawmage, a tough, tanned man with blond curly hair, who Tatters called Goldie. The contrast between his scarred face and his lovely hair was too good an opportunity for a nickname to pass up. Goldie suspected Tatters wasn't Lady Siobhan's collarbound.

It was Tatters' fault – he'd been careless. When the cooks served him without question in the apprentices' mess, he started eating there three times a day. When the khers let him in and out freely, he attended festivals at the Nest, to soak up the atmosphere and any free drinks that lay around. When he could get away with it, he witnessed duels, trying to assess how powerful the high mages were. He became a common sight, which meant people ignored him all the more. He was like a stray cat: everyone assumed he belonged to someone else.

The apprentices had spread the rumour of how talented he was at mindbrawl, causing the mages to speculate on who his master could be. They had finally decided that only one person was powerful enough to own a collarbound, and careless enough to let him run amok: Lady Siobhan. Once it had been established – if never openly then at least in everyone's minds – that he belonged to the supreme mage, nobody had bothered Tatters.

Except for Goldie.

One morning, the lawmage had appeared out of nowhere and grabbed Tatters' arm as he was entering the Nest. Tatters didn't try to resist. Goldie dragged him up to the stone walls of the Nest, between the guards' watchtower and the heavy metal grid that served as the prison door. He held onto Tatters' bicep, grinding it against the wall.

Tatters wasn't worried yet. 'How can I help you?' he asked.

Goldie's face hadn't been spared. The lightborn who flew over his cradle had covered his cheeks with smallpox marks, placing creased folds of skin around his eyelids and his lips. As if to compensate, they had blessed him with hair a girl would kill for. He cut it just under his ears, but it was enough length for it to curl and shine.

'I know you don't belong to Lady Siobhan,' Goldie said. 'I've been keeping an eye on you.'

Instinctively, Tatters braced himself for a mental attack. Maybe sensing this, Goldie clutched his arm harder.

'I know you're a Sunriser spy.'

If the situation hadn't been so dire, Tatters might have snickered at that. The Sunrisers weren't one unified force.

The Winged Maidens and the convents under their influence,

the Wingshade, were the Sunrisers that the Duskdwellers were most accustomed to, because they lived closest to the Shadowpass. When a Duskdweller said 'Sunriser', chances were they meant 'Wingshade'. When people talked about the Sunriser language, they meant the Wingshade common tongue.

And we're from the Pearls, you idiot, thought Lal.

'Now, I don't want a war with the Sunrisers,' Goldie went on, 'and you don't want to rot in a cell. So, you're going to run back to your convent and stop snooping around the Nest. And I'm going to let you off.'

Tatters was careful to hide his relief. On the one hand, it was terrible news that Goldie knew he had crossed the Shadowpass. Most people assumed he had to be a Duskdweller – they were too prejudiced to imagine a white Sunriser. On the other hand, it was wonderful that the lawmage believed Tatters was a spy. Much better he believe that, than for him to get to the truth.

'If I ever see you in here again, I won't play nice,' snarled Goldie.

When he let go, Tatters did what was expected of him: he left the Nest immediately and steered clear of it for the following months. But it was too tempting to avoid completely. Everything important happened at the Nest. And lawmages often travelled across the land; it was rare for them to stay in one place for more than a season. So, when summer faded into autumn, Tatters started visiting again.

But not often enough, if you can miss the change of the head of guards, noted Lal.

You know me. I wouldn't have risked dropping by if it weren't for Passerine.

I know you. You would have risked it if a half-decent excuse cropped up.

Tatters smiled; Lal did know him. Despite the danger, or

maybe because of it, he felt full of life. He strode down the corridors as if he owned the Nest. People ignored him. Like the kher guards or the servants, he went unnoticed.

No guards were stationed beside Passerine's door. He was in the wing of the castle reserved for guests and travellers. From the looks of it, he had a giant's alcove all to himself. The room hadn't been divided into smaller chambers with wooden panels. Which meant this was a high mage's room.

Since when is Passerine a high mage? wondered Tatters.

He focused on expanding his mind to the space around him. He couldn't sense another spirit close by. He placed one hand against the door. The wood was dense, unyielding. He tried the handle, but of course it was locked.

At least he knew Caitlin had told the truth. As far as the Nest's official documentation went, Passerine was a high mage. A guestroom meant he might be travelling and soon be on his way; or it could just as well mean that they had run out of chambers in the permanent wing. Tatters needed more than this to decide how much of a threat Passerine was – both to himself, and to Isha. He had taken a liking to the girl, even after only seeing her once. He didn't want her to get caught up in one of Passerine's schemes.

What do you care what happens to some apprentice? Lal asked.

Don't tell me you can't feel it, he answered. Even though he wasn't sure what was special about Isha, he had no doubt there was something to learn. The pattern of her tattoo stuck in his mind, as grating as a high-pitched sound ringing in his ears. He recognised it. Or her. Or both. *It's as if we've met her before.*

She is uncanny, I'll give you that, Lal admitted.

Tatters backtracked until he found a servants' entrance. The narrow backroom corridors mirrored the maze of official passageways but were used only by the maids. They relied on them to bring hot water for the mages' bathtubs, breakfast to their beds, flowers for their desks, and sometimes even letters or presents sent to them by other officials.

Tatters picked his path from memory. Although the doors leading from the servants' corridors to the rooms should be locked, hurried maids often left them open, especially when they were cleaning them. One servant went through all the rooms, taking off the dirty sheets and leaving the door open for the person behind, who would place the clean sheets back on the beds.

Now that the bell had rung and the mages were downstairs, the maids scurried around with bundles of cloth in their arms. A few frowned at him, but he greeted them and explained he had a letter for Passerine. Discretion was overrated – politeness and a friendly smile achieved a lot more. Passerine wouldn't even look at these women. They would never tell him anything.

But he might scrounge through their minds, looking for you, said Lal, ever the killjoy.

Why would he assume they'd seen me?

Lal was being cautious today. She didn't let Tatters' flippant mood overrule her fears. *If he works out you're here, he'll guess you've mingled with the staff.*

Tatters nodded to a young girl in a crisp white apron and gallantly let her pass. *One, I'm unlikely to be at the front of their minds.* He gave way to an older matron, her hands and forearms rubbed raw from hot water and soap. He overacted a bow for her, making her chuckle. *Two, they don't know where I've come from. Their memories wouldn't be much help.*

He reached the door that he assumed to be Passerine's. He pushed it, and was pleased to find it open.

The room was dim; grey light filtered through the window. On the desk, someone had placed a jug of aromatic water with floating leaves. A few cracked-leather travelling trunks were open on the floor, spilling their contents like gutted fish. The ceiling was too high and dwarfed the furniture, which included a carpet on the floor and a four-poster bed that a whole family could have slept in.

Tatters moved carefully. Everything he touched, he put back as he had found it. He kept his thoughts neutral, sifting through his emotions so only their purest, simplest form remained. He doubted Passerine would be able to perceive them.

The trunks contained a poppy-red stana, a few pins, spare travelling clothes, shoes. It was a mix of Sunriser garments – the three pieces of unstitched cloth to wrap around the legs, waist and shoulders – and Duskdweller ones. Some rice-cakes and dry tea leaves were loosely bundled in a towel.

He must have lived in Wingshade territory recently, said Lal.

Although they hadn't been back in years, as far as Tatters was aware, Hawk and Passerine were originally from the southern side of the Inner Sea, the region furthest away from the Shadowpass. Their people were much darker skinned than most Sunrisers, hence Passerine always stood out. But the tea he'd packed was clearly Wingshade.

In the wardrobe beside the bed, he found a spare high mage's outfit, complete with the black robe and belt. It looked new – it might have been a gift from the Nest. There was vellum paper rolled on the desk, and ink, but nothing written down. Not even one of Hawk's poems. Tatters couldn't decide whether he was relieved or not.

This doesn't tell us much, thought Lal.

It didn't. So, Passerine had been travelling, maybe for a long time. The red stana proved nothing. The Renegades' heraldry was red, but without the hawk emblazoned on it, it could simply be personal preference. He must have crossed the Shadowpass – but had he done so recently and gone straight to the Nest, or had he been in Duskdweller territory for a while? And why had he brought Isha with him?

Tatters needed to talk to someone who had met Passerine, who would know his story. Someone who wouldn't be surprised to see a collarbound in the Nest.

It was time to chat to the supreme mage.

***

After breakfast, Isha would have liked to stay with the disciples, but other tasks were expected of her. All newly arrived apprentices had to gather in the library, where they were divided into three groups based on how well, or poorly, they knew how to write. Part of a mage's life consisted of working as a scribe, painstakingly copying reports sent from across the country to be centralised at the Nest. Any interesting documents – books, sensitive information – were done by disciples. But apprentices were still good for copying vade mecums and instructions, accounts and grain tallies, eye-splitting small texts seeped in boredom.

Isha could read, albeit slowly. Passerine had made sure she polished her reading skills on their way to the Nest. Her handwriting was awful, though, so the mage in charge of the library placed her in the mediocre-but-not-useless group as a compromise. While the light was good, for most of the morning and well after noon, she earned her place at the Nest as a copyist.

After a couple of hours, she was thoroughly sick of it. Her fingers were cramped, her eyes stung, her head ached. Every mistake had to be scratched out of the vellum, skimming the page so to not damage the paper. By the time Kilian dropped by to fetch her, with a group of older disciples assigned to help the young apprentices find their way, her courage and energy had drained out of her.

'Still up for seeing old Daegan?' Kilian asked.

She massaged her stiff hands, trying to muster a smile. 'Of course.'

As she was led into Sir Daegan's class, Isha compared this meeting to the one with Tatters. Instead of being pressed together at the same table in a crowded tavern, she joined the group at a given time, in a chamber on the ground floor of the Nest. The room had been built within a larger one, and only one of the walls was the original stone of the giants – the other three, and the floor, were made of wood. The walls had been plastered in a white paste, a mix of limestone and water. Opposite the door was the heraldry of the Nest, blue and gold, painted on the pale background by an expert hand.

Inside the room, there was no furniture. The apprentices were expected to stand in a semi-circle facing the door, waiting for it to open. It meant that they wouldn't miss their teacher's entry, of course; but it also meant that every new face coming through was studied in detail.

When Isha crossed the threshold, she sensed the apprentices' gazes dismantling her, analysing each feature. Even though she hadn't come alone, even though she was partly shielded by Kilian, she stood out. The tattoo made sure of that. As if that wasn't enough, she was the darkest person there – the rest were as white as the walls. Everyone kept a step away from her.

Kilian told Isha all the training rooms were the same, to stop mages from setting up their own heraldry in the alcoves, creating more divides in the Nest than there already were. She nodded, thankful for his conversation.

They waited. Isha had to stand at the front of the group – disciples were at the back. Kilian placed himself behind her, playfully saying 'I've got your back!'

She was with a row of apprentices – new, like her, but not quite as new, having already done a couple of months or even a year at the Nest – gawking before the door. The stares of the people behind her were tangible, like a sting on the nape of her neck. She could only see the whitewashed wall and the lonely door, but she knew from the whispers that the disciples were watching her.

The first two times the door creaked open, her heart leapt. But they were only latecomers, who slotted themselves behind the row of apprentices.

At last Sir Daegan entered. Silence fell across the room; feet shuffled, robes were smoothed, spines straightened. Isha crossed her hands behind her back, breathing deeply.

Sir Daegan was an ageing man with a belly pushing against his black robes. He had a receding hairline with pale flimsy hair around his temples and down the back of his head. He was a greying man in a Nest full of other greying mages. Like wolves, Isha couldn't always tell them apart. And like wolves, they were always fighting to become the alpha.

The regulars saluted Sir Daegan, speaking nearly as a chorus. He nodded and waved until they fell quiet. He then turned to the first row.

'Let's meet the new recruits,' he said.

He seemed to know the name of most apprentices eager to join his class. He nodded to some and indicated the door to others, on criteria Isha couldn't work out. It was obvious he had pondered each case beforehand. She swallowed. Maybe inviting herself without asking him in advance was a worse breach of manners than she had realised.

When it came to Isha's turn, Sir Daegan glared at her. She didn't turn her head away. His eyes were washed-out blue, tinged with grey.

'Step forward,' he ordered.

She did. When she stood before him, she showed her profile to the class – the tattooed side. She wondered if he had done this on purpose. From the corner of her eye, she could make out the other apprentices, all the way to the disciples lounging at the back, leaning against the wall. They were the only ones to seem comfortable.

'You are expected to clean your face before coming to my class,' said Sir Daegan.

Caitlin raised her eyebrows, an 'I told you so' expression on her face. Someone snorted a laugh. Sir Daegan lifted one hand to hush them. The noise faded into deferential silence.

In Tatters' class, if it could be called that, everyone had interrupted each other. They shared the same space – the Coop, of course – but also the same verbal and mental space. Tatters talked, but he didn't expect people to stay quiet. Sounds and smells and colours surrounded him. Maybe that was the difference between legal and illegal mindlink.

'It's a tattoo, sir,' she said. 'I can't take it off.'

In Tatters' eyes, her tattoo was what made her interesting. In Sir Daegan's, it was what made her distasteful. He poked her cheek; he had withered, wrinkled skin. She tried not to flinch away from the unwelcome touch. He rubbed finger and thumb together, his lips pulled down in a pout.

'Have you got hornblood?' he asked suspiciously.

'No, sir,' she answered. She forced the 'sir' out of her lips.

'How could you imagine a cow tattoo would suit you?' Sir Daegan shook his head, as he would before a poor furnishing choice, as if he were speaking about something impersonal, not *her face*. She didn't bother telling him she hadn't chosen it.

'I guess you wanted to be special.' He spoke with such venom that Isha felt it like acid splashed across her chest. Her lungs tightened. She tried to ignore the amused glances passing between the disciples, and the low chuckles some of them couldn't – or didn't bother to – hide.

'What makes you think you're good enough to train with me? I don't take on first years. I'm sure you were told.'

I survived. She thought of someone ripping her mind as if it were cloth; of tears appearing down the seams. She couldn't say it – not to him, not here. She knew she was good at mindlink because they had pillaged minds and memories and she was still here to tell the tale.

'I'll prove myself, if you want,' she said instead. Anything, rather than spending a year scratching paper with a reed pen.

Sir Daegan shook his head. 'None of that, young lady. I'm not interested in cheek.'

The high mage spread his feet and rested his weight in his toes. He filled the space with his presence, but it wasn't the magnetism Passerine exuded. The way the apprentices were placed around him, with Isha isolated in front, with the door open like a wound, letting in a draft of cold air – this constructed his impression of power.

'I arrived at the Nest two days ago,' Isha said, 'and I've already done a mindbrawl. It's not cheek.'

From the way everyone looked at her – and the horrified expression on Kilian's face – maybe that had been the wrong thing to boast about.

Sir Daegan didn't seem impressed. He was taller than her, and he stood too close, forcing her to tilt her chin upwards to hold his eyes.

'You arrived with Sir Passerine, didn't you?' he said.

She nodded. He graced her with a curt smile, as if that explained everything.

She sensed his intrusion in her mind like a stranger's hand running down her back. She didn't know what he was trying to find, but she knew he was there, rifling through her memories.

Instinctively, she tried to contain herself, to make herself into a shape, a silhouette, something he couldn't access, that had boundaries. It was like falling. The ground disappeared beneath her, and the world went dark. She was herself, she was a body at least, she was the kind of self-contained figures we are in dreams.

She could feel herself spill. Scraps of thoughts escaped her. Kilian – but taller, blonder, and wearing darker robes. The classroom, inconsequential like a reflection in glass. Passerine was there too, giving Sir Daegan a disdainful look. And Sir Daegan himself manifested, the same as he was in his class. He had a bit more hair, that was all. Isha could sense it was him, and not her projection of him.

A settled mind, he said. *That is a good first step. Although it lacks structure, the most essential ingredient.*

It felt very different having someone in her mind instead of fighting on neutral terrain. Isha could sense the strain of keeping herself together in one shape. She had to prevent her mind from wandering, because each stray thought gave away information. She had already betrayed that Passerine was important to her, that she had come with Kilian. There was the stench of spilt beer from the tavern, and Isha consciously focused on alcohol, nothing more, drinking and getting drunk, so nothing else would proffer itself before Sir Daegan.

To her relief, he exited her mind. It was like breaking off from an unwanted kiss. She could breathe again.

When she opened her eyes, she felt mildly sick. She wavered

on her feet, struggling to push down the lump inside her throat, aware of people staring. She wanted to throw up, but she wouldn't give him the satisfaction.

She wondered if he had been able to see it. That she was broken; that she had been hurt. Did a wounded mind limp forever? Could you see the hole where memories had been, like you would a missing limb?

Sir Daegan's expression unglazed. A flicker crossed his face as he stepped out of mindlink.

'I see why you've come to me,' he said. 'You've come searching for what you lack: discipline.'

Isha was shaking. But she was still standing, and he hadn't been able to invade her spirit. She could see from the spark in his eyes that he was interested, at least. At last.

'I'll teach you,' Sir Daegan decided.

**

A roof terrace stretched between the high towers of the Nest where, according to the legends, feathered giants would take flight. It was curved like a soup plate and painted myriad colours, to figure the setting sun. It was hidden from the ground by turrets and battlements.

When Tatters reached it, it was empty. It was the supreme mage's personal terrace, where she spent a few hours every day to rest from the bustle of the Nest. This meant no-one was allowed to loiter. No-one wanted to. There were no benches, no chairs, no flowers. There was no view. All that met the eye were sandstone walls and the pale sky.

Tatters went to stand in the centre of the pictured sunset. He looked upwards and breathed in. Something about the space plucked the strings of his heart, leaving him humming. It was as if the sky would suck him upwards. He threw his head backwards until his neck hurt. The clouds were uniform and grey like a ceiling clamped over the world.

As Tatters didn't know how long it would take Lady Siobhan to come to the rooftop, he practised some fighting stances. He started by stretching, then he went through the basics. Without a target, or something to stand in for a sword or a spear, it wasn't much use. Still, it was better than nothing. Although Tatters had been doing mindbrawl, he hadn't worked on any physical fighting for years. He wondered if it was Passerine's presence that made him want to check he was fit.

Which you're not, if you ask me, said Lal.

He needed someone to train with. But wanting to practise physical brawling didn't match with his happy-go-lucky image. Plus, the apprentices wouldn't get it. They didn't consider the fact that they were helpless if a kher decided to punch them in the face. Or charge at them horns forwards, for that matter.

But Hawk did, which was why the Renegades included kher soldiers.

Passerine being here doesn't mean that Hawk is on her way, said Lal. *There is no need to panic. Yet.*

It took nearly an hour before Lady Siobhan arrived.

He watched as Lady Siobhan tottered across the terrace, leaning heavily on a wood-and-bone cane. A maid was hovering beside her, ready to help if need be. Lady Siobhan was bent over, shoulders hunched. What was left of her white hair clung to her skull in patches.

My favourite collarbound! When she spotted Tatters she smiled, showing teeth blackened by sugar. *I haven't seen you in ages.*

Lady Siobhan's rotten teeth and venerable age meant that, when she spoke, the words came out mushed together. Her mutterings were difficult to understand, but to compensate, she always mindlinked as she spoke. She projected her words directly into people's skulls. It was sometimes unnerving to hear everything twice – once out loud, as indecipherable mumblings, and once in your mind.

Tatters bowed. He waited for Lady Siobhan to come closer before kissing the old woman's hands. The maid, obviously unsure about Tatters' status, dropped him a half-curtsey.

During his many visits to the Nest, Tatters had cultivated a friendship with Lady Siobhan. The supreme mage was drawn to anything powerless, from children to khers, from ungifted to collarbounds. She spoke tenderly to them and offered them baina, often forgetting that, not being mages, they wouldn't be able to spend it. Tatters had worked hard to maintain that closeness. For one thing, it didn't hurt for people to see him in Lady Siobhan's company. It kept the rumours fresh.

How are you and your friend? asked Lady Siobhan. A strong mindlink was like a shout without sound. Emotions, colours and sensations crashed through from her. When she mindlinked, Tatters always had to brace himself.

Good to see you, answered Tatters. He put as much honest pleasure into his message as he could. Because Lady Siobhan was growing steadily deaf, mindlink was the easiest way to answer her. By 'friend', Lady Siobhan meant Lal. *My friend is well.*

Lady Siobhan was a talented mage, talented enough to sense Lal. Sometimes she even called Lal 'your daughter'. In this she was wrong, although it meant she had perceived enough of Lal to see the family resemblance: the same red hair and narrow shoulders, the muddy brown eyes, matched pointed faces.

Tatters suspected Lady Siobhan was the reason Goldie hadn't dragged him straight to the dungeons when he had the chance. As the supreme mage, she would get to judge anyone charged with political crimes, such as spying. Goldie must have known

Lady Siobhan would be loath to condemn Tatters. And the old woman was so unreliable that she might decide to pardon people she liked. Maybe she was even confused enough to have forgotten whether Tatters was her slave or not.

Where have you been? Did you leave? You will forgive me if I forgot you had to leave, thought Lady Siobhan.

I wasn't far, only busy, thought Tatters. Lal kept well away from the foreground of his mind, to avoid Lady Siobhan spying more of her. *I suppose you are busy too, with the new apprentices joining the Nest?*

Yes.

Lady Siobhan sighed through her grey teeth. Some of them were only half or a third of their original size. They were like dirty icicles, waning with the coming of spring.

Yes, Lady Siobhan repeated. She shuffled across the roof terrace, towards the centre of the circle. Tatters followed, staying behind her. The supreme mage was so used to this sign of respect that she didn't notice it. She didn't give any indication that she noticed the maid, either, although she steadied herself by holding her arm. The servant didn't seem taken aback by their silent conversation. She must be used to it.

Lady Siobhan stopped at the centre of the rooftop. Her crooked back meant she couldn't look at the sky. She strained her eyes upwards before giving up. She scratched at the paint with her cane.

Tatters made some small talk – if mindlink could be called talk. He mentioned the cold autumn weather, the number of newcomers, how much louder they were than the old crowd, how much less respectful. He was trying to prepare the ground to ask about Passerine, transitioning from the new apprentices to the new high mages.

It was easy to talk to Lady Siobhan. Everything had been

better when her back was straight and her fingers free from arthritis. Lady Siobhan thought the world was crumbling around her; it was she who was growing old.

It's very difficult to look after everyone, said Lady Siobhan.

It only gets worse, doesn't it?

Lady Siobhan's mind washed over Tatters' like a dull, cold wave. *My boy, it is going to become much worse.*

The image projected with this sentence was a sea of quicksilver, with foam like metal blades. It moved sluggishly, lapping against a wooden dock. In the distance, boats lit up with lanterns glowed on the mercurial waves.

Tatters couldn't make sense of the message, but he perceived the most essential part of it – fear. Lady Siobhan was afraid.

What is it? Tatters asked.

Lady Siobhan patted Tatters' shoulder as if he were a puppy, something nice but dumb. *There is a war coming*, she mouthed and mindlinked. Her breath was stale and sweet, like fermented fruit.

Tatters' heart crawled down to the soles of his feet and settled there. *A war? Who is it?*

The two lands on either side of the Shadowpass weren't allies, as such, but they weren't foes. On the Duskdweller side, the Nest was the central power. It was a simple hierarchy: mages owned fiefdoms, from which they took tribute in exchange for protection. The mages then gave higher mages tribute, in exchange for protection from other fiefdoms. And high mages gave tribute to Lady Siobhan, who owed everyone protection, and unified them into the Duskdweller kingdom, which ran from the Edge, through the Meddyns, all the way up to the Ridge.

On the Sunriser side, the mages were organised into convents, each controlling a small share of land. The Sunriser Edge was huge; people from the Nest often didn't realise how narrow their territory was in comparison. The Sunrisers had enough space for five Nests, and had nearly ten times as many powers vying for dominance.

The various groups, ethnicities, languages and beliefs didn't have a central force to organise them, so they were always involved in border skirmishes to extend their territory. The problem with the Sunrisers was that anyone could stake a claim on a piece of land. Nothing could prevent the Renegades from trying to set up their own convent and make it legitimate by force.

Lady Siobhan shook her head. Her despondent mindlink seeped through. She thought the convents were in danger. That they were dead, or dying.

Which meant the Renegades' territory was growing closer to the Shadowpass, threatening the only Sunrisers the Nest cared about. But that didn't explain what Passerine was doing here. Surely, if Hawk was taking over the Wingshade convents, Passerine should be with her, helping with her conquest?

Lady Siobhan gave him a pointed look, and Tatters struggled to hide his thoughts. He was discreet, as mages went, but he would never be subtle enough to conceal anything from Lady Siobhan on her good days.

The old woman shuffled back to the battlements. Tatters walked behind her. The maid held Lady Siobhan's arm to help her creep out of the stone circle. The cane scraped against the floor, a small, grating noise that followed each step. They rested against the castle walls, Lady Siobhan wheezing from the brief exertion. The maid curtsied and announced she was going to fetch some water. Lady Siobhan didn't acknowledge her.

So, you know Sir Passerine? thought Lady Siobhan.

Well, this was what he had come for, after all. Tatters tried to lie, but lying with your thoughts was different from lying with your voice. He focused on the pockmarks across the sandstone, banishing everything else into his unconscious mind.

Only by name, Tatters said.

He held his breath.

I am sorry for Sir Passerine, thought Lady Siobhan. Her mind had lost its sharpness. Her eyes were clouded. She was looking at something only she could see. *Forced to leave your land. Living as a refugee. It's terrible.* With Lady Siobhan's words came the image of a crowd slipping out of the Shadowpass, coughing up sand. Passerine in torn black robes, his hair whitened with dust. *He is only the first, you know. Two more mages sent word to me today that they are travelling this way. There will be more.*

Tatters forced himself to nod in agreement. Passerine, a refugee? He was Hawk's greatest ally. He had been by her side longer than Tatters himself.

Luckily, these stray thoughts didn't reach Lady Siobhan. She was lost in reminiscence – her own memories, or someone else's, or a constructed version of what she believed had happened.

Tatters leaned against the wall. The supreme mage stood still as a statue, staring straight ahead at the line of sunlight cutting across the terrace. Her fingers were knotted around her cane, clenched like bony claws. Tatters enjoyed the cold autumn sun across his skin. He half-closed his eyes. It might take time for Lady Siobhan to emerge.

Do you know the Shadowpass? she asked.

Tatters hadn't been prepared for her mindlink; it hit him like a shock of cold water. It was unusually strong, more so than a friendly message should ever be. With the question, the sense of the Shadowpass rose within Tatters, the rustling sound of waves, the liquid drops of light landing in pools of shadow. The recollections were his own, but they surged at Lady Siobhan's call. Before Tatters could contain them, memories of crossing the Shadowpass rose within him, lifting him like the tide.

It was a long time ago, yet it was still vivid. He left during the night. He waited, lying on the floor of his master's tent, until everyone's breathing sank into the rhythm of sleep. He pushed himself off the furs. He breezed through the front of the tent, brushing against its cloth. Outside it was cool. The scent of summer, tinged with dying blossom, clung to the air.

At this altitude, halfway up the Ridge, the days were hot and the nights were cold. Stones emerged from the low, flower-strewn grass like the backs of long, grey fish dipping out of the water. Some Renegades had chosen to stay outside, resting their heads on the rocky outcrops. They nestled together, these scarred men and women, nearly hugging. They were toughened by war but softened by sleep.

Tatters stepped away from the circle of sleeping bodies. He moved like a cat, treading softly, not because he was stalking prey but because he *was* prey. If anyone woke up, he would never escape. The punishment for this might not be worth the attempt.

That evening, three or four orders were active within the bind – orders such as 'I forbid you to hurt me' or 'I forbid you to run away'. Tatters wasn't afraid of being caught, but he was fighting a visceral feeling: shame. What he was doing was shameful. It deserved to be curbed. He sank his nails into the palms of his hands so the pain would distract him from the collar.

The shadows from the night-tide etched away at the collar's power. Since they had come to the edge of the Shadowpass, Tatters had felt the bind slackening. It had been a long climb from the shores of the Inner Sea up to the pass, but with each day, the collar had loosened its hold. For the first time in weeks – months? – he sensed Lal within him. Her voice was too faint to be made out, but it was there. Lal wasn't under the influence of the collar, but she was a part of him. And now that the collar's power waned with the shifts of light and darkness, she grew in strength. She coaxed him on.

He left the military encampment and followed the path winding up the slope. Trees didn't like it here, and only grew in hunchbacked, stunted shapes. There was a small cluster of them, like an audience at a hanging, moaning as the wind brushed through their leaves. Above him loomed the Ridge.

The Ridge was the highest mountain-range of the land. Where it rose, all the eyes could see were rock formations. The horizon was cut in two: black sky, then stone.

Tatters saw Mezyan before Mezyan saw him. The kher was standing in front of the Shadowpass, staring down its gloomy mouth.

The Shadowpass was a long tunnel dug into the Ridge. When the sun rose in the Sunriser lands, the light-tide started at their end of the tunnel. Light flowed slowly, like waves, and travellers could walk with it through the Ridge, deep underneath the earth. But if they didn't keep step with the sun, they would find themselves lapped by shadows. As the sun set, the night-tide started pouring through the Ridge – a nightfall such as could never be found above ground.

The darkness of the Ridge didn't only take away people's sight. It tore their souls to shreds.

Tatters stopped when he saw Mezyan in front of the pass. Another day, another place, Tatters might have backed down and returned to his tent, maybe even felt relieved at having been caught. But here, the night-tide ate away at the edges of his self, leaving Tatters feeling fuzzy and undefined. His thoughts were not quite his own. The shadows eroded him like water over stone.

So Tatters didn't try to hide. He walked up to Mezyan.

'You're up,' said Mezyan.

'I'm leaving,' said Tatters.

Mezyan didn't answer. On impulse, Tatters took off Hawk's scarf, his nasivyati. He uncoiled the long piece of red cloth from around his neck, like an impossibly long scab torn off a wound, until it revealed the collar underneath. He handed it to Mezyan.

'You can have this.'

Mezyan looked at the nasivyati, then at Tatters. He nodded. When he took the cloth out of Tatters' hands, their fingers touched. Without the scarf to hide it, the bright gold of the collar reflected the moon. It dappled the ground with specks of light. Mezyan's skin glowed like embers, his white horns like ivory.

'You've got a few hours before they find out you're gone,' said Mezyan with a sigh. 'I'm sorry it came to this. I hope you make it.'

Tatters was light-headed. He stared down the Shadowpass. A few strides in, the tunnel became too opaque for him to see. Guides helped people across the pass during the light-tide, but for him, that had never been an option.

Tatters entered the darkness.

Setting foot inside the Shadowpass sent a shock of cold through his body. His eyes snapped open as he was suddenly flung away from his memory, back into the real world. No line of light slid across the rooftop. It was chillier now, without the sun. Tatters rubbed his face. He glanced at Lady Siobhan, who was standing in the same position, her eyes unblinking and dry. Her mouth was half-open, and spittle filled her lower lip. She didn't drool. At first Tatters thought she wasn't breathing, before hearing a faint rasping sound at the back of her throat.

The maid was beside them. She had a silk handkerchief to dab at Lady Siobhan's mouth, and she had draped a cover around the supreme mage's shoulders. She cast Tatters a reproachful glare, as if any of this was his fault.

Tatters stretched stiffly, then rubbed his fingers and forearms. How long had he been standing there? He craned his neck to check the sky. Every muscle ached. His spine cracked when he turned his head. They had been standing together, Lady Siobhan and he, a few hours at least. Fear clasped his heart. It was an old fear, one that had been his companion before, that would follow him his whole life. He stamped his feet, trying to shake off the pins and needles crawling down his legs.

Tatters watched the supreme mage. It must have been what Tatters had looked like, a few minutes ago. A statue carved out of human flesh. A thing that was alive, certainly, but only as plants are alive – soaking up air and sunshine and water, doing nothing else.

There was a name for mages who had lost their minds. For mages who stared into the void, and saw and heard and breathed nothing but the void. He shouldn't be afraid to use it.

A lacunant. That's what the supreme mage would become soon. And it was what Tatters would become too, one day.

Mages who used too much mindlink might mindramble. They'd daydream more often, they'd forget things. They wouldn't recognise new faces, or they'd get stuck on old ones. But those who abused mindlink turned into lacunants.

You're mindrambling more often, thought Lal. *And longer.* He sensed her worry.

And Tatters wasn't Lady Siobhan. Lady Siobhan would be tended for until the end. She would be nursed and protected as her mind fell apart. If Tatters degraded enough, he would join the lacunants at the front gates – they were the fallen mages without power, without homes. Sometimes their minds were ruined through no fault of their own.

This talk had solved nothing. Tatters worried his thoughts were decaying as steadily as the supreme mage's mouth. The image of sugar melting in a cup of water stuck inside him. He shook his head to clear it, slapped his cheeks. He needed to get out of here.

When he left the roof, Lady Siobhan stayed behind. Her maid continued to fuss over the supreme mage, who stood and stooped and stared. She was, in a way, already dead.

Chapter Four

A week went by before Isha returned to the tavern. Tatters knew she would: people who'd tasted mindbrawl always came back for more.

The Coop was quiet – three or four tables had groups around them, but the main floor was empty. He spotted Kilian's flash of blond hair and Isha leaning against the counter. Tatters waited, nurturing his beer. A few apprentices came to sit with him; one boy wanted to do some mindbrawl. Tatters wasn't in the mood to fight, but he might as well earn the money.

About half an hour passed before Isha and Kilian headed for his table. They pulled stools over, slotting in between the people already huddled around his booth. She was now wearing the same yellow belt as Kilian.

'Isha's been training to fight you,' said Kilian, looking proud, as if that wasn't entirely down to her own merit. Even the best training in the world, in this short time, wouldn't make Isha much of a threat. Still, it was the difference between having never held a sword and having learnt how to distinguish the blade from the hilt.

'But I want to see you duel someone else first,' she said. 'Kilian told me we could watch.'

'You've picked the right night,' said Tatters. 'I've got my first challenger.'

The boy had been there before, as a member of the audience. He wasn't expecting to win, only to gain some experience. He'd made little impression on Tatters. But now this wasn't only about gathering some money and making sure the apprentices wanted to learn from him – this was about impressing Isha enough that she would stick around, at least long enough for him to work out what Passerine's plans were.

So, he stood up on the bench and called for attention, asking people to place their bets with the innkeeper, giving as much importance to his opponent as possible. They freed a circle in the centre of the tavern, pushing back the tables, placing two chairs face-to-face.

Chairs, chuckled Lal. *We used to fight while running.*

Hawk would stomp through the Nest, thought Tatters.

It sounds like she's stomping through the convents, too.

He decided not to pursue that unhappy line of thought.

'What's your name?' he asked his challenger.

'Alistair.'

'Let me buy you a drink before we start.'

He bought a jug of beer, which they drank leaning against the counter. The trick was to win before the duel, not during. Tatters had seen women reading tea leaves who would, whilst preparing the brew, glean the details they needed from their client's private life. In the same way, he gathered snippets of information about his opponent long before they sat down to duel. Anything that could be used against Alistair was useful – be it his body-language, his vocabulary, his stance. Tatters didn't consider this cheating. It was part of the game.

'So why do you want to mindbrawl, lad?'

'The Nest might be sending people to the other side of the Shadowpass,' said Alistair. 'If they do, I want to be with them.'

'Really?' said Tatters. The Nest was always talking about sending mages through the Shadowpass, but they never did. He watched the innkeeper, who was listening to their conversation, wiping some grimy cups against his sleeve. Behind him, he'd piled the dry ones on a wooden plank nailed to the wall.

'There's a group of unlawful mages, the Renegades, and the convents need us to deal with them,' said Alistair. 'Lady Siobhan is considering sending fighters to check how bad the situation is. My family is from the east side of the Meddyns, near the Ridge. If they're in trouble, I want to be able to help.'

The innkeeper put the cup on the shelf behind him, pushing the rickety pile into shape.

'I heard about the Renegades,' he said. 'Nasty bunch, from what it sounds.'

'They are,' agreed Alistair.

'Roasting dead khers on spits and eating them, they say, to make them stronger.' The innkeeper seemed rather proud of his grisly story.

'Don't be silly,' laughed Tatters. 'No-one eats khers.'

If anything, the Renegades are better friends to the khers than most humans, said Lal.

The innkeeper shook his head. 'Don't be so sure. Protects you from mindlink, does kher flesh.'

'Oh really?' said Tatters. 'What happens when you shit it out?'

The innkeeper pursed his lips. His fingers went to his kher bracelet and tapped it thoughtfully.

'Not sure,' he admitted.

They talked for as long as it took to finish their drinks. Then Tatters invited Alistair to take a seat in the chair in front of him. The settler was Caitlin, as she was used to hosting duels for Tatters. She earned money off the bets, whoever won. Aside from the money, she wanted the practice and prestige.

Choosing a settler was difficult, because it needed to be someone trustworthy. Tatters didn't trust Caitlin, but he'd picked her because she was ambitious – and that blinded her. She was too driven to spend time worrying about other people's secrets. She was also convinced that he was an average mage, and didn't like to be proven wrong, even by herself.

Caitlin closed her eyes first; Tatters entered her mind. Most settlers had a signature arena to host other mages. She had a stone amphitheatre, with beaten earth at the centre and an eerily blue sky above them. The seats filled with the audience – including Isha and Kilian, side-by-side. Alistair joined them last.

In reality, the boy was chestnut-haired and mild-spoken. In mindlink, he didn't wear robes but chainmail. His face was hidden behind an eyeless helmet. His voice, when he spoke, was rougher. The chainmail gave away that Alistair still had a physical approach to mindbrawl. Tatters didn't need to imagine himself armoured to be confident no-one could harm him. Still, it sometimes helped apprentices, as their imagined protection was enough for them to be, in effect, protected. The faceless figure was a nice touch. It wouldn't give anything away.

'Are you ready?' Tatters asked.

Alistair nodded, but didn't attack. Tatters gave him a few seconds to make up his mind.

From their conversation before, Tatters surmised that Alistair wasn't too bothered about losing, which meant that trying to shame him wouldn't work. Going by his quiet personality, Tatters guessed he wouldn't be much of an invader, either.

We'll have to lead the offensive, said Lal.

Tatters was aware of the crowd's growing impatience. He crossed his arms.

'I'm not going to go down on my own, you know,' he told Alistair. The boy took a deep breath which hissed through his helmet's mouthpiece. A few people shouted encouragement from the edges of the arena.

You want to impress the girl? asked Lal. *Then let's do this together.*

On the poor kid? Isn't that overdoing it?

You want to be a nice person, or you want Isha's attention?

Alistair attacked.

He charged towards Tatters, pulling a long sword from his scabbard. Tatters glanced at it with interest. When the weapon drew an arc in front of him, he imagined the blade shorter, so it wouldn't reach him.

He was surprised to find the weapon was clearly pictured in Alistair's mind, imbued with precise feelings – the pain of being cut, the weight of a real sword. It wasn't that easy to change. A bit late, Tatters ducked to avoid the hit. The tip of the sword caught him. It struck like a real blade. Of course, the sensation was a fake one, made by Alistair. But it still stung, and Tatters heard his body gasp as the metal ripped against his ribs.

Tatters jumped backwards. In his place, he drew a figure, which he strongly invested with the sense of 'motherness'. She was a mother. Someone's mother, Alistair's mother. She didn't have a face – but she didn't need one. She shrieked in pain as the sword tore through her and she collapsed to the ground. Tatters was liberal about painting blood. He filled the image with the conviction that this death was Alistair's fault. Alistair shuddered to a stop; his helmet gave nothing away.

For extra safety, Tatters took a few steps back, out of reach of the sword. From the corner of his mind, he felt Lal as she manifested behind Alistair. She chose to picture herself wearing a male page's outfit, complete with the little feathered cap.

Her long red hair was tied in a bun under the hat. She was young enough that it was difficult to pinpoint her gender.

Some members of the audience spotted her, but Alistair didn't. Those who had seen Lal before leaned forward excitedly. Tatters saw Kilian nudging Isha and pointing, to show her what was happening.

Alistair remodelled the figure before him, so its features shifted from a woman's corpse to Tatters'. Tatters' limbs grew heavy. Cold spread across his fingers like frost – Alistair's idea of death. The ground underneath his feet cracked, as if it were as brittle as ice. Alistair imagined Tatters falling – not only falling through a hole in the floor, but falling as a corpse, draped in colourful fabric, flung over the Edge to the underworlds where his soul would be trapped.

Tatters let himself drop. But as he fell he became lighter and, as the Temple told them they might one day, if they were good enough, he imagined becoming a lightborn. From time to time, lightborns could be seen flying at night. They were a moving ray of light, dashing back and forth across the sky. The aurorae, as they were sometimes called. The Temple worshipped the lightborns like gods, but to Tatters that was like worshipping birds. They existed, yes, they were beautiful, that was true, and they could fly. But that didn't make them sacred.

Tatters rode the ray of light, which deposited him softly before Alistair. Lal was right behind. It was time to strike.

Tatters decided that if arrogance wasn't the issue, maybe low self-esteem was. He sent Alistair a vision of a mediocre mage in his home village, ordained, certainly, but unremarkable. He used petty tricks to extract money from his serfs. His wife was his parents' choice; she didn't love him, and he didn't love her. His children lived with their nurse and barely knew his name. Every day was exactly the same. And every day he wasted his life, and his mindlink talent, being nothing more than a local administrator, doing nothing more than what was expected of him.

Before Alistair could counter this image, Lal pushed her hand through his back, her fingers curled like the talons of a bird of prey. She grabbed his heart and tugged it out of his body, shredding flesh, with the disgusting sound of his vertebrae tearing.

Alistair screamed. He might have been able to block one of the attacks, but he wasn't expecting two of them at the same time, from different angles. Mental and physical pain flooded him. The solid knight dissolved into a mush of insecurities. This sometimes happened – it was called soulsplintering. When a person broke in mindlink, parts of themselves unravelled suddenly. Images flashed through Tatters' mind – bits and pieces of Alistair, memories and dreams and fears.

The face of another disciple as they did an impressive display of mindlink. Staring at his hand as he sat on his bed, the tinge of envy colouring his skin. Someone, maybe his father, a tall silhouette with greying hair, hitting him hard – too hard – and knocking him off his feet. A voice roaring in his ears. Liquid-hot fear running down his spine.

Normally only Tatters and the settler could see these images – that is, if Caitlin was doing her job right. That's what a settler was for: to prevent the loser from splintering in front of the audience, and eventually to protect them from the winner, in case they decided to abuse their power and trash their opponent's mind as it snapped. Tatters backed down, as was required of him.

That was too brutal, he scolded Lal. They were children. Misgivings about their future or who they might have sex with was enough to destabilise them. No need to go for the kill.

He's learnt something, she said.

Tatters didn't insist, but he let Lal perceive how annoyed he was.

This was why he tried to avoid including her in mindbrawls. In some ways she was like Hawk. She didn't do practice shots.

He focused on his sense of touch – rough wood under his legs and against his back, the warm glow of torches against his skin. He left Caitlin's mind.

In the tavern, Alistair had fainted. The innkeeper took out a wet cloth to dab at his forehead and neck with the quick, expert hand of someone used to dealing with Tatters' mess. There were a few coughs and chairs scratching the floorboards, but no-one dared look Tatters in the eye. Soulsplintering was considered bad luck at best, bad form at worst. Caitlin clapped, and a few apprentices followed, if only out of habit, but the applause was lukewarm.

They're clients, not enemies, he grumbled. *Look at what you've done.*

Lal was smug. She was pleased with the effect she'd had on the crowd. The problem with sharing the same mental space was that they couldn't lie to each other. She could've said she was sorry, but he already knew she wasn't.

Once they'd put the chairs away, he made a point of checking Alistair was all right. He and Caitlin helped Alistair to the counter, where they bought him another drink and spent a few minutes giving him advice. Unsurprisingly, he didn't want Tatters' company – he left quickly.

'You're in a good mood today,' Caitlin scoffed, as soon as Alistair was out of earshot. She spent her recently-earned money on a bowl of food, with a splash of red wine inside the soup, which the innkeeper gave her for an extra coin and which made it edible. She laughed it off, but it meant no-one else would fight Tatters this evening. They'd wait for a better day to challenge him, one where he was more playful, less intent on winning.

When Tatters returned to his booth, Kilian and Isha were deep in conversation.

'He's done it a few times,' Kilian was saying, 'but it's difficult to maintain, so he usually doesn't.'

Tatters sat down beside them. Isha glared at him. She wasn't impressed, or at least, she didn't want to seem that way. Maybe Lal was right. This girl rose to a challenge like hares jump over fires.

'Kilian said you can split your mind in two.' She made it sound as if she doubted it.

'That's pretty much it.' Tatters nodded.

Isha crossed her arms. 'I thought Caitlin was cheating.'

It wasn't very funny, but it made Tatters smile. 'If she ever cheats, I hope she does it more discreetly.'

That was one of the problems when picking a settler, of course. How could you be sure someone was impartial when it was your mind you were entrusting them with? There was no good solution. Audience members could sometimes spot cheating and discredit the settler. When the duels had higher stakes, two settlers were appointed, one picked by each opponent. And, of course, the settler must have no interest in the duel's resolution – hence Caitlin was paid the same sum whoever won.

It wasn't in Caitlin's interest to help Tatters. She would gain an outlawed man's favour but lose her chance at becoming one of the Nest's official settlers. The trade wasn't worth it, and most apprentices understood this. They tended to trust her for that reason. It didn't hurt that she was a good settler. She was, amongst the disciples, one of the best.

'How did you do it?' asked Isha.

He explained that the idea was to fragment your mind into several versions of yourself. In mindlink, dividing your personality into facets meant that, if you were damaged, only part of you was – and if you attacked, you could do so from several different places in the opponent's mind at the same time.

Which was the truth, but not what Lal was.

'And in your case, it's your adult self and your child self, right?' asked Kilian.

It was a convenient lie. Tatters assented.

'That sounds useful,' Isha said. 'Why don't more people use it?'

Tatters shrugged. The Nest lacked imagination. High mages didn't believe in evasion, in breaking themselves down to shards. Maybe they feared it would hasten their change into lacunants.

Kilian piped up: 'It's difficult to get right.'

That was also true. Creating items or armour, or even ideas like 'a mother' or 'someone dying', was relatively easy. But creating something that acted independently, trying to think two actions at once, and imagine them as coming from distinct people, was a tough trick to pull off.

'Do you want to try?' he asked.

Isha pinched her lips together. She didn't want to say no, he could tell. But the duel had shaken her after all. As it would.

'You do training, as well as duels?' she said.

He explained the difference to her – he won money on duels by people betting for or against him, and keeping part of the innkeeper's commission. But people paid for training. Isha put some coins on the table.

'Kilian, my good man...'

'I'll be the settler,' Kilian said, before Tatters could even finish his sentence.

Doesn't want anyone else prying in his girlfriend's mind, said Lal.

It's rather touching, actually, said Tatters. *I've never seen him act protective.*

Lal did the mental equivalent of rolling her eyes.

Tatters projected himself into Kilian's settled mind. The theatre, despite its gold and silver ornaments, was as shabby as ever. When Tatters paced the stage, the hollow wood didn't echo under his feet. Kilian had been too lazy to imagine sound inside his arena. As Tatters waited for Isha, he noted that all the seats were the same colour, however far from the light source. It made the place too bright; flat and unfinished in more than one way. As was his habit, Kilian sat in the front row of the theatre.

When she joined them, it was clear Isha's mindlink figure had improved. It was about her size, but thinner and more elongated, with a chiselled face. The tattoo was fudged, as if it were a light scar. Her grey robes fell more comfortably around her. It was a tame projection, with nothing original about it, but it was still better than her previous incarnation.

'Not bad,' said Tatters.

But a terrible giveaway, said Lal.

Of course.

Tatters lifted his hand. It wasn't hard to imagine Isha with her tattoo – it was such an important feature of her face that he could see it with his eyes closed. He drew her tattoo with the tip of his finger. It crawled from underneath her hair like small black insects, a swarm of ants or flies spreading on her skin. Shuddering, she backed away from him. She radiated – not shame, as he had expected – but rage, helpless anger at having been branded, at belonging without choosing to belong.

When she pushed against him, Tatters let go. The tattoo faded.

'Look at it this way,' he said. 'It's like the collar. People see it. They know it's important. That's where your strongest defence needs to be.'

She rubbed her face. She tried to hide that she hadn't been expecting this.

'No-one went for the tattoo before you,' she protested.

Tatters couldn't help smiling at that. So, people had played nice so far? What did they think training was for?

'Right. People pretend they're polite. But when push comes to shove, they'll fight dirty. They'll go for the tattoo first.'

Isha took a deep breath and nodded. She replaced herself in the centre of the stage, legs spread to take up more space, fists lifted before her, ready to fight.

'Show me your other you.' She presented it like an order, not a request.

Lal came of her own accord. She took shape beside Tatters, her bare feet stark on the dark wood of the stage. She stuck with the young page imagery, which was probably safest. Removing her feathered hat, she gave Isha a bow.

'I do like the bold ones.' Lal smiled.

Isha glanced from Lal to Tatters and back. Kilian leant closer to the edge of his seat.

'Your double is a girl,' Isha pointed out.

Tatters was surprised that she was so perceptive, but he only shrugged. 'She represents my feminine side.'

'So, she's a part of you, but she hasn't got the collar,' said Isha.

'She's a free spirit,' said Tatters.

Isha joined her hands and closed her eyes. Her tattoo reappeared across her face. First, it deepened in colour. It grew darker and darker, pitch-black. Then, it started growing. It shivered like a living thing and spilled over Isha's skin. It was as if the ink was boiling, and the pressure building up was pushing it out of her, until the tattoo dripped onto the ground. Tatters examined the process, which mimicked the technique Hawk had taught him – she advised breaking up the procedure of making a double by imagining steps the mind could follow.

Soon, ink was flowing from Isha's face to the floor. Kilian

watched in awe. 'She's good, isn't she?' he said to no-one in particular.

'Yes,' said Tatters. 'She is.' He had never seen an apprentice capable of splitting their mind after one week.

The ink solidified into a black-fleshed figure, which turned out to be a bird – something hefty and clawed, a bird of prey or a crow. This ink-bird Isha was the colour of the night sky, even its eyes and beak.

The bird had achieved something else: it had taken the tattoo off Isha's skin. She had split herself into the person who was what the tattoo represented, and the person who wasn't.

'That is ... excellent,' said Tatters. 'Can you move independently?'

Isha nodded. She approached Tatters from the left, circling him as if they were going to wrestle with punches and kicks. The bird took flight, heading for Lal.

Is she going to be able to fight like this? wondered Tatters.

Lal was brimming with excitement, primed for battle. But Tatters wasn't sure this was such good news. Isha could complete a complicated mindlink technique that required months to stabilise. She couldn't have spent only a week learning it. It was impossible. But during her last fight, Isha had behaved like a first-timer. How did those two elements fit together?

Maybe Passerine had taught her. It was uncanny to know Hawk, whose blazon was a bird, and to see this girl, who had picked a bird to be her double. It was the sort of sick humour that Passerine would indulge in.

While he was distracted, both Ishas pounced. Tatters wasn't sure what the bird did to Lal, but she'd been ready – which was more than could be said of him, taken completely off-guard.

Isha sent him a picture of his life at the tavern, growing older as apprentices grew younger. She projected an unambitious, drawn-out life, in which he took petty pleasure in humiliating younger mages, who then went on to be ordained and rule the Nest. They grew in might and glory while he continued to pretend he was a great mindbrawler by bullying kids. He was nothing but an impostor.

Tatters was lucky, because Isha miscalculated. Growing old in a modest setting wasn't what he feared – it was what he hoped for.

Although he withstood it, Tatters was shaken by the unexpected flood of images. Isha's mindbrawl was still too amateur to evoke all five senses; she didn't drag emotions from the core of his chest. But it was a decent attempt.

Isha's attack subdued, like the moon waning. Lal laughed in delight.

'Still think you can afford not to focus when we fight?' Isha asked. Her voice was defiant. 'Do you still think…'

Before she could finish her sentence, she collapsed. The bird dissolved. The tension of maintaining herself and a double, all the while crafting two distinct assaults, had been too much. She couldn't sustain it. Her concentration failed her; she couldn't stay in Kilian's arena, as she couldn't focus enough to project her mind outside of herself. She disappeared suddenly.

Tatters opened his eyes. Isha hadn't fainted, but she'd nearly fallen off her chair. She held onto the table with one hand, moving erratically.

'You killed another one?' asked Caitlin. She was drinking the dregs of her soup, sitting on the opposite side of the table. 'Go easy on us, or there'll be no-one left.'

A few apprentices turned to stare. Isha shook her head in frustration. She opened her mouth, but she couldn't bring herself to speak.

'Take your time,' said Tatters.

What did she do? he asked Lal.

She pictured my childhood of pain and poverty.

Best childhood ever.

Exactly.

It hadn't included much food or heating, of course. But their mother had carried a warmth, a light, which their whole family had bathed in.

Kilian opened his eyes. He rubbed Isha's shoulder to help her return from mindlink. It took a few minutes before she could string coherent words together. When it was established Isha wasn't permanently traumatised, most of the apprentices lost interest.

'This is so frustrating,' she managed. She pressed the flat of her hands against her temples, as if to crush the sensations spinning there.

'It was very good,' said Tatters. 'Nothing to be upset about.' He turned to Kilian. 'Go buy the girl a drink, she needs it.'

Kilian seemed reluctant to leave, but Isha muttered: 'I'll pay you back.'

He got up, pale-skinned and golden-haired, a white shape in the grimy tavern. He was handsome, Tatters supposed, if you liked tall, gangly and mismatched.

While Kilian was waiting at the counter, Tatters turned to Isha. The frown between her eyebrows seemed carved there. When her face tensed, the tattoo moved in surprising ways, underlining one eye, pulling the corner of her lips down.

'You did well,' he said.

'But I couldn't keep it up.' She crossed her arms, and her fingers dug into her elbows, creasing her sleeves.

He wasn't sure what to think. The clues around Isha were disparate and strange. She had a kher tattoo, a farm girl background, incredible mindlink talent. A link to Passerine. None of it added up.

Let it go, said Lal. *If Passerine finds you, he'll beat you to a pulp and drag you back to Hawk. It's not worth it.*

He won't need to beat me, Tatters thought bitterly. *He'll get the collar to do it for him.*

He watched Isha as she sulked. He still didn't know what it was he recognised about her. He wished he could follow Lal's advice and leave Isha alone, ignore the tug inside his chest, the uncanny feeling that there was something he had to do, something he had to say, before it was too late.

You shouldn't follow your heart, said Lal. *You're old enough to know better.*

But despite Lal's advice, he found himself asking: 'Have you ever visited the lightborn Temple?'

Isha shook her head, keeping her eyes averted. The Temple was a landmark. New apprentices would want to see it, even though mages didn't share the Temple's beliefs.

'Would you like to go for a walk with me tomorrow afternoon? We could go up to the Edge and visit.'

He spoke cautiously, conscious she would read more into his words, but hoping she would be too curious to turn him down.

'Why did you wait for Kilian to go to the counter before asking?' she said.

'He's not invited.'

She held his gaze. Her scowl softened.

'What is it you want?' she asked.

He didn't think she knew it, but she was difficult to lie to. She stared right through people, in a way that dared them to trick her. Her asymmetrical face made her hard to read. Because he couldn't tell when she was and wasn't buying what he said, Tatters struggled to dose his mix of falsehood and truth. This time, he settled for the truth.

'You want to learn from me. I want to learn from you. Is there anyone in the Nest who can teach you what I'm teaching you right now?'

She shook her head. He knew it, of course. It was, in part, why so many apprentices flocked to him: because he taught them something no-one else would admit to, or maybe didn't have the creativity to imagine.

Hawk's legacy, said Lal.

He recoiled at the thought. *Don't put it that way.*

Tatters focused on the here and now, the sounds and scents of the tavern. He lowered his voice. Isha moved closer. 'The Coop is great, but not private. We could chat in peace.'

Kilian came back. Tatters gave him the place on the booth closest to Isha. She thanked him for the beer and sipped it, leaving a smear of foam across her upper lip.

She had been taught how to send a message through mindlink. As Kilian was congratulating her on her successful double, she projected her answer towards Tatters.

Yes.

Kilian perceived it, of course. Isha was as subtle as a herd of horses. She would have to learn how to use mindlink without it reverberating around her. Kilian narrowed his eyes at her and glared at Tatters.

Tatters only smiled. He added to Kilian's praise, saying he'd never seen a puffin with a double. He spoke loudly. His diversion worked – a few apprentices wanted to know what this was about. When they asked about it, Tatters advised them to interrogate the settler, Kilian. Soon a group of five or so people had clustered around their table, eager to hear the story of Isha's double.

While Kilian and Isha were busy dealing with questions, Tatters slipped away. It had been a long evening. It was time to go to bed.

***

Tatters knew he was dreaming because he didn't cast a shadow.

He was walking down a stone corridor. High stained-glass windows lined the walls, and the moonlight streaming through projected a mosaic of hues – green, blue, yellow – onto the paved floor. The atmosphere of the place was solemn. His steps splashed softly, as if he were wading through water. There was no water in sight.

He didn't like dreams. They were a form of uncontrolled mindlink. Either he had connected with someone else's mind, or they had connected with his. They were both sleeping. Neither of them had meant for this to happen.

'And they must be near.'

Hearing Lal's voice spooked Tatters more than the setting. There she was, as if in the flesh. A girl wearing a white nasivyati, one cloth folded around her legs like a skirt, another around her waist like a thick belt, the last knotted over her chest. Her red hair fell in an unkempt bundle across her shoulders. The windows cast a patchwork of colours across her face, covering it like a mask.

'What are you doing here?' he asked.

She shrugged. She touched the smooth stone wall, watching the light filtering through her fingers.

'It seems this dream is for both of us.'

Tatters didn't like the sound of that. Their dreams should be distinct. If Lal had been a projection of his mind, she could have followed him in his sleep – she would have been nothing more than another part of himself. But she was more than that.

And she was right about the other dreamer being near. Sharing dreams only happened when the two mages were close, both geographically and emotionally. A shared intimacy was required to share a mental space. Even then, dreams could only travel short distances.

The corridor stretched on, with no doors, with windows too high to reach. Tatters and Lal resumed walking. There was no point in searching for a way out. Dreams were dead ends.

Suddenly the passageway flared bright blue. A rippling ray of light brushed past them like a large, twisting snake flying above their heads. As soon as it had appeared, the beam was gone, becoming only a glow at the end of the corridor, fading out of sight. Lal took Tatters' hand. He squeezed, but he couldn't feel her. This dream didn't allow for touch.

'That was a lightborn,' she said.

Now Tatters knew who the dreamer was. 'He'll find us, or we'll find him.' He had to admit he was glad Lal was here, whatever the reason.

They continued down the corridor, holding hands like they hadn't in years, like siblings.

They entered a great hall, greater even than the Nest. Pillars rose at regular intervals, like the carved pillars of a temple, representing animals and trees and vines. At the centre of the room, a skylight broke the uniformity of the ceiling. It was a dome made entirely of glass. The moonlight cast a shape on the ground, as it had in the corridor. Before the circle of light, with his back to them, was Passerine.

Tatters and Lal froze. Passerine was talking, but not to them. He was addressing the skylight.

'I've done nothing wrong. What I did, any of you would have done, if you weren't cowards.'

Passerine interrupted himself, as if he were listening to answers from the dark sky above. His voice was angry, with an edge of despair to it. Tatters had never heard him so stirred.

'You can't do this to me.'

Passerine took a deep breath, as if about to speak, but cut himself off again, holding in the air. He let it out slowly, listening intently to the silence.

'No,' he whispered. 'No. It's humiliating. I don't…'

He stopped again. Tatters wasn't sure whether to make himself known. Dreams often had a set pattern, and dreamers could either let them follow their course or struggle against them, to no avail. It was often easier to let the dream unfold.

Passerine laughed, a sound like stones shaking in a metal bucket.

'Humble? Why should we, of all people, need to be humble?'

Passerine went down on one knee. He lowered his face. His black hair was at the very edge of the pale circle, and where the light struck, it shone silver-grey.

Tatters felt something sliding around his heart. It was fear.

'There,' said Passerine. 'You've got your humble. Please, I'm asking you to reconsider. I didn't do anything wrong. If it was wrong, I did it for the right reasons. It's… I didn't want any of this. All I wanted was a new aurora.'

His heavy breathing was the only sound in the hall, rasping like wind through the room.

For the first time, Tatters felt Lal's fingers. They were holding his tightly. His collar was radiating a faint yellow aura. The silence stretched on and on; Passerine was unmoving, the black of his cape like a shadow cast by a pillar.

Tatters decided this had lasted long enough, and that whatever Passerine was experiencing was private. He had never seen Passerine vulnerable, and he knew the man enough to know what it meant – if someone saw him bow, it would be someone powerful enough to coerce him, or it would be someone dead. This dream had been unwanted. If Tatters left quietly, Passerine need never know this was anything but another nightmare in which he knelt before the moon for a grace that never came.

But as soon as Tatters took a step backwards, the spell of silence was broken. His foot touched the stone as it would have crystal; ringing echoed across the hall. Passerine was on his feet before Tatters could even turn to run – not that running would be much use.

'Who...' Passerine didn't finish his sentence. When their gazes met, the hall shuddered; the walls shimmered like a reflection in water disturbed by a tossed pebble, before settling again, as solid as before.

Tatters lifted one hand as a sign of peace. The other still held onto Lal.

'This isn't what it looks like,' he said.

Tatters heard how thin and worried his own voice was.

Passerine stared at him, his face settling into a mask, his back straightening, any giveaway of emotion cleansed out of his posture.

'You,' he spat. He couldn't keep the fury from his tone. The words quivered like a clenched fist. 'Where have you been?'

Tatters shook his head. Although they were several strides apart, although they were sleeping, he backed away. Passerine didn't follow, but kept his gaze riveted on Tatters.

'You can't be far,' said Passerine. 'You're in the city, aren't you?' Liquid light, the colours from the dome, framed his face. With each step away from him, Passerine's features became more indistinct.

Passerine snapped his fingers. Despite himself, despite everything, Tatters felt the collar constrict around his neck. He stopped. The magic flowed through him like blood. This wasn't a dream anymore. This was a nightmare.

Passerine spoke in a low voice, but it resonated across the hall.

'Come grovelling for forgiveness, and you might get it. But if you don't come, I'll find you.'

'Don't you dare threaten him,' said Lal. She placed herself between them, a shock-pale figure in the hall of shadows.

Passerine's stare moved from Tatters to Lal like a living thing, like a snake or a rope coiling around her neck. 'You are dead,' he told her.

As Passerine focused on Lal, Tatters felt the collar's pull slacken. He tried to run backwards, not wanting to turn, intent on keeping his attention on Passerine. His back smashed against something hard, and for a moment he thought it was a pillar from the hall, before he felt the lines between the wooden floorboards where he slept. Through half-closed eyes he saw the moonlight filtering through his window, grey lines on the floor beside him.

The last image of the dream was Passerine's face, close-up. In the two circles of white around the well of his pupils, Tatters could make out Lal's ghostly reflection.

Tatters woke up suddenly. He started coughing, and was soon taken by a fit of hacking, his lungs fighting as if they were revolting against air. When he struggled to his knees, the rough wood caught his shins. He tried to control his coughs, but it only brought tears to his eyes, which were soon streaming down his face. He brought his hands to his neck. The collar was burning hot, growing tighter.

He's trying to summon me, panicked Tatters.

He hasn't got any power over the collar, said Lal. *It's broken. It belongs to Hawk.*

Tell that to the collar!

Tatters wondered if he would die choking on dust and bad dreams. An urge called him to the door, ordered him out of the tavern and into the moon-streaked streets.

Never, said Lal.

He felt her pull against the collar, straining as if she were a physical being, holding Tatters down with all her weight while the collar choked him.

For a moment Tatters wasn't sure who to side with. It would be easy to yield to the collar and walk the road to the Nest. It would be less painful.

But he would have crossed the Shadowpass for nothing. Tatters coiled into a ball, pressing his fists against his diaphragm. He rested his forehead against the floor. His lungs hurt. His throat hurt. Each cough cut like a blade. He curled around the pain, into it, and closed his eyes. He'd done this before. He could do it again.

And Lal was right. The collar hummed with magic, but it was nothing compared to what it had been. They hadn't broken it, he wouldn't go that far, but they had damaged it. Its light dimmed. Tatters breathed deeply, pressed against the floor, shivering in his room which let everything – air, smells, the cold – inside.

He sat up. He rubbed his neck. The gold was still hot. Tatters pulled his covers around him. Despite the collar, he felt frozen to his bones. He nestled against the miscellanea from the Coop, staring at the door he hadn't opened.

We did it!

Tatters didn't share Lal's enthusiasm.

But now he knows we're here.

Chapter Five

Tatters stood before the Nest's front door, in the shade of the gates, waiting for Isha. He tried to ignore the lacunants crouching beside him.

They held up wooden bowls but, unlike most beggars, they weren't begging for money. Most of them wouldn't know how to spend it. Apprentices sometimes put a stone in their bowls, for the fun of watching them try to eat it – and sometimes succeed.

He always felt ill at ease with lacunants. They wore clothes bleached by rain and foul weather. They didn't huddle together, instead staring at the wall or their hands. Most of them talked, but only to themselves, in low mumbles sometimes interrupted by a scream or a fit of giggling. Amongst them, one could find petty criminals with the gift and high mages who had broken the Nest's laws. If a person was gifted, the Nest never condemned them to death. But the lawmages tore their minds to shreds and left them in front of the castle gates, speaking sweet nonsense to the stones.

If a mage became a lacunant because they abused mindlink, they might also end up here, if they lacked friends or family to tend to them.

If someone stepped on their hands, they didn't whimper. They ate what was given to them and drank the rainwater gathered at the bottom of their bowls. Some of them, the ones most far gone, died quietly, curled in a ball against the wall.

Tatters spotted a woman in vivid red, the dye of her robes not yet faded, which meant she had recently joined the shore of driftwood souls. She was laughing, a hard laughter like sobbing, which raked through her body. The sharp angle of her shoulder blades poked out underneath her cape. He wished he had food to give her.

She was what he would become, if the lawmages caught him.

Or maybe even without their help, said Lal.

Passerine knew he was in town, which meant the Coop might not be safe anymore. But Tatters hated the prospect of running away. He had clientele, he had a bed. Going back to sleeping rough wasn't something he looked forward to. And he was easy to recognise – the collar was too difficult to hide. Leaving might prompt more rumours, attracting attention, achieving the opposite of his purpose.

He sighed. He hoped Isha had answers. Life, as far as he was concerned, needed to be conducted like mindbrawl – he wanted all the information long before he started the fight. For one thing, he might decide the fight wasn't worth it.

At last, Isha joined him outside.

'May you grow tall.'

They touched wrists before setting off towards the Temple.

The path wound across the moorland. Tatters led the way, while Isha let the brambles lining the track scratch at the hem of her clothes. It was a cool autumn day. When the sun shone it was pleasant enough, but as soon as the wind lifted they felt the sharpness of winter to come. The shrubland was orange and red, and each gust of wind tugged a few leaves from the trees' branches.

They weren't alone on the path. Pilgrims trekked across the

moor, small groups in single file, pious men. People carrying their dead. No mages.

At first they walked in silence, but Tatters wasn't shy.

'So, tell me,' he said. 'How are you finding the Nest?'

He watched as she focused on the well-trodden path, trying to steer her thin leather soles clear of the mud.

'It's like any other place. There's bullies and idiots and good people and bad people.'

Tatters plucked some blackberries as they walked, picking the berries from the thornbushes as carefully as he picked his words.

'Have you been to the Temple before?' he asked.

She shook her head. 'I'm told it's beautiful.'

'It is. Didn't Kilian offer to show you?'

Her foot slipped and mud spattered up her ankles. She rolled her eyes, maybe at Tatters or maybe at herself.

'You know he didn't,' she said. 'He thought it wasn't safe for apprentices on their own. Apparently believers can get a bit rough.'

'To be fair, they can.' Although they didn't have much power against a mage, and the priests had to share their grounds with the Nest, whether they liked it or not.

Kilian must have been afraid Isha's tattoo would bring them even more trouble, suggested Lal.

Tatters gave Isha a reassuring smile. 'We'll be fine.'

With the long lights of autumn cutting across the country-side, everything seemed flusher – the copper shade of her skin, the brown of her irises, even her cloud-grey robes. The mud on the side of the tracks was as black as the long, dark slugs beneath the trees.

The breeze picked up again. On instinct, Isha and Tatters moved closer. He offered her some crushed blackberries.

She took a few, and he threw the others in his mouth, licking his palm clean. They weren't ripe, but he didn't mind their tang.

As they grew closer, the track changed from mud to stone. The paved path started abruptly, indicating the end of the land belonging to the Nest, and the beginning of the sacred grounds the priests tended to. The road was made of white flagstones.

It was also a road khers weren't allowed to walk, in case they unhallowed it.

From here, the roofs of the Temple were visible, their mirrored surfaces catching the late afternoon sun. A bunch of people with temporary stalls were selling scented candles, charms, lotions, mirrors. Although the Groniz festival wasn't for another month, the stands were scattered with bracelets of green cloth. A continuous flow of mourners drifted past; either family members carrying the bodies in shrouds or, if the dead had travelled far, professional mourners.

Tatters and Isha wove between processions as the mourners jostled for space, avoiding bodies wrapped in wood and cloth, shaking their heads as stallholders called out to them. Tatters bought some scented candles; they were made on the grounds and supposedly helped the mind ascend when breathing in their perfume. Not that he believed they worked, but they would make a nice gift for Arushi.

Most high priests or priestesses would be sleeping, as ceremonies were conducted at night, but there were always people of the faith around to welcome visitors. One of their main duties would be to collect bodies that were brought to them by grieving families. And to prevent khers from entering the Temple, of course, if any were dumb enough to try.

Once in sight of the Temple, Tatters counted his strides. He reached five before a priest called out for them to stop. He spun on his heels with a smile.

'What's this?' asked the priest. He was a middle-aged man, lean, with sunken eyes that didn't sleep enough. 'Halfbloods cannot come here, as you very well know.'

'May you grow tall,' said Tatters. Isha was pale, but she held the man's gaze without flinching. 'She isn't a halfblood,' explained Tatters, 'she's a mage. Don't you recognise the robes?'

The priest took this in. It was difficult to tell if he was more offended at the idea of an apprentice on his grounds or a half-kher. One had no soul; the other had a sinful soul.

'Please,' said Tatters. 'We're not looking for trouble.'

Priests liked collarbounds. Legends even told of a collarbound prophet. Being bound to obey wasn't unlike being bound by flesh, physical desire, and the humiliation of being only human. The man bit his lips and considered Tatters.

This priest was an ungifted. Tatters nudged his mind in the right direction. He sensed Isha's attention turning to him.

Don't get caught for illegal mindlink, warned Lal.

On a priest? Mages do this all the time, when they think they can get away with it.

'Very well,' said the priest. He glared at Isha. 'But do not be disrespectful.'

They passed more stalls with carved figurines, wooden trinkets with crowns of woven grass, tamed magpies who could tell you your fortune.

'That was a mean trick to play on him,' said Isha as soon as they were out of earshot. 'Do you often mindlink people to think what you want?'

Tatters shrugged. 'He was in the way.'

And you're going to play an even meaner trick on her, said Lal.

I wouldn't say mean. I would say it's a necessary precaution.

Now the Temple was visible in full. It was made of pale marble, with domes covered in mirrors. In the sunny afternoon, the roofs shone enough to burn their eyes. On the left, a shrine hung from the Edge; on the right stood an oblong building with a slate roof, in which the novices prepared the bodies for their flight.

Pink-veined marble steps led up to the entrance. The doors and windows of the Temple didn't have frames or glass to close them, but were left gaping open, so the wind could whistle through. Wooden wind chimes were hanging underneath each porch. Their chorus of hollow, sad ringing was an answer to the birds' happy chirruping.

A few novices were cleaning the grounds. One of them pointed out the wicker baskets placed across the front steps. She reminded Tatters and Isha that they had to leave behind what made their souls heavy. They took off their shoes, as was the custom. A few belts, coats and other items could be found in the baskets, from people too poor for shoes. Devout folk left everything behind to enter the Temple in their undertunic, shivering and freed from their worldly possessions.

Inside, the sound of wind chimes echoed like muttered prayers, as if the souls trapped in the underworlds were begging to be set free. From the corner of his eye, Tatters saw Isha hugging her elbows for warmth.

At the centre of the Temple was a mosaic floor. The green and blue melded into a pattern like twisting vines. It was a representation of two lightborns. The priests had used different shades to imitate the ripples of light running down a lightborn's body, in precious and semi-precious stones. The green lightborn was Groniz, the Giver. The blue lightborn was Byluk, the Taker. They were dance-fighting.

This Temple was devoted to the living as they grieved and to the dead as they left. Groniz gave the gift of life; Byluk took it back. Groniz gave you blessings to help along your path; Byluk took your burdens from you.

Blue and green lightborns existed, of course – the believers revered them indiscriminately, as if all green aurorae were manifestations of Groniz, as if the same went for Byluk. To Tatters, it was akin to worshipping clouds, or the colours of the sunset, the reds and yellows one day, the purple horizon the next evening, although the clouds had long since changed, blown away by the wind.

People were praying, their foreheads pressed against the mosaic. Touching a lightborn, even a picture of one, was supposed to make the soul lighter.

Why don't you try to find a picture of the lightborn Raudaz? teased Lal.

Don't. The Temple served his purpose today, that was all. He avoided it when he could.

He knew he had made the right choice when Isha knelt to touch the Giver's portrait. Her curly hair was tousled by the wind, repeatedly pushed across her eyes. She had to tuck it behind her ears to see before she laid her hand flat against the stones.

Praying opened people's minds. It was one of the reasons why priests were vulnerable to mages.

When Isha got up, they headed for the Taker's shrine. The wooden structure reached out over the emptiness of the Edge, as if trying to bridge it. It was decorated with mirrors that caught the yellow autumn light. Shards of sunlight mottled the ground around it, as if a gold vase had been smashed there.

A woman was waiting beside the shrine, but for the time being the shrine itself remained empty, which served Tatters' purpose perfectly. He needed to be alone with Isha, somewhere where no-one could hear their conversation.

'Do you want to go inside?' Tatters asked. 'I imagine you had one of these at home.'

Isha studied the sacred shrine. It didn't have walls, as such, only a few wooden beams, well spaced-out, to indicate the end of the platform. It had been painted blue, but erosion, wind and rain had faded the colour from the grain of the wood.

'Ours didn't require us to step off solid ground,' she said. 'But I'll give it a go.'

Tentatively, Isha entered the shrine. Tatters followed her. His heart beat harder. It wasn't flying – it could never be – but it was as close to flying as the believers could get. The wind caught his cloak, tugging it this way and that like a living thing, pulling him in different directions.

Isha was pale. 'This is ... something,' she muttered. As she'd grown up by the Shadowpass, this would be the closest she'd ever got to the Edge.

Tatters went to sit beside a wooden pillar. He invited her over. She moved slowly, arms apart. The wind wailed.

They rested at the edge of the shrine, at the Edge of the world. As far as the eye could see was mist, fading into the light blue of the sky. The wind was so fierce that, for a moment, Tatters could believe it would rip his soul out of his body and carry it upwards. Part of him longed to jump.

Below them lay the underworlds. According to the priests, the low clouds beneath their feet were the souls of great men, but not great enough to ascend. They drifted in limbo, regretting past mistakes that prevented them from flying any further. His mother was always adamant that ghosts and hauntings were due to unruly souls rising to reach the world of the living. She had been a superstitious woman, with good reason, all things considered.

Who knew what his father had believed?

Tatters glanced at Isha. She was still the colour of watery porridge, but she nodded when he asked whether she could cope with the dizziness. He didn't feel any unease himself, as he swung his legs in the emptiness below him.

Now is the time, said Lal.

'Shall we do an Unburdening?' Tatters offered.

They had to squeeze close to hear each other above the wind.

Isha shook her head, but she didn't say no. She clung onto the wooden platform until her knuckles blanched. 'You don't strike me as a believer.'

Tatters shrugged. 'It could be interesting. We could get to know each other.'

An Unburdening had simple rules – it had to be done with someone you didn't know, or didn't know well. You spoke of the things that weighed down your soul; it was the mental equivalent of discarding clothing and shoes. You spoke the truth. Once the Unburdening was over and you left the shrine, you never mentioned what had been said to a living soul.

The priests encouraged letting go of gold, of goods, of secrets.

'Very well,' said Isha. She was putting up a good show of being unimpressed. 'How shall we do this?'

'We could trade questions and answers,' said Tatters. It was one way of doing it. The other was simply to let each person speak, in turn, of what they felt was most important; but that wouldn't help Tatters find out what he wanted. Isha was right – he cared little for the usual ceremony and gravitas surrounding an Unburdening.

Lying was, after all, what being a mage was all about.

Are you ready? he asked Lal.

When am I not? He felt her reach out to Isha.

'What does the tattoo mean?' he asked.

Isha frowned. 'That's not how you're supposed to do it.

There are questions for the hands, the eyes and the heart. Deeds you've done, scenes you've seen, feelings you've felt. And you Unburden the hands, the eyes and the heart in turn – letting go of what you've done that you regret, what you've seen that has scarred you, what you've felt that has hurt you.'

Tatters smiled. 'You don't strike me as a believer,' he teased, repeating her own words.

'If you're going to do this, you should do it right.'

'Nice try,' he said. 'You want me to believe there is no emotional weight linked to your tattoo? Doesn't it count as a question for the heart?'

Isha's expression closed, like someone slamming a book shut. 'I don't know what it means,' she said. 'That's the truth.'

It didn't matter. Tatters was more interested in what thoughts the question stirred. Lightly, ever so lightly, Lal touched Isha's mind. Lal unearthed a huge silhouette, a woman. The smell of horses when she picked Isha up and crushed her into a hug. But no face, not even a vague contour or colour. Tatters had the taste of horsehair on his tongue. Isha's mind was loud, tumultuous. If he wasn't cautious, it would swamp him.

Spying wasn't fair, but Isha hadn't mastered mindlink enough to sense Tatters doing it. Which was in part why mages, in each other's presence, kept their minds closely guarded.

He sensed Isha eyeing him. The wind pulled her hair back tightly, revealing the full length of her tattoo, snaking down her ear and her neck.

'Who is your master?' she asked.

One for the heart, said Lal.

It was too late to back down. *I hope this lie holds*, he thought.

'Lady Siobhan,' was the answer he gave out loud. 'Who else?'

Isha studied his face. She was starting to think like a mage, trying to read his thoughts, to spot mistruths. But she wasn't doing it right. She needed to use mindlink, not facial expressions, to pick up clues.

'I don't believe you. How come Lady Siobhan lets you do illegal duels?'

Luckily we spent all that time thinking up a consistent lie! Lal was being ironic. Tatters never answered questions, which was much easier than getting caught out lying.

'I was trained for mental sparring.' And physical, of course. And both at the same time. 'That's what my master wanted me to do. To learn new mindbrawling techniques and teach them to other mages.' The truth, again; only a half-truth, as always.

'I guess you can't do anything your master doesn't approve of,' said Isha.

Unless they forget to forbid you from doing it, corrected Lal.

Tatters didn't give Isha time to ponder the answer he had given her. 'Who are your parents?' he asked.

She kept her eyes averted, which was an ungifted's impulse. Mages knew mindlink didn't need eye-contact, and when they wanted to hide their emotions, they outstared you. Ungifted believed the eyes were the windows to the soul – although in truth the window, the front door and the key were all in the mages' hands.

'I was brought up by two people I wasn't related to.' Lal was hovering close to Isha's mind. Memories floated to the surface, more neatly defined than the previous ones. Faces. Rough hands. The colour of the apron, the weight of the wooden clogs. 'They took care of me. My parents paid them for the service, I think.'

So, she was a foster-child. He wondered why anyone would bother paying farmers to look after their daughter if it wasn't to claim her back, sooner or later. If someone wanted to abandon a babe, they left her on the step of a lightborn temple. They only spent money if they hoped to see her again.

She shook her head. 'I don't know who my parents are.'

'That's two questions you've answered with *I don't know*,' he pointed out.

'Maybe you should ask better questions.'

He laughed. That was what he enjoyed about Isha – the sheer cheek of her.

Unprompted, Isha added: 'When I was small, my father used to visit. I think.' She didn't say it, but her mind did: *Crossed the Shadowpass to see me.* It explained her darker skin and hair, at least. There was Sunriser blood in there somewhere.

Mentioning her father roused complicated feelings inside her. They welled suddenly, not unlike Lady Siobhan's erratic mindlink, and for a moment neither Tatters nor Lal could think their own thoughts. They belonged entirely to Isha.

It was Passerine. He was older, but age hadn't softened his face, only given his expressions a sharper edge. His hair hadn't whitened. He was wearing a red travelling stana, wrapped around him in the Sunriser style. He was seen from afar, maybe walking up to her farm; or maybe walking away, a smudge growing fainter in the distance.

Tatters pulled away from Isha's mind, trying to hide his shock under a cough. Thankfully Isha seemed focused on the depths beyond the Edge. She was watching the seagulls nesting in the cliff-face, emerging from the clouds like spirits, then dipping down and fading back to white.

She's strong, thought Lal. *She'll be dangerous when she knows how to use that strength.*

If she's Passerine's daughter, she's dangerous already.

But he wouldn't tattoo his child – would he? asked Lal.

Despite the sun, Tatters was cold. *If we mess with his daughter – if she is his daughter – then he'll rip us to shreds.* Passerine hadn't been much interested in kher artwork, but something might have pushed him to it. But then why would Isha be hiding her relationship with him, when she would gain more prestige by saying she was kin?

I don't know what this is about, said Lal, *but it isn't good news.*

Isha was speaking. Tatters forced himself to listen.

'Let's assume you lied to me,' she said.

'Perish the thought!' He was trying to make her laugh, but she didn't even smile.

'What would be the consequences? If you weren't Lady Siobhan's collarbound, but an illegal mindmage?'

'The Nest turns you into a lacunant,' he said. 'That's the theory. Or you're taken down as you try to flee, which is what happens in most cases. Because of how lawmages work, it probably means that you end up a lacunant anyway.'

He kept his voice free from bitterness and held the memories at bay. Him running, and the cold touch of Lal's hand in his, her fingers so much smaller as he dragged her behind him. The way she'd begged for him to stop, the mist from her breath hanging around her face. The crashing sound of hooves behind them and the fear – the knowledge – of what came next.

If the Renegades hadn't been there, he would have died. Hawk had saved his life. But she hadn't been able to save Lal.

It's all right, said Lal. *What is done is done. Give it to Byluk – one for the hands.*

She pushed the moment away from them. But still, that was the last night she had been herself. If he had been less careless, that evening might have ended differently, and their lives would have taken a different turn.

'Would you take that risk?' Isha asked.

He smiled, as if she were sweet and sassy, but wildly off the mark. 'What do you think?'

Her face was as serious as a lawmage's before the block.

'I think it would be foolish to openly practise mindbrawl if there wasn't someone powerful to protect you.' She watched Tatters closely. A good thing she wasn't yet trained to spy on his mind and feel the shiver of fear that cut through him.

'My turn,' he said.

If Isha wasn't playing nice, neither was he.

'What's the deal with you and Sir Passerine? Or are you going to say you don't know, again?'

Her expression froze. Her mind was awash with images. The silhouette was there again, faceless, smelling of animals and leather. As Isha reached out for a hug, the hair, wet from the rain outside, dripped on her small fingers.

An even older memory, or if not older then more distant, buried under these surfacing ones: a middle-aged woman standing in the middle of a path between two orchards, staring into the distance. Isha shaking her, touching her shoulders, asking what had happened. The woman not answering, eyes empty, as if her soul had been sucked out of her.

You're going too deep, worried Tatters.

Lal ignored him.

Isha running. Unknown silhouettes clustered around her home, with people she loved inside, repairing the barn. A chilling silence where screams should be. She was running faster. When she reached them, the people had black holes where their faces should be.

Someone's tampered with her mind.

As Lal spoke, Isha gasped. She'd sensed the intrusion. Lal returned to Tatters' mind, cutting the links.

Isha looked around her, towards the long rip through the earth, as if a jagged knife had cut off a chunk of the world. She was frowning, but not in anger – she was confused about what had happened. Maybe she hadn't seen Lal. It was difficult to guess what she had or hadn't perceived.

'Are you all right?' he asked.

Isha glanced around her, as if she would be able to see what had invaded her mind.

'I'm not sure,' she answered. She studied her surroundings one last time. But her reluctance to speak to Tatters was what saved him. She shook her head. Awkward now, and embarrassed at being awkward, she said: 'It's nothing.'

She didn't ask a question, and Tatters left her in peace. He wasn't sure this had been such a good idea.

Lal disagreed. *Someone has cut memories from her mind. I'm sure of it. She knows something someone doesn't want her to know.*

They sat together on the shrine, listening to the wind. The sun was setting, bleeding gold across the sky.

Abruptly, Isha spoke again:

'What does my tattoo mean?'

Tatters stretched, holding himself to the shrine with his legs. The wood, although it was varnished on the top of the shrine, was rough on the underside of it. 'I asked that one first,' he said.

Isha shrugged. 'There is no rule against asking the same question. And you know something. You've recognised it, haven't you?'

When she turned to glare at him, her face was achingly familiar. Maybe she was right – if he focused, he believed he had seen the tattoo before. But where? It was like trying to recall a melody. He could hear the first note of the tune, but not the second. Instead, all he heard was the hiss of waves, of the tides rising in the Shadowpass.

Uneasy, he answered, 'No. I don't know it.'

Isha glowered, and he knew he would never have anything of hers if he didn't give her anything of his.

'Is it something to do with kher magic?' she insisted.

Tatters nearly laughed, before catching himself, and remembering that most humans knew very little about the khers. 'No,' he said. 'The tattoos don't help or hinder fleshbinding, any more than the mages' robes help or hinder mindlink.'

An idea started to form in Tatters' mind. 'But you've got a point. The khers would know about your tattoo. I could get you to meet them, if you want. They might be able to tell you more.' *To tell us more.* Why hadn't he thought of it before? He was meeting with Arushi this evening, but he might as well bring Isha with him, to see if the khers recognised the tattoo. If they did, it would make his search a whole lot easier – and avoid having to shuffle through Isha's mind, which was considered poor manners at best, criminal at worst.

Do you think Passerine knows what it means? asked Lal.

That was something to consider. Tatters thought of Isha running through her farmland. Of the woman standing in the middle of the path, a trail of spit running down the corner of her mouth.

And one for the eyes, said Lal. *Scenes we have seen. The priests would be proud.*

'Why did you decide to come to the Nest?' he asked.

Isha pinched her lips.

'I think I've had enough.'

He didn't push. He suspected they were both reaching the end of their tethers.

'Maybe it's time to go back,' he offered.

When they left the shrine, the woman stepped in, followed by an old man, eyes milky with poor eyesight, who had arrived while they were inside. Tatters briefly wondered what burdens they were both carrying, heavy enough to want to share with strangers.

Once they were on solid ground, Tatters decided Isha needed to collect herself; her face was bloodless, her pupils wide. They went back into the room where Groniz covered the floor and sat down on the outline of the mosaic. It was cold here, although not as cold as inside the shrine. Unless they tried to get invited into the priests' quarters, they wouldn't find anywhere warm to rest. Tatters took off his stana and placed it across Isha's shoulders. It was longer than a Duskdweller cloak, because it had to be long enough to fold across the chest, so it completely covered her.

'Thanks.' She sounded surprised. Maybe she hadn't wanted a dirty cloak which Tatters walked, ate and slept in. But she tugged the hems closer and blew on her hands.

Isha stared at the mosaic before them. With the lights low on the horizon, the sun sinking over the Edge set the stones ablaze.

'I'll tell you why I came to the Nest,' she said. This was a breach of the Unburdening's rules. 'But I have a question for you first.' She was serious again, now she had stopped shivering.

He had to admit he was curious. 'Very well. I'm listening.'

Pious folk and priests milled around the Temple, but everyone kept their distance. She spoke with her hands still cupped in front of her mouth.

'Can I touch your collar?'

For a moment, Tatters didn't know what to say. No-one had ever asked that. His collar was intimate. Even he didn't touch it. Oh, at the beginning he'd tried to tug it off often enough. Now that he knew he would never be able to remove it, he avoided it.

It was an odd request, and oddly frightening. Collars were one of the most powerful pieces of giant magic. It was difficult to know how it would react.

No, said Lal.

But I want to know why she came to the Nest.

No.

Why not?

I have a bad feeling about this, warned Lal.

But life was made of risks. Tatters cleared his throat:

'All right. Tell me why you came to the Nest.'

For a moment it seemed as if Isha would protest, and they would be stuck in a stalemate. But then she pulled the cloak tighter, and stared at the stone lightborns, and said:

'I was running away from the Renegades.'

Since when is Hawk bold enough to attack farms on the other side of the Shadowpass? he wondered.

Since when does Hawk attack farmers? added Lal.

Maybe that was why he felt so close to Isha. It was the kinship between people trying to get away from Hawk, fleeing to the end of the world to escape her.

'I came to the Nest for protection,' Isha went on. 'But I won't be at peace until I know what's going on, or until I can fight back.'

Before Tatters could come to terms with what Isha had said, she wiped her right hand on his cloak and extended her fingers towards his neck.

Tatters' throat tightened, but he pushed down the fear swelling inside him. This wasn't such a big deal. He would be fine. He braced himself. The collar would react, but it would be nothing he couldn't handle.

When her fingertips touched the gold, the world burst.

It was as if a thunderbolt had hit him, not a girl's light fingers. The violence of it was ten times what he had expected. Memories rushed from his mind in a flood. Colours flashed before his eyes and he became heavy, leaden, as if he were turning into metal from the inside out. The feeling of heaviness propagated like rust, across his chest, his shoulders, his hips, his arms, until he landed with a thud.

He was lying on the floor. Lost, he opened his eyes. He was inside a tent. Red light filtered through the cloth. It was a large tent, if sparse, with a bedroll and covers to pad the ground for the sleeper.

He got up. His rags were nowhere to be seen. In their place he wore a linen tunic, tight around the chest, which flowed out like a skirt from the waist downwards. The clothes were comfortable and clean, although they were undyed. His legs felt numb, unused to walking. He stumbled outside the tent, where the brilliant Sunriser sun greeted him, and into an encampment.

Tatters stood and stared. The camp consisted of a couple of tents, and several horses tethered to the maple trees. He knew he was still in the Rohit Pattra forest because all the leaves were red. A space had been cleared to build a campfire – a circle of stones and a trivet with a cauldron. Although the fire wasn't burning, there was something in the cauldron, and the lingering smell of food. The people walking back and forth weren't wearing a uniform, but Tatters didn't doubt for one moment this was a military camp. Everyone had a weapon hanging from their belt, and a rack of shields was resting against a tree, with the same repeated heraldry: a bird painted black on a red background. He was, as was often the case, the only white-skinned Sunriser in sight.

Someone spotted him and shouted. Tatters backed towards the tent. It made no sense – he wouldn't be safer there – but he didn't know where to go. He was barefoot. They had horses.

Where was Lal?

Hawk came up to him. This was a memory of the first time he'd seen her. This image of her overlapped with other, later recollections. She was wearing a shirt that was loosely laced at the front, and leather gaiters strapped around her shins. Before she could explain anything, he blurted out:

'Where is she?' It was all he could think of. The circle of bruises around her slim wrist. Slipping on the blood-red leaves. And her begging for him to stop running. 'She was with me.'

Hawk's smile faded into a frown. 'Who are you talking about?'

'Did you see this girl, young girl...' He waved his hand at a vague estimation of Lal's height. 'Red hair, rather long, she can't be far...' Panic was rising inside him. He'd thought they'd be safe in the Rohit Pattra because it was a sacred forest. Rohita was the Wingshade name for the lightborn Raudaz. He didn't think they'd hunt him down here.

'This is important, she was with me. Where did you find me? Have we travelled far? She must be near where you found me.'

She's a child, he thought. She's a child and she's alone in the woods and they were hunting us down and I beg you, I beg the lightborns and all the winds from all the underworlds, I beg all of you, let her be alive, let her be alive.

I promised I would look after her.

Hawk put a comforting hand on his shoulder. In part to soothe him and in part, he suspected, so he wouldn't bolt. 'There was no-one but you.' As she said it, in her rough voice, something broke inside Tatters. She'd protected him, but not Lal. He thought he would faint. His legs gave way, and it was all Hawk could do to stop him from splitting his skull against the stones from the firepit.

He couldn't see. He couldn't breathe.

'Calm down,' said Hawk. 'It's all right, it will be all right.'

But it wasn't, and it wouldn't be.

That's enough.

Lal stormed through the memory, shredding it as she did so.

For the first time, Tatters realised Isha was present inside his mind, an unwitting witness.

I knew this was a terrible idea.

Lal raised barriers inside Tatters' mind, separating what she wanted Isha to access from what was personal. She placed them in a circle of darkness, with nothing below or above them.

Isha goggled at Lal. But then, she was a sight. She carried the tantrums and fury of childhood inside her, as well as the confidence of thirty years of existence. She was wearing a green dress with a worn leather belt, no shoes. It was a poor child's outfit, but she wore it like a warrior. Her long red hair floated around her as if she were standing in water.

Return to your own mind, before I collapse this, spat Lal. Tatters wondered if he should intervene, but he was still shaken.

It took Isha a while to leave, and he noticed how interwoven they'd become, in that split moment of her touching his collar. She took her hand away. He emerged from mindlink with faded emotions still sticking to his skin, as if there were something inside his mouth, his ears, his lungs. She hadn't meant for this, he was sure, any more than he had expected it to happen.

Isha and Tatters looked at each other. They were sitting close together, with the wind screeching through the Temple, and the interwoven mosaic glowing before them. Half of Isha's face was in shadow, the dark tattoo made darker still in the dimming light.

'She isn't your double, is she?' whispered Isha. 'She's real.'

Tatters' tongue was thick inside his mouth. He didn't know why he told Isha the truth. He didn't know why she extended her hand and squeezed his, as if to comfort him.

'Lal is my sister.'

Chapter Six

When they finally left the Temple, they walked fast, to outpace the setting sun and reach the city before nightfall. Not a word broke their stride. Isha was mulling over what had happened that afternoon as, no doubt, was Tatters. There was an ache at the tip of her fingers, like a burn. She pressed them together to dull it.

She had felt what it was like to be Tatters, the different shape of his body, the weight of his limbs and the emotion that had clung to his heart, like something planting its fangs there, like two holes across his chest. She could picture the encampment as clearly as if she had been there, feel the gritty earth underneath her – his – bare feet. She wondered who the woman was. It would be unthinkable to ask.

Something about the recollection was jarring, but she couldn't put her finger on it. It was stilted. It had a piece missing from it.

And she was still reeling from the truth about Lal. What was his little sister doing inside his mind? Was it possible to live – to be sustained, at least – without a body? Unless she kept her body somewhere else. Could she do that? Keep her body in one place and roam the world in someone else's mind?

That's when Isha pinpointed what had troubled her. In the vision, Tatters hadn't been wearing his collar.

She tried to run the moment through her mind again, but she couldn't find any hint that he was wearing gold around his neck. She couldn't see it, she couldn't sense it. But being a collarbound must be impossible to ignore, must be as intrusive as a hand clasping your throat.

This memory predated Tatters becoming a collarbound.

'So?'

Isha blinked. She had no idea what Tatters had just asked. He repeated his question:

'Do you want to eat with some khers?'

He sounded guarded. He usually made a show of being carefree, but what had taken place was enough for him to stand a few feet away from her and to seal off his mind. Now that she had met Lal, she could perceive that he was shielded by something that wasn't him, or not just him. This young girl – this Lal – was present. Isha wondered how she could have missed her before.

She was exhausted. But on the other hand, she had come here to learn.

'Yes,' she said. If the khers could tell her what her tattoo meant, why shouldn't she meet them? She had never talked to a kher before; she had never even seen one before reaching the city.

'Nothing slows you down, does it?' His tone wasn't quite light enough.

'If you don't want me to come...'

'I offered.'

When they reached the outskirts of the city, he guided her towards the kher quarter: the Pit. It was set apart from the rest of town, with mudbrick walls marking the border between the stone houses of the humans and the shambles of the khers.

There were gates, of sorts, although no-one would have called them that – it was more an opening in the wall where two khers were lurking. Isha had only seen female khers at the Nest, but these were male. Stories of male khers committing gruesome murders sprung to mind, tales she had heard at the farm or on the road. These had horns with ochre paint across them, and tattoos snaking around their naked torsos, heavily stylised, which made it difficult to know what they represented.

One kher studied Isha's face, his gaze moving down her cheek. People stared at her tattoo the way they might stare at a horse before buying it. They might as well test her teeth, tug at her hair to check its thickness – it was as if she were a curio, not a person.

When Tatters drew closer, the male khers didn't block the entrance, but they shifted their weight on their feet, their pose changing ever so slightly from lazy to threatening.

'What is it, flatface?' spat the first one.

Tatters gave him a broad smile. He touched his forehead with his thumb. If any awkwardness remained, he hid it well enough.

'Idir. I have a meeting with Arushi,' he said.

The kher word sounded rough in Tatters' mouth. The khers didn't answer. One of them was cleaning his nails with his teeth, close enough to listen in, but acting as if the conversation wasn't of interest to him. The other one glared at Tatters, then at Isha.

'You want to come through?' he asked her.

She didn't know what to say, and wasn't sure why the kher was ignoring Tatters to speak directly to her. She nodded, but the kher didn't seem satisfied.

'Are you aniybu or taniybu?' he insisted. Isha turned to Tatters for help; she didn't even understand the question.

'Neither,' said Tatters. 'She's not a halfblood.'

The two khers looked at each other, clearly thinking this over. One of them shoved his chin towards Isha.

'You a soulworm, then? Is that why you've got the robes?'

The kher blew out of his nose, and she was reminded of a bull before it charged. She attempted a smile, but she couldn't match Tatters', not with nervousness writhing in her stomach.

'Yes,' she managed. 'I'm an apprentice.'

'Huh,' said the kher. He nudged his friend with his foot. The friend shrugged.

'What do I know?' he answered. 'But I'm not blocking the gates to that girl.' He said it matter-of-factly, as if it was obvious why he wouldn't want to get in Isha's way.

The first kher turned around and called over his shoulder, 'Yua! Come over here!'

A female kher ambled over from inside the Pit. She was a petite woman, with skin as deep red as a blush. She seemed younger than the other khers. Although all khers appeared young anyway, she seemed to be more around seventeen than twenty. Her horns were much shorter, too, two stubs poking upwards out of her forehead, with a small spike growing behind them. She had polished pebbles tied around her horns, the kher equivalent of earrings.

She glanced at the guards, then at Tatters. Her eyes went to the gold around his neck.

'Oh yes, the collarbound! Arushi mentioned you.' She turned to the guards. 'He's a guest.'

'What about the other one?'

The kher called Yua squinted at Isha. 'I dunno.'

'She's my chaperone,' said Tatters, keeping a straight face.

The two male khers didn't laugh, but Yua did. 'All right, let her in. Who can say no to that?'

The men shuffled out of the way to let them pass and Yua waved her guests inside.

Isha's heartbeat picked up as she crossed the gates; she was frightened of what she might see. The rumours about khers weren't flattering – they were supposed to be lustful, mating at any time of day, in public spaces. Although Isha supposed what she'd heard must have been exaggerated, she wasn't sure how much was true. She soaked up every detail, conscious that she would never have entered the Pit without Tatters.

The houses were mudbrick for the most part, with planks of wood holding up collapsing roofs, and cloth blocking the windows. Most khers, she'd believed, preferred to sleep in tents. Carpets were thrown across the road, with groups of people sitting on them, cracking walnuts on a plate together, sorting out the shells from the food. Trees had been planted down the centre of the road, casting shade and providing cover. In the early night, the breeze carried a strong smell of spices. The streets seemed to belong to men – they were gathered in circles on the floor playing board games, or standing, resting their horns and heads against the trees. Isha and Yua were the only women in sight.

Yua had tattoos across her neck, with curves and swirls and interlocked lines that could symbolise a current, wind, or maybe someone running. Movement, at any rate. The tattoo started at the rim of her chin and went down to her collarbone, like a choker of fine black lace. She was quick and curious, and walked with swift, half-danced steps.

'So, tell me,' she said. 'How did you catch Arushi's attention?'

'I guessed her age,' said Tatters.

How come Tatters knew this much about khers? Kilian kept telling her Tatters was a low-stakes mage who knew a few fun tricks, who could only help with her studies, not replace them. But it seemed there was nothing Tatters couldn't lecture about.

'Someone tells Arushi she's old and she takes a shine to them. Typical. Well, give her that, she'd rather have a truth than a compliment.' Yua cocked her head to one side with a cheeky smile. 'How good are you at guessing? Care to tell me how old I am?'

Tatters made a show of thinking about it. Isha watched, to see if she could work out how he did it. When he counted under his breath, she struggled to understand what he was counting – the number of tattoos? Yua's smile only widened. She had very white teeth, tiny and pointed in her little mouth.

'About twenty, more or less,' said Tatters. Isha had to admit she was disappointed. She could have guessed that.

Yua laughed. 'You couldn't be more wrong.' She continued guiding them through the Pit. People lifted their heads as they went by, but didn't interrupt them or leave their games. Children followed them like shy animals, from a distance.

'I'm forty-seven,' said Yua. Isha tried not to gape. This kher was smaller than her, and seemed younger, and she was over twice her age.

Tatters didn't seem taken aback; he laughed with her. 'You're a longlived! That is completely unfair.'

'You could have known from the tattoos,' she said. 'But you're only human, after all.' It was meant as a joke, but it was double-edged.

Animals roamed the streets, mostly hens, with the odd goat munching on the bark of a tree. Now Isha could see a few women, throwing food for the birds, or cooking around firepits set in the shade of the trees, with dogs lying at their feet.

Yua turned her attention to Isha. When she moved her head, the pebbles caught in her horns clicked against each other. Isha supposed they were polished quartz, sanded down so they reflected and caught the light. 'Tidir, chaperone,' she said, letting the irony filter into her voice. 'Tell me what I should beware of with your ward.'

'He's a terrible liar,' Isha said, which she hoped was enough of the truth not to be taken seriously.

Yua laughed. 'That's nothing special. All humans are liars.'

'If I may,' said Tatters, 'what's your relationship to Arushi?'

'Ucma,' answered Yua, still smiling. She had answered in her own language on purpose, Isha could tell.

Tatters wasn't one to back down before a challenge. He barely hesitated before saying: 'Sister?' He made it sound like a guess, but it must have hit its mark, because Yua nodded in approval.

'You do know some things, then.'

As far as Isha knew, khers didn't have families, or sisters for that matter. They just slept with anyone they felt like sleeping with; they didn't remember who had given birth to who. Maybe that was just a myth that humans believed. She would have to ask Tatters.

They stopped in front of a house, less shabby and more house-shaped than the others. It had two storeys, which meant it loomed above its neighbours. Its small windows – holes in the mudbrick wall, but still, they were square holes – were draped in patchwork cloth. The door was a curtain of beaded threads, not quartz this time, but plain grey pebbles.

Yua pulled back the bead curtain, inviting them in.

The chatter of conversation stopped abruptly when they entered the room. The place was filled with women and children. A chimney at the back hosted a smoky fire. The children were gathered on a carpet, where they were chopping up vegetables, or pulling the fibres out of celery sticks. The whole place was hot, filled with vapour from the cooking pot, and smelt of unknown spices that made Isha's eyes water. A few adult women were present, including a plump lady in a corner, who was sitting on a pile of goatskins.

It was to her that Yua first introduced Tatters and Isha. She had the perfect face of a young woman, with the largest spread of horns Isha had ever seen. They were shining black and smooth, shaped like antlers, their intricate branching-out reminding Isha of a stag. They added two feet to her height, and evidently weighed so heavily on her head that she had to rest them against the wall to be comfortable. Beads and coloured threads hung from her horns, along with hand-knitted pieces of wool.

The two horns curved down her chin, followed her jawline, then turned back towards her face. Two wounds marred her forehead, above her eyes, where the horns were starting to grow into her skull. The flesh was swollen and bruised, with a thin sheen of blood around the sores. Her eyes were bloodshot. Her hair grew thinly across her skull, stuck down with sweat. It hurt to watch; Isha's teeth ached.

This was an old kher.

'My mother, the mother of this household, and our uaza,' said Yua. 'This is the collarbound Arushi talked about, and a friend of his.'

Now the family lounging on the carpet were muttering, staring whilst pretending not to stare. They were waiting to hear what the matriarch would say.

Tatters bowed to the old kher, touching his forehead with his thumb as he had before. Rather too late, Isha copied him. He opened the purse tied around his belt and took out the scented candles he had bought at the Temple.

'Tidir, Uaza. Thank you for inviting us,' he said. He held out the candles, palms outstretched.

Uaza moved slowly, but her hands were unwrinkled, without the inflamed knuckles Isha associated with age. She brought the candles close to her face, so she could see them despite the horns growing in front of her eyes.

'They smell very nice.' Her voice sounded youthful, but it had an edge to it, a slight quiver. 'Where did you get them?'

'At the lightborn Temple,' he said.

An eerie silence settled in the room. The khers would never be allowed inside the Temple, as they were considered impure. This was a gift they would not have been able to buy for themselves. Isha wondered if Tatters had done this consciously, and decided he must have. It was a unique present in many ways, but most unique was its message. Why give candles created to help souls ascend to beings who weren't supposed to have souls?

'It is very thoughtful of you,' said Uaza.

With a collective sigh, the people in the room relaxed. A few children jumped to their feet to touch or sniff the candles. Soon they were being passed around, from nose to nose, so everyone could decide which scent they liked best.

As the noise picked up again across the room, Tatters turned to Isha. While the candles were the centre of attention, he whispered, 'When you're invited to eat at an iwdan house, never bring food as a present. It's an insult, as if you didn't expect them to feed you well. But you do have to bring a present. That's just good manners.'

'Iwdan?' she repeated – or rather, tried to repeat.

Tatters lowered his voice. 'The term the khers use for themselves. Kher is fine, but saying iwdan shows you're making an effort.'

'Is there anything you don't know?' she couldn't help but ask.

'Well, I didn't know that you touching my collar would have that effect.' He smiled as he said it, but his voice was grim.

Their aside was interrupted by Uaza.

'So, who are you, then, who knows something of our customs?' she asked.

'Just a human called Tatters,' he answered, 'who is lucky enough to have had iwdan friends.'

Before the matriarch could ask more questions, a female kher pushed through the curtain, holding something in her hands. Her horns, which curved above her head like a ram's, got caught in the beads and she shook her head grumpily. She had a broader, harder face than Yua.

'Someone help me out of this!' she snapped.

A child ran up to her, and she gave him the basket of eggs she'd been carrying. 'Don't break them,' she said. The child caught the basket between his arms and his chest, the handle resting on his chin. The newcomer started tugging at the beads, and Yua came to help.

'You!' she said to Yua. 'Where were you when we needed you for cooking?'

She seemed about to say more, but stopped short as she caught sight of Tatters across the room.

'I was picking up your guest,' said Yua, as she helped untangle the beads.

The kher – who must be Arushi – nodded to Tatters. He smiled and gave her a wave, but she immediately focused on Isha, her face showing everything Isha didn't need to know, from her surprise to her disapproval.

'I wasn't expecting two of you,' she said as the last of the beads fell free.

Walking up to Tatters, Arushi lifted her wrist for him, but he touched his forehead for her. Too late, he offered his wrist, as she changed her greeting to touching her horn with her thumb. They fumbled between the human and kher welcome gestures, before settling on the human one.

'Good to see you,' she said.

Isha was about to extend her wrist, but Arushi turned away. So much for avoiding bad manners.

The guests left the matriarch to settle around the carpet. Above the fire hung a cauldron filled with water. Yua gathered the eggs, and started poaching them with a dexterous hand, spinning the white and yolk with a spoon so they didn't disintegrate in the hot water.

Soon Tatters was chatting and doing his share of the cooking. Isha couldn't find a conversation to be part of, or a way to make herself useful. When she asked whether she could help, Arushi drily told her she was a guest. She noticed Tatters didn't ask, but simply unsheathed his knife to peel vegetables with the younger children, who were the slowest workers. Arushi came to sit beside him, and they were soon engrossed in a conversation which, from the other side of the carpet, Isha couldn't quite catch.

Most khers were wearing trousers and colourful knitted woollen shawls that fell down to their hips, with a hole for the head – no sleeves nor buttons in sight. A few women were bare-chested, and Isha tried not to stare. Everyone was barefoot; the carpet, although threadbare, provided good insulation against the cold.

Isha got up, dusting her robes, to join Yua crouching in front of the fire. There weren't any stools or chairs that Isha could see. Furniture didn't seem to be a big feature of a kher household. Yua swirled a spoon inside the cauldron with one hand and broke the eggs into it with the other. When the eggs were poached, she placed them in a wooden bowl, where they formed a soggy pile.

Closer to the cauldron, Isha could see the water was a dark shade of green, with herbs floating inside it and staining the eggs grey.

The smell was overpowering and not altogether pleasant – mushrooms maybe, something damp and earthy and rotting.

'So, tell me, chaperone,' said Yua as Isha knelt next to her. 'Who are you?'

If only I knew the answer to that question. 'I'm Isha. I joined the Nest this year.'

'Ah yes, the shade of the robes. Arushi told me something about them. You can only start having colours once you're officially part of the Nest, is that right?'

This was a safe enough topic, so Isha explained that grey robes were for apprentices, and that darker robes – or flusher colours – were for mages. Traditionally, newly ordained mages wore blue. And the high mages wore black, the most expensive colour a garment could be. It needed to be dyed time and time again to be dark enough.

'Where did your ward get a black cloak, then?' asked Yua.

Isha glanced at Tatters. She had never considered that. Tatters' cloak *was* black, although whether from dye or dirt it was difficult to tell.

'I don't know,' she admitted.

Yua chuckled. 'No matter. I'm just curious.'

I'm curious too, now. The simplest solution was that Tatters must have been given the cloak by his master. Someone powerful enough to own a collar would be able to afford black dye. But why give him a precious item of clothing and then let him ruin it?

A male kher poked his head through the curtain. 'May we come in?' His tone was low and respectful.

'You can come in when you are invited in,' Yua shouted from the opposite end of the room. The other khers didn't look up from their chores.

'I was only asking. You invited a man inside,' said the kher at the door.

'He's a guest,' Arushi chipped in.

Yua aimed her spoon at the kher at the door. Isha was surprised by the authority in her voice, playful but severe, the one people used with children, not with adult men. 'Off with you!'

The male kher let the curtain fall back across the threshold. The beads chimed.

Yua turned to Isha and explained how cooking went in a kher house. Iwdan meals, she said, were often comprised of dry food that could be put in boiling water when they wanted it to become edible again.

'Dry food is good for travelling. You can store it easily if you're going for long stretches without hunting anything fresh.'

Yua showed Isha long strips of yellow pastry, which were hard and brittle. They had been sun-dried, she explained, hanging from a rack outside. But in the soup, they would become soft again.

Once Yua had finished poaching the eggs, she started putting ingredients in her cauldron – the vegetables the children had prepared, the dry yellow pastry, powders and spices, withered mushrooms like cut-off fingers. She threw everything in the pot, in no order Isha could make sense of.

'In the old days, when iwdan were still nomads, the evening meal would always start with a shared pot of boiling water. Every member of the tribe added what they could, so the result was one soup made out of everyone's donations.'

The ingredients filled with water and swelled. The smell was thick in the air; Isha could taste it on her tongue. Yua put a poached egg, now cold and slimy, into each person's bowl, then poured the broth, making sure everyone had their fair share of the vegetables simmering inside the pot. The children helped her distribute the bowls around the carpet. The matriarch didn't move from her pile of animal skins, but food was brought to her. A few extra spaces were set up, and Isha guessed they might be for the men waiting outside.

Everyone was picking a place Despite Arushi glaring at her, lips squeezed shut, Isha went to sit next to Tatters. Isha wasn't sure why Arushi was being so hostile; she had been invited by Tatters, after all. If anything, it was his fault she was here.

It was only when everyone was served that Yua went to the door to call the men inside.

'You may come in.' She held back the curtain for them. As a group of three men entered the house, Yua spoke words that felt well-used, the words of a ritual: 'We give you the hearth, for as long as you lack a path.'

A change came over the room, which Isha sensed without understanding it. The women fell silent. The three male khers took their place closest to the door. Tatters had been seated far from the men of the household, beside Arushi and Yua – and the warm fire, and the aroma of kher food. He wasn't far from the corner where Uaza was already slurping her soup. Tucked beside him, Isha tried to ignore the feeling that she was at odds with the room, a wrong note in a flawless melody.

The room was quieter than it had been as they cooked. Short questions and answers were exchanged, but the conversations were subdued.

Tatters nudged Isha with his elbow. She watched him as he pierced the poached egg with his knife, so the yolk would mix with the rest of the soup. He then set his knife aside and ate with one of the wooden spoons. Except for porridge, Isha never ate with a spoon – a knife was all she'd ever needed at dinner. If the Nest had the time to make broth, the apprentices drank it from the bowl, or soaked it up with bread. There was no bread here.

She copied Tatters' way of eating, grateful that he had taken the time to show her. The once-dry food – moss, mushrooms, something chewy that might be meat, and the long threads of pastry – was hot and tender. The pastry's texture reminded Isha of seaweed. She couldn't say what the broth tasted like. Iron, maybe, or salt. Like something that had come from the ground.

'You must be Arushi's guests,' said one of the male khers.

He was broad-shouldered, tough from physical labour, with tattoos down his chest and forearms. His hair was long, tumbling down his neck. He introduced himself as Ganez. Isha worked out that he was Arushi's and Yua's brother – or blood-relation, at least – while the two other men were... She wasn't quite sure. Partners? Husbands?

'We don't usually have humans in our home,' Ganez went on.

From the back of the room, Uaza intervened. 'They brought candles from the Temple.'

A child was sent to bring the candles to Ganez, who sniffed them as the women had. He picked one, lit it, and placed it in the centre of the carpet.

'An unusual gift,' he said, watching the thin thread of smoke. He'd picked a candle that was supposed to be rose-scented, although it was difficult to tell with the soup still bubbling and its sharp metallic smell in the air.

'Well, as you've said, we're unusual company.' Tatters smiled.

'I can see that,' said Ganez, nodding towards Isha, as if acknowledging something they both knew but were too polite to mention. Isha had no idea what the gesture meant, except that it was supposed to include her.

'We're both very honoured to be allowed inside your home,' Tatters went on. 'Do tell me if I can ever repay the favour.'

Ganez watched Tatters, licking the corner of his lips absent-mindedly. To Isha, it seemed as if he was trying to make up his mind whether to like him or not. She copied the other women and stayed quiet.

'I don't envy you, collarbound,' said Ganez, 'if humans give you half as tough a time as they give us.'

'I'm not complaining,' said Tatters. It was true, Isha realised. She'd never heard Tatters complain about being a slave. Part of her wondered whether the collar might ban him from talking about his status as a collarbound.

'No-one is free in this world,' said Tatters. 'Everyone has to eat. Everyone has to work. A collar doesn't change that much.'

Ganez brought his bowl to his mouth and gulped down the dregs. 'Very true. Each path has its thorns.'

Isha caught Arushi and Yua exchanging a glance. They looked as if they wanted to speak, but knew better than to do so.

Ganez turned to Isha. 'Do you always follow him? Is there no way for you to control him from a distance?'

That's when it struck her. Tatters was a collarbound, which meant he had a master. And Isha was obviously a mage. So the khers had assumed she was Tatters' master – or his master's envoy, at least. Which explained Arushi's behaviour. As she was friends with the slave, she had no reason to like the slaver.

'No, no,' Isha mumbled, 'Tatters invited me.'

Tatters jumped in to explain: 'She is too junior to own a collar, let alone a collarbound.' He placed a hand on her shoulder, to signal his support. 'I invited her to come because I believed she would be able to learn a lot from you.'

Ganez snorted. Whether he believed Tatters or not, he didn't push.

'What could a mage want to learn from the iwdan?' asked Yua. Her light voice contrasted with the deep rumble of Ganez's words. The three men turned to her when she spoke, but if her interruption was unwelcome, no-one mentioned it.

Isha cleared her throat. 'I wondered if you might be able to tell me if my tattoo had any meaning in ...' She caught herself before she said kher. 'In iwdan.' The way she pronounced the unfamiliar word sounded nothing like what Yua – what Tatters, even – had said.

'Don't you know?' said Ganez. 'Didn't your uaza tell you?'

Isha tried to swallow, but the unusual food was stuck in her mouth. The air she breathed, the soup she ate; everything tasted of earth, as if she had been buried alive. She thought of faceless figures surrounding her farm. About what they had taken from her.

'The tattoo was done to me when I was a child,' she said. That was the truth. And the truth was, she had known at the time why, and what it meant. But not any more.

Only a shocked silence answered her; obviously this surprised the khers much more than the tattoo itself. She lowered her face, a blush already burning her cheeks.

Tatters changed the conversation topic, asking what kind of work the male khers were doing.

'Nothing,' spat Ganez.

It was a subject the men were ready to lament. The mages had banned them from being guards, and even from approaching the Nest. In town, they couldn't hold positions of responsibility nor carry weapons. They couldn't be bodyguards or mercenaries, which meant they were relegated to carrying weights, making walls – anything a donkey could do, grumbled Ganez – or manning the mills and sowing the land for farmers outside the city.

'We have to get up before dawn to reach the fields when the sun rises,' said one of the men.

'Then we work for half of what we could earn inside the city,' said the other. 'Even then, there are farmers who refuse our work.'

Ganez poured himself another portion of soup, and asked if anyone else wanted seconds. Isha didn't lift her bowl; she wasn't used to soggy poached egg and the bitter taste of grit in her mouth. Ganez talked whilst serving some of the children, Yua, Tatters.

'Too many of us are stuck here all day, doing nothing, getting in the women's way.' He shook his head, making a sound Isha had heard khers do before, a sort of sigh through the nose. 'It is unnatural, women outside the hearth like men, men inside the hearth like women. Women should rule within the hearth, not without. And men should rule outside the hearth, not within.'

While the men talked, Isha examined the tattoos around her. She spotted an eye, a triangular leaf from a tree, a circle with five branches that might be a hand. Ganez had tattoos down the left side of his chest, cutting a line across his abdomen. Isha got the impression, from the variations in the black of the ink and the style of drawing, that different parts of the tattoo dated from different times, although each part was linked to the other, the lines and circles woven in tight patterns. In places, especially around his shoulders and his hips, the drawings had something unfinished about them.

Arushi had pushed her sleeves up, revealing forearms covered in black blocks with flesh-coloured designs inside them, and the same triangular leaves Isha had spotted on Ganez's skin. In contrast, Yua's tattoos stood out as softer, curlier, than any of the others.

None of the children were tattooed and none had horns, although they did have stubs on their foreheads where the horns would grow.

Tatters hummed at the right points in Ganez's speech.

'It's stupid,' he intervened, sipping his soup. 'People should want iwdan workers. You're safe to work without being mind-linked.'

'Humans don't care about us while we're alive,' growled Ganez. 'The only thing they want from us is our dead.'

Tatters opened his mouth as if to challenge this, but Isha saw him catching Arushi's eye. Whatever he was about to say, he changed it to a nod. The conversation moved on. When the cauldron was empty, Ganez went to fetch clay pipes from the back of the room and invited Tatters to smoke with the men outside.

Tatters thanked them for their kind offer but didn't get up. He turned to Isha and asked, in a low voice, 'Will you be all right on your own?'

'Can't I come with you?'

He eyed Ganez, who was already heading for the door.

'I wouldn't advise it,' said Tatters. 'But I can stay with you, if you want.'

She shook her head, despite the lump of worry in her throat. She didn't need to be coddled.

'You're doing fine, by the way,' he said as he got up.

When he reached the entrance, Ganez cleared his throat, and spoke words which broke the spell of silence placed inside the room: 'We return the hearth to you and thank you for your gift.'

The men stepped out, and the children followed like a flock of birds, making excited noises, relieved to be allowed to run around again.

'Seshaq!' said Yua as soon as Ganez had let go of the bead curtain. 'Someone was in a good mood.' She shook her head, not quite laughing, as if they'd had a close escape.

'He's an idiot,' grumbled Arushi, getting to her feet. She gathered the bowls and piled them next to the fireplace. Stumbling to her feet, Isha helped as best she could – without asking this time – by collecting the spoons.

'Give it a break,' said Yua. 'You were looking for trouble, inviting those two.' She turned to Isha, taking the spoons out of her hands. 'Who was it who tattooed you, then?'

Isha had answered that question fifty times in these last two days, or so it felt. She shrugged. 'What does it matter?'

In the corner of the room, the matriarch was wiping her mouth with her thumb. Isha went to take her cutlery away. But when she knelt beside her, Uaza placed a hand on her wrist.

'Child. Sit down.' She said it so seriously that Isha couldn't help but obey.

Isha looked at the arm holding her. It had tattoos too, of course. Like Yua, the old kher had spirals and arabesques, silken lines like drifting smoke.

'I'll tell you a story,' said Uaza.

'I'm all ears,' said Yua.

Arushi caught her sister's arm and tugged her towards the dirty washing-up. 'You can listen and do the dishes.'

'I can too,' said Isha. Arushi stared at her for too long before nodding.

Arushi warmed some water by the fire and brought it, with a few knotted rags, to her mother. Isha and Yua took turns dipping the bowls and spoons into the tepid water and rubbing at them with the rags, while Arushi dried them and put them back into a wooden chest beside the chimney. When they were sitting side-by-side, the likeness between the two sisters was more obvious. Arushi had more austere clothing, nearly human in its lack of colour, whereas Yua's polished pebbles glinted when she moved – but still their faces matched, they had the same creases at the corner of their eyes.

Once they were all set up, Uaza closed her eyes. She started talking, her voice flowing amongst the sounds of laughter outside, the splashes of dirty water, the low hum Yua made as she worked.

'Once upon a time there was a powerful king. This was a long time ago, when each tribe was led by a king, and humans hadn't mastered mindlink yet. This king was longlived.'

'She won't understand a word,' said Arushi. 'She doesn't know what a longlived is. I'm not sure she even knows what an uaza is.'

The old kher opened her eyes. 'You shouldn't interrupt.'

'Still, she doesn't. Do you?'

Isha had to admit she didn't. Yua chuckled to herself, singing stray notes from a song as she cleaned the dishes.

'Yua and tasna are longlived,' said Arushi. From the tenderness in her voice, Isha assumed tasna was a term of endearment for her mother. 'Which means,' Arushi went on, 'that their horns grow more slowly than the rest of us. It means they live longer.' Isha remembered what Yua had told Tatters, that he might have guessed she was a longlived by her tattoos.

Pride slipped into Arushi's tone. 'Tasna is more than a century old. And Yua will live to be three times that.'

'And what's an uaza?' asked Isha, trying to pronounce the rough syllables, the sound alien in her mouth.

Both sisters answered at the same time.

'A storyteller,' said Yua.

'Someone who draws tattoos,' said Arushi.

'Can we get back to the king?' snapped the old kher.

Arushi rolled her eyes. Uaza settled comfortably on the goat skins, the pieces of cloth tied to her horns moving like banners in the wind. She went on:

'This king had a son. As was the tradition at the time, to prevent the tribes from fighting, the king had to give away his child to be fostered by another tribe. But he wanted to always remember who his son was and so, rather than wait for his child to be of age, he tattooed him at birth. He tattooed his wrist, as you should, for the first marking must be low.'

Uaza extended her hand. Isha wasn't sure at first what was expected of her; when the matriarch did a gesture of impatience, Isha put down her bowl, shook her wet fingers to dry them, and placed her hand in the kher's. Uaza touched Isha's wrist. 'There,' she said. She pulled Isha closer, so she could tap Isha's hipbone with her hard, dry finger. 'Or there.'

She let go. Uncertain whether an interruption would be welcome or not, Isha went back to her dishes.

'His son grew in might. As there must be, there was a war. The king did not see his son's tattoo behind the strap of his shield, and he killed him, and grieved.' The flickering light from the fire made the kher's red skin redder still, blood-like. 'Then the king had a second son, and he loved this beautiful babe even more than the first. So, to always be able to recognise him, he tattooed him over the heart. But when the time came to fight, he did not see his son's tattoo beneath his armour, and he killed him, and grieved.'

Uaza cleared her throat. Arushi got up to stack some more wood on the fire, and it spat and smoked as they finished washing the dishes.

'Then the king had a third child. This one he loved so tenderly, so fiercely, that he ached at the idea of giving him away. When the time came to leave his third son, he tattooed him once again. But this time he tattooed his child across the face, so that nothing would ever cover that mark.'

Uaza crossed her hands before her.

'That was the one and only time an iwdan tattooed a child's face.'

When she turned towards Isha, her horns moved with her, like an impressive headdress or a crested helmet. The few hanging beads caught the glow of the fire, reflecting shards of light across her shoulders and the wall behind her.

'Who was afraid to lose you, child? Who wanted to be sure they would always know you?'

Isha's mouth was dry. 'I don't know.'

'There is a variant to that story,' said Yua, 'where the three sons have to hide their tattoo three times to be able to pass as members of another tribe to avoid being executed. The first two succeed, and when the king ambushes the enemy tribe, he kills them by mistake. But the third can't hide his rank or birth, and so he's killed by his foes, rather than by his father.'

Uaza nodded. 'Those who love you will know you. And those who wish you harm will know you too.'

I wonder whether Tatters is part of the first or second group. Isha didn't doubt, seeing how Tatters had reacted to the tattoo, that he knew something about it. Maybe he knew which tribe she was part of, even if Isha didn't know that herself.

But she still wasn't sure whether he was friend or foe.

She thanked the three women for the food and the tale. Yua and her mother smiled the same ageless smile, the smile of people who grew so slowly they stayed children for decades.

Arushi didn't smile.

***

Outside, Tatters was sitting with the men, blowing blue-grey smoke into the night air. The stars were brighter than usual. The only clouds were the ones shrouding the men and their pipes.

Isha waited for Tatters to take his leave from the group of smokers.

'What was it like?' he asked. He stretched, yawning to the sky. The gold of his collar glinted in the moonlight.

'It was fine.'

A lot had happened in one day. She thought of the collar, the searing it had left at the tip of her fingers. She thought of a red-haired girl called Lal. She thought of the questions Tatters had asked about her parents.

She thought that those who loved her would know her. And that those who wished her harm would know her too.

Chapter Seven

Isha was inside a tent made of red cloth. An animal skin covered the floor, and a torch had been placed in the centre, casting moving shadows on the flush walls. On her right, she could see the wooden frame of a bed, with furs and cushions. On her left, a rack for drying hides. But the hides pinned on it weren't drying. They were already cleaned and hardened.

She was dreaming. It felt odd, to be conscious that she must be sleeping. It had never happened to her before.

This was the tent from Tatters' memories. Or if it wasn't, it was her version, her dream-interpretation of it. It was more opulent, better decorated than it had been in Tatters' mind, and the rack was a new feature, but everything else she recognised.

She went to study the hides. They were fine work – this was vellum, not leather. Words were scratched across their surface. She squinted at them, but the light was too dim to make out what was written. Sheet after sheet, skin thin, was covered in cursive, cramped writing. The ink looked like insects; the fire from the torch made them crawl.

'Good morning. Or good evening, I suppose. Good night, maybe.'

The voice was as deep as a man's, but when Isha jumped and turned, it belonged to a woman. She was the warrior from

Tatters' memories. She was wearing a whitewashed linen tunic, but no armour.

'This is nice,' said the woman. 'Welcome, my eyas.'

Isha didn't know what an eyas was, but the word struck a chord inside her, in the same way an image or a sound can recall a nightmare.

The woman moved closer. She was dark-skinned, with paler flesh across her face where old scars had healed. Her hair was black, tightly braided then loosely wrapped in red cloth. The cloth was longer than it needed to be and fell over her shoulders and down her back. Isha wondered if it was a nasivyati.

She joined Isha beside the drying vellum and recited:

> *Cackle and fizzle*
> *Grizzle and spit*
> *We're all playing*
> *And you're It.*'

The woman smiled fondly, as she would to an old friend.

'It is only a silly children's rhyme, but it's been stuck in my head tonight. Do you sometimes feel like that? Everyone is playing, and you're It.'

She lifted one sheet between finger and thumb. For a moment it seemed she would read it out loud. But in the end she let go of the vellum and it drifted back down to rest on the rack with a soft rasp.

'Maybe I also like the rhythm of it. It reminds me of the Shadowpass warning song:

> *Wade through shadow*
> *Stay in light*
> *Avoid the waves*
> *Their touch is blight.*'

146

A shaft of sunlight shone through the tent. Everything in its path disappeared, leaving only a circle of dawn-grey light. The woman watched this, smiling to herself, unmoved to see part of her bed dissolve into motes. She was right. It was a nice dream. Isha didn't feel worried. There was light, and warmth, and the background sound of birdsong.

'I know you,' said Isha.

The woman laughed. 'I hope so!'

Another shaft of light speared the tent, cutting through it as if light were a knife, as if it were fire that ate what it touched. It swallowed the torch and the central wooden pillar holding up the tent. It didn't matter for the torch. The two pillars of light let out enough of a glow. The ink on the vellum seemed darker now, and Isha could see through the first transparent pages to the skin spread further down the rack, through layers and layers of words.

Although she knew talking to people in dreams was silly, Isha couldn't stop herself. 'You knew Tatters.' She didn't expect the woman to react. If anything, she half-expected her to turn to the drying pages of poetry and read from them.

But the woman's face changed. The dream shifted; the birdsong stopped. It wasn't as warm now, with the cold bite of morning wind and dew.

'You're with Tatters?' she asked.

Another ray shone through the tent, splitting the ground between them. Isha took a step back. The rack of poetry was gone. Isha heard the sound of waves, and she felt water lapping at her feet, but when she looked down, there was nothing.

The woman stared at Isha from behind the barrier of light. She was frowning. Only bits and pieces of her tent remained, like a ragged banner.

'You found him?' the woman asked.

Isha could hardly say she had found him – it wasn't as if she'd been looking for him. She tried to stay inside the dream, but she could hear a sound above her head, a low growl, and she knew it was her neighbour snoring. Her feet weren't touching water, but they were poking outside the covers, and that was why they were cold. She focused, willing herself to sleep, but the dream was slipping away.

'I've got a question,' said Isha. She thought of what the khers had said. Asking a dream made as little sense as asking a mirror, but she said, 'Is Tatters dangerous? Is he on my side?'

The woman's face creased. Isha could hear the rustle of sheets. As the light grew around them, the tent faded away into nothingness, into one white cloud suspended around them. The woman's outline grew fainter.

'It depends,' she said. She was disappearing, but she stretched out a hand and caught Isha's wrist. Isha saw her do it, but she couldn't feel her. Her arm, she sensed, was really under her pillow, holding up her head. The woman looked Isha straight in the eye.

'What does his bind look like?'

With those words, the light shining in Isha's eyes became too bright. Groaning, she turned on her side. She rubbed her face as dawn light poured through the high windows, then pulled her feet back under the sheet. She was left with a vivid image of the dream, and the aftermath of its meaning.

She could still see the woman's face, dark eyes dark skin dark words amidst the burst of light. *What does his bind look like?*

What should a collar even look like? How would Isha know if it looked any different than it should?

She decided to ask Kilian about dreams. Depending on his

answer, she might know whether to forget this mindrambling or consider it as holding some truth.

But it hadn't been a normal dream. She already knew she wouldn't like Kilian's answer.

* * *

Studying with Sir Daegan didn't, as Isha had hoped, spare her from scribe duties. Unfortunately, she was back in the library.

No carpets nor tapestries to brighten the walls here, only cold stone and rows of books on plain wooden shelves. One wing still held some of the giants' books, each as high as an adult man, and wider. At regular intervals, rough tables had been set up that could have belonged to her farm, with uncomfortable stools. Sir Daegan's followers were gathered around one of them. The disciples had to count tithes which, despite the thrill of handling money, looked as boring as her own chore copying out their payment summary. If anything, doing the accounts was worse, because it also required checking the sums for mistakes.

The task was hard and asked for a lot of focus, so nobody spoke much. Sir Daegan hadn't arrived yet. He would join them, Isha imagined, once the brunt of the work was done, to sort out any unresolved issues.

'Your handwriting is terrible, puffin,' Caitlin pointed out, leaning over Isha's shoulder. 'No surprise, coming from a farm girl, I suppose.'

Isha gritted her teeth and let that one pass.

As they neared the end and started filling up the coffers, the disciples relaxed enough to chat, Kilian and Caitlin included. They were gathered around one table – in the library, each area belonged to a different high mage, just as they did at breakfast. Here, only Sir Daegan's followers were welcome.

Once Isha had handed in her summary, she went to sit at one end of the table. At last she had a chance to practise mindlink, rather than mathematics. She closed her eyes and, breathing deeply, she tried to settle her thoughts. Her mind was a plain with grass blowing in the wind. There was nothing else. She held the air in her lungs before breathing out. She opened her eyes. She listened to the ongoing conversations. After a few seconds, she closed her eyes again.

She wanted to be able to jump in and out of mindlink at a moment's notice. It was like learning to use a muscle she'd always had but never cared for.

'Not tired of being a good girl yet, puffin?' Caitlin chirruped.

Isha lost her concentration. If Caitlin calling her a nickname could unsettle her mind, she needed more practice.

'Come have a chat,' said Kilian. 'No need to be so serious.'

'No, let her be,' said Caitlin. She placed one hand on Kilian's arm, her fingers fluttering like butterfly wings. 'She's so hard-working, right? Maybe I should get her to copy that report again; that would keep her busy.'

Isha turned to address Caitlin. 'I've got a question for you.'

Caitlin lifted her eyebrows and made an 'oooh!' noise. She was probably expecting some jibe about her hair or clothes. People stopped to stare and listen. Isha shook her head – why would she bother teasing Caitlin? She had serious questions to ask and needed serious answers.

'Don't get the wrong idea,' she said. 'It's about mindlink.'

If anything, the group grew quieter. Isha had called out a disciple on mindlink knowledge. And not any disciple – Caitlin, whom Sir Daegan always praised, who was Tatters' underground settler.

It was too late to back down. In any case, Isha wasn't sure she wanted to.

'Go on,' said Caitlin. She rested one elbow against the coffer beside her, tucking her chin into her hand, and she smiled like cats do, when they ready themselves to pounce.

Isha had been planning to ask about dreams, but she decided to make her question more difficult, to avoid sounding naïve or ignorant.

'Can dead people live on in someone's mind? Like, I don't know, mindlink parasites?'

By the way Caitlin paled, Isha knew she had put a tough question. She felt smug. *Ha, you expected something dumb coming from me, didn't you?* Caitlin made a split decision. Isha saw the idea cross her face; or maybe she was more tuned-in to mindlink than before, and could sense the flow of her thoughts. Between admitting to ignorance and lying, Caitlin chose to lie.

'Why, are you afraid of ghosts?' She laughed. The disciples around her snickered. Kilian gave Isha the sorry look one gives the fox being thrown to the hounds. 'Sorry, when your mummy took flight, she didn't hide inside your head.'

Isha had heard people say that when an emotion got too strong, the person snapped. In her case, it was the opposite: something inside her that was flexible and soft suddenly grew hard and sharp. Maybe it was the mention of her mother, when she didn't even know who that woman was, when all she could think of was her foster mother with blank eyes.

'You're right, joking about people's relatives dying is hilarious, Caitlin, I should try it some time.' She got up from her stool, laying her hands flat on the table. 'How about you just answer the question?'

Caitlin straightened and folded her hands in front of her. Around her, the disciples did the same, leaving their stools to stand. They moved like a pack. Isha stiffened. Were they going to bother closing the gap? The library was eerily quiet. She glanced at Kilian, who was grimacing. She narrowed her eyes at him. He mouthed something, turning his fingers in front of himself in the air, drawing a circle.

She felt the draft of cold air behind her, too late.

Isha turned around so fast she nearly tripped over her own feet. She hadn't heard his steps on the stone floor. Sir Daegan stood in front of her.

'May you grow tall,' he said.

The disciples diligently echoed his greeting.

'Are you having a nice morning?' Sir Daegan asked, pleasantly enough. He towered over Isha, leaning his heavy frame over her, close enough for it to be awkward. Although she knew it was what he wanted, she didn't take a step backwards. She was stuck against the table anyway. 'Please, tell me what's been going on. It sounds very interesting. More interesting, no doubt, than a boring old man. And the boring old work he entrusted you.'

Sir Daegan's starched black robes touched hers. She craned her neck to hold his eye.

'I was asking the disciples questions.' She tried to sound meek. If she wanted it to work, she should look down and back away. But she couldn't bring herself to. 'I was only keen to learn more.'

Sir Daegan snorted. It turned into a cough, and he lifted a hand before his mouth to clear his throat. Isha felt his breath on the top of her scalp. She cringed.

'We should all be trying to elevate ourselves. I'm all ears. What was the question?'

Isha forced herself not to look around, not to search the room for support. She could do this alone. There was no point in hoping for help – she had to help herself.

'Is it possible for someone to project their mind into someone else's mind, and stay there after their death?'

Sir Daegan frowned. His grey eyebrows joined. He knotted

his hands in front of his stomach. They were big hands, with obvious blue and purple veins, and nails with white stripes at the tips.

'That is an interesting question,' he said. He pushed closer, this time forcing her to step aside, and settled on the stool at the head of the table. As soon as his attention shifted away from her, Isha relaxed. She only realised her shoulders had been halfway up her neck when they sagged.

'It is possible to project yourself into someone else's mind, as you very well know. What would happen, then, if your body was killed while you were mindlinking – not while you were sending a message or emotions from your mind, no, but after you'd stepped out of your body to visit a stranger's mind?'

He addressed the question to the class. No-one offered to answer; even Caitlin didn't try to reply. Sir Daegan let the silence drag on to indicate his disappointment. Then he resumed. 'Theories vary. The experience has never been attempted. The problem is, what you project is only a part of yourself. Even if you found yourself stuck inside someone's mind, you would be a shadow, hardly better than a lacunant. They would be able to ban you easily.'

'But what if they didn't want to ban you?' asked Isha. She had shuffled to the side but hadn't taken a seat again. She didn't dare.

Sir Daegan's eyes were the colour of a dry winter sky when it is too cold to rain.

'What do you have in mind?' he asked.

'What would happen if the person who died was a friend, a relative, and they were welcome inside your mind?'

Sir Daegan stared at her for too long, then studied the shelves lining the library. He smacked his lips.

'In theory, a mind could survive, if nothing tries to uproot it. Do you know what collarbounds are?'

Isha wondered if she had let something slip about Tatters. Her heart beat harder. She loosely held her wrists, left wrist in the right hand, right wrist in the left hand. It prevented them from trembling. 'Yes, sir.'

'You know who made the collars?'

She nodded. 'The giants, before they alit and joined the lightborn.'

'Exactly. We know very little about the giants, except that they managed to break away from the shackles of flesh and take flight. But we know that they left magic items behind them. It is believed that the incredible power emanating from those artefacts comes from giants' minds, trapped within the metal.'

Now that Sir Daegan had started, he wouldn't stop. His teaching voice boomed across the library.

'Gold seems to be one material into which giants could project their minds, as is quicksilver. That is why both metals are known to be alive, even if their form of consciousness must be low or dormant. If giants could project themselves into, and live within, the metal after their bodies had died, why shouldn't a mage be able to repeat that feat, by mindlinking into an animal, a lesser being or another mage?'

Sir Daegan combed his grey hair with one hand. 'So, it is a possibility,' he said. 'Anything else?'

It was a rhetorical question; he meant to resume the work at hand. But Isha wasn't finished. It was usually impossible to ask Sir Daegan anything as he only listened to the disciples, never bothering with the small fry, especially Isha, who was barely legitimate enough to be in his presence. But he seemed to be in a talkative mood today, so she had to take advantage of it. Her head was still spinning with possibilities, ever since her outing with Tatters yesterday.

'Yes,' she said.

She heard someone's intake of breath; it wasn't quite a gasp. Sir Daegan glared at the assembled apprentices, before bringing his grey-blue eyes to rest on Isha's face.

'I'm listening.'

'Is it possible to mindlink in dreams?' she asked.

Sir Daegan glanced past her, at the rows of apprentices lining the table or standing behind his coffers.

'Can someone answer this?'

'Yes.' A sharp voice cut in, polished around the edges, servile to her masters and dangerous to her lowers. Caitlin. She cleared her throat, the sound weirdly similar to the one that had come from Sir Daegan's old, square jaw.

'Two powerful mages, who have been in close contact through mindlink, or have an intense relationship that involves thinking about each other, can inadvertently share a dream,' said Caitlin.

'Interestingly,' added Sir Daegan, nodding his approval, 'dreams rarely cross the Shadowpass. Even mages who often share dreams find the Shadowpass severs their connection. As you can imagine, this makes coordinating with mages on the Sunriser side more difficult than it might have been. In the few instances when it has happened, it required a relationship strong enough to cross the night-tide.'

Wade through shadows, stay in light. Isha's mouth was dry. Why would she, Isha, have a relationship with someone from Tatters' memories? A relationship strong enough to cross the Shadowpass, if that was where that woman was? She should have asked for her name. She tried to remember if she had ever seen the face before, without it being linked to Tatters. She couldn't recall – but then, after the incident, there were many things she couldn't recall.

'Are you going to let us start the session?' asked Sir Daegan.

His question was playful enough, but his tone indicated that Isha had overstepped.

'One very last thing,' she heard herself say.

The library was as silent as a kher grave. In the background, a peal of laughter from another group was quickly muffled. Sir Daegan turned to her slowly, as if his limbs were made of stone. Before he could order her to be quiet, Isha asked:

'Is it possible to spy on someone's mind?'

Yesterday, as she had been talking with Tatters, she had sensed something. It had been like someone slipping their fingers through her hair – light, barely a touch, but it still left her ruffled and changed.

Sir Daegan's grey lips broke into a smile. *Who is the collarbound?*

Although he was sitting in front of her, looking her in the eye, the mindlink reached her as if he were whispering inside her ear, a step behind her. She could nearly feel his stale breath against the back of her neck. The hairs on her arms stood on end. He projected an image of Tatters towards her as he had gleaned it from her thoughts: someone in rags, with a ragged beard and lank red hair, nondescript features. And a collar.

Does that answer your question?

Sir Daegan readjusted the cuffs of his robe. 'We are ready to begin,' he announced.

**

Once Sir Daegan was satisfied that his funds had been properly counted, and once he had assigned the payments due to servants, craftsmen and city folk who laboured for him, his followers were given permission to scatter. The disciples would escort Sir Daegan around town as he went to collect the remaining or incomplete tithes in the quarters he controlled. Isha was about to leave the library with the other apprentices who had recently joined, when Sir Daegan stopped her with a swish of his fingers.

'Come with us,' he ordered.

Isha stopped awkwardly in the doorframe, blocking the way to the apprentices wanting to step out.

'Excuse me?' she mumbled.

'You are *so* eager to learn,' said Sir Daegan. He was smiling, but his tone was ironic. The apprentices sensed a threat and looked away. 'Maybe you will find some answers to your questions.'

There was nothing Isha could do but bow and thank him for this great honour.

Sir Daegan led his disciples out of the Nest, Isha trailing behind. Kilian walked beside her, bounding along the path like a dog happy to be let out. They crossed the bridge separating the Nest from the moors. The river below churned white foam, screaming as it threw itself over the Edge. Isha breathed in spray. When she stepped off the bridge, her robes were damp. The sky was pale blue, with flimsy clouds strewn across it, like flowers scattered in a grassy field. It was growing colder every day.

Isha watched as the sun lit up the blue clouds beyond the Edge. She had lived for so long below the Ridge, with the rock escarpment rising above her, its crushing shadow stretching across the land, that she was unused to the sky.

'You're such a tough one,' Kilian said. He playfully pushed against her. She slipped in the mud and shoved him back. He laughed. They stayed at the back of the group, far from Sir Daegan.

'Look at you, already one of the collectors!' teased Kilian.

'Sir Daegan just wants to get back at me for asking too many questions,' said Isha.

Kilian shook his head. His hair was the colour and texture of hay. 'If he wanted to punish you, he could make you copy out something or do mindlink squatting or whatever. I mean, I'm sure he's pissed-off with you, but bringing you along *is* an honour.' He glanced at her. He couldn't stop smiling. 'Hey, puffin? You want to bully seagulls? You ever seen the size of a puffin?'

He showed her with his hands: a puffin – a small, round bird – and a seagull, spreading out his arms to encompass the full range of their wings. Then he swapped between the two, repeating loudly, as if to an idiot: 'Puffin. Seagull. Puuu-ffin. Seaaa-gull.' She swatted his hands and he stopped, chuckling.

'Don't you take anything seriously?' she asked.

'Don't you take anything lightly?' he answered.

She smiled. The group went their way, down from the Nest, towards the town. The city lay low, like a squatting toad with towers for warts. The rooftops were red and yellow, the ramparts were brown. The mud was black and squished underfoot. On the road, they crossed carriages and men on horseback, poor folk and guards on foot. Most people moved aside to let Sir Daegan and his disciples pass, but started closing in again near the end of their formation – by Isha and Kilian. They had to quicken their pace to avoid being bumped into.

When they reached the city, a slow, low-grade headache clamped around Isha's skull. The mages had filled the city with invisible messages and warnings addressed to each other. Now that she was more attuned to mindlink, she could sense it in the air, permeating the streets, as thick as smog.

They headed for the quarter Sir Daegan controlled.

'In his area, he goes to the meetings between merchants and oversees transactions with mindlink, to check no-one is lying or cheating,' Kilian explained. 'He judges cases between them.

In exchange for fair treatment and good justice, the merchants pay a tithe.'

'Who decides where each quarter is?' asked Isha.

Kilian made a sound like a horse snorting through its nose. 'Ah, they're old borders. They were drawn up by some supreme mage ages ago. People just stick to those.'

'Can't the ungifted send money to Sir Daegan through their servants?'

Kilian shook his head. 'Sir Daegan collects them in person at each door. It's traditional.' He passed his arm around her shoulders – because he was taller, he could do so and use her as a crutch. He leant all his weight on her, until she could hardly walk. 'He has to remind them who's in charge. Can't hurt. Hey, puffin, it can't hurt to remember who's in charge, all right?'

'Get off!' She tried to push him away. They squabbled in the street as she struggled with his bigger size and strength. None of the mages played; none of them touched. Isha had to admit it was a relief to know someone to whom human contact came so easily. She finally got rid of him by slamming her elbow in his sides until he relented, wincing in pain but laughing.

'She's got bite!'

'Don't underestimate the puffin,' she said.

Kilian squished his lips into what he thought looked like a beak. 'Squawk squawk.'

She couldn't help but laugh, until she noticed that a few disciples had turned to glare at the roughhousing. She lowered her face. Although Sir Daegan didn't mention it, she felt that he disapproved. He was talking in a low, serious voice with Caitlin. He walked with a cane plated with gold, as well as heavy rings with pearls across his fingers, which he didn't wear for training. The black of his robes only underlined these riches, the jewels radiating against the dark backdrop.

'You'll get me in trouble,' she whispered to Kilian. He only shrugged.

'You're friends with Tatters, right? You love trouble.'

'I'm not his friend,' she corrected.

Especially not if he spies on my mind. She wondered why he'd done it. What was he hoping to uncover? She pictured the woman of her dreams asking: *Did you find him?* People were trying to find Tatters – but what was he trying to find?

Part of her was furious with Tatters for luring her far from the other mages to mess around with her. But part of her was sorry for him. He had seemed so frightened in the Temple. His sister had died and he had grieved for her and then she had never left. What could have happened for her to die while inside his mind? He was like a clay pot with a crack inside it that no-one could see from the outside, but that meant the whole structure could shatter without warning.

'You're joking, right?' Kilian's lively voice pulled her out of her daydream. 'Didn't you have some secret get-together or something yesterday?' When she frowned at him, Kilian only tapped the side of his nose. 'I know everything.'

'You mean disciples don't mind their own business,' she said.

Kilian chuckled. 'That too. And everyone knows Tatters. Soon enough, everyone will know you, by the looks of it.'

I'm too obvious, she thought. *But then, so is Tatters. And he seems to be able to keep secrets.*

When they reached Sir Daegan's territory, there was nothing to indicate that one quarter stopped and another began – no street signs, no walls, no locks. Yet when Isha crossed the road, she felt the transition in her teeth. It was as if the air around her had changed taste.

'Weird, isn't it?' said Kilian. 'It spooked me at first.'

'What is it?' she asked. It had been easier to walk through the city when she was less receptive.

'All mages have influenced their quarters. Especially the borders,' said Kilian. 'You can sort of…' He did a vague gesture with his hands. 'Infuse the place with emotion. Like the emotions of mages you've defeated, for example. Think of ink in water. It colours the space where other people's minds are.'

Here the road was paved with regular flagstones, worn down on either side where carriages had eroded them. Although people emptied their sewage into the street, servants threw buckets of water to rinse it away. Sometimes the houses had front gardens planted with grass and flowers.

'What do you actually know about Tatters?' she asked. 'Is it common for mages to hide their name?'

Kilian shrugged again, his hands clutching his belt, his elbows relaxed and open along his sides. 'It depends. It's a Sunriser tradition. People don't really believe in it at the Nest.'

Sir Daegan stopped before an impressive building of red sandstone. Caitlin went to lift the copper knocker to call forth the household. Kilian went on:

'It's a bit like having a double. The idea is, if you use a fake name, all the memories attached to your real name – childhood memories, your siblings and parents, stuff like that – are more difficult to access, because they're linked to another name. But it's not been proven to work.'

At the door, Sir Daegan was engrossed in a conversation with a servant, who was wearing colourful livery. Every now and then, the servant nervously glanced at the gathering behind Sir Daegan, which spilled over the doorstep and into the street. As far as Isha could tell, most of the disciples didn't bother with Sir Daegan's conversation. They were there as a mob, to intimidate the ungifted. They weren't expected to have duties, only presence.

'So, you think Tatters is from the Sunriser convents?' she asked. If she wasn't required to worry about what Sir Daegan was doing, she might as well chat with Kilian.

'No, let's face it, he looks Duskdweller.' Kilian tousled his hair, shaping it so it didn't fall in front of his eyes. 'There are other reasons for changing your name, you know.' He winked at her. 'If you were on the run, for example.'

'How come he hasn't been caught by the lawmages yet?'

'They don't want to catch him,' said Kilian. 'Simple as that. He belongs to Lady Siobhan, you know – it's an open secret.'

Kilian went on to tell her his version of what had happened to Tatters: he had been on the run for illegal mindlink. When Lady Siobhan came to oversee the punishments inflicted on criminal mages, she thought it would be a shame to waste such talent. She offered Tatters the choice between becoming a lacunant and begging at the gates, or accepting the collar and becoming a slave.

'How do you know he was given a choice?' asked Isha.

Kilian lifted then dropped his hands, in a 'who knows?' gesture. 'Maybe he wasn't. Maybe the supreme mage said, "I want this one", and they put the collar on him rather than mindscrew him.'

Isha distractedly watched the servant wiping his brow against his sleeve, blocking the threshold with his body, muttering towards Sir Daegan. Caitlin stood beside the high mage, her lush hair tumbling down her back, glinting auburn in the sunlight. Kilian was still talking.

'Either way, he belongs to the Nest. And he would have died if not for Lady Siobhan.'

Isha's attention was drawn to the conversation at the door. It dragged on longer, she felt, than was comfortable for the servant or the high mage. Kilian followed her gaze. The other disciples seemed to have come to the same conclusion, because they assembled in a tighter group around Sir Daegan. Slowly, they fell quiet. The servant was obviously ill at ease. He kept touching his forehead, his hair, the buttons on his jacket. His hand fell back limply at his side, only to go up and fiddle with something else the moment after.

'Very well,' said Sir Daegan. 'I will resolve this matter and come back to you.'

The servant's shoulders sagged in relief. He bowed low before closing the door.

'Someone is meddling,' grumbled Sir Daegan. His lips were pushed over his teeth, and barely opened when he spoke. 'Let's find out who.'

The disciples whispered words of support. From what Isha knew of Nest politics, this meant another mage was patrolling Sir Daegan's area and making a claim over it. They could, in theory, fight him to take it as theirs. Sir Daegan waved his group forward, heading without a moment's hesitation down one of the roads.

This was different from the casual ambling that had brought them to the first house. Everyone was silent and grim-faced, even Kilian. Sir Daegan's cane hit the cobbles with a click as regular as a clock ticking. He studied every front door, every window, every carriage, as if counting them. Isha stayed close to the group.

They found him soon enough. He was standing beside something that could have been a birdbath, but wasn't. Her heart missed a beat when she recognised him. What was he doing here?

Passerine was trailing his fingers along the rim of the basin. It was placed at the centre of a square of pale flagstones, its pool of quicksilver grey and still.

'What's that?' Isha hissed, pointing towards the smooth, shallow bowl of mercury.

Kilian made a movement to shush her, but he still answered. 'It's a marker, of sorts. That's where the boundaries stem from.'

Passerine looked up at the sound of their steps. His black robes fell straight from his shoulders, as if he were a dash of ink. His belt was dyed dark blue – the belt of an outsider.

When he locked gazes with Sir Daegan, he flicked the mercury with his fingers.

Isha felt the ripples as if the world around her were made of water and someone had just dropped a stone. She saw Kilian grit his teeth. The emotions that had been invested in the quicksilver, which generations of mages ruling over this quarter had soaked into the metal, echoed around the square.

Even Sir Daegan stumbled, although he pretended never to have missed a step. Passerine shook his fingers clean.

'May you grow tall,' he said.

'May you grow tall,' repeated Sir Daegan, his words like spilt acid.

Passerine was younger than Sir Daegan, taller. His jet-black hair was thick where Sir Daegan's grey was fraying. His voice was a drum where Sir Daegan's was an oboe.

The two high mages touched wrists. Passerine didn't acknowledge Isha, but she knew he had seen her. He graced Sir Daegan with a small, condescending smile. 'It is a lovely area of the city, is it not?' His robes folded like bats' wings when he crossed his arms.

'It is,' said Sir Daegan. He was forced to cock his head backwards to address Passerine. 'You are a newcomer, so I won't hold it against you. As a member of the Sunriser convents, you might think the Nest is one large convent. But it is not the case.'

Because of his dark skin and irises, the white of Passerine's eyes gleamed. 'I am well aware of the differences between the Nest and the convents.'

Isha sensed that this wasn't the right answer. Sir Daegan had been offering Passerine a way out, but Passerine hadn't taken it. He was prowling another mage's area of influence and had just admitted he had done so knowing full well what it entailed. Sir Daegan clenched his jaw.

They were standing very close. Isha observed how tense Sir Daegan's shoulders were, how his fingers were gripping his cane, how he held himself, pushing his weight into his heels. She wondered if that was what she looked like when she confronted him – defiant, but shrunken.

Kilian took her arm. Her first instinct was to pull away, but the expression on his face stopped her. The blood had drained from his cheeks. She let him guide her towards the back of the group.

'What does this mean?' she asked, as quietly as she could.

'Sir Passerine is claiming the quarter,' said Kilian, keeping his voice low. 'That means Passerine and his disciples will fight us and Sir Daegan. And the winner gets to keep the quarter. The money, the fame, all of it. The losers are, well…' He swallowed. 'Well. It's not as if the *winner* was going to put themselves in the quicksilver.'

'They're going to make lacunants out of the losers?' Isha whispered, horrified.

Kilian shook his head. 'No, no, but… but bits of us will be gone. It's like a wound, if you like, it's a shard of you forever lost.'

So the mercury would be filled with pieces of people. An eye. A tooth. A scream. A finger. Of course, it would be sensations, not flesh. Metal could only contain feelings and wants, longings and griefs. But it didn't make it any less sinister.

'But Passerine hasn't got apprentices,' she pointed out.

Kilian nodded. 'I know. We're just meat-shields. But without a shield, I guess ... I guess it won't be nice to watch.'

He squeezed her arm.

'Isha,' Sir Daegan called.

She hadn't been expecting her name; she jumped. She felt Kilian tense. The disciples around them parted. Reluctantly, Kilian let go and shuffled to the side. Isha was worried enough without the fear in his eyes, which only made her feel worse.

She went to the front of the group. Sir Daegan rested a bejewelled hand on the small of her back. He pushed her forwards.

'You are acquainted, I believe?' he asked.

Passerine nodded – but whether in greeting to Isha or to answer Sir Daegan's question, it was difficult to tell. She was surprised when he extended his wrist. The ligaments there were taut, visible under his skin. The gesture was formal, when their relationship wasn't. She touched wrists with him.

'Now that we're done with the niceties ...' Sir Daegan shoved Isha's back, his rings digging into her skin. 'Isha, do your duty.'

'W-what?' she spluttered.

She turned, as she preferred showing her back to Passerine than having Sir Daegan behind her. He smiled, his grey eyes still narrowed in a thin line. Belatedly, Isha realised what he meant. He wanted her to duel with Passerine.

'With all due respect, sir,' she said, unsure how to refuse, 'a more senior disciple would represent you much better. I am unprepared to bear such a heavy responsibility.'

She glanced at Caitlin, but Caitlin didn't step forward. Sir Daegan did his usual little wave of dismissal. His pearls caught the sunlight.

'No, no. I trust you will find this enlightening.'

So, this is my punishment for asking too many questions. Isha was torn. She didn't want to be loyal to anyone but, if she were to pick a side, then she was with Passerine – now, and always. She owed him that much.

'Sir, Caitlin is a much stronger choice.' It was worth a try, at least. 'She will be able to defend you to the fullest.'

Sir Daegan's lips froze into a snarl; his eyebrows pushed lower over his eyes. 'Are you defying my orders?'

This was it. She would lose her teacher before her first month at the Nest. Before Isha could answer, she heard a voice – a whisper, nothing more.

I don't mind. Accept the duel. The tone was warm and encouraging. The expression on Sir Daegan's face didn't change. He hadn't sensed Passerine's intervention. She didn't risk answering through mindlink, as she would give herself away.

'Of course not,' she said. 'I am more than happy to be your champion.'

With a deep breath, she faced Passerine. His smile, his posture, didn't change.

She projected herself into his mind.

His settled mind was the bleakest she'd encountered. There was no grass; there were no pebbles. Passerine's mind was an empty space. Its ground was flat and shiny like the surface of a lake, with no depth and nothing to reflect. It didn't have walls. Its sky was uniformly grey.

She suddenly remembered that she had been here before. Confused memories spiralled inside her. She had trained with him, before the incident. She remembered something of the texture of his thoughts.

This wasn't a duel with an audience or a settler. Their blows would only be for them to see. The mages around them would perceive the outlines of their fight – the shape of the attacks, maybe, the parts of you that leaked and spilled out of yourself. But for the most part, this battle would be their own.

In mindlink, Passerine didn't wear his mage's robes. Instead, he was dressed in a rich Sunriser outfit, with a blue nasivyati rather than black, slim sandals hugging his ankles. He cocked his head to one side, his faint smile unwavering. He was waiting for her.

Isha wouldn't harm him, but she had to pretend to try, at least. She focused on her tattoo. The ink quivered against her cheek, moving like something alive. It simmered, scalding her, overflowing out of her face. She shed her tattoo like snakes shed their old skin.

I am me. Isha. I was born, I will live, I will die. That's all.

And I am something else. I am what people see of me. I am a name, a symbol, a black line on fresh skin.

She saw Passerine through two prisms at once. She saw him with tenderness, as the Isha who felt protected by him, whom he had brought to the Nest. And she saw him with pride, as the Isha who knew he followed her because of who she was, because she had earned his guardianship.

She also viewed Sir Daegan as if through two mirrors, each with a different reflection. He was her teacher and master, certainly. But he was also no-one special. The black inkborne bird felt only disdain for him, for the man who had made the mistake of scorning her, as if she were some ungifted halfblood.

It was like walking on a wire. The slightest distraction pushed her one side or the other, and she struggled to maintain both shapes, outweighing each thought with another to keep her balance.

Passerine eyed her carefully. Isha moved first, aiming for a symbolic hit.

She sent him a constructed version of himself as a refugee, after having crossed the Shadowpass, shivering under his stana, with nowhere to go, no home nor stronghold nor friends to rely on. She crafted the dull ache down his legs, the taste of grit in his mouth, the vague scent of burning wood that was all that remained of his convent turned to cinder. She hoped she hadn't misjudged. Surely now that he had found shelter within the Nest, this shouldn't harm him?

She sensed his amusement. She knew – she hoped – the onlookers couldn't perceive it. *Safe*, he thought. *The Nest isn't safe.* Within the message, a vision was threaded, of a small nest of twigs at the end of a branch, shaking in the gale, threatening to come undone. In Passerine's mind, the Nest was only a temporary hideout, not sturdy enough to withhold the Renegades, or maybe not strong enough yet. He let her images wash past him.

She stood panting, focusing all her energy on keeping her mind divided. He must have felt how confused she was, as to why he was doing this and why this fight was necessary, because he explained:

What do you think I'm trying to do today? We need power. Isha was both pleased and surprised by the 'we', the admission that they were together in this. *We need control. That is the only way to be safe. I am sorry. I didn't think you would be with a high mage – certainly not this one.*

He sighed.

I hope you'll forgive me.

To her shock, Passerine hit back. He overcame the weak imagining she'd sent him and replied swiftly. It was harder than she had expected. It was based on truth.

She was at the farm with her foster parents. Her foster mother went to fetch the pot with the soup three times, forgetting each time that she had already served them. Her foster father hadn't touched his food. The bowl was placed against his elbow, and he nearly spilled it as he turned to address his wife. Isha felt sick.

Each time she looked up at her foster parents, she wondered: *Who are these people?*

Passerine's attack created a rift inside her, from which memories came gushing like blood.

The neighbours had found them wandering their grounds, all three of them, eyes glazed over, talking nonsense. Her foster father had been trying to pick fruit from a barren apple tree. Her foster mother had been sweeping the front step until her hands bled. Isha had been roaming the mountainside above the village and wouldn't speak a word to anyone, not until her foster brother was called back from his apprenticeship and took her hand and led her back inside.

No-one knew what had happened. Something had attacked them – wrecked a peaceful household, left their minds to rot. The village was astir. Someone had crossed the Shadowpass to reach this remote farm, too far from the centre of the village to be heard, too isolated by orchards and fields of wheat.

Because of her, of course. Who wanted to harm a couple of farmers? They wanted Isha.

The only reason they didn't take her was Passerine. Isha remembered, afterwards, that he had been part of the struggle. She vaguely recalled him pushing her behind him, screaming 'Run!' and launching himself at the attackers. He had come to bring her yearly upkeep fee and had arrived at the same time as their enemies. Without him, Isha would have been snatched away from her home. She knew that much.

A few nights later, in the aftermath, she found herself talking to Passerine as he was seated before their fire, his feet close to the flames, his stana thrown across the back of the chair. He had tried to explain what had occurred to her foster parents, but they were confused, still, with frightened smiles. Minds slowly healing, with bits of life missing, like holes in a piece of fabric.

'We need to regroup at the Nest.' His deep voice, and the spitting flames. The smell of the broth. Warm bread from the oven on the table. 'The Renegades will secure their power inside the Wingshade convents, then they'll come for the Duskdwellers.'

Isha sat cross-legged before the fire, pushing the ashes back inside the grate with a stick. The damp wood let out too much smoke. An ember landed on her arm but didn't burn. When she smothered it, it left a black line down her wrist.

The weight of his hand on her shoulder, with the added weight of his words. The flame reflected in the white of his eyes. 'They will capture you, by force if need be.'

And so she had fled. She had followed him to the Nest.

She would never know what they had taken from her, what she had lost. They had left her shattered in their wake.

Isha broke; her soul splintered, with a sound like wood splitting under the axe. But she didn't fall apart. Something held her together. When she looked down, black threads were sewing her back into one piece. Or maybe it wasn't threads but veins, pulsing black blood.

It was ink.

It doesn't matter. I don't need to remember.

The part of her that was the tattoo didn't yield.

The world will remember for me.

Half of Isha was on her knees, yielding to Passerine. But half of her was still flying, smiling with a crow-black beak and talking with a crow-black tongue.

The thieves were wrong to think they stole from me.

I was the treasure.

Her bird-self stared Passerine down. Before she could strike, he lifted both hands and said:

I surrender.

She was so stunned she took time to leave his mind. Pulling herself together was like picking strewn pieces of clothing flung around the room, struggling to get dressed under Passerine's gaze, naked and vulnerable. She returned to her own mind. She dimly heard Passerine addressing Sir Daegan:

'You will want something of mine, no doubt, to mark your victory.'

Sir Daegan's voice was terse. 'I do not know about hospitality in the convents, but at the Nest, it is considered poor manners to belittle a guest, even if they brought it upon themselves. You may leave.'

She opened her eyes. The autumn sun was stark. Her fingers, clenched like claws, hurt. She rubbed them until they unstiffened.

Kilian closed the gap between the disciples and Isha, worry and awe fighting for a place on his face. 'That was wonderful.' After a beat, he added, 'You're going to be fine.' He didn't reach out to her. He wrung his hands instead, glancing from the other disciples to Sir Daegan. The high mage was tapping his cane on the flagstone before him like a cat taps its tail when it's annoyed.

Passerine graced them all with a brief nod. Isha was still recovering her breath. Her knees were trembling.

'I will not trouble you any further.' To Isha, he said, 'I look forward to duelling with you again.'

He could have fought her; she was grateful to him for conceding the match.

Passerine smiled. 'You are a quick learner.'

She smiled back, albeit weakly. If someone had pushed her, she would have collapsed. It was as if her bones had been sucked out of her legs.

Sir Daegan watched him leave, his lips pinched, until Passerine was out of sight.

Chapter Eight

Isha, Kilian and the other apprentices bumped into Tatters as he was leaving the Coop. He was pushing a small barrel in front of him, which reached up to his knee. He greeted them with one hand, using the other to stabilise the cask.

'Where are you going?' asked Isha. There was little point staying at the tavern if she couldn't train.

'To see Arushi,' he said.

Kilian was on the tavern's threshold. The friends they had come with went inside, but he lingered.

'You coming?' he asked Isha.

She glanced from him, in the golden light of the inn, to Tatters, who already had his back to her, and was bent awkwardly to pivot his barrel.

'Go in, I'll join you later,' she said.

Kilian pulled a face. He stayed, scuffing his shoes on the doorstep; for a moment, it looked as if he was about to offer to come with them, but Tatters was leaving, and Isha couldn't wait for Kilian to make up his mind.

'See you soon,' she promised.

She ran to catch up with Tatters. She could see him smiling.

'I'm flattered,' he said.

She walked alongside him. The beaten ground wasn't too

difficult to navigate, but once they reached the cobbles the barrel either got caught in the irregular stones or bounced out of control. Isha leant over to help Tatters. The cask was heavier than she had expected, and she had to use all her weight to roll it. They each held one end as the alcohol sloshed inside.

'They invited you again?' Isha asked, in part to make conversation.

'No, I'm inviting myself.' Tatters guided them towards the Pit. They had to avoid people on foot, carts pulled by horses, kids who kicked their barrel as they pushed past. 'You still need a present, though. And it still can't be food if it's khers.' When folk spotted Isha's robes, they moved out of the way. A few cart drivers called out to Tatters as he went past, and he waved back without breaking his stride. 'Can't be the same present as before. Beer is always popular. Plus, the innkeeper gave me a good price for it.'

Isha spotted the mudbrick walls of the Pit, then the two kher guards. They weren't the same ones as before. As before, however, they lurked in the shade of the wall, arms crossed, heads lowered so their horns pointed towards the humans ambling past.

The city is full of locks, thought Isha. *Locks and doors.*

'I get stopped by lawmages at the Nest and by khers here,' she said.

Tatters smiled again. She could tell he was in a good mood.

'Power is the number of thresholds you can cross,' he said.

As they got within earshot, the khers shuffled towards the entrance. The nearest one called out:

'You with them?'

He shoved his chin, indicating something behind them. Tatters and Isha turned.

A group of humans were drawing closer – nearly ten of them, including one lawmage. His undyed belt stood in stark contrast to his rich outfit. They walked three-by-three, in rows, surrounding one man at the centre. At first Isha mistook the man for a smith, because of the leather apron knotted around his chest. At second glance, she decided he was more likely a butcher, as he wore a thick belt on which several knives were hanging. On either side of the procession were kher guards with the Nest's heraldry. Amongst them was Arushi.

Tatters drove his barrel out of their path, Isha in tow. They tucked themselves away to let the procession pass. The humans were chatting amongst themselves; the khers who guarded them kept their mouths shut. The butcher laughed raucously, slapping his bulging stomach with the flat of his hand, as if testing the bounce of his beer-gut.

Arushi was at the front. She looked from Tatters to the khers at the gates before nodding. The khers nodded back. They stood aside when she entered the Pit, followed by the humans.

Isha studied Tatters' face. The glow had left his expression. He rested one hand on the lid of the barrel, lightly, with his fingers spread apart. He bit his lower lip as he watched the group walk past.

'This might be more instructive for you than I'd thought.' He didn't say this as if it were good news.

The procession seemed to share his foreboding. As they crossed the mudbrick porch, the humans fell silent. The butcher gave everyone – including both kher guards, Isha and Tatters – a long, hard stare. It was the sort of stare that examined every feature so that, when the person punched, they could aim for the nose.

The group's khers weren't the only ones armed. Except for the lawmage, all the humans were carrying swords, and a few even had crossbows. Isha had rarely seen a crossbow, so the triangular wooden frame seemed more weighted, more threatening, than the blades. The bolts gleamed in the sunlight like teeth.

Head cocked to one side, Tatters waited until a noticeable distance stretched between them and the intruders. Only then did he tilt the barrel onto its side; the cask spun easily on the smooth earth.

Instead of the route for Arushi's house, Tatters followed the human procession.

'You know what this is?' whispered Isha.

'All I'll say is, maybe this is not the right day to be wearing mages' robes.' Tatters kept his gaze on the road. He sighed. 'But then your tattoo says something different.' He stopped, blocking the barrel with his foot. 'Look, if this was someone else, any another apprentice, I'd send them home now. Do you think you're ready for this?'

The streets were quieter here, without any carts, only a few lazy dogs stretched out in the evening sun. A goat was scraping bark off a tree with its horns.

'Yes.' She didn't know what this was about, but she was here to learn.

They resumed struggling with the barrel until they reached the central square. It was where khers set up tents during the night, hemmed in by mudbrick walls, half-crumbled houses, and the high fortifications that circled the city. On the battlements, the khers had splashed paint and sculpted the stone, creating a vibrant, striking mural. Eyes, silhouettes, trees, beasts and birds were drawn in a mess of vivid hues. They towered above the square, dwarfing the people; Isha's breath caught in her throat.

In the centre of the yard, a few khers were arguing in their own language. Two women were trying to reason with a younger man – Isha thought she could tell, thanks to his shorter horns. He was half-naked, with a tattoo running across his back and his spine, nearly all the way around his waist. At first she couldn't make out the design, then she worked out that the circle around his bellybutton was an eye, and the large spiral down his side was a chunk of muscle from an animal. The two lines across his stomach must be horns. The tattoo was a stylised version of a bull, she decided, or some other horned, thick-shouldered beast.

Tatters pinched Isha's sleeve. He steered her towards a chicken coop, a wood and wicker structure with hay inside it. They stood partly hidden between the barrel and the pen, where they had a decent view, but were out of the khers' line of sight.

I need to remember how Tatters does this, thought Isha. *There's crossing the threshold, and then there's not outstaying your welcome.*

When the human procession reached the square, the khers parted, and Isha spotted what the disagreement was about. A body was laid out on a wooden stretcher, resting against the floor, with a piece of linen in place of a shroud covering it up to the neck. The horns rising from the head curved back in two neat circles.

The man who might have been a butcher took a step forward. 'What's the problem, young man?' He had a booming voice, with an edge of laughter to it.

One kher woman turned to address the men. 'It's nothing, sir. It was his idewran who died. His ...' She seemed to struggle to find the right word. 'You would say father, sir. Like his father.'

The man made a sound between a grunt and a laugh. 'I thought you all screwed each other until you couldn't tell who's your father, or even whether you're sleeping with your sister.'

The kher kept her voice neutral. 'He is very upset.'

The other woman pulled the young man back. He spat on the dust in front of him, which made her gasp and slap his hand.

'As long as he lets me do my work,' said the man. He used his voice like he used his eyes: to warn that worse could be to come.

The humans formed a semi-circle as the butcher knelt beside the body. He lifted the head and placed it on his lap. He fingered his knives, running his coarse hands across their blades, until he settled for one that he unhooked from his belt. It was a stocky cleaver. He held one horn in place, yanked it towards him, and hacked at it with the knife.

Isha didn't know what she was expecting, but it wasn't that. She felt each hit in her teeth. The blade sank into the horn. The butcher hefted the cleaver out, grunting, jiggling the handle to free it. The khers were silent. He worked close to the dead kher's forehead. The son watched his father without a word. He breathed heavily, the creature tattooed on his chest heaving like a living thing. He watched as a human chopped the horns off his father's head.

A buzzing echoed in Isha's ears, the start of a migraine or a spell of dizziness. It was like falling through glass, hearing her world shatter.

When the base of the first horn was cut through, the butcher tugged to remove it from the forehead. Because of the way it had grown, curving back inside the kher's skull, it wasn't easy to extract. Dark blood, oozing like pus, seeped from the wound. As the butcher turned the head between his hands, his rough work bruised the dead skin.

She should feel worse. She should be sick. But she was numb.

The second horn proved more difficult. Even with its base at the temple removed, it wouldn't leave the kher's skull. It must have grown at an awkward angle. The butcher shook it, trying to loosen it. The deceased kher's head lolled above his desecrator's knees, spraying black drops on his apron.

The body was in that strange in-between state where it looked, still, like someone. But the butcher treated it as he would an animal carcass. Like a picture that could be seen two ways, Isha saw both scenes in her mind – the carving up of meat, and the grim funeral. If she focused on the butcher and the horns, she could nearly forget the victim was someone with a son watching the scene, someone like Ganez, who worked as cheap labour on the farmlands, who was afraid of what came after death. Those dark lips had kissed people's hands as their life faded away.

Isha turned to Tatters. He was pale, but he stared as if it were his duty.

'Why?' she asked.

He shook his head. 'Don't you know? Mages don't like paying with normal money. Too easy to mindlink. Too easy for the older mages to manipulate the apprentices, changing the shape or colour of the coins in their thoughts.' His hair fell across his eyes. 'So, they use something that is immune to mindlink.'

Baina. Isha had wondered, of course, what kind of cattle was used to make those small, round coins. But like a lot of the strangeness of the Nest, she had taken it for granted.

The realisation crept along her arm like a ghost. She was carrying dead kher horn in her purse.

The butcher was still struggling with the second horn. He placed one hand against the kher's cheek, pushing one way, pulling the horn the other. His hand slipped; flesh across the face broke. He swore, wiping skin off the palm of his hand.

The kher women winced. The young man snapped: 'Be careful!'

The father's face now had a red patch from the cheekbone to the corner of the eye. His horn, half ripped out, hung limply from his forehead.

The boy lunged suddenly, shoving the butcher off the body. With the tenderness reserved for a living person, perhaps a child or an elderly family member, with a gentleness which left Isha raw, he lifted his father's shoulders. He rested the bloodied skull against his chest.

'That's enough,' he said. 'You have one horn. Take it and leave us.'

One woman knelt next to him, touching his hair, replacing stray curls behind his ear. She whispered something. The young man shook his head. He hugged his father closer, unaware that he was smearing blood across his naked chest.

The butcher cleaned his hands on his apron as he hoisted himself to his feet. 'Give us the body.'

Menace rose like static electricity. The humans lifted their crossbows and their swords. The kher guards took a step forward.

The young man looked up at the khers from the Nest. Arushi was at the front of the group, and he must have known she was the head of guards, because he asked her:

'How can you do this to your own people?'

'Don't make this difficult.' Her voice was deep and quiet.

She knelt beside the young man. She tried to prise his father from his arms, with all the care she might use to lift a newborn. When he clutched his father, she placed her hands on his forearms and left them there, saying nothing, not trying to take away the body.

Long, tense seconds drifted past. Isha saw the shoulders of the young man sag. Tears clouded his eyes. Arushi was clearly about to lean over and delicately slide his father out of his hug, when the butcher lost patience. He wasn't watching the khers carefully. From his point of view, Isha imagined, this was slow work, which meant he wouldn't get home and grab a beer as early as he hoped.

'Move out of the way, cow.'

He strode towards them. The young man tensed and held his father harder. Without casting the butcher a glance, Arushi got to her feet. Her arms were stained with damp patches.

'Let the body go,' said the butcher. 'Now. It's the property of the Nest. If you don't, you're breaking the law.'

The young man said nothing. His arms were clenched around his father.

'He is sorry,' said one of the women. She leant over the young man, touched his fingers, tried to loosen them. He wouldn't budge.

'You think I won't put you to the pillory?' asked the butcher.

'Give him some time,' said the other woman. She had horns that nearly reached her forehead, which meant they would, in time, start growing inside her skull. Soon she would be the one on the ground with a half-sawn horn drooping from her brow.

Isha couldn't know for sure, but she guessed this meant the female kher was about the same age as the deceased. Maybe she was the young man's mother.

The lawmage joined the butcher. His scarlet robes shone in the low evening sun. 'You don't want to be arrested, do you, lad?'

The young man kissed his father's forehead before setting him down. He got up.

'That's better,' said the lawmage.

The young man threw a punch at the lawmage's face. He hit his mark.

It went fast. Tatters barely had time to drag Isha out of the line of fire. The lawmage stumbled backwards, swearing, his arms folded in front of his face to protect himself. The butcher ran behind his guards. A human shot a crossbow, and the women shrieked and threw themselves to the ground. Several khers ran out of their houses or from nearby streets when they heard the screams. Isha saw Yua dash around the corner, only to dive down to avoid a crossbow bolt.

Someone must have been shot, because they started howling in pain. Two bolts hit the wall above Isha, sinking deep into the rammed earth, with only small shards of wood poking out. She lay flat on her stomach, tasting grit. The kher boy managed to kick the lawmage in the shin before Arushi deftly caught his arm and twisted it behind his back. She didn't take out her sword. With her free hand, she grabbed his hair and forced him to his knees.

'Everyone calm down!' she shouted.

Silence, like dust, stayed suspended above the scene. Only one kher was still moaning – the one who had been shot. It was an elderly male kher who had been sitting with his back against the fortifications when the fighting begun.

'Someone tend to him,' said Arushi. She nodded to the two women who had been with the young man, and who were closest to the body. 'You. Go.' From the way she said it, the urgency in her voice, Isha guessed this was to protect them as much as to help the wounded.

They scrambled away, their colourful woollen attire white with sand. Not far from where Isha was lying, Yua rose. She did it slowly, but not because she was hurt. She moved like a cat deciding whether to pounce. Her face was sour.

'We should arrest…' started the lawmage. He was pressing his sleeve against his upper lip. Blood – fresh blood, bright red, the blood of someone standing and breathing – tarnished his robe.

'I have already arrested the person responsible,' interrupted Arushi.

The lawmage glared at her. She glared back. Around them, khers spread like shadows across the square. They stood up, dusted their clothes, and stared at the assembled humans, the desecrated body.

Unhurried, but never lowering their eyes, the human guards placed their crossbows on the ground, each putting their foot in the stirrup at the front of the weapon, and pulling the strings back into place, using both hands. The tension increased as they pulled the bows taut.

The lawmage made a split decision. 'Very well,' he said. 'We are leaving. We are taking the body for further examination.'

'No!' shouted the young man.

Arushi pushed down on his head, forcing him to press his chin against his chest. It held his mouth closed.

Isha spat out sand. The smell of violence hung in the air. Tatters had drawn them both behind the chicken pen, although its wicker walls wouldn't have offered much protection. When she rose to her feet, he kept one hand gripped around her forearm. She could hear him breathing fast.

'I'll be all right,' she whispered, so as to not attract attention. He let go.

'Sorry. It's just…' Shaking his head, Tatters kept his eyes on the square. 'I shouldn't have brought you here,' he muttered.

Arushi and the lawmage were standing facing each other. The lawmage, like most humans, was taller than the kher. But her polished horns reached up to his eyes, and she angled her face downwards, moving the points ever-so-slightly towards him. She handed over her prisoner to another guard, who tied his arms behind his back with rope. The young man didn't fight back.

'Let this man finish his work, and let the people grieve their loss,' Arushi was saying.

'We can't do it safely here,' argued the lawmage. 'If we are attacked…'

'As the head of guards, I hereby declare it safe to finish retrieving the horns.'

The lawmage folded his arms over his chest. Around him, a patchwork of people in yellows, blues and reds were gathering. The khers stood at a safe distance, but with their heads lowered. The colour of their garments echoed the mural, whose bright painted eyes all seemed turned towards the lawmage. At the bottom of the wall, below the drawing of a tree spreading its branches, the old man was still whimpering. His pain was muted, covered by the two women fussing over him. One, the older, kept looking over her shoulder at the young man kneeling on the ground.

The lawmage turned to the butcher. 'What would you rather do?'

'I'm not afraid.' He spoke loudly, addressing the square.

He took a step towards the body. No-one stirred. He sat down, pulled the dead kher towards him, and untied a hook from his belt, which he plunged deep inside the kher's skull. In the silence, it was possible to hear wet, fleshy sounds, as well as the scrape of blade on bone. The hook caught the horn like nails across slate.

Tatters mindlinked towards Isha. *I hope Arushi knows what she's doing.*

She sensed the emotions within his message – worry, for Arushi of course, and for her. He'd tried to conceal it, but it was visceral, like the jump someone might make when something crashed to the floor close to them.

She focused. Sir Daegan had taught her how to mindlink without drowning the recipient with information he wasn't interested in.

I'm sure she does, Isha answered.

The lawmage frowned and skimmed the crowd for the source of magic. Tatters immediately went down on one knee, half-hiding behind the barrel. The lawmage ignored him, staring straight at Isha, the apprentice who had nothing to do in the Pit, and surely wasn't welcome there. She felt his gaze like a physical thing, a heat, touching her cheek and remembering the detail of her tattoo. She wasn't difficult to identify in a crowd. Even as he turned away, she knew he wouldn't forget her.

The butcher finished his business. He got up, hands stained up to his elbows, leaving two gaping holes in the kher's skull. After wiping the horns, he tucked them under his arm. They could have been two hoops for children to play with.

Yua crossed the square as soon as the butcher moved away. She went to place a piece of linen across the dead man's forehead, to hide the wounds. Other khers closed in. The humans backed away, giving ground. Arushi followed the humans, the young kher bound between the guards.

'I'm going with her,' said Tatters, 'but I'll escort you to Arushi's house first. If you stay inside, you'll be safe.'

'I'll manage on my own,' said Isha.

Tatters hesitated.

'I know Yua. I have the tattoo.' *I need to see this through. I need to say sorry.* She didn't share her thoughts, but held Tatters' gaze. 'I mean it. I'll be fine.'

He nodded. 'Stay safe.'

He followed the human procession as they left the Pit, a lot faster than they had entered it.

Isha joined Yua beside the body. The khers moved across the square as if in a choreographed dance, each conscious of their role in the drama. While one kher was building a small fire, another brought metal pliers, probably to retrieve the crossbow bolt from the wounded man. Others brought herbs and water.

'Tidir. What a day to come, soulworm,' said Yua.

Isha knelt beside her.

'Tidir. I'm sorry,' she said, although she wasn't sure what she was apologising for – for intruding, for what the mages had done? 'Tatters brought beer. We were going to, err...' Invite ourselves? She could hardly say that. '…see if you wanted some.' Then, because Yua stayed quiet, 'He followed Arushi.'

Yua glanced at the barrel, then at Isha. 'What does he see in you, do you think?' she asked.

Isha's tongue died in her mouth. When she didn't answer, Yua looked away.

The two kher women had returned as soon as the wounded man was in safe hands. They were arguing as they wiped blood from the dead kher's face. Yua held the linen over his brow, pressing down with both hands.

'Such a shame,' one said, lightly touching the rip across his cheek. Where the skin had come off, the face was distorted in an unnatural smile, flesh pulled sideways and crumpled like paper. 'Such a shame,' she whispered again. A sob broke her voice. The other kher hugged her. She started crying like a child would, with abandon, with tears and wails and shaking shoulders.

Yua ignored them. She worked on. Once she'd tied the cloth around the man's forehead, she spat on a folded square of linen and dabbed at the damaged skin. It left a brown stain on the fabric. The body was on a stretcher of wood and cloth, although the butcher's work had left him askew. She tidied the sprawled limbs.

'Is there any way I can help?' Isha asked. She couldn't hold Yua's gaze. 'I don't want to be disrespectful. I want to help, but I wouldn't want to …' She didn't know what to say. The humans who had handled the corpse hadn't treated him well. 'I could understand if he didn't want humans to touch him anymore.'

Yua's expression softened. 'So maybe that's what Tatters sees in you.' She wiped her hands on her tunic. 'You needn't touch him. Help me bring him inside.'

They picked up the stretcher and carried it together. The two women followed, still crying, tears dripping off their chins. Yua didn't look at them, keeping her eyes fixed on her feet, until they reached one of the crumbling houses.

Once inside, they put the stretcher down and Yua, with Isha's help, rolled up the carpets to free space for the body. Other khers – family members, Isha assumed – mainly women and a few children, gathered around the corpse. Yua stepped aside as they crammed closer to the body. They kissed his forehead and stroked his cheeks, they took his frozen hand and brushed his fingers against their horns. Some of them, obviously older, brought jars of oil to clean the body, combs to brush his hair, clippers to trim his nails.

'Get me some charcoal from the fire,' said Yua.

Isha crossed the room. Yua kept her eyes lowered and spoke to no-one, so Isha copied her, biting down on her lips to stop words of sympathy from escaping her. She didn't want to attract attention. She knelt by the fireplace to retrieve a piece of charcoal.

'Let's leave them in peace.'

They left the family to their mourning. Isha was relieved that they wouldn't have to help clean the body. She had done it once before, at the farm. It hadn't been pleasant.

Outside, Yua scribbled a symbol with the charcoal on the front door and on the doorstep. Isha didn't ask any questions.

Yua let out a deep sigh, as if she had been holding her breath since the humans left.

'Seshaq. You mentioned beer?' she asked. 'I think I need some.'

***

Tatters paced himself, keeping in step with the procession. The guards escorted the humans out of the Pit, to the central square, where the statue of Lady Siobhan stood. In front of her there were three empty pillories; two others already held guests.

Both were men, and both had been there long enough to receive lashes on their backs. Their shabby clothes hung from their sides, torn by the touch of the whip. One hung his head low, lips parted, dribbling. The other was younger, but his knees kept buckling and he struggled to maintain his footing.

The lawmage and the human guards dragged the young kher out of Arushi's grip.

'We can handle it from here. You should escort the baina back to the Nest.'

Arushi acquiesced. Her face gave nothing away. From the dimming sunshine, Tatters guessed this would be her last task before the end of her shift. When the khers marched the butcher away, Tatters stayed behind. He would be more useful here. He couldn't mindlink to Arushi and he didn't want to be too easy to spot, so he wasn't sure she saw him as he settled amongst the beggars at the foot of the statue.

The kids moved aside. Tatters crossed his legs in front of him, holding them loosely in his arms. No-one asked him any questions. They were used to seeing him, if not to having him sit with them.

He already had an idea of what he could do to help the young kher, which Lal already disapproved of. It involved a couple of illegal things, such as fleshbinding and aiding a criminal, and of course it broke that big taboo, the line drawn between humans and khers.

This has nothing to do with you, said Lal. *You shouldn't stay.*

The lawmage recited some rights to the kher. 'And don't try any fleshbinding,' he spat. 'That's strictly forbidden. It would be punished as severely as an escape attempt.'

Heard that? asked Lal.

The young kher said nothing.

The lawmage sentenced the kher to three days at the pillory

and forty whip lashes. He droned out his verdict, apparently bored with the whole proceeding. Mages were required to be put on trial, but for minor offences khers and ungifted could be judged by lawmages. They could always appeal against an unlawful ruling, of course. If they were found innocent, then the lawmage was condemned to the sentence they had pronounced. If found guilty, the criminal could be punished for wasting the court's time. Most people didn't bother with appeal; all in all, it was better not to annoy the lawmages.

Yet you are planning to annoy them. Lal wouldn't let go.

Listen, the kid's grieving his dad.

So what? That happens all the time. If not today, tomorrow. If not this kid, then another.

Tatters ignored her.

The executioner, who also did the whippings, wasn't there. The lawmage told the kher he would get his forty lashes the next morning.

'If you want, you can get fifteen on the first two days, and then the last ten on the third.'

When the kher didn't answer, the lawmage shrugged.

'Waste of breath being nice to you.' Which meant, Tatters guessed, that he would receive all the lashes in one go. The lawmage left, but not before ordering one human guard to keep watch.

The guard grumbled and sighed as his colleagues dispersed. Tatters supposed he was also nearing the end of his day, and this extra piece of work was keeping him from his dinner.

For a while nothing much happened. A few children circled the new arrival, poking the kher's ribs or tugging at his horns. He didn't fight back, even when one kid kicked his ankles. Merchants closing up their shops gave unsold fruit and vegetables to the beggars, who ate most of it, but lobbed the rest at the pilloried criminals. Because a newcomer was always more fun to persecute, and it was less frowned upon to mistreat a kher, the young man got more than his fair share.

One child, older and bolder than the others, thought it would be fun to see how many rotten fruits he could plant on the kher's horn. The guard helped him. They managed to fit six fruit on the young man's left horn, by squashing them a bit. The juice ran down the side of his face. They gave him a crown of apple peelings before losing interest.

Tatters waited for the curiosity of the crowd to dull, for the merchants to close their shops. In order for his plan to work, he needed secrecy. The sky was dark grey when he jumped off the statue's base.

The guard noticed him before he reached the pillories. He wasn't stupid. He spotted the collar first.

'I've seen you around,' said the guard. He didn't look the bad type. He was square-jawed, with light brown hair, hazel eyes. Life had roughened him around the edges, but not broken him.

'I've been around,' said Tatters. He rested his back against the pillory, as if it were a comfortable piece of furniture.

The guard eyed Tatters, then the kher. 'You got business here?' he asked.

Tatters unknotted his pouch from his belt. He took his time. As he sorted through the money, he nudged the man's mind. There wasn't any resistance. Tatters pushed the balance between concern about the consequences of a bribe and greed – in his favour.

If you're doing this, at least be subtle, said Lal.

I am subtle, said Tatters. *I've barely brushed him. It's the softest mindlink he's ever had, I'm sure.*

He had some baina from his work at the tavern; the apprentices didn't always pay him with regular money. He counted out three coins into the palm of his hand, now with the guard's full attention. Even the kher was watching, his teeth clenched. He must be thinking about his father, who would soon be reduced from man to money.

But baina was his best bet. It was impossible for ungifted to earn, and it was illegal for them to handle it – which only increased its value. The black market paid good money for even a few coins, and individuals sometimes wanted baina to wear against their skin, as protection against mindlink.

When Tatters touched the baina, his capacity to do and receive mindlink shut down. Lal suddenly became silent. The guard's mind was sealed off from him, unreachable.

'Why don't you go grab yourself a beer somewhere nice?' asked Tatters. 'I'll keep an eye on this one.'

The guard hesitated. Tatters held up the baina, pressed together between finger and thumb. At the Nest, it would be worth a meal, maybe half a training session with a mediocre mage. But for an ungifted, it was precious.

As the uneasy pause lengthened, Tatters wondered if his mindlink had been *too* subtle.

'You seem like the right kind of sort,' said the guard.

'That's exactly what I thought when I saw you,' answered Tatters.

The guard nodded. He extended his hand, palm stretched out flat. Tatters put the coins on it, but he didn't let go of the money.

'Do me a favour,' Tatters said. 'My master is interested in this one. He'd be upset if he got damaged.'

A glimmer of understanding flashed through the guard's eyes. Some khers had well-shaped horns, too interesting to be sawed into baina. Instead, they were carved into shackles or other items useful for mages. It was easier to make certain items if the horn already naturally followed the curve the craftsman required.

Better the guard believe that the orders came from a powerful mage; a plot to get their hands on kher horn fitted. Mages were always plotting.

'Of course,' said the guard. 'I'll make sure I'm around for the next few shifts.'

Smiling, Tatters let go of the baina. Lal resurfaced.

'He won't need much. A bit of food, a bit of water.'

'They're animals, really, aren't they?' laughed the guard.

The kher tensed. As far as Tatters was concerned, that wasn't an insult. Animals were better company than most humans. He chuckled. 'Drink to my health,' he told the guard. 'Maybe, say, for an hour or so?' Tatters probably wouldn't need a full hour, but it would give the young kher some peace and quiet, if nothing else.

'May you grow tall.' The guard thanked him and left. His heavy trudge brought him to a tavern spilling light and laughter into the square, inside which he disappeared. Tatters didn't budge. He rested against the pillory and stared out into the night. He listened to the kher's raspy breathing.

That was stupid and rash.

But it was the right thing to do, Tatters said. Lal grumbled at the back of his thoughts. He surveyed the tavern, in case the guard changed his mind. After a while, Lal fell quiet.

When the guard didn't run out of the tavern with armed men and a lawmage, Tatters tended to the young kher. He plucked the fruit off his horns. He wiped his face with his sleeve. 'Do you want water?' he asked. The kher shook his head.

'He should keep an eye out for you the next few days,' said Tatters.

'I heard.' The young kher's voice was hoarse.

Tatters rested one arm beside the kher's hand, where it poked out of the pillory, caught between the wooden shackles. Now all that was left was to ask. He couldn't help someone who didn't want assistance.

But just by offering, you'll already be giving too much away, said Lal.

'I know it's rather intimate. I'm not family. But you're getting forty lashes tomorrow, so I'll ask.' He paused. Mezyan had warned him this could be a sensitive subject. The Renegades used it between themselves, but then, they were a clan. A unit, at least. Tatters licked his dry lips. 'Do you want me to fleshbind with you? No-one else will get close enough.'

The young man tried to lift his face to meet Tatters' gaze, but craned his neck against the pillory in vain. Tatters leant over to make it more comfortable for the kher.

'Humans can't fleshbind,' said the young man.

A common misconception. Tatters shrugged. 'I can do surprising stuff.'

'My family has shared blood with me,' said the young man. 'They'll come tomorrow.'

Tatters shook his head. 'You can be sure they won't let khers attend a kher beating. You know they don't.'

A long silence. Tatters straightened; his back hurt when he bent over. He stretched, waiting for the kher to answer.

'What's your name?' asked the young man.

'Tatters.'

'What kind of name is that?' The kher tried to shake his head, but winced as the pillory held his neck in place.

Tatters smiled. 'Why? Have you got a better name to offer?'

The kher managed a smile back. His face had a soft, bright, youthful smile. His eyes remained sad. 'Yeah,' he said. 'I'm Ka.'

'Not much of a name. I've got more letters.'

They laughed, although in Ka's case it produced a choked sound, like a sob.

'It would be interesting to see a human try fleshbinding,' said Ka. Tatters nodded.

If they catch you doing this . . . Lal warned.

They won't.

Tatters checked the square for passage. It was night now. The sky was black, with a few stars poking out between the clouds. The beggars had built fires between the cobbles and huddled around them. The shops were closed. In the buildings around him, windows shone with candlelight. The people in the other pillories were sleeping, or trying to. No-one was watching.

Still, he acted carefully. He didn't take out his knife, instead placing his thumb on the tip of one of Ka's horns, sharp, stained with fruit-juice. He pressed until he drew blood. Hopefully the red drop would be hidden by the other liquids on the horn.

'Would you mind biting the inside of your cheek?' he asked.

Ka nodded. Khers were used to fleshbinding and, because of that, to pain. Ka's left hand, like most khers, had a crisscross of scars across the palm. When fleshbinding with someone else for the first time, he cut a line across his skin, and they shook hands to share blood. Tatters avoided that technique, in part because it left such recognisable scars.

Ka bit the inside of his mouth. A bit of blood dribbled at the corner of his lips. As if he were cleaning Ka's face, Tatters wiped it away with his thumb. Their blood mingled. It only had to happen once. From now on, Tatters would always be able to fleshbind with Ka.

And Ka will always be able to fleshbind with you, said Lal.

That was true. Fleshbinding wasn't used to fight, because it involved sharing. It always went both ways.

Tatters dipped into Ka's sensations as if bringing up water from a well. His neck was stiff, and he was cold, especially across the back, as if he'd removed his cloak. He felt tension in his arms, something rough against his wrists. He rolled his shoulders, but couldn't remove the dull pain in his spine. A cold and wet line, like dried slime, slid across the side of his face.

Most importantly, he felt Ka's grief. The last living beings Tatters had fleshbound with were animals, so he hadn't been expecting more than physical discomfort. He had assumed grief was inside the mind, not the body. But it was as if someone had carved out a hole inside his chest. He could feel the edges of the wound as surely as though the butcher had sliced his flesh, not the old kher's horns. There was an aching gap, an emptiness within.

It was a pain he recognised. He had hoped never to feel it again.

'No,' whispered Ka. 'You can leave that.'

Tatters let go; it was like dropping a stone into very deep waters. He felt the ripples as the grief sank into Ka.

They were silent for a while. They stayed next to each other in the night and, although one was standing straight, they were both pilloried. When Tatters gave Ka some of his heat, they both shivered. Fleshbinding with khers always dulled Lal, sometimes muzzling her completely. For the first time in years, Tatters was close to someone other than his sister. They breathed air like icicles, which cut through their lungs. The half-moon rose.

Arushi crossed the square towards them, still wearing her guard's uniform. She must have come straight from the Nest. Her sword bumped across her thigh with each stride. Tatters placed his thumb against the palm of his hand and closed his fingers around it.

'Idir. I thought I would find you here,' said Arushi.

She extended her arm. Keeping his hand closed in a loose fist, Tatters touched wrists with her. She glanced across the square. He could see her mind at work: she noted the absence of guards, the rotten fruit on the ground, Tatters standing beside Ka. She nodded to herself and a small, tired smile tugged at her lips.

'Thanks,' she said. 'I'm glad someone was here.'

She turned to Ka. She placed a hand on his forehead, her fingers in the tousled hair between his horns. Although Tatters watched her closely, he couldn't decide whether she was fleshbinding or not. Unlike mindlink, fleshbinding couldn't be perceived by outsiders, only by the people involved.

With Arushi standing before him, Ka looked younger. They were both youthful, of course, but Ka's face was still unsettled, the changing features of childhood not quite fixed. A difference could be found in their gazes too, in depth and seriousness. Arushi's face wasn't old, but her expressions were.

'You are like the bull,' she said. Ka sucked in a deep breath, and the tattoo across his back arched, glowing faintly in the moonlight. Arushi lowered her voice to a whisper. 'I know it feels like it, but this won't break you.'

When she took away her hand, Ka was crying.

Chapter Nine

After the skirmish, the Pit was eerily quiet. Isha rolled the barrel; Yua walked beside her. When they reached the khers' house, Yua motioned for Isha to wait outside. She went to fetch a small chopping axe, which she held with both hands. Yua pushed up her sleeves, tucked her hair behind her horns, and lifted the axe. When the first hit landed, foam spurted around the blade. White frothy beer spilled on the porch and around Yua's feet as she broke the barrel open with a few deft strokes to the lid.

Yua and Isha placed wooden cups in a circle around the barrel, in the wet patch of spilt alcohol. Isha wasn't sure if it was the smell of beer, or the sound of chopped wood, or the commotion outside – but soon Ganez was there, and a few other men, and a group of curious children.

'What's this?' asked Ganez.

'A gift from Tatters,' said Yua.

Ganez nodded his thanks towards Isha. The men clustered around the barrel, dipping cups inside the drink, passing them around so everyone had their share. Yua filled an earthenware jug from the barrel and went inside the house. Ill at ease, aware her welcome only extended as far as the khers granted it, Isha followed Yua inside.

Yua knelt beside her mother. Uaza moved her head slowly,

and the heavy interlocking horns shifted, scratching against the wooden wall. Spotting Isha, she greeted her with 'Tidir.'

Yua poured her mother a glass of beer before turning to Isha. 'Do you want some?'

Soon the three women were chatting together in a circle, their glasses in front of them, using animal pelts for seats. They were in a corner, slightly removed from the thick woollen rug at the centre of the room, tucked to the side of the hot chimney as it warmed the house. A group of children were seated around the hearth, playing with knucklebones.

The beer was bitter and strong. After a few gulps, Isha's head was swimming.

'Beer is all very good,' grumbled Uaza, 'but next time, tell your collarbound to bring us some human cloth. There's a shop in the textile market which won't sell to the iwdan, and they have the softest rolls of fabric I've ever touched. Old Maria, the human hag is called.'

Yua smiled. One of her horns was decorated with coloured woven thread, knitted like a glove. Maybe, Isha mused, the ornament for her other horn had fallen off when she threw herself on the ground to avoid the crossbow fire.

'Old Maria is probably long dead,' Yua said. 'And you can't ask for a present, tasna.'

'I don't see why not,' answered Uaza, shifting her weight with a grunt. 'And if he's so desperate to please Ganez, he should get him a new clay pipe.'

'He likes the old one,' said Yua.

The old kher harrumphed. She brought her cup to her lips and drank slowly, wincing when she had to push her head backwards to swallow.

'His old pipe is no good,' she said at last, as if she had thought long and hard on the subject, and couldn't come to another conclusion. 'It's broken. When he pulls on it, half the smoke pours out through the crack.'

Yua asked if Isha wanted to help with the cooking, so soon the two of them were cutting up carrots and adding them to the broth. Yua sent the children on errands to fetch eggs, borrow herbs off the neighbours, bring out the dried paste. She corrected Isha on how to hold a knife, and instructed her on the order in which to put the vegetables into the soup.

Uaza got up. It was the first time Isha had seen her do it. Despite her lithe, young features, she moved as if her limbs were stiff with arthritis, tottering like the elderly do, as if they need to learn how to walk again. One hand against the chimney, she lowered herself beside Isha. The children scattered to give her some space.

Isha shifted uncomfortably, trying to keep her hair in front of her cheek – Uaza had placed herself on her tattooed side. The inky patterns burned against her skin like a rash, until she couldn't help but brush against the tattoo self-consciously. She knew each curve of it by heart; it was slightly swollen under her fingers, the skin different to the touch.

'Do you know what the world is made of, child?'

The old kher's voice broke the silence. Not for the first time, Isha was surprised by how full it was. The quiver at the end of the words could have been due to a light cold, a rough throat – it didn't sound like the voice of old age.

'No,' said Isha.

Of course, she knew the world was made of mind and matter. If elevated enough, mind became independent from matter and turned into a soul. She suspected Uaza wouldn't like that answer. The Temple believed the horns that sprouted out of the khers' heads was a failed attempt at producing a soul, which was why they interfered with mindmagic.

'The world is made of three things,' said Uaza, lifting three fingers. Yua tended to the fire, throwing bright sparks into the air.

'Sar, aman, asemmid. Earth, water and air.' With each element, Uaza lowered one finger, until her hand was closed into a fist.

Isha found it curious to think that earth, water and air were equivalent. According to the Temple, wind elevated the mind. Living creatures breathed and dead creatures didn't, because breathing was what enabled the mind to flutter in and out of the body. Even lesser beings – animals, khers – breathed, in the hope of enticing a soul to enter their flesh. Air was a thing of the mind; water and earth were simply matter.

'And the world is destroyed by one thing,' Uaza added. She pointed to the smoky fire. Above it, the cauldron simmered. Chunks of orange and white vegetables floated to the surface.

'Fire,' said Isha, like an apprentice during a lecture, because it was what was expected of her.

'Timessi,' repeated Uaza. 'It eats the world. But three guardians keep it in check – with earth you can stifle a fire, with water you can drown it, with air you can blow it out.'

There was a brief silence while they watched Yua add the last ingredients to the pot. Isha noticed a small kher, with stubs of black horn pushing out of his forehead, listening to their conversation. His dark, unkempt hair fell across his face. In his eyes, she could see the reflection of the flames – red fire, black pupils; black hair, red skin. Isha looked at her own forearm, deep brown in the glow of the chimney, so unlike Kilian and Tatters' pale skin.

Uaza went on to tell the tale of how fire was first tamed by the three true gods, how they kept fire under control to feed and warm their people. About how the khers, to honour their three guardians, tattooed themselves according to their chosen god.

The child listened intently. Yua didn't interrupt, but paced quietly, preparing the room for dinner. She swept the carpet, cleaning off the crumbs from the previous meal, the soft rasp of the broom against the fabric whispering stories of its own.

'So Yua and you are both linked to water?' asked Isha.

The old kher smiled.

'Longlived are like a man – they flow, seemingly forever,' said Yua, leaning on her broomstick and pausing in her work. 'So yes, we are children of water. There aren't many of us.'

'Most iwdan are children of earth, the great giver of life, the first true god and the first to forge a world for us to roam over,' added Uaza.

Isha didn't need to believe in the tale for it to be an engaging one. Kher faith wasn't as severe as the Temple's. For human believers, their only choices were to elevate themselves to a pure soul – or fail. As a kher, whatever happened, you belonged. The world loved you. It was an enticing notion.

Uaza was still staring at Isha's tattoo, and she pushed closer now, too close for Isha to be at ease. The old woman sucked her teeth, entirely focused on the tattoo, not caring that it was drawn on skin. Unexpectedly, she reached out. Isha tensed. As Uaza was leaning forward, her tunic drooped somewhat around her neck, revealing black lines underneath the fabric, too sombre in the dim light to make out the patterns. She pressed her thumb against Isha's jawline, following the lines of the tattoo.

Isha glanced sideways at Yua, who had paused in her cleaning to watch. She stood barefoot on the carpet, the bright wool dulled by dust and time, the dye blushing in the firelight. Beside her, the child sat still, straining his ears and eyes to catch every word coming from Uaza.

'Tawa asemmid. You are a child of air,' said Uaza. A wave of heat rose inside Isha, her heart beating harder. The old kher's eyes were like obsidian stones.

'No wonder,' she continued. 'Mages believe they are birds; they would think of themselves as children of asemmid. They knew when you were born that you would fly.' Isha swallowed. She wanted to say that it was impossible, that no-one knew, at birth, whether a child would bear the gift. But she was sucked into that gaze, as dark as the Shadowpass.

Uaza followed the outlines of the tattoo with her thumb and spoke slowly, as if she were reading.

'You will be a ruler, a leader of the flock. Your fate is to do great deeds, as your blood requires.'

Isha had seen her tattoo often enough to know it had a jagged outline, scratched back and forth in spiked triangles. But as Uaza retraced it, she understood for the first time what it was. An outstretched wing, the tips of the feathers cutting sharply across her face.

'You will change how the mages fly.'

The old kher's thumb trailed down the tattoo until it reached the end of Isha's jawbone. She pressed her finger there as if checking Isha's pulse. Disappearing down her neck and into her hair, there was the strangest part of the tattoo – something which she had long believed to be a withered tree, with four visible roots running from its trunk.

Uaza watched it intently. Before she spoke, Isha knew what she had seen.

'And you will be a killer.'

The talons of a bird of prey.

When Uaza took away her hand, the atmosphere changed. The world had paused, the flames had stopped flickering; everything breathed again. Yua shook her head.

'You'll spook the soulworm,' she chuckled. The child laughed with her. The broom brushed against the carpet again.

Isha crept away from the fire. She felt hot. Her tattoo was a bird of prey plunging towards the thing it was about to kill. The smell of spices rising from the cauldron made her feel faintly sick. She stared at the bubbles breaking its surface and tried to calm herself.

It's such a violent fate, she thought. *Blood and claws.*

Her head was spinning with images, the illegal mages coming to her farm, burning through her memories, stealing her life from her; the woman in her dreams, dressed in leather; the weapons lying around the military encampment. What would have happened if they had taken her, if Passerine hadn't been there to stop them?

The beads of the front curtain chimed.

'We're back,' said Tatters as he entered. He gallantly held the curtain so Arushi could cross the threshold, then flashed Isha a smile. 'Did we miss anything?'

***

The meal followed the same pattern as the previous one. Although Tatters knew this was how a kher household lived, he found it difficult to adapt. Arushi, who was fierce and determined, who had a sharp tongue about her and twice her brother's wit, didn't speak a word as they ate. Ganez was decent enough, but his main conversation subject was what the khers suffered from the humans. It was justified, of course, but it wouldn't have been Tatters' first choice of topic.

He tried to steer the discussion to recent events of interest. Unfortunately, that turned out to be just as unpleasant.

'The town crier said there's refugees up East,' said one of the kher men. Three of them had joined the evening meal. Tatters had gathered they were Yua's lovers. They changed often; that made sense, as a longlived would be a prized companion, and she must have more than enough khers head over heels for her. As far as he could make out, none of the beaux in the household were Arushi's. At least, never when he was around.

Sometimes kher women also left their household to spend the evening with Ganez, although that was less common. Traditionally, men travelled between hearths, not women. Maybe being a longlived's brother entitled Ganez to some special treatment.

'Refugees are coming out of the Shadowpass, their brains rotted through, gibbering nonsense,' one kher was saying. 'Lots of them.'

Ganez nodded vigorously, his mouth full of soup. 'There's a few iwdan from the Meddyns, and traders from there too, who say they've got refugees trickling into their cities, but only the ones sane enough to make it down the Ridge.'

The war between the convents had intensified, everyone agreed, which was why Sunrisers were pooling through the Shadowpass. No-one seemed to know that these weren't the usual squabbles for power – that this was most probably one woman's work, one woman's dream. It boiled down to the Renegades. To Hawk.

As another flagon of beer was opened and shared, the gossip circled back to Ka. It was unavoidable, Tatters supposed.

'A very decent boy, that one,' said Ganez.

'Only one of us with a decent job, too,' added another guy.

'What does Ka do?' asked Tatters. It was a strain to sit across the carpet from Arushi, to watch her eat without lifting her head, when she was the one who had prevented the whole incident from spiralling out of control. He checked on Isha, who was copying the kher women, although she could probably speak up if she wanted to – the khers would allow some leeway for a guest, surely?

She is a mage before she is a guest, said Lal. *She's right to lie low.*

'Ka helps a falconer from a rich farm outside the city,' Ganez explained. 'He gets to do as much as some of the humans. But if he misses several days in a row, he might not have the job when he goes back.'

Another kher shook his head. 'Forget the job, he'll be missing the grieving rites.' If Tatters remembered correctly, the funeral would be prepared by the bereaved family, who would isolate with the body for a couple of days until everything was ready.

They discussed the whipping the next day, the unfairness of baina. The khers received a token payment for their deceased's horns, but not enough for the grieving family to make a living, certainly not enough for the indignity of serving as mages' coin.

'Do you have some on you right now?' Ganez asked Isha.

It was a gruff, sudden question. Maybe he didn't expect her to have brought any. A hush descended on the room like a curtain being drawn, blocking the light. From Isha's dismayed reaction, there was no doubt she had baina about her. Tatters' mouth went dry.

One child gasped, and Yua glared at her, although she seemed as shocked as her daughter. Arushi shifted on the carpet. No-one broke the silence. Blushing, Isha muttered something, but she spoke so low no-one could hear her.

Don't, said Lal, sensing Tatters' thoughts before his decision was even made. *If you show them you have baina, here, today, after what happened, even a lightborn's blessing won't protect you.*

But Tatters didn't have a choice. *What else can I do? Let Isha deal with this? I brought her here. I owe her that much.* And he owed the khers that much, too. He owed them the truth.

'We do,' he said.

His voice was quiet, but not as quiet as Isha, and it seemed to echo, bouncing off the shaken expressions, the grim faces. He reached out for his purse and opened it, spilling the metal coins on the carpet, pulling out the baina to set aside. Ganez watched without a word. He picked one of the round coins and lifted it before his eyes. It was dark, smooth; it could have been sawn off his own dark, smooth horns.

He handed it to Uaza, who rubbed the coin with her thumb before kissing it. Ganez observed her, his jaw tense, his fists pressed against his thighs.

'Before, our horns showed where we had lived, where we had suffered, where we had been loved,' he said. His words were powerful, angry, contained.

Khers buried their dead. It was something humans never did and that, even now, Tatters found vaguely sinister. They had discussed it at length with Mezyan. The khers buried the bodies, carving a wooden simile of the horns that they planted in the ground to mark the grave. Tatters couldn't get used to the idea of leaving a body to rot, to the mercy of worms and beetles and maggots. But Mezyan was just as troubled by the way humans threw their loved ones over the Edge, so that they could take flight.

'It's as if you're chucking them away so you don't have to deal with them anymore,' Mezyan had said. 'At least underground they are hugged by earth, where they came from, which loves them. At least there is a trace left.'

Still, Tatters would rather fly than be trapped underground.

He snapped out of his reminiscence at the short, stark sound of Yua cuffing one of her children. The boy took back his hand, wincing. 'Don't touch it,' she said severely.

'A young life shouldn't deal in death,' Ganez agreed. He took the coins back from Uaza and pressed them between his palms, head bowed. His lips moved without shaping full syllables. After a while, Tatters realised he was praying.

Isha looked as if she were about to throw up. Tatters tried to give her an encouraging smile, but a heaviness had sunk inside his chest, the memory of Ka holding his father, the hole of grief like a seeping wound, and he couldn't bring himself to.

Once Ganez had finished his prayer, he held the baina in his fist, close to his heart.

'What would you do, collarbound, if I showed you my collection of human vertebrae, and I told you I played knucklebones with them?' he asked.

Tatters wondered if Ganez would attack him. He would never hit Isha – not a mage, not a girl. But a collarbound who had brought the remnants of the dead into a family home, thinking he might wave it away with beer and a shrug? Given the chance, Ganez might beat him blue.

'I would wipe the bones clean,' said Tatters, 'and I wouldn't let children touch them.' He glanced at Arushi. She had paled, her face a sickly pink. She must have had enough fights for one day. 'And I would probably punch you,' Tatters concluded.

He held Ganez's gaze. He braced himself for violence.

It didn't come. Ganez snorted. 'I won't take away a slave's money.' He placed the baina on the carpet, beside Tatters' purse. 'Treat them with respect, at least.'

Tatters bowed his head. The rest of the meal was terse, subdued. When the men left the room to smoke, with the usual ritual words – *we return the hearth to you and thank you for your gift* – Tatters decided it was wiser to stay with the kher women and help clean up.

Isha and Yua gathered the bowls, while Arushi scraped the cauldron clean and filled it with water. He helped Uaza to her seat in the corner, before returning beside the fire, where the water was warming. When it was hot enough, he started washing the dishes in the cauldron, rubbing them with rags to get the food off while Arushi rinsed them. From time to time his skin brushed against hers, and Lal disappeared, flickering back and forth in his mind, like a candle when someone quickly passes their finger through the flame.

'Come help me feed the hens,' Yua told Isha. They left Arushi and Tatters by themselves, with only Uaza snoozing in the corner, swathed in layers of woolly covers.

As he worked, Tatters cast his eyes around the small home. The narrow wooden walls were rendered cheerful by colourful cloths pinned to the beams, as well as the carpet in the centre of the room. The fire cast a warm light across the red and orange threads. Hanging from rusty nails beside the chimney, bunches of dried herbs and wreaths of garlic let out their aromas, set beside wicker baskets and pans. Above him, Tatters could see a trapdoor leading to the attic, which must be divided up into bedrooms for the adults – the children would sleep together downstairs.

In the pot, the water was tepid. Soon a shine of grease covered the surface.

'I'm sorry I didn't choose a better day to visit,' Tatters said. He spoke softly, so as to not disturb Uaza – or be heard by her.

Arushi was leaning over the cauldron, her starched shirt rolled up to her elbows. Because of the heat, and the water that had splashed her arms, her bark-like tattoo was visible through the white linen, running from her wrists to her shoulders.

'There is never a good day between iwdan and humans,' she said.

Her long hair was tied back with a leather band. She was still wearing the thick guardsmen's trousers, but she had taken off her belt and hooked it up on the wall, with her sword still in its sheath.

Is that what you like about her? The soldiering? Didn't you get enough of that with Hawk?

He tried to ignore Lal.

'It must be difficult for you,' he said.

They were both bending over the pot, their hands in the dirty water. Sighing, she used her wet wrist to push a stray curl out of her eyes. It stuck to her forehead. She placed the clean bowl upside-down before the fire to dry.

'The others don't understand,' she said.

She didn't say it, but Tatters heard: *Ganez doesn't understand.* He wasn't the one working with mages to feed his family. There would be arguments, Tatters guessed, if Arushi were allowed to argue.

'Can I ask an ignorant human question?'

Arushi smiled. 'Please do.'

The curl fell in front of her face again. She frowned, shook the foamy soap off her right hand, then placed the lock behind her ear. Only the cutlery was still dirty; she took a handful of spoons to scrub clean.

'I thought hearths belonged to women in iwdan culture,' said Tatters. 'How come you don't speak when the men are present?'

Arushi sighed. 'It's a long story.'

But when she spoke, she made it brief. Before, when khers were nomads, the tribes were organised differently. When they were travelling, women kept silent and men made decisions, and the families hunted according to the male bloodlines. But when they set up camp, men became quiet, women decided on how to feed and who to tend for, and the families gathered around the firepits according to the female bloodlines.

'But now we don't travel,' she said, 'and men hardly work. So, we have to give them some of our space for it to become theirs, or there would be an imbalance.'

The imbalance seemed on the female side, as far as Tatters could tell, since they worked all day before being forced to become mutes in their own homes come evening – but he kept his opinion to himself. As Arushi spoke, a loose coil of hair dropped across her eyes once more.

'Oh, come on!' she grumbled. The wet hair slapped against her cheek when she shook her head to get it out of the way.

'May I?' he asked.

Tatters couldn't help but feel amused at her annoyance. Arushi relaxed enough to smile back. He leant forward and picked the strand of hair, deftly twisting it and tucking it behind her ear.

Just as he was doing so, Yua and Isha walked back inside. Retrieving his rag, he continued wiping the spoons.

'Not finished yet?' asked Yua. 'What are you doing, sweet-talking the dirt off?'

Yes, Lal insisted. *What are you doing?*

Tatters only laughed and finished the work at hand.

***

When Tatters announced he would escort Isha back home, Arushi offered her company. All three of them walked side-by-side out of the Pit. The city was quieter at night. Laughter and scraps of drunken song from the taverns echoed from far away, and sound moved sluggishly, as if rather drunk itself. The never-ending, never-dulled crash of the river over the Edge muted everything else.

In their group, only the soft splash of their feet could be heard. Tatters wanted to broach a few subjects with Isha, but he didn't want to do so in front of Arushi.

There is one thing you have to say, at least, said Lal.

'Isha.' In the semi-darkness, the tattoo made it seem as if

shadows were eating away at her face. 'Sorry for having dropped you into it, today. I didn't mean to drag you into the middle of iwdan and mages' fighting.' He felt he owed her some protection, at least. He could have done with a friend, too, when he'd been running away from Hawk.

Isha shook her head. In the night, only her teeth showed when she smiled. 'It's all right.'

'No, it isn't,' Arushi interrupted.

Arushi strode faster than them both, so she kept having to stop to let them catch up. Tatters sensed her anger in the same way he might sense the sharpness of a sword by the glint of its blade.

'The situation between the iwdan and the mages isn't all right,' Arushi went on.

Placed as he was between the kher and the apprentice, Tatters felt it was his role to help the conversation run smoothly.

You put yourself in that impossible position, don't forget it, said Lal.

And where else would I be, anyway?

He turned to Arushi. Her boots clicked on the flagstones. Each step was the same, heel first, a military walk the guards must have taught her.

'Don't go too hard on Isha,' he said. 'Everyone has it tough. Iwdan work hard hours for little pay. Ungifted work hard hours for little pay. Mages finish as lacunants. Everyone has a spouse or child to tend for, someone they grieve, someone they hate. Everyone suffers.'

Isha listened, but didn't intervene.

Arushi snorted. 'That's naïve.'

'It's not. It's life. We live in the same world, after all. We all have problems.'

But Arushi has a point, said Lal. *Some problems are worse. Some people suffer more.*

They stepped around a muddy puddle that took up half of the street. Isha bunched up her robes and held them well above her ankles to avoid dirtying them. When they were on the other side, Arushi asked:

'So, you're happy with things as they are?'

'That's not what I said. If we were all nicer to each other, that would help. If every master treated their servant right, if every mage treated ungifted decently, if every human lent a helping hand to iwdan, we would be better off.' Tatters was enjoying this conversation. It reminded him of the atmosphere amongst the Renegades, before, when they weren't yet an army, when Hawk was a visionary rather than a leader. He let himself be carried away. 'I don't think the mages are right. They think you need to ascend to become better, and that you ascend through mindlink. But you become a better person by being a better person.'

Isha chipped in. She sounded young, without the rough edges of the Renegades, without their broken teeth, their scarred faces, their hard words.

'You mean you don't believe in using mindlink to free yourself from flesh to become a pure spirit?' she asked.

Tatters remembered when he had asked the same question, or close enough, and heard Hawk's loud baritone laugh. She'd slapped his back and told him he had a lot to learn, but at least he was starting to ask the right questions.

'I guess I believe in balance,' he said. 'Mages think you should study and elevate your mind and ascend. Without letting your body hold you back. But what's wrong with a good shag? Some people like it. You should enjoy both the good shag and the good read.'

Those were Hawk's words. The good shag and the good read.

She'd spoken loudly and punched his arm and squeezed him roughly across the shoulders when she talked.

You were completely smitten by her. If not her, then what she represented, said Lal.

We all were. A taste of bile rose in his mouth. Those had been happy memories, soured now by everything that had come after.

Tatters shook himself back to the present.

'We should go for the best of both worlds, flesh and mind,' he concluded.

Isha and Arushi burst out laughing.

Tatters was taken aback. Isha had a high-pitched, merry giggle, which came from her mouth; Arushi's was deeper, curiously similar to grunts, coming from her nose. They glanced at each other, and the fact that one was laughing made the other laugh harder. They had to stop in the middle of the street to wipe their eyes.

'You can't seriously believe that,' said Isha. 'What do you mean, we can never ascend? So, all that's left to us is to grovel before the lightborns and give up trying?'

Before he could answer, Arushi added, 'I never thought you were the romantic type. Everyone acts nicely and the world gets better? Really?'

People never laughed at Hawk, thought Tatters.

Lal shrugged. *Charisma. It does a lot for you.*

He didn't try to reason with them. They teased him for the rest of the trip, and he answered good-humouredly, avoiding the political implications of what he'd said. When they reached the city gates, a lightborn flew overhead, shimmering blue and green. They gazed after its arc until it disappeared over the Edge.

They left Isha at the gates. Outside the city, at this hour, only apprentices or mages would be on the moors. Neither were a threat to her. She could walk the wasteland up to the castle by herself.

'Before you go,' said Tatters, 'I want you to note that I've achieved something no-one else has ever done.' He pointed to Isha, then to Arushi, wiggling his finger to underline his point. He let it draw out as long as he could before saying, 'I got a mage and an iwdan to agree.'

Arushi rolled her eyes. 'We agreed that what you were saying was stupid.'

'Still, it's an achievement,' he insisted.

They touched wrists with Isha and bade her goodnight. Tatters watched as she headed out. No torches lit the path; she would only have the stars to make out the grey, uneven ground. But then other apprentices were passing through the gates, and some of them held their own torches, or lamps hanging from their belts – she might be able to follow them.

They started the long walk back to the Pit. The silence, induced by an evening of eating and drinking, was comfortable; it was the kind of silence that descends when the body tires, but the tang of alcohol in the mouth remains. Tatters breathed in the cold but thought of the warmth of the khers' hearth. Now that Isha wasn't there, he matched his pace to Arushi's. As they neared the Pit, however, she slowed down, or dallied to kick pebbles into the gutter.

'I needed to talk to you about something,' she said.

They stepped into a pool of light cast by an open tavern window. For a second, the roar of people clinking glasses and the smell of stew enveloped them. Then the moment passed and they were back in the still, scentless darkness.

'A high mage asked me whether I had seen a collarbound,' she said.

Tatters made a non-committal sound, popping his lips

together. When Arushi didn't continue, he asked: 'What did you say?'

'That I had seen a collarbound. That I had done my duty, and checked he belonged to a mage. That I had let him into the Nest.' Arushi was studying his reaction. He tried to smile, but his brow was stuck into a frown.

It must be him, he thought.

That dream was a stroke of bad luck, said Lal. *Now that Passerine knows you're around, he'll try to find you.*

'He asked me who the collarbound's master was,' said Arushi.

Screw the underworlds. He was sure his face betrayed something, because she went on:

'I told him that kind of information was confidential.'

'Did you tell him the collarbound had great kher manners at dinnertime?' asked Tatters, trying to turn it into a joke.

Arushi didn't smile. 'It was none of his business.'

His relief was palpable, as if it were a physical thing curled inside his chest. He stopped in his tracks. Arushi stopped too, cocking her horns to one side, as he turned to her and took her hand. As always when he was in contact with khers, Lal disappeared. It was disconcerting, like discovering that a house he had long shared was now deserted, and all the space was his to fill.

He squeezed Arushi's hand, brought it to his lips, and kissed his thumb – not her skin.

'Thank you,' he said. 'You didn't need to do that, or warn me about it. It's much appreciated.'

He expected her to snatch her hand away. Judging by her expression, he half-expected her to slap him. But she did neither. They stood still for a while. Shapes and shadows, firelight and lamps, flickered in the gloom. His collar shone dully, as did the polish across her horns.

Tatters became conscious of her warm skin inside his icy fingers, of the cold wind hissing around them, as if autumn were cupping them both between its palms, keeping them pressed together.

Arushi took away her hand. 'You put me in an awkward situation,' she said, gently.

Tatters supposed she meant with regards to Passerine, but her tone made him unsure.

'I'm sorry,' he said. 'I ... Let's say not everyone in the Nest is on my side.'

Arushi waved to dismiss his words. Her sleeve slipped, showing the leaves tattooed across her arms. 'We all have enemies.'

'And we all have friends,' said Tatters.

She smiled. He smiled back. His slight drunkenness made him stupidly, euphorically happy. He threw his head backwards. He felt like hugging the sky.

'We do,' she agreed.

'Maybe what I was saying earlier wasn't that stupid, then?'

Arushi shook her head. 'Don't get excited. It was nonsense.' But there was a different spark in her eyes.

Tatters kept his face angled towards the sky as he breathed in the wet air of the city. He hoped for another lightborn to bless them.

But it was only once he'd waved Arushi goodnight and was on his way home that a rush of red flashed high above, briefly lighting up the sky. It was like a low-flying comet, but one made of ripples, liquid in its grace, not a ball of fire and stone.

I feel it too, said Lal. Her tone was unusually soft.

What?

The nostalgia.

They watched the lightborn as it disappeared over the Edge, taking its light with it.

Chapter Ten

Every morning, Isha worked as a scribe, copying handbooks, tallies, reports. She sharpened reed pens, she corrected other people's notes. The Nest was an administration before anything else, centralising and harmonising the rule of mages from the Northern to the Southern Edge, from the Meddyns to the Ridge. Amongst the new apprentices, some were either too old or too set in their ways to learn writing, late bloomers to whom the gift had come in adulthood, and who were sent to do other tasks instead. Isha wondered if that was how the Nest chose its butchers to saw kher horn into baina, by selecting members who were better at manual labour.

In the afternoons, once the sun had turned and it was too dark to work without straining her eyes, she trained with Sir Daegan. She learnt to send messages, to settle her mind, to strengthen it against intrusions. Sir Daegan talked about some of the theories around mindlink. He encouraged the apprentices to practise on their own and in pairs. Then at the end of the session he left, often taking the disciples with him. Not since he had brought her to collect his due had Sir Daegan required Isha to accompany them.

But today, when the session ended, he beckoned her over. 'I have a task for you,' he said.

Caitlin and the other disciples waited in a circle around him.

'Just you,' Sir Daegan said. Then, to the disciples, 'You are dismissed.'

The looks Isha received made it abundantly clear what everyone thought. Kilian grimaced and shook his head behind Sir Daegan's back, mouthing 'you are in trouble'. Caitlin's mind scraped hers, suddenly – a quick hit that was soon over. The shock of it settled in Isha's stomach. It was the equivalent of a kick under the table that no-one saw but still stung. Isha glared at her. Caitlin was busy talking to someone else as if nothing had happened, but the smile at the corner of her lips was proof enough.

Isha mindlinked towards her, striving hard to keep the message private. *What's your problem?*

She failed. Caitlin turned to her, raising an eyebrow in mock surprise. Kilian goggled.

'Now, now,' said Sir Daegan. He put a hand on Isha's shoulder. His skin was wrinkled and cold, and he held her too close to the neck, fingers clutching her collarbone. 'We should be on our way.'

He steered her away from the disciples and out of the door. He kept his hand uncomfortably placed against her neck as they crossed the Nest, which meant she had to stay one step in front of him, where she couldn't catch his eye.

He led her to his personal chambers, in the wing of the Nest that accommodated high mages, only letting her go when they'd reached their destination. He plucked the ring of keys off his belt to unlock the door. He invited Isha inside, locking up again behind her.

'We wouldn't want to be interrupted.' He smiled with lips the colour of dead worms.

Isha's mouth was dry. She had never been inside Sir Daegan's private quarters. The front room was decorated lavishly, with tapestries, a carpet to fend off the cold, gilded artwork hanging on every wall. A couple of low armchairs circled a table where branches of evergreen and holly berries had been strewn. A bookshelf rested against one wall, a liquor cabinet against the other. This was a room designed to receive guests. Lamps were placed on every available surface, kept burning by the maids. They let out a faint glow and the scent of perfumed oil.

'To the right,' said Sir Daegan.

Two doors led off from Sir Daegan's living-room – one to the front and one to the right, behind the liquor cabinet, which had a crest carved above it. Gingerly, Isha made her way across. She glanced at the colourful glass inside the cabinet, the small hand-carved barrels of hydromel, the thin bottles of wine. She could sense Sir Daegan behind her, hear his felted steps on the carpet. She pushed the door open.

This second room was barren. It was also much colder, and the ceiling was much higher, although the space was relatively narrow. It took time for Isha's eyes to adjust enough to see the contraption lurking at one end. She could make out its shape, tall and threatening in the weak light, but not what it was.

The floor and the walls were stone. Isha supposed it was a chunk of giant's corridor that hadn't been renovated – surplus building, unused. When Isha looked upwards there was light filtering through the half-crumbled roof. That explained the draft.

Her whole face must have been a question.

'We will come to that later,' Sir Daegan said. 'This is what I want you to do.'

He confidently headed for the corner of the room furthest away from the hulking shape. She followed. Fear was crawling up her spine; a small, beetle-like thing that was the realisation that she was alone, that Sir Daegan was stronger than her, that this could be a dungeon. That no-one would hear her scream – not through walls as thick as giants' fists.

Sir Daegan stopped in front of a crate at the back of the room. The crate was open, full of what looked like pieces of wood. Isha leant in closer. It contained long bars, carved at each end so it would be possible to fit them together.

'Don't be shy,' said Sir Daegan. In the dark, his skin had a pale glow, like a ghost. It was as if he were a pair of floating hands and head. 'It's not like you. Pick one up.'

Isha obeyed. The bar was heavier than she expected, and it wasn't wood – its surface was smooth and dark and ivory-like. It was kher horn.

She nearly dropped it, only catching herself when she remembered Ganez, his sombre entreaty: *Treat them with respect, at least.* She put it down carefully, trying to stop her hands from trembling.

For a moment, Isha wondered if Sir Daegan murdered khers for leisure, and this was his pile of bones, wrought into trophies. A sickness filled her stomach, clotted her mouth.

'Ingenious devices, aren't they?' said Sir Daegan.

He sent her an image through mindlink. It showed her the way the pieces could be assembled, how the nooks at the end fitted together to build a larger structure out of the bars. He showed her, also, the final shape it should have.

It was a cage.

The wind from the roof rasped and wheezed like a dying man.

'Why would you need a cage?' she asked.

'You're a smart girl. Think about it.' Sir Daegan gestured towards the crate. 'You can work while you're considering it.'

It was a disturbing task. Daegan stood beside her, never lowering himself to touch the bars, but sending her precise technical images of what she should be doing, and how. Following his mental instructions, she started building the cage. There was a mallet beside the crate, and she assembled the pieces before hammering them together so they would be difficult to unpick.

No sound but the scratch of bone against bone. She could hear the thump of her heart, smell her own sweat. Sir Daegan watched over her, breathing slowly, his hands knotted behind his back, his long robes sometimes shivering in the breeze, their shade of black shifting against the paler black of the stone. She tried to think of nothing. He would be studying her mind as closely as he was her handicraft.

When she had finished about a third of the structure, Sir Daegan interrupted her.

'It is probably better if you place it where it should be. Otherwise it will be difficult to move.'

'Why me?' She felt relieved to hear her voice, even as it echoed in the silent, abandoned corridor.

'Why do you think?' Sir Daegan waved towards the device at the back of the room. 'This way.'

Isha carried the partially-constructed cage. She had the four walls and the ceiling, but they weren't linked together yet. When she dragged them across the floor, the polished horns caught in the cracks between the stones. She was scraping the surface of the bars, but Sir Daegan didn't seem to mind. He didn't offer to help her carry them.

'It's because of my kher tattoo,' she said. It seemed obvious, now she thought about it. 'You don't want to touch this much kher horn.'

Sir Daegan didn't smile, but she sensed his amusement. 'It is commonly believed exposure to khers and kher horn can diminish mindlink powers.' He glanced at her with his colourless eyes.

'You must be immune, considering you can mindlink even with a kher tattoo.'

She bit her lips and didn't answer. She carried the bars across the room. The contraption she'd spotted wasn't that ominous seen up close – it was only a chimney. A human-made chimney, stuck against the giant-made wall. It stood out starkly, carved out of smaller stones. Each brick from the chimney was about a fifth of the size of the ones making up the wall. When she lowered the bars beside it, the hearth shone. She crouched closer. The inside of the chimney was bright as silver, even in the dim light.

'Silver melts and darkens,' said Sir Daegan. 'Try again.'

Isha cursed her mind for being too easy to spy into. She tried to close it down. She extended her hand to touch the back of the chimney. Something moved inside the hearth, like a ghost reaching out – but she realised it was only her reflection.

'A mirror,' she breathed. Its surface was perfectly even.

'Mirrors,' corrected Sir Daegan. 'Running all the way up.' Isha peered further into the hearth, but the rare autumn light didn't illuminate the funnel.

'I trust you know what mirrors and kher horn have in common?' asked Sir Daegan.

She forced herself to think fast.

'Lightborns can't fly through them,' she said.

Stories told of men sealing lightborns into bottles and forcing them to grant their wishes. It usually ended badly for the person doing the wishing. But these folktales all involved mirrors. It was common knowledge that lightborns were attracted to mirrors, and sometimes tried to fly into them, only to find themselves bouncing off in the opposite direction. And khers blocked all minds – especially pure souls like the lightborns.

'It's a lightborn trap,' she breathed. She was shocked, if only because she hadn't anticipated that Sir Daegan was superstitious. Who could buy into these old legends of caught lightborns and unthinkable magic? He was too down-to-earth to believe a lightborn would bless him or grant him new powers.

'There is a lot we don't know about lightborns,' said Sir Daegan. He was using his teaching voice; it boomed in the narrow space. 'But we know enough. They are pure souls, but they can take on human shape, if it takes their fancy. They can mindlink, but it is impossible to step inside their minds, for if you enter a lightborn's mind and they alight, you will be ripped from your body and die a gruesome death. They can fly. They are fast. They are arrogant. And they are beautiful.'

When she turned towards him, Sir Daegan was smiling, showing white-grey teeth and white-grey skin. He noticed her staring.

'Now get on with it,' he said sharply.

Sir Daegan wanted the cage to cover the front of the chimney. If a lightborn did fly down, attracted by the mirrors, it wouldn't be able to leave with kher horn all around. If a lightborn had been drawn to the chimney before the cage was in place, it would have slipped harmlessly through the walls – the giants built thick structures, but not thick enough to prevent a lightborn from crossing them. They could fly through gates, through houses, through people.

'Couldn't it fly back up the chimney?' Isha asked.

'Not with the way the mirrors are angled.' Sir Daegan was proud of his creation, she could tell. 'A lightborn trying to fly up this would be reflected back down.' Despite his distaste at the idea of touching kher horn, he helped her lift the makeshift ceiling of the cage, so she could finish building it.

'The funnel behind is not a chimney,' he explained. 'It's a lightlure.'

Hinges and a lock for a door had to be assembled at the front of the cage. It was excellent craftsmanship, but confusing. Isha put it together wrongly the first time, then spent time-consuming minutes undoing and rebuilding it. Once the structure was complete, placed against the wall, she still had to nail it through the cracks in the stones, with metal nails as long as her hand, which riveted the whole piece to the ground. By the end, her palms were dark with powdery metal.

They took a step back to admire the result. The cage was a sinister thing. It made Isha think of a kher buried under the stone, their horns still growing after their death, curving in on themselves to shape this prison. The bars were dark; the hearth the colour of moonlight.

She didn't want to be a part of this, of making cages, of desecrating dead khers, carrying baina, treating people like currency. She didn't want to be a part of the Nest. *Yet here I am. This is what I have done.*

If Sir Daegan heard her thoughts, he didn't answer them. On the contrary, he sighed with satisfaction. He patted Isha's shoulder with a heavy, ring-laden hand.

'One last touch, and the lightlure will be complete,' he said.

They went back inside the living-room. Here the atmosphere was warm and cosy, with none of the black-and-white bleakness of the side-room.

Isha helped him heave a rolled carpet up from underneath his bed. They carried it back to the cage and unfurled it there, revealing shards of mirrors that had been woven into the carpet's threads, at regular intervals, presumably so it would be impossible for a lightborn to go through it. This too had to be nailed to the ground. Isha knelt on the hard stone to work. The task was all the more challenging because she could only drive the nails between the flagstones, and so she had to stretch the rug in awkward places to make it fit. The threads were coarse, the fabric was undyed – but the mirrors must have been expensive, and the weaving was exquisite. When she took a step back, the mirrors shimmered, drawing patterns of silver-light and shadow against the floor.

'Dealing with lightborns is dealing with beauty,' said Sir Daegan. 'All in all, a very satisfying business.'

Dealing with the Nest is dealing with ugliness, she thought, but she did her best to stifle the words before Sir Daegan could hear them.

When they left the side-room, he locked it behind them.

'Do you want a drink?' he asked, amiably enough.

He poured her a glass of wine while she stood, uneasy, beside one of the armchairs. The tapestries on the walls showed the Nest hanging above the Edge, with mages gathered around it, stars and the sun and lightborns flying beyond the cliff. Another tapestry was a hunting scene, with horses, deer, dogs, and trees. These mundane items, the musty smell of books, the crunch of hay inside the chair when she sat down, couldn't quite dispel the eeriness of the side-room they had just left.

Sir Daegan handed her a glass. It was real glass, not wood, with wine as dark as blood inside it. He had served himself one too.

'You understand,' he said, as he sipped his drink, 'that this will remain between us.'

He licked the corners of his mouth as he watched her closely. She brought the wine to her lips, although she didn't feel like drinking.

'Do you know why I picked you, aside from the obvious kher tattoo?' he asked.

He didn't sit down, but stood beside his chair, one hand

against the headrest, the other playing at swirling the wine inside its glass.

Isha shook her head.

Sir Daegan stared at her with unflinching eyes. 'Because you have more to lose.'

He mindlinked as he spoke, his mind like a whip. She flinched despite herself. It wasn't much, if anything at all – a brief image of Passerine striding down a corridor, Tatters sitting on the floor inside the Temple. But the images cut through her sharply. He hadn't meant for it to be a pleasant experience.

'I have not questioned you about this. You will not question me, either.' Sir Daegan's voice was affable, unthreatening. If it hadn't been for the fierceness of his mindlink, she could have believed he didn't really mind either way, that this was only a pleasant conversation between friends.

'I will ask again. Do you understand me?'

'Yes,' she whispered.

***

The sky was clear and white, with the smell of snow in the air. The square hummed with voices. Tatters didn't try to get a good view of the pillories; that would have been too much of a struggle. The children would be at the front, sitting on the ground, or holding onto their mothers' aprons, as the women paused in their morning duties to enjoy the show. Adults of all ages crammed around the square, leaving a respectful circle for the lawmage to do his work.

Tatters headed for a stall laden with vegetables, fruit, cheese, different ingredients picked from the farm early the same morning, or maybe the previous day, and collected in miscellaneous piles. The wares were autumnal – pumpkins, late apples, walnuts.

At the foot of the stall were rotting gourds of various shapes and sizes, which the shopkeeper gave away for free, to throw at the criminals. It attracted passers-by to his stand.

Brushing the midges aside, Tatters went to stand beside the stall. The shopkeeper waved at his gourds, but Tatters only shook his head. He tucked himself at the mouth of the narrow alley running alongside the shop. It was impossible to find a quiet corner in the square when it was this full, but hopefully the busy shop would distract anyone looking this way. He crossed his arms, in part to fend off the cold, in part to brace himself.

There's still time not to do this, said Lal.

First the town crier gave the news for the day. It was the usual: there were refugees in all of the Meddyns now, choking the towns huddled between forest-covered hills, slowly pooling down the Sunpath towards the Nest. A skirmish had taken place with a small retinue of bandits who had red banners and might or might not have been Renegades.

Tatters tried to ignore the twist of fear in his gut. The town crier reassured everyone they had been dealt with by the local mages, earning Lady Siobhan some 'praise be' and 'long may the Nest stand'.

After the crier, a bored, sniffling lawmage announced the punishments for the day and how many whip lashes each petty villain would receive. He also listed their crimes for the crowd, who shouted 'shame!' with delight, especially when it came to thieves. Ka got a lacklustre response – impeding a lawmage in his duty wasn't a wrongdoing anyone cared for.

The executioner will hit him harder, warned Lal. The popular belief was that khers felt less pain than humans.

Tatters wasn't looking forward to it. But he had told Ka he would be there.

Don't tell me you're afraid of a flogging, he answered Lal. *We've had worse.*

You've become soft.

Well, this is a good way to find out, isn't it?

The hangman, whose duties included beating, cracked his whip above his head. The crowd muttered in excitement, whilst Tatters clenched his teeth. He could see, in the distance, the red smudged shape of Ka, leaning into the pillory. There wasn't another kher in sight.

Tatters fleshbound. Suddenly his neck was stiff from a night of sleeping in an uncomfortable position, his spine ached. His knees kept wanting to buckle, but when they did, the pull on his shoulders became acute. Wincing, Tatters rubbed the nape of his neck, trying to keep the movement natural. Lal was right. He had become soft.

What is it? Do you feel that guilty about being a mage? Lal was growing angry. Maybe she hadn't thought he would stay true to his word. *Is that what this is about? Do you think suffering with Ka makes up for everything else you've done?*

She was furious but faint – the fleshbinding muffled her voice. She spoke as if from far away.

It's not about suffering, said Tatters. *It's about sharing the load.*

The first person to be beaten was one of the thieves. Tatters supposed Ka would be second or third. He listened to the sharp sound of the whip and the screams of the pilloried man. The crowd thumped its feet in time with the lashes.

When the hangman stepped up to Ka, a few people cheered.

Tatters let himself slide to a crouch on the floor, as if it were more comfortable. He tensed his shoulders, pressing his back into the stone. He was so focused he lost Lal entirely. He held his breath.

The shopkeeper misunderstood his change of posture. 'Khers

always give a good show, don't they?' he said. He was trying to be friendly. Tatters tried to smile.

The whip cut through the cloud-white sky. When it landed, Tatters felt the burn of it from his shoulders to his hips. The shock of the hit, and the sound of it, shuddered through his teeth. Despite himself, he gasped. He hadn't felt pain in a long time. He remembered when he could take it; now he wondered how he'd done it. What had numbed him? Habit? Disgust? Why didn't it matter then, how hard they tried to break him, and why did it matter now, one blow across someone else's back?

By the second strike he wanted it to be over. It could be, if he wanted it to – he could drop the fleshbinding. He doubted Ka would force his agony onto him, although it was possible, of course, to share your feelings with someone against their will.

The third strike. The fourth. The crowd was whistling and shouting abuse. Because of his position, Ka's blood was rising to his face, drumming inside his ears. Tatters shared every heartbeat. He hugged his knees against his chest to hide that he was flinching; he couldn't afford to draw attention to himself. Ka didn't shout out. The fifth strike was harder. Tatters could sense hot liquid crawling down his back.

He wouldn't be able to keep this up.

Shuffling further into the alley, Tatters closed his eyes. It wasn't discreet, but it would help. He detached his mind from his body, visualising himself elsewhere, with other thoughts, other fears. The skin off his back was cut in thin, bloody stripes. But he wasn't there to feel it. He wasn't under this pale autumn sky, but enjoying the warmth of a summer afternoon. The excited voices were insects buzzing around the overripe fruit. It wasn't blood he could smell, but pollen, drifting in the hot, heavy air.

At first his mind resisted. Fleshbinding and mindrambling together was like trying to draw squares with one hand and circles with the other. But Tatters had practiced. Slowly the city faded away. The wall against which he was resting became bark; the hard pavement he could feel through the soles of his shoes melted into soft earth and thick grass.

He was sitting in the shade of a tree, in the Rohit Pattra, the Forest of Red Leaves. Where his bare feet poked out of the protection of the branches, the sun scorched his skin. The colours were bright – green grass, blue sky, bright red leaves from the maple trees. His eyes half-closed, he listened to the lazy drone of bumblebees. Lal was sleeping at the back of his mind, curled in a corner like a cat.

Mezyan was lying on his stomach beside him. He plucked idly at the maples' winged fruit, splitting them in half, or tossing them in the air for the pleasure of watching them spin to the ground. Other Renegades were scattered across the grove. It was too hot for training; they had done most of the day's work this morning, at dawn, and would finish the remainder at dusk. Hawk herself was sitting, cross-legged, a few feet away. She didn't seem to mind the sun beating down on her.

She was beautiful. Coarse, certainly, like a roughly hewn piece of wood, but beautiful still. She wore the mantle of leadership better than most women wore dresses. Her black hair shone in the sun. Her dark skin shone darker still, tanned by a summer of training outside.

They had discovered humans could fleshbind, if taught. They were excited like children before snow.

'I think we'll use fleshbinding to resist pain, rather than inflict it,' said Hawk. 'If one of us is tortured, but twenty people share the pain, it should be manageable for everyone involved.'

These were the early days, with only about fifteen Renegades, most of whom didn't live at the camp, and couldn't be called upon if there was an emergency. They were hiding in the Rohit

Pattra because it was a sacred forest, which stayed empty outside of festival weeks.

'They can make torture last a very long time,' Tatters said doubtfully. 'I don't think it'll work.'

Her gaze was hard as iron; it was a hardness that didn't come naturally, but had been hammered through fire. 'Maybe we need to find a way to kill the person being tortured, to shorten the ordeal,' she said.

No-one could answer that. Hawk had suffered, and she was intent on never suffering again. Everyone in the encampment assumed the mages had harmed her, although what had happened wasn't clear – but she hadn't renounced her convent for nothing.

'There is a story that fits this situation,' Mezyan said. 'Once, this king negotiated peace with another tribe. The two kings met, and they shared blood, so the deal would be sealed with fleshbinding.'

'How many kher kings were there, exactly?' interrupted Tatters. 'All your stories start with a different king.'

'There were as many kings as there were tribes,' said Mezyan.

'Chieftains, then.'

'Kings.'

Tatters didn't argue. He played at combing the grass, enjoying the feel of it. Red, five-fingered leaves dappled the ground.

'But the other king was an oath breaker. He went to war against his ally. The night before the battle, the evil king couldn't sleep. He turned and turned in his bed, until in the end he spent the night awake, standing beside his tent, jaw clenched. When his lovers asked him what the problem was, he refused to answer.'

Hawk had closed her eyes, soaking up the sun. Mezyan pushed himself up on his elbows, resting his chin in his hands.

He checked whether Tatters was listening before pursuing his story:

'On the other side of the battlefield, the good king's lovers woke to the sharp, stark sound of a whip. They couldn't see anything in the dark and assumed he was beating a thief for sneaking into their tent at night. They went back to sleep. But the next morning, they found him standing beside his tent, his back bloodied. He had spent the night whipping his foe and spoiling his sleep. His back was torn; but the pain belonged solely to the other side.'

Tatters shook his head. 'I would have thought beating yourself all night isn't the best way to make a point.'

Mezyan laughed. His laughter was young, still. They were both young, still.

'You don't think it's noble to sacrifice yourself to punish your enemies? Come on, Tatters, honour and glory. Who needs to become a pure spirit when your great deeds fly through people's minds forever? Isn't that the ultimate flight?'

As Mezyan pushed himself up into a sitting position, his white horns reflected light in Tatters' eyes. It burned; he blinked.

'I don't have enemies.' But it was a lie. The Red Belt, an alliance of Sunriser convents where kher slavery was permitted, would destroy them if they found out there was an illegal convent of mages, founded without their permission, living outside of their rules. But it was difficult to think about it on a day so full of the smell of summer, so achingly bright.

Tatters tried to change the subject. 'You could be an uaza. You're good enough at telling stories.'

Mezyan shook his head. 'I'm aniybu. I will never be an uaza.'

Aniybu designated a halfblood through the male line, with a kher father, whereas a taniybu was a halfblood through the female line, with a kher mother. Taniybu were usually accepted into kher homes and taught kher culture – aniybu weren't. If a kher father had gone off with a human woman, it meant he expected the halfblood to be cared for by humans. Khers didn't want anything to do with the child.

Mezyan ripped out a clump of grass and let it rain between his fingers onto Tatters' foot. Ticklish, Tatters took his foot away.

'You don't always need to sacrifice yourself to fight back,' said Hawk. 'You can sacrifice someone else.'

They both jumped; they had assumed she wasn't listening. She was still sitting in the sun, breathing in as the wind ruffled the trees. Tatters could see beads of sweat on her forehead, but she didn't wipe them away.

'I am sick of paying the mages' price,' she said. 'Next time, I will make sure someone else bears it.'

He remembered her profile, cut out neatly against the summer sky, her cropped hair, the patches where her stana stuck to her skin. The dreamy look in her eyes at the thought of kings and honour gained through injury. He remembered thinking he wouldn't want her as his enemy.

But you did become her enemy.

He shivered. It was as if the colours and the heat were sucked out of the world. First the grass faded to grey, then the trees, then even Mezyan's red skin and glinting horns, until they were a dulled and dirty white. Winter was setting in the midst of summer. There was a discomfort between his shoulders where the bark caught his skin, but when he moved to relieve it, it only became worse. Soon his back was throbbing, and the ache spread through his muscles, down his arms and legs.

The hangman had finished. Tatters had remained mind-rambling, present but absent, during the rest of the beatings. Ka was in the pillory, panting, bleeding – alive.

It worked, said Lal.

It did.

It hurts, though.

It does.

Even half of Ka's pain was difficult to bear.

The crowd was breaking up. The shopkeeper started calling out for people to buy his pumpkins as soon as the lawmage stepped away from the criminals. For a while, Tatters stood beside the stall, watching the press of bodies ebbing across the square. They were normal men and women, with work, with children, with modest lives, who were going back to washing their sheets and cooking their meals. They haggled over prices with the same voice they used to scream 'shame'.

He spotted the guard he had bribed the day before. The man tried to prevent children from throwing rotten fruit at Ka. Instead they simply lobbed them over his head, but at least he put some effort into chasing them off. Tatters felt a sharp sting, like salt, when the guard rinsed Ka's wounds with his pouch of water.

At least that money was well-spent, he thought.

But you can't protect everyone, said Lal.

Tatters waited until the square had returned to its usual state – beggars beside Siobhan's statue, women gathered around the shopping stalls, men returning to work, servants escorting mages or buying wares for them.

When he crossed the square, the guard noticed him and gave him a nod. Tatters answered with a brief wave. A huddle of guardsmen were chatting together, and he briefly wondered whether they were discussing the rumours around Lady Siobhan's collarbound.

Ka was stuck in the pillory. The wounds that cut across his back scarred his tattoo with long, slim lines. Tatters wondered if he would need to re-ink the tattoo, or if he would let it stand incomplete, as a reminder.

'Idir,' said Tatters.

For a while Ka didn't answer, too busy taking deep, harsh breaths. 'You came.'

Tatters rested one arm casually against the pillory, although the movement strained his sore shoulders.

'How are you feeling?' he asked.

Ka smiled. Lines of dried tears marred his cheeks.

'I'm fine.' He repeated Arushi's words: 'This won't break me.'

It wasn't safe to mention fleshbinding, or kher-human friendship, or anything else that might attract attention. They stared across the square, at the low clouds.

'You know, normally this is something we do all together,' Ka said. Tatters guessed he meant the fleshbinding. 'We always share, good or bad, with everyone else in the hearth.' Ka squeezed his eyes shut; the aftermath of tears wet his eyelashes. 'It must be so lonely, being human. It feels so lonely now.'

Tatters didn't know what to say. He would have to leave soon, to keep people from prying, and Ka would be lonelier still. A faint drizzle started to fall, as fine as mist, hanging in the air and pervading everything with damp.

Ka lifted his head inside the pillory to meet Tatters' gaze, although the wood pressed uncomfortably against his throat.

'I won't forget what you did today.'

***

The last thing Isha wanted to do was to face the other apprentices. They would be curious and she didn't have any answers to give them. Furthermore, she had someone she needed to see. She headed for the city, sharing the road with merchants and servants, most of them going the other way, as well as one or two lawmages. Isha kept her eyes downcast while they overtook her.

She found Ka easily. He was the only kher being punished in the central square. Other people had gathered around the pillories, siblings or spouses, helping the criminals eat and drink, sometimes cradling their heads. One was even tending to a prisoner's wounds.

One of the guards stared at her, but she was entitled to be there as much as anyone else. Isha walked up to Ka.

'Tidir,' she said.

Ka made a choked sound. At first she thought he was sobbing, and fear crept along her spine, fear that she had done something unforgivable. But then she saw he was laughing. It was, in a way, even more unsettling.

'You are a friend of Tatters, I guess,' said Ka. His voice was hoarse, as if the rough wood had left splinters in his throat.

'Is it that obvious?' Isha asked.

Ka let his head sag in his bounds, still chuckling, the thick laughter rattling through his nose. It was obviously an effort to keep his head upright.

'Yes,' he said. 'But he should have told you that tidir is the female greeting, and that idir is the proper way to greet a man.'

Isha blushed. How could she know that? She spent all her time at Arushi's home with the women. Everyone welcomed her with tidir.

'Sorry,' she said.

He didn't answer, which she hoped meant he accepted her apology.

The guardsmen seemed suspicious, glancing in her direction and whispering amongst themselves but, maybe thanks to her apprentice's robes, they left her alone.

'I'm Isha.'

'I'm Ka. As I'm sure you know.'

She lifted the water pouch she had been carrying. 'I've got water.'

'I won't say no.'

After bringing the water to his lips, she took some apples that she'd stolen from the common mess out of her pockets. She held an apple to his mouth so he could eat.

'Why did you come?' Ka asked.

'I thought you might like some company,' she said.

'Who wants a soulworm for company?' he answered, his mouth full of half-chewed apple.

She had been expecting this, and she didn't let it hurt her. He had cracked lips and lines of dirt down his face, whilst she had baina in her purse and the grey robes of power.

'I'm trying to help,' she said.

'Maybe I'm better off alone.'

It stung, but she thought of what mages had done to him, today, and to his father, the day before, and to his people, the years leading up to this day. It didn't matter that she had never lifted a finger against a kher. They both carried different legacies.

'If you want me to, I'll leave,' she said. 'But I thought I could keep your mind off things.'

Ka spat out the apple core and pips. He did it nonchalantly enough, but Isha wondered if he had meant to spit at her.

'Why would you want to help?' he asked. 'Go back to your Nest, eyas.'

My eyas. Isha heard it as clearly as if someone had spoken behind her, with their mouth against her ear. *My eyas.* She felt it like someone defiling her funeral, in her bones. But she knew even as she heard it that there was no-one behind her. She checked over her shoulder, all the same, and saw nothing but the guardsmen and the merchants, carrying on with their lives.

'What's that?' she asked. 'The thing you just said. An eyas?'

Who had used it before? It took Isha a moment to recall – it was the woman from her dreams.

'It's not an insult, don't worry,' grumbled Ka. His smirk was angry, defiant. 'And even if it was, I doubt you can make my life any worse right now.'

'No, that's not it.' She hesitated. 'I heard someone talk about an eyas the other day.' It was true. But she was becoming a mage, so it was only part of the truth. 'I'm curious, that's all.'

She kept her voice as neutral as possible, trying to pretend this was small talk. He seemed to believe her. She had learnt with one of the best teachers, after all. Tatters could make small talk until people gave him their soul.

'An eyas is a baby hawk before it leaves its nest,' explained Ka. 'Before it becomes a fledgling, you start training it. It has to be before it can fly. That's the only way to get a bird of prey to be tame.' His voice turned hard; his face closed. He shook his head as much as the pillory allowed him to. 'Like iwdan. You beat us while we're young, you reap us when we're old.'

The conversation stalled like a cart caught in a muddy path, and Isha wasn't sure how to push it forward again. His family would come to visit him soon, now that the guardsmen were relaxing their hold over the square. She should leave.

Yet she stayed. She wanted to tell Ka that she didn't have a father either. That she was sorry for the baina. That she wasn't one of *them*.

Inside the pillory, most of what she could see was his back, with lacerations across it, still oozing blood. She could also see the outlines of muscles and tattoos down his sides, his shoulders and his neck. His thick black hair turned into stubble which wasn't yet a beard as it reached his jaw.

'I'm sorry,' she said. 'I know it doesn't make up for what happened but, for what it's worth, I'm truly sorry.'

His eyes were darker even than Passerine's.

'Go home, eyas,' he said. 'Go back where you belong.'

She bid him goodbye, but she didn't know where a tattooed mage belonged.

Chapter Eleven

The day after Ka's beating, the mages were celebrating the Groniz festival. Isha felt uneasy knowing that while the khers grieved, the humans rejoiced.

Groniz was the Giver, the lightborn of spring and fertility, who flew over babies' cradles to grant them gifts – beauty, luck, strength. According to the Temple, a long time ago, Groniz had been tricked by a jealous soul, a dead spirit who couldn't ascend, to believe a child had been born in the underworlds. Which was why, every year, during winter, Groniz disappeared over the Edge for a season, to check for children in need of her blessing. During her absence, everything died and grew cold.

The festival was devoted to Groniz, to bid her goodbye and good luck. Although the mages weren't always in agreement with the priests, both communities liked celebrating the Giver. The Temple opened its doors to everyone, mages included, for dance, prayer, and food. The priests would be breaking their fast; the mages would be eating even though they hadn't fasted.

The priests do the fasting, the mages do the feasting, as the saying went.

The countryside mages, at least those from nearby towns, made the pilgrimage to the Nest for the festival, which meant the apprentices were kept busy guiding visitors to their rooms, greeting them in the name of the high mages they represented, and of course collecting their gifts and reports. They also went to pick evergreen, holly and mistletoe, to hang on the Nest's walls. Kilian dragged Isha to the popular activities – gathering greenery, dying cloth, drying seeds to save for spring.

On the evening of the festival, Kilian was buzzing with excitement. He went to fetch Isha at the doors of the female dormitory.

'I thought mages weren't supposed to worship lightborns,' she said, as she stepped out of the room. She was amongst the last girls to come out. While the others had been busy braiding their hair with plants and ribbons, she had practised mindlink and lost track of time.

Kilian laughed. 'This is Groniz. Everyone likes Groniz.' He gave her a critical once-over. 'You aren't even wearing something green?'

Isha pulled up one of her sleeves. Around her wrist, she was wearing a thin bracelet of green threads, with a carved wooden bead. It was a present from... someone. Someone whose face she couldn't exactly place, but who had been important, whom she had admired. A woman, Isha believed. She always wore this bracelet at the Groniz festival. Or at least, so she thought. She could remember past festivals, her foster-family dancing, snippets of scenes that might cover several years or only one night. Maybe crucial moments had been stripped away from those memories, or maybe not. It was frustrating, like trying to catch motes of dust that flew away by the time her fingers came close.

At the farm, she would also put on a green dress – but mages always kept their robes. Instead, she had slipped on a green belt. During the festival, the mages made a conscious effort to loosen tension between factions. One way to do so was to abandon, for one night, the belts that marked them out.

Kilian shook his head. 'That's not enough,' he said firmly. 'Where is the wacky hairdo? If there isn't at least a holly bush in your hair, it doesn't count.'

'My hair looks like a holly bush anyway. It doesn't need actual holly.' It was one tradition Isha was glad she could skip this year. She hated the hassle of placing leaves around her head, which were then a nightmare to take off.

'Well, where's the embroidery down your robe?' asked Kilian. He crossed his arms, mock-severe, with an exaggerated frown.

'You're one to speak,' she said. 'What's your contribution?'

He had been waiting for that question. He grinned. 'Can't you see it?'

He spread out his arms so she could admire him in full. He had the green belt, of course, but that didn't count – it was just good manners. She studied him. At first she didn't spot it. But then her eyes caught a flash of colour near the bottom of his cloak. He lifted it for her.

He had dyed the leather of his shoes. They shone emerald-green.

'It's very good,' she had to admit.

'Isn't it?' Kilian beamed. 'This took ages. And it probably won't hold. It cost me a fortune in dye. But isn't it worth it?'

She laughed. Kilian was so uncomplicatedly happy, it was contagious. And the shoes were a thing of beauty, if only for one night. 'Yes,' she said.

As they ambled towards the Temple, Isha's shoulders relaxed; maybe she would enjoy the evening. When she was with Kilian, her spirits lifted. His most important concern was whether his shoes made an impression. She wished that could be her most important concern, too.

The path to the Temple was different from when Isha had taken it with Tatters. Garlands had been tied between the trees' branches, and kher guards with unlit torches lined the road at regular intervals. They would stay all night, to help drunk mages find their way back to the Nest. She supposed they would set fire to the torches when the sun started setting, creating a pathway of light from the Nest to the Temple.

Around them, a variety of costumes were on display – some apprentices, like her, had only put on a necklace or a shawl in honour of Groniz. One man had a wreath of thorns, which he wore like a crown. Another held a decorated staff, the wood painted with Groniz's symbols: roots, flowers, pine trees. A girl had made earrings out of small, varnished pinecones, which she kept readjusting.

A group of disciples was sitting at the foot of a tree, sharing a wineskin. Isha's heart sank as she recognised them.

'Hey guys!' Kilian waved at them.

'You took your time,' said Caitlin. 'Any longer and we would've finished the booze.' She handed them the wineskin; Kilian took a few hungry gulps out of it.

Caitlin looked wonderful, of course. Two plaits ran around her forehead, joining at the back and falling down her shoulders, threaded with deep green ribbons. Twigs and wispy old man's beard were artfully tucked behind one of her ears. She had embroidered green threads along the usual gold of her disciple's robe. And yes, on the brooch holding it up were autumn leaves, freshly plucked, Isha noted wearily. Her lips were the colour of crushed berries.

Caitlin gave Isha an appraising look. 'No green?' she asked. 'You're an unbeliever, puffin?'

Isha answered with a tight smile. It didn't seem worth pointing out the bracelet.

'So? What happened with Sir Daegan last time?' added Caitlin. 'We're all dying to know.'

Kilian was busy showing off his shoes, the wineskin in one hand, the other pulling up his robes so the green leather glinted.

'Nothing much,' said Isha.

Caitlin made a sound that would have been a snort if it hadn't come from her perfect mouth. 'But only you could get it up for him, it seems.'

A boy beside her laughed at the implication, but Isha heard the jealousy in her tone. It was better, she decided, to give Caitlin an answer of some sort, if only to stop her from prying.

'He wanted to move some kher horn he'd just bought,' Isha said, truthfully enough. She kept her mind closely guarded and her voice sullen. 'He only wanted the tattooed girl to touch it.'

She sounded bitter enough. From the way Caitlin smirked, Isha knew she'd given her a satisfying answer. As long as the reason Sir Daegan chose Isha was that she was spoilt, unfit to do a mage's task, Caitlin was pleased.

'Ah, he's old-fashioned,' said Kilian. He gave her the wineskin. 'Take some of this and forget it. When you smash us all at mindbrawl, he'll have to admit you're a great mage.'

Isha smiled. Kilian understood her better than he thought. She *did* plan to best them all at mindbrawl.

* * *

Everyone was on their way to the festival, so only loners and unbelievers like Tatters stayed at the Coop. A few apprentices were around too, drinking, working up the mood to head to the Temple. All in all, it had been a quiet evening before Arushi stormed in.

She was the last person Tatters had expected to see. When she entered the tavern, conversations abruptly stopped. The apprentices turned to her, noticed the uniform, and craned their necks to spot the lawmage who was bound to follow. But she had come alone.

What does she want? grumbled Lal.

The innkeeper didn't budge from his place behind the counter. He shouted from across the room: 'This isn't your kind of place, hon.' Tatters wasn't sure if he'd addressed her as 'hon' or 'horn'.

Arushi put her fists on her hips. Before she could answer the innkeeper, Tatters scrambled up from his booth.

'Tidir! Welcome,' he said, with overacted enthusiasm. 'What can I do for you?'

He was conscious of the gazes of the apprentices around him. They were gawking, trying to assemble the pieces of the puzzle – collarbound, kher guard. Skies knew what they would imagine his relationship with Arushi was. Nothing that would elevate their minds, that was sure.

'I need to talk to you,' she said.

She can't boss us around. Lal's animosity was palpable. She had been enjoying the prospect of an evening of beer and mindbrawl. *Tell her to come back later.*

Tatters had to admit he would rather Arushi didn't address him like she did unruly disciples, but he didn't want to upset her.

'Of course,' he said. 'Here? Shall I buy you something?'

Arushi narrowed her eyes. It seemed to dawn on her that everyone was listening to their conversation. She studied the faces of the apprentices, took in the variations in grey amongst their robes, the fact that the clientele were exclusively mages in training. In honour of Groniz, the innkeeper had placed bushels of flowers on each table. But there was no doubt this wasn't a festival crowd.

'I know somewhere more private.' Her tone was as unyielding as steel. Most apprentices ducked when she glared at them, hiding behind their glasses like children caught stealing sugar.

Get lost, snapped Lal.

'I'd be happy to,' said Tatters.

I'm not.

Oh, really? Tatters answered. *Would you believe it, I got the hint?*

Lal sulked. Tatters followed Arushi out of the Coop. She moved with swift, long steps. Although she was shorter than him, she forced him to make longer strides, her walk one pace short of a run. Her head was held low, as if she were about to run someone through.

The streets were lively. They passed by a makeshift creature of hay, with a pumpkin head, supposed to represent the evil spirit that had tricked Groniz. The scarecrow was much higher than a man. There was a heavy two-handed sword on display beside it. For a coin, people could try to cut the pumpkin. A small crowd had gathered to watch the attempts and clap along. The entertainer overseeing the activity wiped the sword clean between each strike. People were cheering, but Arushi didn't so much as glance their way.

Tatters had lived long enough with Hawk that, when a strong-willed woman was upset with him, he kept his mouth shut. Arushi did the same. It was only once they reached a tavern closer to the centre of town, in a cleaner neighbourhood, that she relented enough to say: 'Here.'

The tavern was large. The main room wasn't covered in dried-up beer and puke. The owner had decorated the tables with sprigs of wildflowers in tall vases. The tablecloths all matched, bright green with yellow flowers. A cook was at work beside the chimney, roasting meat on a spit. The place smelt of sizzling food and freshly chopped wood.

Although it was comfier than the Coop, it sent a shiver down Tatters' spine. The people sitting along the wooden benches, or leaning against the long, varnished counter, or peeking through the lace curtains, weren't his kind of crowd. They were guards. A few khers, a few humans. Even those who weren't in uniform had the hard faces of people who killed for a living.

With our luck, we'll meet Goldie, Lal said. She wasn't at her most supportive.

Upstairs, private quarters were reserved for more important clients. That was where Arushi brought him, after having ordered a bottle of wine.

A servant unlocked a room for them, before handing Arushi the key. Tatters guessed that unofficial questionings sometimes happened in these comfortable, quiet spaces.

And if there's corruption amongst the guards, this is where they settle their arrangements, prompted Lal.

What do you mean, if?

Arushi closed the door with her foot, placing the bottle of wine and the glasses on the table. She didn't uncork the bottle. The table was pushed against the wall furthest from the exit, with two wooden benches on either side. Arushi picked one, Tatters picked the other.

Once they were seated, she didn't bother with padding.

'You're a mage, aren't you?' she asked.

'Nice to see you too,' he answered. There was only so much he could take.

She shook her head. Her horns gleamed.

'This is important,' she said.

Through the window, they could hear the ruckus from the street below. A square of sunlight framed the bottle of wine. Tatters ran his finger along the shape cast by the window, as if the distinction between light and shadow could be smudged away. Leaning over, he retrieved the bottle.

'I see you've decided we're friends today,' he said. 'Yes, I can mindlink. Is that all, warden?'

He uncorked the bottle with a clean round plop. He put the wine down again so it could breathe before being served.

Arushi was stern. 'What were you doing with those kids back there?'

'Training.'

Tatters didn't like the turn the conversation was taking. Arushi hadn't locked the door, but the space was narrow to manoeuvre in, and of course he couldn't mindlink a kher. She was probably stronger than him. After all, her sword was there, by her side, pushed up at an awkward angle because of the bench. He could smell the faint scent of leather from the sheath.

'Don't lie to me.' She rested her weight into her elbows, which brought her horns uncomfortably close. The light caught the bright-black tips.

'Mindbrawl,' he said. 'Which is, technically, training. Why? Planning to arrest me? I must say you're very civil about it. Most people don't bother with the wine.'

Maybe she's found out about Lady Siobhan, said Lal. *She did promise to kick you over the Edge.*

But Arushi surprised them both.

'Do you remember Ka?'

Tatters nodded. Arushi picked up the bottle of wine, sniffed it, and filled the two glasses.

'For someone who keeps secrets, you're terrible at it,' she said.

At last something we agree on, said Lal.

Tatters took his glass. The wine hadn't had enough time for all the flavours to express themselves, but he needed a drink, so he gulped down half of the glass. It was better stuff than he was used to; he regretted quaffing it. Arushi didn't drink hers.

'Humans can't fleshbind. The iwdan can't mindlink.' Arushi crossed and uncrossed her hands before her. She stared at Tatters, as if reading his face, maybe hoping to find answers there. 'Care to explain?'

Tatters fidgeted. The square bench was uncomfortable. It didn't have any cushions – maybe that was on purpose. He felt an ache between his shoulders that he couldn't accommodate. When he tried to lie back, his legs got caught in the bench on which Arushi was sitting.

'What exactly did Ka tell you?' he asked.

Arushi shook her head. Her hair was ruffled, sprouting around her horns in a mess. 'No, you don't get it. I'm asking the questions.'

Tatters held his glass in front of his lips. 'No, *you* don't get it. This is a conversation. If it's an interrogation, then do it properly, and drag me to prison first.'

It was a dangerous gambit, but it worked.

Arushi sighed, then reached for her glass. As a sign of peace, Tatters clinked his beaker against hers. When she sipped the wine, it left a purple-black line on her upper lip.

'All right. You should know, mister secret-hoarder, that iwdan tell each other everything. Ka told his family, who told mine who, against their better judgement, told me. It's now common knowledge in the Pit. You can fleshbind.'

I knew this would be trouble, said Lal.

I forgot khers share absolutely everything, admitted Tatters. *You would've thought the kid knew better than that.*

'The good news is, most iwdan don't put two and two together, and they just assume you're a halfblood.' Arushi drank more wine. Tatters copied her. The alcohol left a warm glow inside his chest. He appreciated Arushi going to the trouble of buying it. This wasn't a pleasant conversation, but the wine dulled the edges of it, allowed him to believe it wouldn't be too disastrous.

'But I know that's impossible,' she concluded. 'Because you can mindlink.'

Tatters took a deep breath. He thought of Hawk extending her hand towards him, her palm cut open, bleeding freely down her fingers. The way they shook hands when they shared blood. Her laughter, the pure joy of it, when she showed him humans could fleshbind. In some ways, she was like a child. New things filled her with glee. It softened her warrior features, broke her serious demeanour. He could see the girl she had been when she smiled.

'Humans can fleshbind,' said Tatters. 'All of them. They just don't try. They've got no-one to teach them. They can't do it intuitively, like iwdan, but they can learn.'

Arushi gave him the look Hawk loved: the look of people whom Hawk would have so much fun proving wrong.

'Actually, if you want to fleshbind with an animal, you can do that, too. I don't know if iwdan sometimes try?'

Arushi lifted one hand to shush him. He fell silent. She used the same hand to scratch the base of her horns, further tousling her hair, in a delicate, self-conscious gesture that contrasted with her military outfit. He watched her for too long; he realised he liked watching.

Don't you think you have other things to worry about? moaned Lal.

'Let me get this straight,' said Arushi. 'You can fleshbind and mindlink and you're human?'

Well, human enough. 'Don't I look human to you?' He smiled.

She drank some more, as if she could wash down his words with wine. He finished his glass. When he put it back down on the table, she poured him another one.

'Does your master know?' she asked.

Arushi had caught him off-guard twice in one conversation. Her voice had softened.

'I don't want you to get into trouble.' She didn't catch his eye. 'But you make it hard to watch out for you.'

She was steadying his glass with one hand. On impulse, he bent over to touch her fingers. Lal disappeared; his connection to mindlink faded. When they touched, a warmth spread between them, crawling up his arm like a blush, like the feeling of alcohol getting to his head. He didn't take his hand away. She didn't remove hers.

Arushi met his gaze. Something in her expression made Tatters' heart leap, pound in his ears and temples. He was taken aback by the strength of his own reaction. He didn't think of Arushi as more than a friend – a fun friend, certainly, with a pretty face, no doubt, but not…

She kissed him.

He closed his eyes. Her lips were hot. Soft. The curve of her horns pressed against his forehead. He cupped her jaw in his hand. Her skin was soft. Hot.

Emotion rippled through him like a stone breaking the surface of a lake.

She interrupted their kiss and sat back down on her bench. There was a pause.

By the underworlds, said Lal. *Tell me she messed around with your memories. Seriously? A kher? Now? Skies and thunder, I can't believe it. You're so immature.*

Tatters left his bench to settle beside Arushi. *Oh, you think you can get rid of me by—*

He let his arm rest against Arushi's. Lal was silenced.

'Do you mind if we stay like this?' he asked.

They finished the wine.

* * *

The line of kher guards ended at the border of the Temple's lands. Beyond, paper lamps were swinging in the trees, and bowls of water had been placed on the ground with candles floating inside. The lights in the water resembled small, earthbound stars. Wind chimes and mirrors were tied to every branch of every tree, reflecting people and faces at surprising angles. As the sun set and the night grew dark, walking across the grounds became like walking through a maze. The Temple itself had been washed until the mosaic floors gleamed. Despite the cleansing, it still smelt of blood.

The animals that wouldn't survive the winter had been slaughtered that afternoon in the designated area outside the Temple's main building. Where the killings had happened, the earth was choked with blood, wet and muddy underfoot. There were firepits with roasting meat and racks of smoking food along the Edge. Lightborns didn't eat, of course, but it was believed Groniz could taste the feast from the smoke.

The priests had fasted for days leading up to the festival, so they looked even leaner than usual. The food comprised offerings that ungifted and mages had donated, and which would serve to break the fast.

Isha followed Caitlin and the others as they ambled towards the Edge, admiring the decorations, commenting on people's clothes – until someone hailed her.

'You! With the tattoo!'

She recognised the priest coming towards her: he was the man who had barred their way last time she'd visited with Tatters.

'What is it?' she asked, conscious of people staring.

He seemed more tired than last time she had seen him, half-starved, skin on bone, eyes bruised black with lack of sleep. Like all the priests, he was wearing a green cowl. Like all the priests, there was a mask of dried blood across his face.

'You need to purify yourself,' he said. 'I cannot have a half-blood walking the grounds without following the cleansing rites.'

Of course, no other apprentice would have to observe this formality. Part of Isha was annoyed, but another part of her didn't want to make a scene. She did the cleansing rites at the farm; she could do them here.

'Go ahead,' she told Kilian. 'I'll catch up with you later.'

Kilian nodded. Caitlin had already turned away.

The priest led Isha towards the Temple's entrance. Across the front steps, poor folk from the city burned offal and washed their arms in pails of blood. They lifted mirrors above their heads when they prayed. The priests tended to the fires and sang woeful, aching choruses into the night. They cried for the death of Groniz, and the fact that humans are flesh and blood. *Though we hope to ascend we are doomed to being vile, doomed to bodies, rot, and death.*

The priest helped Isha kneel beside a bucket of blood. The stone stairs cut into her legs as she removed her bracelet. She washed her hands in the slimy liquid, already thickening into a paste, while he stood beside her and sang about loneliness, about longing to belong, about fatherless sons, motherless daughters. She waited, her hands in the blood, the acrid smell of it turning her head, until he had finished.

When at last he paused, she got up and pressed her fingers to his cheek. She added another, brighter line of red onto his mask.

Her arms were stained with gore up to her elbows. 'I need to rinse this,' she said. The priest didn't answer at first. 'I understand it is not common practice, but I cannot join the other mages covered in blood,' she insisted.

His face was impossible to read, marked with bloodied fingers from ungifted, from other priests, from her.

'So, you are a mage, but not so proud that you don't cleanse yourself,' he said. 'And you are tattooed, but not so deeply that you can't use mages' magic.'

'I am a strange one,' she admitted.

He went to fetch her a bucket of water. 'What is your name, strange one?' he asked, as she crouched on the blood-streaked steps for the second time. The water was cold and clear, where the blood had been coagulated and had clung to her.

'Isha,' she said.

The priest nodded. 'I am Osmund. If you ever wish to pray here, ask for me, and I will vouch for your right to stay.'

She tried to thank him, but he was already focusing on the next person coming to purify themselves. After retrieving her bracelet, she left him to it.

At the top of the staircase, above the ungifted cleansing themselves, a platform had been set up for Lady Siobhan. The supreme mage sat on a silk brocade armchair – not quite a throne. She was wearing a heavy malachite-and-gold necklace, which matched her malachite cane. The throng of servants and courtiers around her was so thick that Isha couldn't get a good view; all she could see was wispy white hair and bright green stone.

Beside Lady Siobhan, there was a woman dressed more poorly than the servants. She was as thin as a child at the end of winter, in a ragged linen tunic, head and feet naked. She didn't have a seat, so she stood beside the armchair. From time to time,

Isha could see Lady Siobhan's white crown of hair turn as they spoke, probably steering away from controversial subjects, in a show of goodwill.

She was the head priestess, although priests would not call her that – her official title was the Doorkeeper. She guarded the threshold between the worlds of the living and the dead, to help people cross over to the underworlds. Like her people, her arms and face were dyed red with drying blood. It was the only dye she wore. Unlike her people, she didn't wear green, even for Groniz.

Isha found Kilian with the other disciples, in line for the gifting ceremony. The first part of the festival belonged to the priests, and the mages went through the motions, waiting impatiently for the food to be cooked. Before being able to eat, everyone had to throw an offering over the Edge. Priests lined the cliff, overseeing the rituals.

'We believe we are lightborns,' sang a priest with a loud baritone. His voice carried across the crowd, languid notes drifting in the night. 'We believe we are beasts.' Like the smoke from the fires, the song stained everything it touched. Isha carried it with her long after he had stopped. 'We are both. We are neither. We are torn.'

'I do wish he would stop whingeing,' said Caitlin. She was growing tipsy; her cheeks were flushed, her words harsher than usual.

The others laughed. Isha hid her sigh behind another chug from the wineskin.

'And to think the unbelievers are ready to miss this,' said another girl, who had tied vines around her ankles.

Not attending the Groniz festival was a statement, but not an uncommon one. The line between believers and unbelievers was a thin one at best. People were free to walk on either side of it, as long as they didn't defile the festival.

'Do unbelievers even dance?' asked another boy. He extended his hand towards Isha and wiggled his fingers. Reluctantly, she gave him the drink she'd been hoarding.

'Must be boring if they don't,' said Kilian.

'That's why khers are always sulking,' said Caitlin. 'They're shithorn bored.' She gave a pointed look to the only person who wasn't smiling, the only one who had a tattoo. Isha ignored her.

They were nearing the front of the line. Most people gave Groniz an item that they had made themselves, be it only some needlework or a wooden tool. People hoping to join the Temple, or devout folk, would throw their shoes. The mages usually tossed a few coins.

'Give me the wineskin,' said Caitlin.

She stepped up to the Edge, her deep brown hair floating in the wind, the candles making it glow like polished copper. She stretched backwards, finished the wineskin and, in the same disdainful movement, flung it into the void. Some of the apprentices laughed and clapped. Isha caught the expression on one of the priests' faces, and only felt ashamed.

When she opened her purse to gather a handful of coins, as was expected of her, she realised that she was carrying something that made her soul heavier, which she should return to the lightborns, which was, in its own way, sacred.

She threw the baina over the Edge.

Chapter Twelve

If possible, Tatters would have stayed with Arushi in the tavern. But the head of guards had duties to attend to during the Groniz festival, including, surprisingly, freeing prisoners.

'We've had permission from the lawmages to set loose anyone in the pillories,' she explained. 'Whatever the time they were supposed to spend there, it doesn't matter. This is a pardon from the Giver. At least human feasts are worth something, I guess.'

She had received firm instructions to do it at dusk – not before. The sun wasn't quite setting yet, but it was close enough, and she was impatient.

'Shall we tell Ka the good news?' she asked.

Outside, the sound of singing drifted through the streets. At first, they didn't see anything unusual for one of the biggest celebrations of the year.

As they headed for the main square, they encountered a Sunriser family cuddling in a porch, mother, father and three children tightly snuggled under one blanket. Tatters watched them as they curled up to sleep. They must be from the Samudra territories, on the shores of the Inner Sea. He recognised their driftwood jewellery, strung into necklaces and belts, tied around their waists or necks. The Pearls – the network of sea-trading convents that Tatters came from, the most mixed area on the

259

Sunriser side – weren't far from the Samudra lands. These people were nearly kin.

Despite their trinkets, they had wan faces, deeply set eyes. Beggars. They would stand out, poor things, when they tried to find work and money. People rarely saw Sunrisers this far from the Shadowpass.

The further they went, the stranger the city grew, as if they had changed sides of the Ridge: more Sunriser faces filled the streets, carrying makeshift tents and bundles of cloth over their backs. They wore traditional outfits, too, where knotting the fabric was favoured over stitches, and small scarves of bright nasivyati were slung around their shoulders.

A kher guard, who had been waiting in the main square, stood to attention when she saw Arushi. 'These are the first ones,' she said. 'They've been arriving in dribs and drabs, but I'm told more are on their way.'

The square had been overtaken by twenty or so Sunrisers who huddled together in the biting cold. They had built fires where they could, blackening the pavement with ash. They were desperate enough to set up sleeping areas next to the criminals, and one enterprising family had even pulled a piece of cloth between two empty pillories to create a makeshift roof.

The shopkeepers were only just closing their stalls, a few of them whispering amongst themselves. It was as if it were snowing, and the landscape was changing – but instead of snow, it was families who were falling from the sky.

Arushi and Tatters avoided the circle of Sunrisers to reach Ka. He was awake, wincing in his pillory. His knees were red and torn. Yesterday evening, his mother had brought him a cloak, but someone had stolen it for themselves. His hairs stood on end, his naked skin like a plucked chicken.

You should ask him how he feels about keeping a secret, grouched Lal, unsympathetic.

'Idir. Are you all right?' asked Tatters.

'I'm fine,' said Ka. 'My tasna will have a fit when she sees they took my arrud, but I'm fine.'

Tatters glanced towards the Sunrisers. 'Do you want me to find it for you?'

Arushi nodded. 'While you do that, I'll finish my duties for the day. Ka, let's get you out of here.'

It was easy to find the thief. Amongst the Sunrisers, there wasn't one kher. An arrud was a distinct, square piece of cloth with a hole for the neck, unlike any human garments. The person who had taken the cloak was an old woman with few teeth, snoring with her mouth open, leaning against Siobhan's statue. With only a grimy stana and no shoes, she must be frozen. Tatters could see cuts and bruises on the tender underside of her feet. He tried to wake her up as gently as possible; but although he swapped between Duskdweller, Samudra dialect and the Wingshade common tongue, she didn't seem to understand what he was saying. She let him pull the bright kher fabric away from her, shivering but not fighting for it.

By the time Tatters returned, Arushi had read out the pardon and unlocked all the pillories. Ka was stretching, cringing at the ache in his shoulders and back.

'Do you have any idea what this is about?' asked Tatters.

Arushi shrugged. 'All I know is there are more on their way.'

Tatters handed Ka his cloak. The scars along the young man's back were healing, black-brown lines on the red skin, purple bruises along the edges, some wounds still seeping. Ka pulled his arrud over his head.

'From what I gathered,' said Ka, his voice muffled by the fabric, 'they are running from the Renegades.'

Tatters' gaze went from the old woman – knobbly hands, wrinkled face – to the people squatting around her and beyond, clogging the square with muddy covers. He listened to the raspy breaths, like those of sick or suffering men. A couple of them were muttering prayers to Harita, the name the Wingshade gave Groniz.

He thought of the first time Hawk hugged him. The first time he smiled at her.

Could I have guessed it would come to this? Could I have seen it coming? Could I have stopped it?

Before Lal could answer, Ka went on: 'Do you know there was a messenger with them? He didn't go through the main gates, but to the entrance near the Pit. He wants our people's help to get through the city without trouble.'

A messenger. This was getting worse.

Who did she send? said Lal. They both felt the same secret horror at the idea she might have come in person.

'How do you know all this?' Arushi asked.

Ka smirked. 'My family came to let me know I'd be missing all the fun. They didn't stick around, though.'

'Let's go see this messenger,' Arushi decided, undaunted.

This was the worst news Tatters had heard in a long time. He crossed the city in a daze, behind Ka and Arushi. For the first time in years, the collar shone. It was only a dull glow for now, but it was steadily growing stronger. Already it was too hot to be comfortable.

Calm down, thought Lal.

Tatters didn't feel like calming down. He was running out of options. The Winged Maidens hadn't been able to fend off Hawk, and now she was sending her soldiers across the Shadowpass.

The Nest is still safe, said Lal.

But for how long? It's hardly a stronghold.

Hawk was a brilliant mage; worse, she was a brilliant teacher. Her army was trained to counter mindbrawling techniques. And they were good. Not all as good as her, but good enough to break through the Nest, if they had the numbers.

What's Passerine's role in all this?

Neither he nor Lal had the answer.

For all Lal's talk about keeping their emotions under control, Tatters could sense she was febrile. A weight had sunk in the pit of his stomach; it was as if he'd swallowed a stone and his throat was roughened by its grit.

'Are you coming?' Arushi asked.

Tatters detached Lal from the forefront of his mind. This was not the time to be mindrambling. He rubbed his eyes. When they were closed, he felt a lurch, as if he were falling. He kept them open.

No-one was guarding the entrance of the Pit, which was unusual. Tatters spotted a few children milling not far from the front door, probably so they could warn the adults if humans approached the gate. Amongst them, he recognised one of Yua's sons, so he waved at him. Shy, the child didn't wave back.

'Where is your tasna?' asked Arushi.

The kid stared and wouldn't answer.

'The messenger must already be inside,' said Ka, striding ahead.

Arushi paused. She frowned at Tatters. 'Are you sure you're all right?'

He nodded, although it made his head swim. Maybe he shouldn't come any further.

'There's a banner,' Ka called out from the end of the street, pointing.

Tatters could see it if he squinted. It had been planted beside a tree. The wind caught it, a dash of red and black in the twilight.

He didn't need to look at the heraldry. The messenger had tethered their horse to a branch, and it was grazing the leaves.

Ka ambled back towards them, hands resting on his belt. 'What are you doing?' he grumbled. 'Are we going to see what's going on, or not? There's an iwdan sent from the Sunriser side, and you're not curious?'

The messenger was a kher. It was a small relief. 'You never said the messenger was iwdan,' said Tatters.

Ka lifted both hands, palms up, in a 'what does it matter?' gesture. 'An aniybu, from what I heard. But it'll be easier to see with our own eyes.'

Mezyan. It has to be him, said Lal.

'Ka is right,' said Arushi. 'We should just go and check out what's happening.' She studied Tatters thoughtfully. 'Unless you don't want to come.'

Tatters weighed his options. Mezyan wasn't Hawk. He had let him go once before. Lal grumbled that they couldn't trust an old, unused friendship; that it was as reliable as a rusted weapon, or a shield of rotted wood.

I need to know what's going on, Tatters thought. *Otherwise, I'll never be able to protect us from Hawk.*

Lal was bitter. *You were never able to protect people from her.*

Despite the risk, he muttered that he was coming, that he was sorry for being awkward. Ka turned away impatiently, whilst Arushi lingered to walk beside him. The Pit was empty: there were no men seated in the doorways, no women carrying babies over their hips, no games happening in the shade of the porticos. It was uncanny.

They found the khers in their main square. The adults had gathered, standing or sitting around the plaza, some resting against the walls, features framed by the painted mural, some cross-legged on the dusty floor.

Arushi picked someone's front door to lean against. A group seated across the landing shuffled aside for her. Settling beside her, Tatters spotted Ganez further down the circle, with the other men from Arushi's family. He had crossed his hands behind the nape of his neck and spread his legs, his posture not altogether friendly.

'What's happening?' Tatters asked.

Arushi kept her eyes focused on the centre of the square. 'We'll know soon enough.'

Tatters stood next to her, so close their shoulders touched. When she didn't move away, he leaned some of his weight on her. She smiled.

There was a clank of metal, something bulky being dragged across the ground. It was Mezyan, as Lal had guessed. He was carrying a cauldron that was nearly his size and, judging from the liquid sloshing down its sides, was full of water. Tatters watched with the khers as Mezyan lugged his weight through the square. He blackened his hands with the soot of the pot. He lost a lot of water on his way.

At the centre of the square, a fireplace had been built. Mezyan hoisted the cauldron above the pit, then lit the wood. He fussed around the flames for a while before they caught, spilling thick smoke. At last, the logs were burning, and he stood panting beside his pot, wiping his soiled hands on his trousers.

Tatters sat down at Arushi's feet, so he would be less visible in the crowd. He pulled his cloak up over his neck to hide, as much as possible, the glint of the collar. From the relative safety of this position, he observed Mezyan. The halfbreed looked older. Even from afar, Tatters could tell his face had heavier lines, with wrinkles down his mouth and eyes, white and grey lines in his hair. His armour, padded leather with velvet on the outside and steel plates on the inside, lay in chunky flaps over his arms and thighs, dulled with use.

He still wore Tatters' old scarf.

Arushi let herself drop down next to Tatters. Casually, she took his hand and squeezed it, not looking at him, as if this was nothing much. He squeezed back.

'What's the water about?' he asked. 'Is he inviting you to dinner?'

'He wants to talk. Whoever cooks with him is ready to listen.'

It didn't look like anyone was. Mezyan waited on his own with his simmering water while the khers watched. Arushi stroked the back of Tatters' hand with her thumb.

Ka, who had been talking with other members of the crowd, came to stand in front of where Tatters was crouched, towering above him.

'You know the aniybu,' he stated. 'I'm sure you do. You've been acting strangely since you heard there was a messenger. Tell me about him.'

Arushi let go of his hand. Several conversations whispered across the square, but everyone kept their voices low. To Mezyan, scraps of words must be coming to him from all directions. He must know they were about him. Still, he stood patiently beside his cauldron.

Tatters considered Mezyan, then Arushi's tense, tired face.

'Do you know him?' she asked.

Don't, said Lal.

Tatters nestled closer to Arushi. She let him rest his shoulder against hers. Lal was cut off.

'You know the iwdan who taught me about your culture?'

She nodded.

'It's him.'

Her eyes widened. She turned towards him so fast she nearly

266

bashed her horns against his nose. Even when her face was guarded, she was lovely.

'Is that true?' she asked.

'I knew it,' said Ka, sounding smug.

'Is what true?' Yua said, skipping up to them. Arushi moved away from Tatters, letting Lal resurface. Yua's eyes were laughing as she nudged Tatters with her elbow. 'Don't go flirting with my sister, flatface. I'll carve out the horns you haven't got.'

Today she'd tied long ribbons to her horns, which fell down her shoulders, plaited with her hair. At the end of the ribbons she'd threaded colourful pebbles, which rested against her collarbone.

'You look wonderful, as always,' said Tatters. Yua chuckled.

'Shouldn't you be saying that to Arushi?' She turned to her sister, who gave her a no-nonsense look. 'You know flatterers are the worst ones,' Yua added.

Arushi didn't crack a smile, instead catching her sister's horn in her hand and tugging it, the kher equivalent of boxing someone's ears.

'Ow, ow, I get it!' laughed Yua. 'I'll stop, I promise!'

When Arushi let go, Yua turned to Tatters. She pulled her braids back in place. 'So, tell me. What's true, O great liar?'

Tatters pointed towards the centre of the square. 'The iwdan over there ...'

'The halfbreed,' corrected Arushi.

'You're open-minded for someone hitting on a human,' teased Yua.

'Well, he is.'

'If you're not interested, don't let me bore you,' said Tatters. He couldn't help smiling. He liked Yua's easy laughter, the way her face shone when she smiled, the tenderness she displayed towards her sister.

'No, no, do tell,' said Yua.

'Tatters' iwdan manners come from that man,' explained Arushi.

Ka was quiet and serious. He kept his eyes on Tatters.

'What's his name?' asked Yua, taking a seat beside them, placing her hands behind her back to recline against the floor.

'Mezyan,' answered Tatters.

It was as if uttering his name had brought him to life. Mezyan spoke up, projecting his voice across the square.

'I understand why you don't trust me,' he said. 'So, I will not bother you for long. But first, let me bring you word of the Renegades. I will be brief.'

Arushi sat with her back straight, stiff. Next to her, Yua slouched happily. When Ka focused his attention on Mezyan, his eyes gleamed in the slanting light of dusk.

'We believe that the only people who'll ascend are the ones who do good in this world, whether you can mindlink or not.'

It had been a long time since Hawk had talked about this. A long time since Tatters had believed these words.

'All creatures are equal. Iwdan are equal to mages.' Mezyan had caught their interest. Not a murmur interrupted his clear, confident plea. 'Lightborns are equal to iwdan, too. We are all siblings. This is what we fight for. This is why we need your help.'

Mezyan fell silent, standing alone beside his pot. Vapour drifted from the surface of the cauldron. Tatters wondered if he would give up when the water boiled dry, or before that.

It was interesting to see the khers' reactions. Ka was shocked. Arushi was thoughtful, but not altogether won over; a restraint remained. She needed time to consider the implications. But Yua's eyes glittered like semi-precious stones, like the beads decorating her plaits.

'I think I need to hear more of this,' she whispered.

'Don't get excited,' said Arushi.

In the air, Tatters could taste violence. Unsaid ideas hung there – revenge, retribution. What people deserved. What they would take, if it was not given.

It soured the Renegades, said Lal. *It will sour this place, too, until it's a battlefield, not a home.*

'I wouldn't listen to the Renegades,' Tatters found himself saying.

Ka shook his head. 'What would you know about it? You're human.'

Yua got up, patting Tatters' shoulder as she did so. 'It's not your story, collarbound. We'll choose how this tale ends.'

Ka nodded, a grim set to his jaw. 'I'll talk to my family.' The way he announced it made it clear he would vouch for Mezyan.

With a dance-like step, Yua hopped up to Ganez. Arushi followed her with her eyes, but only sighed.

'This will get us into trouble,' she muttered.

It's done now, thought Lal.

Tatters studied Mezyan. He had short, straight hair; a short, straight silhouette. He was watching the people watching him with soft brown eyes. Having spotted the sole human in a crowd of khers, Mezyan kept coming back to Tatters as he glanced around the square.

He hasn't recognised you, said Lal.

She was interrupted as Arushi placed a hand on Tatters' forearm. He pretended he hadn't felt it, although it was impossible for a mage not to react to kher contact – it was as if the sun was suddenly dulled. His senses were diminished and Lal, of course, was silent.

Arushi's touch was gentle. Tatters didn't always need Lal.

In a corner, Yua chatted excitedly with Ganez. Then she pushed on and out of sight, while Ganez got up and headed for another group of men. If Mezyan noticed, he didn't show any signs of impatience or eagerness.

It took some time before the khers agreed on what to do. Groups came and went, whispering like waves. A slow tide of folk grew closer to Mezyan. Women discussed what the longlived wanted, then broke apart, and debated it with other women from other families. Ka stood beside Yua as she went from group to group; a longlived's words and wants were taken seriously.

Arushi stayed beside Tatters. With her armour from the Nest, she was no better than him at talking to her own people. He took her hand. It was her turn to pretend she didn't care. Her fingers, callous from military training, brushed against his skin.

In the end, Yua made the first move. She walked up to the cauldron, a small sack of dried beans under her arm. Once she'd emptied her bundle in the bubbling pot, Mezyan touched his horns in thanks, and let himself smile at last. She sat down beside his fire.

After her came Ganez, with a handful of dried mushrooms. Then a kher Tatters didn't know, carrying a bowl of soft cheese. Then Ka with a pouch of salt, and someone else with dried meat. An old woman brought a wooden ladle to stir the soup. Soon a circle of khers had formed around Mezyan.

Arushi got up, dusting her trousers. 'I'd better see what he's on about.'

'If nothing else, you'll get a meal out of it.' Tatters smiled.

He rested against the wall, arranging his stana around his legs. Bits of earth and hay stuck to his hair.

Arushi went to fetch her mother; Uaza used Arushi's arm as a cane, holding a sprig of sage in her free hand. She added the herb to the pot. Arushi helped her mother sit down beside the fire, tucking covers and cushions around her until she was at ease. Yua stood beside Mezyan, her high-pitched voice carrying above the rumble of conversations. As she talked, she threw her head back and smiled, showing her teeth, or toyed with the pearls woven in her hair.

When the broth was ready, the khers brought out wooden bowls. Everyone took their share and drank standing up, talking to their neighbours, debating what the Renegades believed and what they planned to do. They questioned Mezyan, before discussing what he'd said far from earshot. All the while, Yua stayed beside him, sipping at her bowl with small cat-licks, not using a spoon.

Arushi poured Uaza a share, before bringing Tatters an empty bowl.

'Come and have some,' she said. 'You might as well.'

Ready? he asked.

Lal wasn't amused. *Are you sure it's worth it?*

I always trusted Mezyan.

But people change.

Tatters accepted the bowl Arushi was handing him. *We'll see, won't we?*

Even though Tatters wasn't tall, he stood out. Khers tended to be smaller than humans. When he strode past them, all he saw at eye-height was a forest of horns, all different sizes, like the leafless branches of a winter forest. Their tattooed skin and their colourfully woven clothes contrasted with his sober attire. Most khers had dark hair, too, making his red locks easy to spot.

Mezyan caught sight of him well before he reached the cauldron. As he came closer, Mezyan's expression changed. It was like watching a cloud pass in front of the sun – colours drained and greyed, and the light of the world subtly shifted.

Now he's recognised you, said Lal.

Tatters dipped his bowl inside the cauldron, careful not to

burn his fingers. The dried chilli floating at the surface let out hot, spicy fumes that stung his eyes. Arushi picked up a bucket of cheese from the floor and served Tatters a spoonful. The thick, creamy white melted in the soup.

'Thanks,' he coughed.

He wiped his face on his sleeve. Kids shoved each other around the broth as they struggled to catch the best pieces, leaning over dangerously, bashing other people's spoons out of the way until they caught the pepper, mushroom or herb they wanted.

Arushi dunked a cup into the broth and thickened it with cheese, using only one hand to ladle it in her bowl. At her feet, a few hens were pecking at the crumbs. A rooster with a brilliant green tail walked over her toes, ignoring the blazing fire.

Yua joined them, sweat on her forehead from the flames. Mezyan and Ganez were behind her.

There was an awkward pause.

'It's been a long time,' said Tatters. He expected Mezyan to tap his horns, but instead the halfbreed extended his arm.

'It has,' he said.

They touched wrists. Mezyan had a new tattoo coiling around his elbow, depicting the half-open wing of a bird taking flight. His red nasivyati – Tatters' scarf – was resting across his shoulders, above his padded leather jacket. His hair was cropped short, rising a few inches from his skull. It was streaked with white and hardened his features. Amongst all these flawless, youthful khers, he looked older than he was. His human blood aged him.

They were all standing in silence: him, Mezyan, the two sisters, Ganez. Everyone seemed to be waiting for him – or maybe for Mezyan – to do something.

'So, you made it,' said Mezyan.

Tatters wondered if Mezyan had thought he'd died crossing the Shadowpass. If Hawk believed that. That might explain why no-one had come after him. The underworlds were the best kind of hiding-place: who hunted after the dead?

'From what I heard, you made it too,' said Tatters.

Mezyan nodded. 'We have. Our dream has come true. Iwdan, mages and ungifted, living in harmony together, sharing the workload.' Mezyan shone with inner light. Tatters had only seen the faithful glow like this before. Mezyan turned to address everyone in the group, and somehow his heat matched that from the fire. 'We're building a stairway,' whispered Mezyan. 'So, we will ascend together.'

In other words, the Renegades have won, said Lal.

In other words, those who opposed them were hanging from gibbets, with wind playing through their hair. Hawk was seated on something akin to a throne, passing judgements and laws, giving out orders, and writing poetry about the glorious unification of the convents under one ruler. Poor folk probably sang those poems, too, when they saw her ride past.

'You know you are always welcome back,' said Mezyan.

Tatters stiffened. There was a sound like metal shackles closing with a snap. When he checked, both sisters were staring at him. Yua was smiling, but a rather severe smile; the one a mother would give a child she knew was lying to her. Smirking, Arushi lifted an eyebrow.

'You were a Renegade?' She sounded like she couldn't bring herself to believe it.

Tatters gritted his teeth. 'An honorary Renegade, I think would be the right term. I wasn't exactly one of them.' He wished he could mindlink to a kher, and tell Mezyan to hold his tongue.

Mezyan's eyes were still as liquid as before, pale brown, like something melting. But his voice and his stance were more military. He sounded scarred. The childlike softness Tatters remembered was gone.

'You were always one of us.'

Tatters had to force himself to keep his tone even. 'Always. Forever. Never. They're tough words.'

As are 'good' and 'evil', prompted Lal. *As are 'dreams come true' or 'everyone living in harmony'. There was barely harmony between the Renegades when there was a handful of them. They bickered like tomcats.*

Tatters couldn't say he disagreed. He found it difficult to believe the convents would bow to Hawk's rule without putting up a fight – especially not the Winged Maidens. And khers and ungifted would be baying for revenge. Did Hawk encourage them to murder mages, or did she turn a blind eye? He doubted she would stand in the way of her supporters to prevent them from tearing their old leaders to pieces.

'If harmony is the rule, why have all these Sunrisers fled?' asked Arushi. 'They're flooding the streets.' It was the question Tatters had wanted to ask.

'There are some compromises that are impossible. The iwdan have compromised for too long,' said Mezyan. 'It's time for us to reclaim what's ours.'

'Hear, hear,' said Ganez. His voice echoed like a stone falling down a well. 'We live locked up like beasts, when before the whole world was ours to roam. The mages owe us our land.'

Tatters held his tongue. What people thought should be theirs, what they felt they were due – that was treacherous ground. It was a trail that led into quicksand. He listened as Yua and her brother discussed what khers deserved and what the mages refused to give them. Arushi didn't voice her opinion.

If they were tackling tricky subjects, he might as well bring up the one he had come for. Tatters drank some soup. The thick beans and spices made a mushy paste that burnt his tongue, only softened by the melting cheese. He asked: 'And Passerine, in all that?'

Either Mezyan had become a better actor, or he hadn't been expecting this. 'Passerine?' he repeated.

'Sir Passerine, I guess. The high mage. The one living at the Nest.'

The one who fought with double-handed spears and no shields. The one who didn't understand the concept of training and would beat me to a pulp. The one Hawk couldn't get enough of. Shall I give you three guesses?

Mezyan paled. He seemed sincerely taken aback; but then, sincerity was an emotion, and all emotions can be faked. He rubbed his white horns, like a human would scratch their nose, to buy themselves time before a lie.

'I didn't know about that,' he said. 'I thought he was ... It doesn't matter. I didn't know he had come here.'

'Who is Sir Passerine?' asked Arushi.

'No friend of mine.' Mezyan didn't shout or growl, but he spat in the fire. He did it in a quiet, humble way; most soldiers spit at a name to show how tough they are, but he did it like people throw salt in the air for a lightborn, to dispel a curse, because it was something he had to do. Tatters couldn't remember Passerine doing anything that would justify that kind of reaction.

Mezyan stared straight at Tatters. 'I'm sorry.'

It was Tatters' turn to be bewildered. Why should he suddenly be sorry?

'What are you sorry about?' Arushi asked, obviously trying to put the pieces together.

Rather than answering, Mezyan changed the subject. Soon he was engrossed in a conversation with Yua and Ganez about what the Renegades might mean for the Nest, and how the khers could gain more independence from the mages with – and without – outside help. He shared stories about khers stealing mages' weapons, about convent guards turning against their masters in a coordinated attack, about trying to ally with human folk from the farmlands who shared their grudges.

'We are planning on breaking up their little festivities tonight,' Mezyan announced, a playful glint in his eye. 'I've got some men in the woods. With your help, we could give the mages a scare.'

Arushi didn't respond. Tatters could feel her looking at him; if she were a mage, he would be prepared for her mindlink, for her trying to read his emotions.

As the sun sunk over the Edge, Mezyan talked to all the khers, one by one. Tatters went to sit in a corner with Arushi. They must have been the only ones not to mention politics, commenting instead on the colours of the sunset, the brilliant reds and golds and pinks that cut across the sky, then dimmed to purple. When the sky was black, salted with stars, Arushi talked about her work. Tatters made fun of the lawmage Goldie. She laughed, and said she knew exactly who he meant.

Tatters didn't finish his meal – it was too spicy. Arushi drank the tepid soup for him.

'You keep a lot of secrets, don't you?' she said, apropos of nothing.

'I'm not a reliable friend.' *Or a reliable something-more-than-a-friend, either.*

Around the dying fire, children were lying against each other like sleepy dogs, wreathed in smoke.

'What is Mezyan sorry about?'

Tatters shook his head. 'I don't know.'

He wasn't sure she believed him, but she didn't insist.

When the moon appeared, a podgy, not-quite-full moon, Yua came to warn them that Mezyan was leaving. He had a small retinue of men, whom the khers had agreed to let through the city without alerting the town guards. Arushi and Tatters exchanged a glance.

'Thanks to your friend, my sister is going to cut off her hair,' grumbled Arushi. 'And become a highwaywoman.'

'She'll hang mages' brooches on her horns,' added Tatters. He didn't say: *He is not my friend.*

Yua laughed; Arushi rolled her eyes.

'Don't be so glum,' Yua said. 'Anyway, I like my hair.'

Mezyan said goodnight to the assembled khers. He gave each of them a word in private, an encouragement or a promise of better days. Their hope was his best leverage against them. Hope had always been the weapon Hawk wielded best.

Tatters felt mildly ill. It might have been the soup.

'I'm going to bed,' Arushi told him. 'It's been a long day. And I don't want to be a part of what happens next.'

'You could stop it, if you wanted.' It was wishful thinking. She was the head of the guards, but she wouldn't pick her lords over her family.

As he expected, she shook her head. But her answer surprised him.

'You know, I was thinking about what you were saying the other day: if everyone was kinder, the world would be a better place. That's true. But you would still have servants and slaves, powerless ungifted and iwdan.' Arushi had eyes as deep as the night. 'Surely, it's better to break the bond, rather than rely on the master's goodwill?'

Tatters' mouth tasted of ash. He'd thought something similar, before he'd seen the cost of breaking the people who were part of the bond. Hawk wanted to change the world, but she burned what didn't bend.

'A collar isn't the same,' he said. 'It's not made of people.'

'No.' She let out a quiet, hushed sigh. 'Still, I can't stop this.

Ka is right. This is not for you or me to decide. It is more than us. It is about the whole Pit, and everyone must choose together.'

From her tone, this was the end of the conversation. He leaned in to kiss her, on the lips maybe, on the cheek if she had turned. But she lifted a hand to stop him.

'I don't know about this,' she said. 'You've said it yourself: you're not reliable.'

Tatters tried to ignore the satisfaction coming off Lal.

'I need some time.' Arushi wasn't angry, only stating a fact. 'You didn't tell me about the fleshbinding, or about the Renegades. Maybe I don't know you as well as I thought.'

There was only one thing he could answer. 'I understand.'

It was strange, stilted, to touch wrists with Arushi, when they had been so close before. Tatters watched her as she walked away, never turning back.

We need to deal with Mezyan, said Lal. He could tell she was relieved by Arushi's reaction. It was just the two of them again. Tatters felt old; an ache throbbed in his chest, as if he had been running for too long and had only just stopped and found out it hurt.

Mezyan was beside his horse, a few feet away from the main square. Tatters joined him, as if only to help prepare for his departure. The mount was a small bay mare, bred for endurance over long distances. Nervous, she jerked her head, tugging at where the reins were tied to a branch. With a shushing noise, Tatters reached for her neck and mouth, holding her close to the bit. He petted the mare until she calmed down, only swishing her tail against the flies now and again.

There had been a time when he knew all the horses in the Renegades' herd, but he didn't know this one.

What did you expect? said Lal. *It's been years.*

Still, a pang of nostalgia seized him at the idea that even the horses were different now. Mezyan was busy tightening the strap of his saddle, preparing to return to his men-at-arms. Tatters used some hay to rub down the white lines in the mare's coat, left by salt and sweat. The warmth of her, and the smell, took him back to when brushing down a horse after a day of riding was his routine.

Don't dwell on it, advised Lal.

For a while, nobody spoke. The cold dulled the smell of the gutter. Tough winter midges flew in small clouds around them.

When Mezyan unknotted his reins, ready to climb back onto his mare, they stood in silence for too long, each trying to find the remains of the friends they had been in the adults they were.

'So, you didn't make it, after all,' said Mezyan, shaking his head.

Lal was as confused as she was frustrated. *What does he mean, we didn't make it?*

'This is why you're here, isn't it?' Mezyan put a hand on Tatters' shoulder. It was their first friendly contact in years; it felt alien. Maybe sensing this, Mezyan took away his hand. 'Look, when you get back to Passerine, give him a message. From Hawk.'

He gazed at Tatters as if he wished to find someone else inside him, as if he expected Passerine himself to be there, and he was trying to see one man through the other.

'If he doesn't give back the eyas, the Nest will burn. That is her promise.'

Before Tatters could ask for an explanation, Mezyan had a put a foot in his stirrup and was throwing one leg above his mare's back. Once he was astride the horse, he looked more like a warrior and less like a friend – the moment to talk was lost, and Tatters stepped back as the mare moved away, snorting against the flies which clung to her.

What's an eyas? asked Lal.

Chapter Thirteen

After the rituals, it was time for the feast. At that point, the Groniz festival was reclaimed by the mages. They brought in musicians playing the viola or the harp. They gossiped while they wolfed down meat, trying not to stain their robes with the juices. Mages believed they would ascend. Their minds, already elevated by their gift, were only one step removed from a lightborn's. They had no reason to cry.

The priests ate silently and tolerated the profane music. The ungifted didn't mind swapping the singing for instruments, or the praying for eating. Only they were able to enjoy each part of the festival to the full.

The apprentices assembled around one of the firepits. Despite the uniformly green belts, followers belonging to high mages didn't mingle with lower-class disciples. With or without the belts, they recognised each other. Kilian sat with his legs spread out, the precious shoes poking out in front of him, where he could admire them. The girl with the vines around her ankles was now removing them to rub her sore feet.

On the other side of the fire, Isha caught someone staring at her. She glanced through the flames at Passerine, leaning against a tree.

When he'd got her attention, he moved closer to the fire,

silence following in his wake. The apprentices didn't seem to know whether to rise for him, or sit and stare.

'I believe we are gathering for the dance.' His voice was not unlike the priest's – deep, quiet, unbroken by emotion.

Isha understood this as a cue. 'We're on our way,' she said, as she leapt up. She followed Passerine away from the firepit, the apprentices behind her scrabbling to grab their shoes and wine.

'How have you been?' he asked.

She swallowed. She thought of herself, memories in pieces like brittle hay, wafting away despite how tightly she tried to bundle them. After the attack on her farm, he had anchored her. Somehow, he was still an anchor, even without meaning to be. In his presence, the questions fluttering in her mind stilled.

'I have been learning,' she said. 'It's not always easy.'

He nodded. 'It never is.'

A silver brooch adorned his usual robes. The brooch had a precious stone so dark it took her some time to realise it was green. He was stronger than most high mages, broader, and he moved with purpose, like cats do when hunting, sleek and silent. He looked at everything intently.

'Your teacher . . .' Passerine offered Isha his hand to step up the slight slope leading to the Edge. His skin was surprisingly hot. 'Are you happy with how he treats you?'

Isha pictured Sir Daegan in an abandoned room as she nailed a cage in place.

'He doesn't treat me badly,' she said.

'Was he the one who taught you how to do a double?'

He let go of her hand. She wondered what to say. Apprentices never talked about Tatters to high mages, but Passerine wasn't any high mage. And she wanted help. She wanted answers.

'No,' she said. 'I . . . I have another teacher.'

At the front of the Temple, the Doorkeeper called out for

the dance to begin. Lady Siobhan echoed her words, urging the mages to join the priests for the heart of the festival.

Everyone drifted together for the first and last time that night. A lightborn flew above their heads and people cheered. It was a blue lightborn, and far away, but it was still a good omen. Hopefully it would fly back down once the dance began. Passerine didn't look up.

They reached the space, arching between the trees, that was reserved for the dance. Passerine placed himself beside Sir Daegan, Isha in front of him. The other apprentices clustered around. They were forming two lines face-to-face, which twisted through the Temple's grounds, stretching all the way along the Edge.

The priests were giving out lamps cut from green paper, which would glow brightly when lit, and give out the smell of incense. Isha held hers with both hands.

Lady Siobhan remained in her seat to watch the dance. She was offered a lamp, which she immediately handed to one of her maids. Even from afar, Isha could see how stooped she was. Her thin neck seemed to struggle to hold her layered necklace.

Sir Daegan and Passerine exchanged stiff, polite greetings. They didn't touch wrists; the lamps made for a good excuse not to touch. Each high mage was flanked with disciples protectively gathered around them. Passerine was the only high mage by himself. Because of that, and because he was the only Sunriser there, he stood out. He stood out nearly as much as a girl with a kher tattoo. Isha smiled at him. They were strangers here, but they were together.

Passerine answered her smile. His mindlink was as soft as a feather brushing against her skin. *At another, less crowded time, we should talk about your progress here. You can tell me about this other teacher of yours.*

Her mindlink skills were better, but she still didn't dare answer him. When she nodded, she was aware of Sir Daegan's eyes narrowing at her.

'Bobbing your head to the music, are you?' he asked.

Isha pretended to be absorbed by the paper lamp between her hands.

She sensed Passerine's amusement. *You don't need to nod. You can simply lower your defences around the thoughts you would like me to access. It's a subtler way of talking through mindlink.*

And a smart way of doing it, too, if one of the mages was less experienced than the other. She was proud that Passerine wanted to share mindlink techniques with her, however modest. She let him perceive her agreement and her happiness. Such a method had its limits, though. The person unguarding their mind would have a hard time lying. She wondered how they were supposed to prevent unwanted knowledge from slipping away.

Do you need to lie to me? Passerine asked. She glanced at him, but he wasn't looking in her direction.

On the other hand, Sir Daegan was still staring. Although he tolerated her link to Passerine, fraternising too openly with another high mage might try his patience. She turned away.

She focused not on sending the message, but on thinking it clearly, so that it would be easy to spot. *That's what mindlink is about. Lying.*

She heard him laugh, although his lips didn't move. *Yes, you have a teacher who isn't old Daegan.*

Two lines of apprentices, disciples, mages, priests and ungifted were now spread out along the Edge. Young priests bearing candles were walking down the line. It was like watching a snake uncoiling as the lamps were lit, each scale radiant.

The humming began with the priests, soon picked up by the crowd. Isha added her voice to the chorus. The dance had variations, but the baseline of the song, and of the steps, would be the same everywhere. She lifted the lamp above her head. In front of her, Passerine did the same. She spotted Kilian, mouth half-open, humming loudly. They started hitting their feet on the ground to keep time. When everyone was holding the tune, the priests started singing, and the dancers started spinning.

Swapping place with the person in front of her, stepping sideways and forwards, backwards, twirling – Isha had done it every year. She could have done it with her eyes closed without bumping into anyone. Mages and ungifted repeated the core of the dance, while the priests wove between them according to a more complex pattern.

It was the only time of the year when mages and ungifted danced the same steps, to the same sound. For a short, precious spell of time, they behaved like equals. As they swayed, the Edge blurred. There were stars above them. There were stars below them, beyond the abrupt end of the cliff. And they were stars. They were a creature of light writhing on the ground.

The Groniz dance wasn't about finding a human partner: it was about inviting a lightborn to dance with them.

The song vibrated through Isha, as if she were an instrument and the whistling wind was playing her, thrumming against her ribs. She breathed in the sickly scent of blood and fragrant smoke.

When they'd celebrated Groniz at the farm, a lightborn had never come. But lightborns were more common beyond the Edge.

A flash of bright yellow light, like a slow thunderbolt, lit up their procession from tip to toe. Sir Daegan's smile was hungry, eating at the light. His wrinkled features shone vivid gold for an instant. He caught Isha watching him and his grin widened, showing teeth that glinted yellow before dulling back to white.

The priests sang louder. People strained, raising their arms in the hope of touching the aurora, even though it was flying well above the treeline. Looking up was like staring at a mirror. The golden pattern against the backdrop of the sky matched the green candlelight against the backdrop of the grass. The lightborn rippled colours and light across the night sky. Isha felt as if she were falling upwards, as if she had been caught out standing on the wrong side of the Edge, treading the sky, and she needed to find solid ground again. Everything was the same liquid darkness, everywhere stars glinted. Green and gold mingled while lightborn and humans danced together.

Then the lightborn left, and they were on the cliff once more, and it was cold. A cloud crept over the stars and wrapped itself around the moon. The dancers were out of breath; the dance slowed. Isha found herself out of time with her neighbours. She struggled to find her footing again.

Some commotion further down the line was breaking up their rhythm. That was what had caused the discrepancy in the dance. Some people slackened the pace whilst others stopped altogether, craning their necks to spot the cause of the trouble. A group was wading through the procession, heading for Lady Siobhan's platform.

Sir Daegan's mind let out a short, stark instruction. His followers moved immediately, with the coordination of a flock – even Isha found herself reacting. Sir Daegan closed the distance between himself and the supreme mage's platform. He was the first to move, but all the high mages had the same instinct, bringing their apprentices with them, blocking the way to their leader. It reminded Isha of the way bees flew to defend their queen. Mindlink meant they behaved like a swarm of insects, like one entity.

Passerine followed as if he were one of the disciples, despite the glare Sir Daegan cast him over his shoulder. Now Isha could make out someone on horseback, reining in their mount at the bottom of the steps. Lady Siobhan pushed herself up from her chair, trembling as she rested her weight on the malachite cane. The priests and ungifted didn't seem to understand what was happening – they hadn't been told about this part of the choreography.

At last, the intruders were close enough for Isha to see them. She felt something like a kick in her stomach; painful, sudden. It was a kher. Khers were forbidden to tread the hallowed ground of the Temple, yet here he was, his hair cut so short she thought for a moment he had shaved his head. His horns gleamed white.

Isha had never seen a kher with white horns. Maybe he sanded down the outer layers, revealing the white keratin beneath.

The kher sat astride his horse, soldiers flanking him on either side. His escort was a mix of humans and khers in full brigandine armour, with helmets from which mail-curtains hung. Nobody wore clothing Isha recognised; none of the khers, as far as she could tell, were from the Pit. Behind him, a line of five or so prisoners, dark-skinned, albeit all lighter than Passerine. They were wearing stana, but the wrapped robes were frayed at the bottom, dusty, bleached by sun and bad weather. They had been ripped off at the elbows, revealing scarred forearms.

They were tied to each other by a rope, which was fastened to the kher's saddle.

They were Sunrisers.

Isha noticed the mages were trying to mindlink the intruders, but the few humans in the group were close enough to touch the khers, and thus become immune to magic. The captives only stared, dull-eyed, at the throng of believers. The ungifted and priests whispered curses, but they didn't press too close. No-one was armed except for the intruders, their blades glinting at their sides. The Doorkeeper didn't seem to know what to do. No-one did.

The white-horned kher cut the rope from his saddle and tugged at it. The line of prisoners stumbled forward, tripping over each other's feet.

'My greetings, good folk of the Nest, good men and women of the Temple,' said the kher. His voice, which carried across the grounds, was that of a middle-aged man.

The Doorkeeper answered before anyone else could, her bony fists curled tight in rage. 'You are committing blasphemy. Do you not know this land is sacred?' The crowd muttered in agreement.

'Yes, I know this is a violation of Temple rules, but rest assured it will be a short one,' said the kher, untroubled. His gaze trailed past the Doorkeeper, on to Lady Siobhan, where she stood quivering with age and cold, her necklace like a yoke.

The kher lifted his arm. The people attached to the rope were forced closer to his horse. Isha noticed tattoos inked down his fingers, but she was too far to see their design.

'Lady Siobhan. I have brought you a gift. These are not free mages but hostages. As a show of goodwill, I hereby release them. Please be aware that there are more left behind, and that if you refuse to listen to me, they will be slaughtered like the cattle you killed today.' The kher smiled, and the white of his teeth echoed the white of his horns. 'Who knows, we might even roast and eat them.'

The kher waved to one of his soldiers, who unsheathed a dagger to cut the binds holding the prisoners. Lady Siobhan watched; her followers, waiting for an order, watched in silence with her.

Isha glanced at Passerine. He was very still, as if the kher's words were weights pinning him to the ground.

'This is Sir Cintay of the Redstone convent, and what is left of his followers,' the kher said. 'I suggest you listen to what he has to say.'

A soldier pulled a prisoner out of the line, then thrust him in front of the horse. Sir Cintay had torn shoes and exhausted, hopeless eyes. His arms bore pale lines where the skin had been roughened by rope.

One knee on the ground, he mumbled something through thirst-broken lips.

'You can't hear him, can you?' the kher interrupted. 'When could you ever hear the voices of the lost?'

Lady Siobhan lifted a hand; the kher fell silent. Leaning heavily into her cane, the supreme mage threw her mindlink to every mage present, sharing her words effortlessly.

You are home, Sir Cintay, amongst your people. Tell us what happened.

Her words flowed through the crowd like ink on a page. And Isha felt Sir Cintay's answer, too, sensations more than words. The smell of fire and burning flesh – but it wasn't the hot ash and juicy meat of their celebrations. Shadows lapping at a shore of silver-grey sand. A banner, blood-red as it unfurled to the ground.

He kept one fist planted in the dust, his head bowed low. The other prisoners, worn and wary, circled him.

Pictures swept through their minds as Sir Cintay shared them. Lines of men and women tied to posts along a road. The stench of excrement, knees pressing down on stone. Sweat pouring down their backs during the day, feverish shivers through the night. Glaring sun and moon, like two eyes of one smirking, unpitying face. The tiny feet of flies as they crawled across lips and eyelids.

Lady Siobhan was clutching her cane with both hands. She was a frail old woman, her face bloodless white.

You are our brethren. Relief filled Sir Cintay's mindlink. *We have come to beg, although we are not used to it.*

I will beg this of you – hear what the kher messenger has to say. Hear the word of the Renegades.

***

It was dawn by the time the shock of the event at the Temple settled. Lady Siobhan had agreed to talk, but not at the Temple, not when it suited the Renegades – it had to happen on her own terms. She had insisted the khers leave the Temple grounds, and she had delayed any discussion until morning, once the Groniz festival was officially over. Isha was in the breakfast mess when the bell tolled. She gritted her teeth as the sound echoed through her skull.

Although the bell was early, the mages were awake – most hadn't slept. Those who had tried to sneak in a few hours of sleep were still eager to hear the messenger and dragged themselves out of bed for that purpose.

Above the wide staircase at the centre of the Nest, there was a small platform that served as a balcony to address the people assembled below. When an important announcement needed to be made, the large copper bell was rung and mages flocked to the hall to listen. Only high mages, in times of crisis, could thus summon a meeting.

Isha slipped through the mass of light grey robes without recognising anyone. She could hear scraps of conversations around her. Apprentices pushed past as they searched for friends within the crowd. They were the furthest away from the staircase, near the arches leading to the courtyard. In front of them were the disciples, the countryside mages who had come for the festival, and finally the high mages. She had never witnessed the Nest this full.

On the balcony, Isha could see men and women in ebony-coloured robes, with long greying hair, some of them, including Lady Siobhan herself, resting on precious canes. Isha could easily identify the Sunriser mages, now wearing clean robes and standing in a half-circle behind Lady Siobhan.

Beside them was the half-kher. His bright red stana fell to his ankles, only brightening the shade of his skin and the brilliant white of his horns. He had folded it in a way that was unfamiliar to Isha, baring one shoulder, creating a long, square sleeve on the other arm.

Behind her, someone called out her name. She turned to find it was Kilian, still groggy with sleep.

'I knew I'd find you here. Always the good girl.' He patted her arm. 'Want to come to the dining hall for breakfast?'

'Don't you want to hear what they have to say?' She thought Kilian would care for the bell, but he laughed it off.

'Lady Siobhan is going to introduce the Sunriser mages, that's all. And say that we should care for our brethren of the Sunriser convents.' When Kilian smiled, he used his whole face: lips, cheeks, and eyebrows. His robes were becoming too short for him, and stopped well before his wrists and ankles, showing skin. 'I mean, a new Renegade convent is wild, don't get me wrong, especially if they let khers join. But they're just one convent. What can they do?'

'What about the refugees?'

Kilian shrugged. 'It's a squabble between convents. They're always squabbling. Best thing is to not pick a side.' He yawned largely, shoving his mouth into the crook of his elbow. 'It can't be that bad.'

Isha glanced up again. The kher was talking to the supreme mage, his position relaxed, as if he didn't mind being the only member of his species anywhere near the balcony. Passerine was absent. He should be standing beside Lady Siobhan, with the other high mages, but he was nowhere in sight.

'They might have important news,' she said. *About the Shadowpass, and about my home.*

Someone bumped into Isha, penning her in. The press of people around her, clumped close together, added to the dread pushing down on her, made her feel dizzy.

'The Sunrisers are at war,' Kilian said. 'So what? They always are. We know the drill. Each convent has its own set of rules. It doesn't work. They should build a second Nest. The Winged Maidens could do it, but they don't because of weird religious stuff. No-one wants to be the person to cross the Shadowpass and set it up for them. End of story.'

'I see you're an expert on Sunriser politics.' She couldn't keep the edge out of her voice. So, half the apprentices would scoff down the best parts of breakfast while the Renegades stated their demands. The Nest wasn't teaching her mindlink, but the art of slacking off.

'Keep your hair on.' Kilian stayed by her side. 'I'll listen if you think it's important. But by the time we get to the dining hall, there'll only be stale bread.'

They waited. From the stone arches, the balcony was so far away they wouldn't be able to hear what the leaders were saying. This wasn't an issue, as the mages would mindlink the information, sharing it swiftly and silently. It also meant that, although all the mages would be listening to the conversation happening on the balcony, the servants and the kher guards would be kept in the dark as to what had been said.

Lady Siobhan stepped forward. Reluctantly, people fell silent. Around her, Isha heard apprentices whispering, nudging each other in the ribs, sometimes shouting someone's name before being hushed by the other mages.

From afar, Lady Siobhan was a black shape with a white patch for a head. But her mindlink had none of her old age or hesitancy – it was a young, violent thing that spread through the giants' hall.

Today we welcome the Renegades' representative to the Nest. Let me introduce you to the half-kher Mezyan.

There was an audible intake of breath from the crowd. Although Mezyan was too far for Isha to see his features, his image was mindlinked by the mages. She could picture him as Lady Siobhan did; with a square jaw, greying hair and wrinkles round his eyes, the marks of age shocking on a kher's face. White horns curved from his temples, with lines drawn in ink and ochre across them. There was something stark and hard and military about him.

The Renegades have been at war with the other convents, but they freed the members of the Redstone convent as a sign of goodwill.

Because she was near the apprentices, Isha could also sense the hum of their messages. It was mostly jokes about half-khers and horn-humpers. The humour, she suspected, was there to hide how anxious they felt. Isha tried to ignore them, but it was like trying to ignore the seagulls chattering in the sky.

I trust we will be open-minded about what the Renegades have to say and that they, in turn, have come only with good intent, to find a common ground between the Nest, the established convents and their own, young convent.

Kilian put a hand through his hair, as if to comb it. He smiled at Isha, pushing against her with his shoulder. She rolled her eyes and didn't push back.

Suddenly Lady Siobhan's mindlink was cut off. Isha strained her eyes to catch what was happening, but she could only make out movement on the balcony, not the detail of what the high mages were doing. She only understood what was going on when Mezyan placed his foot on the edge of the balcony and hoisted himself up onto the balustrade, leaving the supreme mage and her followers stranded below.

As he did so, the mages around Lady Siobhan mindlinked what had just taken place, outrage clouding their messages. Information choked the Nest and Isha's mind; she didn't have time to disentangle her thoughts from the ones they flung at her.

The half-kher had touched the supreme mage. Mezyan had cut off her mindlink with his unholy, dirty flesh. The mages radiated their anger, and the image of his hands. For a moment, Isha saw those hands, bright red against Lady Siobhan's pale skin. She saw them as if she had been there, as if she had held them. Down each finger, a tattooed line ended in a circle around his knuckles. Isha wouldn't have known what it was, if someone else hadn't invested the tattoo with meaning, a fascinated and excited horror.

It was a representation of hanged men. Eight of them – one for each finger. He hadn't tattooed his thumbs.

The hallway groaned as the mages, nearly in the same breath, gasped.

Mezyan straightened on the balcony's balustrade, where the slightest push could throw him down to his death. He loomed taller than the high mages around him, well above Lady Siobhan hunched over her cane.

He addressed the hall, shouting at the top of his lungs. His voice bounced off the stone walls.

'People of the Nest! And by people I mean not only those wearing robes, but those walking between them, men and women carrying baskets of food and bed linen, iwdan guarding the doors, you – yes, you, who are so used to the mages' silence that you hardly hear it anymore! I am talking to all of you.'

The hall was still, but not because people were mindlinking. The mages were stunned. Isha observed the reactions around her. She spotted, standing beside the pillars, a few maids who had stopped in their tracks. The kher guards who were posted along the arches had turned towards Mezyan – to listen or to prepare to intervene, it was difficult to say.

'There is more than one way to live. I come with an alternative. The Renegades don't tell you to bow to mages. They teach you how to live by your own rules! And mages, those of you who are sick of the suffering, who are aching for change, you are welcome, too. It is only the blind and the brutes who are our enemies.'

A high mage stepped up to Mezyan. Even from where she was, Isha could imagine what it would be like close up – someone fierce standing tall, smiling downwards, all tooth and horn and war-tattoos. A soldier facing someone old, withered, used to empty chambers and quiet, cruel words.

'This is mad,' whispered Kilian, a mix of fear and awe in his voice.

Mezyan skipped aside, and Isha couldn't tell if the mage had tried to push him. He walked along the balustrade, arms spread out, so obviously enjoying himself, so obviously convinced he was right, that he filled the castle with something it hadn't had in a long time: ideas the size of the giants of old.

'You know,' said Mezyan, 'I came here thinking I would die. Thinking these mages would kill me. They might. Who knows? Who cares? We are thousands. We are strong. We are birthing a new world. And you can be part of it!'

It was like at home, on the farm, when a dog started barking and it set off the whole village. The mages had caught onto the fact that they couldn't use mindlink to shush Mezyan directly, as they couldn't access his thoughts. So, they scuttled after him, trying to cut him off, while some of the apprentices around

Isha hooted; whether to encourage the high mages or mock them, boo Mezyan or goad him on, it wasn't entirely clear. Lady Siobhan called the kher guards forward, but although they gathered around Mezyan, they seemed reluctant to interrupt him.

'Why are they letting him speak?' asked Kilian.

'Maybe they want to hear what he has to say,' Isha answered. For the first time, it seemed to strike Kilian, and maybe other mages, that they were helpless if their guards refused to obey them.

Mezyan turned on his heels with easy grace, without stumbling on the narrow railing. 'If you kill me, there will be war. If you let me free, we will give you a choice.' He jumped out of reach and trod down the balustrade lining the stairs, leaving the mages behind. 'We will give all of you a choice!' he shouted. 'Mages can't make you into slaves. You can set yourselves free!'

The hall resonated with sentences like bubbles in simmering water. Some made it to the surface, some stayed caught in undercurrents. The servants were murmuring amongst themselves; the kher guards were closing in on the troublemaker. Apprentices and ordained mages alike were trying to be heard.

Mezyan lifted something that had been draped over his shoulder. For a moment, Isha thought it was his cloak. He unfolded it with a flourish.

The banner opened like a wing. The emblem was a bird of some sort, all claws and evil beak, with its wings spread out on either side. It was a bird of prey, with unmistakable talons.

'I speak in the name of the Renegades,' bellowed Mezyan. 'And in the name of our ruler, the woman who set us free. I speak in the name of Hawk!'

Isha heard Ka's voice as if he were beside her.

An eyas is a baby Hawk before it leaves its Nest.

Suddenly, Isha knew who she belonged to. She wondered if that was what it felt like, to be bound by a collar. To find out one day, in a place where she'd assumed she was safe, that she had a master.

A legacy of blood and claws and birds of prey.
And their leader is called Hawk.

The crowd erupted at Mezyan's arrogance, at his brandishing of a foreign heraldry in the sanctum of the Nest. Isha could see people's mouths moving but couldn't make out the words. It was as if everyone in the hall had turned to beasts. All she could hear was barking and snarling.

Worse, she could feel her tattoo as if the bone needle were piercing her again, her skin freshly cut; she was burning. It was too hot here, too stuffy, with too many bodies closing in around her. Her head swam, and her vision shifted and changed, blurring the shapes around her.

For the first time in her life, Isha mindrambled. It wasn't a pleasant experience.

In the past, she stood in front of her farm, with Passerine and three other soldiers before her. The soldiers were on horseback, whilst Passerine had dismounted. They were all wearing red.

'Your mother wants you to return,' said one of the soldiers.

'Now you have come of age, it is time for you to join us,' said another.

A flash of red as Passerine moved between her and the Renegades, his horse in tow. The thick, stocky body of the animal partly hid the soldiers from view.

'If you don't want this, you don't have to,' Passerine said, his tone low and threatening. 'No-one should be forced to follow Hawk's path.'

One soldier nudged his horse closer. The recollection was ripped and holed, but she remembered the shouting, Passerine pushing her out of the way, him screaming at her to run, them screaming at him that he was a traitor, and her foster parents rushing out of the farm, unwittingly throwing themselves in the path of danger.

And running. Running like her life depended on it, with minds clawing at her, tearing out clumps of memories like a fox pulling feathers out of a chicken.

The only way to survive was to shut down parts of her mind. To protect herself, she had banned her double, her eyas self. She hadn't lost half of her life to them – she had locked it away to save it.

She had sealed away the knowledge of who the woman in leather armour was. Of who had given her a bracelet of wooden beads for the Groniz festival. Of who had branded her like an animal before her life had even begun. Of who had taught her mindlink, well before she arrived at the Nest – now she knew why complicated techniques were so quick for her to assimilate, because she had learnt them once before. The knowledge came flooding back, of the person who had visited sometimes, who had sent Passerine to check on her more often, who had written her destiny on Isha's face before she had a chance to decide for herself.

That was why they had been able to share a dream, because they had a bond that could wade through the Shadowpass: they were flesh and blood. The hawk and the eyas.

My mother.

Kilian touched her arm, breaking the hold the images had over her. 'Let's get out of here.'

Before they could, Lady Siobhan mindlinked to the crowd. Her magic burst across the hall, fierce and violent like a torrent of water, not altogether controlled. It nearly knocked Isha off her feet. She opened her mouth to cry out, but she couldn't make a sound. Too late, she understood they should have left already. A clamp, as firm as iron, stuck her feet to the ground and slammed her mouth shut. Everyone in the room – mages, apprentices, servants – jerked to a halt. Half-finished sentences cut off abruptly. Everyone stood still.

Isha had never met a mage strong enough to reduce people to puppets. Yet that was what had happened: Lady Siobhan had taken control of all the souls within her reach. The only people in the hall immune to mindlink, Mezyan and the khers, stared at the ghostly sight. Every human had fallen quiet. When they moved, it was with the sleek coordination of one mind.

Being a mage, after her initial shock, Isha managed to free herself from Lady Siobhan's influence. Kilian did the same, shaking off the supreme mage's grip. All around her, the apprentices and mages awoke. The ungifted weren't so lucky. They didn't have any mental tools to defend themselves. Lines of servants trickled up the steps, pooling around Mezyan like water running down a sinkhole – every stable boy, maid, servant, cook, human guard took the closest route to hem in Mezyan, pushing the khers aside. They were careful not to touch kher skin, only their clothes. It was like watching a hive closing in on their enemy.

And she can wipe their minds. Her stomach lurched. *Lady Siobhan can cut out anything Mezyan said from their memories. They won't even know what he was offering them.*

Isha found it hard to breathe. On the balcony, Mezyan stepped down from the balustrade, reaching out for the ungifted arms as if they were helping him down, not arresting him. For a frightening moment, she thought they were going to tear him to pieces, lynch him then and there.

But the ungifted simply placed themselves around Mezyan, eyes glazed over, empty shells building a barrier of flesh to block his path. As people brought forward shackles, the kher guards at last agreed to help, although it was clear from their body-language that everyone was unnerved. Mezyan disappeared, too short to be seen amongst the throng of humans. His words seemed to shrink with him, the fire he carried growing smaller and dim.

'We should move, now,' Kilian said urgently. 'In case it gets worse.'

Isha could only nod.

Kilian navigated their way out of the crowd, ducking under people's arms, using his elbows like levers to move them aside. He was taller than her and could see a way out. It was a struggle to keep up with him, questions baying around her, words like grunts banging inside her skull. A man stepped between them and she lost sight of Kilian. When someone walked on her robes, she tripped, her golden belt coming undone. She held onto her clothes with one hand to stop them from getting caught in people's feet again, twisting the belt between her fingers. Under her breath, she cursed the underworlds, the skies, and everything in between.

Upwards, she couldn't see beyond the wall of shoulders and necks, except for the curved underside of an arch. She followed the shaft of sun and the motes of dust outside. The inner court-yard was full of people discussing what had happened, with kher guards struggling to keep the entrance clear.

Outside, at last, she could hear herself think.

Kilian popped out of the crowd behind her. 'You all right?' he asked.

'I thought you were in front.'

'I came back for you.' He took her hand this time. They walked past the Nest's gates and into the grass that lined the river. Here it was quieter. Speech became speech once more, not howls. Kilian was still holding her hand; she pulled it away before retying her robes.

'Are you sure you're all right?' Kilian asked. 'You look like you're going to faint.'

Her head was still spinning, but her thoughts were her own, and it was cooler outside the gates.

'I need to sit down,' she said.

The ground was damp. Groups were chatting on the moors, with apprentices who seemed relaxed; some might even have ignored the bell and didn't know about Mezyan's announcement yet. Taking an unsteady breath, Isha hid her hands, squeezing them between her legs, where no-one could see them shaking.

But it was impossible to escape entirely. The small retinue Mezyan had come with were waiting beside his mount on the other side of the bridge. His horse was grazing beside its standard. The flag was red and black. The wings moved as if the hawk was flying. The Renegades seemed tense.

She couldn't tell if the roar inside her skull was the river or her blood.

Sighing, Kilian placed his arms behind his back, resting his weight on the flat of his hands. He was still wearing his green shoes – it was his only pair. 'Feeling better now?'

She rubbed her cheek, as if she could erase the tattoo there. 'I'm fine,' she lied.

Kilian cocked his head to one side. His lanky blond hair fell sideways over his eyes. For a moment she wondered if he would see it, if by staring at her long enough he would guess at the bird of prey within her tattoo and understand what it meant.

'It's about your family, right?' he said. 'They're much closer to the Shadowpass. I get why you're worried.'

The word 'family' made her flinch. Kilian seemed concerned, but he was putting up a brave front. After all, the Sunrisers were far away. From the Nest, even her farm and the Shadowpass were far away.

'Aren't you?' she asked.

Kilian laughed, but he sounded strained. 'Why should I be? Mages are everywhere. And we can mindlink ungifted to do what we want.'

As Lady Siobhan just proved. She wasn't sure it was a reassuring fact.

'The halfblood isn't going to cause us any trouble,' he concluded.

Isha passed her hands around her knees and hugged them to her chest. 'What are the lawmages going to do with him?'

Kilian shrugged. 'Hang him, I guess?'

Isha didn't answer. She thought of Uaza telling her she was born to become a killer. She thought of the banner, the raptor with its long, square wings spread out as it flew above them. She thought of the Renegades attacking her farm. Of her mother hiding her with a foster family. Of hawks and Hawk.

Of the fact that the Nest would hang its enemies.

'Don't worry about it,' said Kilian. 'It's got nothing to do with us.'

* * *

They didn't sit in the moors for long. Caitlin came to find them. She called them over, but the scream of seagulls and the rush of the river meant they couldn't hear a word. She waved impatiently.

'Shouldn't we get up?' said Kilian.

It was Isha's turn to shrug. 'If it's that important, she'll come and fetch us.' She hoped it wasn't. She didn't want to face other mages right now.

Unfortunately, it was. Red-faced and grumpy, Caitlin stomped closer until they were within shouting distance.

'Get up!' she ordered. 'Sir Daegan wants us.'

So Isha and Kilian picked themselves off the riverbank, and shook the grass out of their robes, and complained about grass-stains, before following Caitlin back inside the Nest.

They had to push through a crowd as thick as mud, which parted reluctantly, then climb up the steps leading to the balcony. The mages and Mezyan were gone, but groups were sitting on the staircase and talking, kher guards were patrolling the hall, and a few maids were rolling up the Renegade banner.

In comparison, the corridors were strikingly empty. Their footsteps padded dully on the stone. Isha could hear Caitlin's short breaths. The passageways were bleak slabs of grey with no windows.

Most of Sir Daegan's followers were already there by the time they arrived in front of his chambers. As they waited, the last latecomers hurried to join them. Soon they were all huddled in front of his door, not unlike the figures bunched in front of the tavern before it opened in the evening, hoping for a beer and some food. Isha wondered why Sir Daegan needed this ragtag band of apprentices clogging his entrance.

The answer came once they heard his controlled voice further down the corridor. Caitlin straightened her posture, and the other disciples copied her. The group was unrecognisable. Instead of slouching youngsters, they looked like a small army, standing to attention in their grey uniforms, forming two columns on either side of his door.

Sir Daegan came into view, with Sir Cintay in step beside him. Although he was wearing a deeply dyed blue robe and had washed his hair, the Sunriser's features were still stark, shaped by hunger, sunburn and fear. Behind the mages, two human servants were carrying a chest, one manservant for each thick copper ring on the sides. From the way they moved, it was heavy.

Sir Cintay saw the apprentices, and the apprentices saw the effect they had on Sir Cintay. He had lost his convent. He must have had followers of his own, who hadn't survived, or who were still suffering at the Renegades' hands. People he had taught and cared for but couldn't protect. He shuddered as if they were ghosts, spirits escaped from over the Edge.

Sir Daegan, still chatting pleasantly, unlocked his front door.

'Please, do come in.' Sir Daegan waved everyone inside.

It was a tight fit. The apprentices had to hug the walls, and only a few people – Caitlin, some of the older disciples – managed to claim an armchair. Sir Daegan took a seat, as did Sir Cintay, while the manservants lowered the chest onto the carpeted floor between them. The packed bodies in the small living-room, and the fire, which had been stacked before they came in, meant the air was stuffy, thick with the smell of burning sap and sweat.

Sir Cintay was tall but thin, as if someone had tied him to a rack and succeeded only in lengthening his arms and legs, somehow contriving to keep him alive. He stooped when he walked; from a wound or from shame, Isha couldn't tell.

'I am glad you were able to retrieve it,' said Sir Daegan. 'I heard it was your convent's most precious possession. It would be a shame for such a relic to be lost.'

Sir Cintay nodded, but his eyes said something else. His shoulders were curved as he crouched in his exquisite seat, amongst silk cushions. As he rubbed his hands nervously, his sleeves sometimes showed the old scars around his wrists.

'We told the Renegades we would be worth nothing as hostages if we had nothing of ours to bring with us,' said Sir Cintay. He spoke low, as if whispering could prevent anyone from hearing, when there was nothing else to listen to but the spitting fire. 'So, Hawk agreed to let us take a chestful – no more, no less – of our goods with us. She confiscated what remained.'

'I am glad.' Sir Daegan smiled and waited.

'Before we do this...' started Sir Cintay.

Sir Daegan interrupted him at once. 'Of course. Let it be known, then, that in exchange for your most generous gift, I will ensure you have a place at the Nest, now and for as long as the trouble with the Renegades lasts.'

Sir Daegan glanced at the assembled apprentices. They were witnesses, Isha realised, who would be able to testify of the terms of the trade.

But they all belonged to Sir Daegan. How fair could such a jury be?

'You know...' Sir Daegan slipped into a fatherly, maybe even tender, tone. 'Lady Siobhan has promised all Sunrisers are welcome at the Nest. But Lady Siobhan is growing older and, by your own account, there will soon be more Sunrisers than guestrooms. What then? Soon it will be about payment and rent and services due. Soon there will be mages who will have to live with the lacunants, or inside the city gates.'

Sinking into his armchair, Sir Cintay seemed to be ageing before them; his features were drawn, and white hair peppered his head.

'I am well aware,' he said.

But I was not, thought Isha. What did that mean for Passerine? Would he be thrown out without money or powerful friends to fight for his place at the Nest? What about her?

'But no vassal of mine will ever be sent away,' added Sir Daegan. 'If you truly have what you promised, you will have proved your loyalty a hundred times over.'

Sir Cintay gestured to the manservants. One of them knelt

before the chest and, after rummaging around his belt for the key, unlocked it.

The apprentices craned their necks. Isha didn't, but she heard their gasps of excitement. Caitlin, who was closest to the high mages, mindlinked to the disciples next to her. The picture went from mind to mind until Kilian shared it with Isha.

Isha perceived two facets of the same scene. From where she stood, she saw nothing of the chest but its leather and metal straps, and the back of the manservant leaning over it. At the same time, she had Caitlin's view of it, the glint of gold and precious stones inside; a folded square of turquoise silk; a glass flask filled with quicksilver, which sloshed with the ungracefulness of metal when the servant pulled it out. She sensed Caitlin's eagerness: sharp, exuberant.

The servant placed both hands under the silk wrapping, holding it that way before Sir Cintay. The Sunriser mage unfolded the fabric, revealing what it had been protecting.

It could have been a child's crown, small and wrought with gold. And then Isha understood it wasn't a crown but a choker, meant not for the brow but for the throat. The pattern was familiar; she recognised the way the gold threads melded together, the intricate carvings scratched in the soft metal.

It was a collar.

'May I?' asked Sir Daegan.

'It is yours.'

Sir Cintay sounded exhausted. *His convent's relic. And he is selling it to pay his rent.* Isha was sorry for him. As a man responsible for lives and treasure, he had decided the treasure was worth less than the lives. If her understanding of Sunriser convents was correct, he had never been anyone's vassal, either. This was the first time he had relinquished his authority to another mage.

And it's the same for me, she thought. *If I don't want to belong to the Renegades, I have to belong to the Nest*. It didn't feel like much of a choice.

Sir Daegan lifted the collar to eye's height. He didn't smile. He didn't need to. He was like a cat licking its lips beside a half-chewed mouse.

'You may leave us,' he said.

Sir Cintay's jaw tensed as he bit down on the retort that might have escaped his lips. The manservants closed the chest, replacing the precious items inside, with the exception of the collar, which stayed in Sir Daegan's lap. Sir Daegan stroked it with the tip of his fingers, as if it were an unlikely pet.

Sir Cintay got up, but didn't leave. When he spoke, the words seemed to come with difficulty, as if he were forcing them through his teeth.

'As your vassal, I have a favour to ask.'

His hands folded above the collar, Sir Daegan displayed a patient smile. 'Please do.'

Sir Cintay swallowed. It was obvious that, whatever it was he wanted to say, he only said it because it was more important than his pride. That was something mages didn't often do.

'Spare Mezyan's life,' he said. 'I know you are Lady Siobhan's adviser. Convince her. Please.' Each sentence was shorter than the one before; each word sounded more painful to speak.

Sir Daegan gave out a curt laugh and, as if on cue, most of the apprentices sniggered. Isha hated the way the sound of laughter drained all colour from Sir Cintay's face.

'Don't kill a messenger.' An edge of desperation filtered into his voice. 'The Renegades won't take kindly to it. They'll wash the ground with more blood than you would need to drown ten khers. It will be … It will be my people who pay that price.'

He lowered his eyes as if he couldn't hold their concerted gazes. The servants also kept their heads bowed. Sir Daegan rubbed at the corner of his mouth with his thumb, as he would to keep himself distracted during a boring conversation – or maybe it was to hide the fact that he was grinning.

'You might find that you need to talk to Hawk and send messengers of your own to negotiate with her,' added Sir Cintay. 'If you kill Mezyan, she...' He stayed silent for a long time, long enough for Sir Daegan to lift a hand, as if about to shoo him away. 'She is stronger than you think. I believe the Nest will be surprised when it comes to dealing with her. We... the Wingshade convents were.'

'I have heard you,' said Sir Daegan.

Sir Cintay glared at him. Sir Daegan stared back. When it became clear that was the only answer he would get, Sir Cintay left, the servants in his wake.

Once he was gone, Sir Daegan lifted the collar towards Caitlin.

'Would you like to hold it?'

The disciples crammed around Sir Daegan's chair, passing the relic from hand to hand, commenting on how the gold was warm, like flesh, and supple, like fabric. Not only did they talk about it as if it were alive, they held it just as carefully. Isha stayed at the back of the room and shook her head when Kilian tried to pass the collar to her.

When the collar was returned to him, Sir Daegan turned to Isha.

'Don't you want to touch it?' he asked.

To her dismay, he winked. The door that led to his lightlure was hidden from view, with a cluster of disciples leaning against it, but neither Sir Daegan nor Isha needed to refer to it.

A cage and a bind. Both powerful, both magic. If Isha hadn't known Sir Daegan was ambitious before, she knew now. She had seen Lady Siobhan during the Groniz festival. Harsh winters had claimed stronger souls.

Everyone was looking at her. 'No, thank you, sir,' she said.

She still remembered touching Tatters' collar. She pressed her thumb against her fingertips, trying to dull the ache.

'Isha's used to collars,' said Caitlin.

It was her usual nastiness, but this time it hit its mark. Caitlin meant that Isha knew Tatters; but Isha heard that she was a collarbound herself, branded as a slave. She blanched. Sir Daegan observed her with interest, studying her reaction.

'What can you tell us about collarbounds, then?' he asked.

Isha shielded her mind from him as much as she could. A lie was difficult to pull off when facing a high mage – but she had learnt the power of untruths.

'I wouldn't be able to tell you more than what Caitlin or any of the others know, I'm sure.'

There, she thought. *If we're doing this, we're in it together.*

But Sir Daegan didn't question her. He went back to admiring his purchase, holding it between his fingers, savouring the power coursing through the gold.

There would be a second collarbound in the city before long.

Chapter Fourteen

The next day, the mages were ready to give the half-kher their answer. The apprentices were teeming along the bank that separated the Nest from the city, standing in the white spray of the river. A circle of high mages, Lady Siobhan amongst them, stood together on the bridge. They brought Mezyan out to where his troops were waiting and undid his manacles, even conceding him his horse. As soon as he was freed, Mezyan climbed astride his mare to face them. One of his soldiers handed him a banner, which he held in one hand like a spear.

They had done this on purpose, but knowing it was artificial didn't make it less effective. On one side, there was a swarm of curious faces, dressed in greys and blacks and blues, the colours of the Edge, of the sky, of the river crashing into the clouds. On the other side, there was only Mezyan and a handful of fighters. Red banner, red skin. The promise of blood.

Blood is thicker than water. Despite its width, despite its current, despite its drawn-out noise that never dulled, Isha wondered if the chasm would protect the Nest from what was coming.

Mezyan put his heels to his horse. As it stepped forward, Mezyan might have spoken – it was impossible to hear his voice above the roar of the waterfall. But Isha saw him throw back his head, as if he were laughing, before resting his banner next to his horse's hooves.

Lady Siobhan wasn't the one to answer him. Her frail mutterings wouldn't carry; she couldn't mindlink to a kher. When Isha saw Sir Daegan stride to the front of the group, her heart sank. The supreme mage wasn't yet dead, but already the flies were buzzing around her corpse.

Sir Daegan was speaking for her today, but soon enough, he would be speaking for himself. Sir Daegan had a booming, easy voice. 'The Nest has considered the Renegades' requests.'

His gaze trailed along the riverbank, along the lines of men and women, arms crossed, stamping their feet against the cold, with the looming shape of the Nest behind them like an overgrown shadow.

'The Renegades asked the Nest to recognise their laws as legitimate for all, and applicable to the Nest as well as the Sunriser convents. Those demands are not acceptable,' said Sir Daegan, 'and the Nest will not yield to them. Tell your master this – all birds belong at the Nest, hawks and sparrows alike, and all should bow to its rule.'

Sir Daegan was good at speeches. When he paused for dramatic effect, people leaned in to catch his expression. His face was stern. He wanted to seem unbreakable, as established and venerable as the gates the giants had left behind. But Isha couldn't help noticing he was an old man, Lady Siobhan older still, and the gates were rusting.

Isha found herself touching her cheek, where her life was inked in black curves. Now that her memories had returned, she was torn about Hawk. About her mother. She had admired her, if not loved her; but her emotions were muddled by the fact that she had been forced to serve Hawk, and had decided not to, and wasn't sure which was truer – the respect from her past or the fear from her present. She wasn't sure how long she would be able to live at the Edge, walking the crumbling line between the cliff and the fall.

'We should take your head for this insolence, but we will let you live. Tell your leader of our mercy. And tell her mercy is only the sister of justice. If she pushes any further, she will find justice isn't as kind as her sibling when dealing with rebels and traitors.'

At the end of the tirade, Mezyan stood up in his stirrups. The high mages stirred, moving closer to Lady Siobhan. Mezyan lifted his banner with both hands and slammed it into the ground, planting the flag in the soft, muddy earth.

Then, without a word, he turned his horse around. His retinue followed. They broke into a trot, then into a gallop, until they were racing down the road, the dawn lights breaking in the distance, above them and above the city. The Renegades left only dust behind, and their emblem bleeding red and black, a wound in the grey light of morning.

Isha knew what it meant.

It meant war.

* * *

That night, Isha woke to a servant shaking her awake. When she pushed back the covers, confused, she assumed the Nest had found out she was linked to the Renegades, and that they were going to throw her in prison. Then her thoughts cleared and she heard the servant saying she had been summoned by Sir Daegan.

'He wants you now,' the servant insisted.

She pulled on her grey robes in a daze. The servant was holding a candle on a saucer, which she handed over. Isha walked by its flickering light, which cast tall shadows down the corridors; large, distorted silhouettes that seemed to be clawing at the walls. Birds of prey. Soldiers. Black shapes, as black as her tattoo, trying to grab her and drag her into the darkness. She shivered, hugging the candle close so she could feel its warmth against her chest.

When she reached Sir Daegan's door, she took a deep breath and cleared her mind of all surfacing worries that she didn't want him to perceive. Instead, she focused on wondering what he wanted. Sir Daegan would like to think she was only concerned about him. People listened to the lies they wanted to believe.

She knocked. Immediately, the door swung open, and Sir Daegan poked his head out. His body blocked the entrance. He wasn't wearing his robes, but darkly-dyed hose and an undertunic. It was a shock to see him without his daytime clothes, with bony shoulders covered in hair, and naked feet with yellowing nails.

'You took your time.' He wanted to sound severe, but his tone came out impatient, elated. He glanced over his shoulder and grinned before turning back and regaining some composure. 'Come in.'

She tiptoed after him, trying to hide her fear. She could feel her heartbeat in her mouth.

The room was different at night. Only outlines were visible – half-empty wine glasses and piles of books, the copper bowl with fruit inside – which merged into one knobbly monster, full of bumps and humps and jagged edges, until the candle revealed the objects for what they really were. The light caught strange items: the crystal in the cabinet, a silver spoon dropped underneath the table. The collar.

'Take it,' said Sir Daegan. She could see his grey, squat body, but not the detail of his features.

She picked up the collar between two fingers. It was hot and pliant, like a snake that had dozed in the sun and absorbed the heat.

Sir Daegan pushed the door to his side-room open. He paused, swinging the door handle in his hand, causing the hinges to whine. Now she could hear noise from within. It had no rhythm to it, it came and went, erratic thuds like wet fabric slapping stone. From time to time, a clanking echo, which sounded to her as if a pile of branches or metal bars were clattering to the ground. As if bones, maybe, were being dropped in a common grave.

Reluctantly, she followed Sir Daegan inside. She lifted her feet high to avoid tripping on his thick rugs. When she moved the candle, the scent of melting wax rose.

The side-room was as cold as if they had stepped outside. It should have been dark, darker than the chambers, with only a sliver of night sky visible from the ceiling. It wasn't. It was bright.

The inside of the cage was lit up. A long trail of light was bouncing inside it, so fast that it filled the small space with lines, crisscrossing inside the bars, twisting itself into knots. The light hit the sides of the cage, producing the thumps, and tried to blast its way through the kher horn, making it rattle. Long shadows extended far beyond the cage, until it loomed larger, until the black lines covered all the walls, enclosed Isha's hands and arms, barred Sir Daegan's face.

Isha's breath caught in her throat. The lightborn was the colour of melting gold, of long sunsets, of lost treasure. It let out a wailing cry, as uncanny as a rabbit screaming. It was high-pitched and mournful, and it stopped as abruptly as it started. The mirror inside the lightlure was cracked from the strength of the blows, but still it reflected the light, trapping it.

Sir Daegan watched the cage as it rocked on its foundation, the nails that pinned it down creaking. He listened as the screeching picked up again, reverberating against the narrow walls like the shrill ghosts of giants. At the same time, the lightborn let out a flood of emotion, as strong against the mages' minds as flames. A wave of heat scorched Isha's thoughts. From the corner of her eye, she saw Sir Daegan wince.

It was beautiful, and it was howling to be set free.

'Go hold the collar inside the cage,' Sir Daegan instructed.

Isha didn't try to hide her horror. She could feel the power emanating from the lightborn – even from the room's threshold, she could sense its strength. Something like that could tear a soul out of a body. It could rip feelings to shreds. Who knew what it would do to her?

Sir Daegan's mind pressed against her, as effective as a dagger pushed against her ribs.

'Don't think of disobeying me now,' he warned.

Isha moved closer to the cage. She could tell the lightlure was too narrow – the lightborn had condensed its light, which made it look smaller, but also fleshier. More like an animal and less like a god. Forced into a thin ray, it appeared almost solid, tangible. If the lightborn were allowed to unfold its full length, it would become transparent. Like mist or clouds, it could both thicken or spread thin.

To get a better grip on the collar, she closed her fist around it, recoiling at the moist touch. It was like holding something alive. She took another step, conscious of the way the bars bowed when the lightborn crashed against them.

'Don't stop,' said Sir Daegan.

'It might kill me,' she answered.

He snorted. She understood it to mean her life would be a small price to pay for such a catch.

Maybe she should try to make a shushing sound? She inched forward and reached out with her mind, trying to share positive feelings, of calm, of quiet, of sitting below a tree and listening to the wind rustling its leaves, of waking at the farm to the sound of the singing cockerel. The lightborn reeled, and Isha was overwhelmed with images she couldn't understand, a primal fear that wasn't hers, disgust. Her stomach heaved. She stamped down on the sensation. Dots flashed before her eyes. She squinted, struggling to focus on the shape writhing within its prison.

'The collar must be inside the cage,' said Sir Daegan. 'Don't drop it.'

She knelt so she could creep closer, afraid she would faint and fall. It was as hot as if she were standing near a hearth. Holding the collar far in front of her, she extended one arm. She was shaking. She swallowed as the heat touched her; she expected burning, but it was a comfortable warmth, like a mother's hug.

Still trembling, she put her hand into the cage, as far as she dared. Each time it flashed through her arm, she shared some of the lightborn's emotions – confusion, anger, frustration. The light streamed through her skin as if she were made of paper. She felt fragile, easy to rip apart. She forced herself to keep breathing.

Very well. Sir Daegan was standing at a safe distance, but his mind was preying on hers, controlling, to ensure she was following his orders. *Now I want you to speak these words out loud. 'Your master is Sir Daegan.'* He tried to take control of her lips and tongue, as if she were an ungifted. She clenched her jaw, not yielding to his pull.

I will do it, if you ask, she mindlinked.

He didn't back down, but his grasp on her diminished. *Do it.*

Out loud, she repeated his words, her voice unsteady. 'Your master is Sir Daegan.'

The collar brightened, becoming incandescent. It pushed against her fingers, swelling to twice its size.

'I have to drop it!' she gasped, as it went from lukewarm to smouldering.

Although Sir Daegan didn't give her permission, she let go. The collar continued glowing and growing. She crawled backwards, wondering what that awful, tearing sound was, only to find out it was Sir Daegan laughing, laughing openly, with glee. Her skin crawled. The collar was now the size of a hoop, brilliant yellow, rivalling the lightborn.

'I am your master,' Sir Daegan repeated. 'I order you to take human shape and to stop struggling.'

The collar shone like a comet. The lightborn squirmed and thrashed; the cage rocked sideways, and Isha scrambled to her feet to get out of the way before it broke. But the cage held fast, and the light compressed into a smaller and smaller space, until all the threads of gold melded, forming something vaguely human-shaped. There were no features at first, only a silhouette of light, like the counterpart of a shadow.

The room dimmed. For a moment Isha saw the white shape of a woman, burned into her eyes as if she had stared at the sun. Then everything went dark. Without realising it, she had dropped the candle. It was cold again. The crack in the ceiling, with the faint glimmer of the moon above, was too far up to see by. Something was slumped on the floor, but it could have been anything, a pile of clothes, an animal, the aftermath of a nightmare.

It started breathing – a raspy sound.

Isha heard the sharp crack of a fire striker. Sir Daegan must have steel and flint in his chambers. She pushed herself to her feet, dizzy, breathing as hard as the thing in the cage.

Sir Daegan returned with an oil lamp. It cast a pale glow through its wrought glass case. Isha glimpsed jutting shoulder blades, gold hair, the curve of a cheek, five fingers clenched like claws against the stone. Nails filled with grit. She turned away.

'I did it,' whispered Sir Daegan.

I did it, thought Isha. *This is my fault.*

***

By the time Sir Daegan requested she fetch the disciples, it was morning. She gathered the people she could find at the common mess. They were reluctant to leave their meal for her, but she shrugged and said it was Sir Daegan's orders. Caitlin seemed more offended to know Isha was acting as Sir Daegan's messenger than she was about leaving her half-eaten plate.

'The puffin is on the rise,' laughed Kilian. 'You're his little favourite now, aren't you?'

There was no point in arguing.

They had to wait in front of Sir Daegan's chambers, like they had before his meeting with Sir Cintay. The disciples chatted amongst themselves, trying to guess what could be so important as to take place during breakfast. A few people wanted Isha to tell them more, but she stuck to the same story – she knew nothing, Sir Daegan had asked her to bring them, that was all.

'You must at least have a hunch,' Kilian insisted.

'No,' she said curtly.

Kilian shook his head.

'You can tell me, you know,' he said. 'You're not gaining anything by keeping it to yourself.'

You're wrong, she thought. *Secrets are more precious than money. They're the currency of power.*

Before Kilian could press her further, Sir Daegan exited his chambers. The disciples greeted him, placing themselves in formation around him.

'We are going into town,' Sir Daegan announced.

He took another step forward, and they saw the woman.

She was wearing a dress, with a wimple that hid her hair, neck and shoulders. Her blue sleeves brushed against the ground, showing slim white hands. Despite the formal attire, she was bare-footed. Isha imagined she must be cold, skin on the freezing stone. She had a golden face and eyes that couldn't decide whether they were hazel or green, and kept shifting from one to the other. She wasn't young; she wasn't old. She didn't look at them.

Sir Daegan led them into the Nest's courtyard without bothering to introduce the woman to the disciples, or the disciples to her. In the courtyard, he asked a kher guard to saddle a horse from the stables. Once it was ready, Sir Daegan lifted the woman into the side-saddle as if she weighed nothing. He helped her naked feet into the stirrups, and she let him handle her without a sound. He took the reins.

The same thought ran through the followers, as clear as the waters rushing over the Edge.

It's a nice mistress he's found for himself.

Seagulls were circling above the Edge, nosediving into the river and emerging with a splash, screaming at each other while they fished. A few were waddling across the bridge too, but they took flight when the humans reached it. Isha could see the horse's shoes hitting the paved road, but she couldn't hear them above the cries of birds. As they left the Nest, the woman looked over her shoulder. Instinctively, Isha copied her. Behind them, the white foam of the river and the white of the clouds gave the illusion that one could walk the waters and step off into the sky.

When Isha turned around again, the woman wasn't watching the Edge anymore.

While Sir Daegan held the bridle, the disciples walked

alongside the horse in a procession that caught everyone's attention. More than one traveller going to or from the Nest stopped to stare.

'My feet are going to fall off,' complained Kilian.

Isha, exhausted from her sleepless night, didn't find the strength to answer.

When they arrived at the city's central square, Sir Daegan asked them to form a cordon of bodies, with enough space in the middle for a demonstration. He didn't explain what kind of demonstration. Obediently, the disciples placed themselves at intervals around the central statue. Lice-ridden children and beggars made up the bulk of their audience, but shopkeepers and marketgoers also loitered at a distance. A few people had even followed them after crossing their path on the moors. Sir Daegan's excitement was like a smell permeating the air around him. Everyone could sense he had prepared something.

Once he had ascertained everyone was in position, Sir Daegan helped the woman dismount. She slid to the floor, not even wincing when the mud licked her feet.

'You can take it off,' Sir Daegan said.

The woman's face was as unmoving as marble. She undid her wimple. She folded it and handed it to Caitlin, who was standing beside Sir Daegan, before placing the pin on top of the square of cloth.

Around her alabaster neck, the woman was wearing a collar. Her hair had been braided so it wouldn't hide it, and the choker cast a yellow light across her shoulders. The crowd didn't show much enthusiasm; the disciples, however, exchanged shocked glances. A mistress was one thing, but no-one wasted a magic relic on a lover. It was slowly becoming clear to them that she must be more than that.

Sir Daegan basked in the interest of his followers for a while, soaking up their curiosity. He cleared his throat. Isha could tell he was enjoying every second, the autumn sun on his skin, the weight of his mage's robes, even the cold bite of the metal rings on his hands.

He gave his collarbound her first command:

'Alight.'

That was when people gasped.

The woman leapt into the air. She didn't fall, but grew slighter as she rose. Her flesh melted into light. She became a ray flashing in the air, whirling above the crowd, creating an ethereal breeze that ruffled their hair. She swirled and swerved above their heads, and they followed her with their eyes as she cut a silhouette as bright as brass in the pale sky.

When she landed, she shifted from light to human, with the gentleness of a ribbon fluttering to the ground. She flowed like water and stilled like the surface of a lake.

She was a wonder. And Isha had helped turn her into a slave.

At first people were too stunned for applause. When they did cheer, they did so with a mix of hooting and praying; a few hymns were sung.

'Dance,' Sir Daegan ordered.

She changed again, drawing a rising arc. Most people tried to grab her as she flew past. Older children lifted younger ones on their shoulders for extra reach. If their fingers came close enough, the light shone through them and was gone just as briefly. Then they kissed their fingertips, pressing them against their heart and lips so the blessing would enter them.

The crowd only grew. People saw the gold of a lightborn and dropped their work, their homes, their spouses. They piled inside the square until Sir Daegan instructed his disciples to hold them back. Isha simply waved her arms to keep people at bay, but she noticed some of Sir Daegan's followers impressing a fear of coming closer in the minds that overstepped. Mages from the Nest spotted the low-flying lightborn and hurried across the bridge, pushing themselves through the throng.

As everyone shoved for a better view, the mages were the ones to get closest, with the shopkeepers next, while the beggars and children were relegated far from the slender, stone-faced woman who sometimes touched the ground before slipping into the sky once more.

Isha heard someone pushing through the crowd, repeating 'sorry' unapologetically as they drew near. It was Tatters, forcing mages aside with his elbows. He greeted her with a nod and used her as an excuse to cross the last rows of men and women pressed together.

'You're not supposed to come closer,' she said.

Tatters sat down at her feet.

'I'm not going further,' he promised. He rested his forearms on his crossed legs to enjoy the show.

Isha hesitated, but decided to let it slide. *How did you get this close?* she asked instead. Some practice in mindlink couldn't hurt, even with this many mages to spy on them.

Tatters answered out loud, maybe aware that mindlink would attract notice.

'No-one stops a collarbound. They assume I'm obeying an order I can't do anything about, so they move out of my way.'

The lightborn landed beside Sir Daegan. The flight had undone her hair, and the stray locks rested across her shoulders like further threads of gold from the collar. Compared to her stark face, the dress was plain. The city itself was colourless.

'And to think you didn't even tell me about this!' He couldn't keep the awe out of his voice.

Isha understood him. Even if he didn't believe humans would ascend, even if he didn't think lightborns were sacred, their shine wasn't something anyone could discard. They were painfully beautiful, like nothing from this world should be – and they weren't, after all, from this world.

But then Tatters said something that startled Isha. To himself, with no less admiration than before, he muttered: 'She's huge.'

Isha tried to hide her frown. As casually as possible, she said, 'You must be so bored.' He looked up at her, still resting on the floor. 'What with having seen so many lightborns already.'

He smiled. 'This is the first one I've seen up close.'

So how do you know she's huge? This wasn't something she wanted to say out loud.

Tatters only laughed. *You're so smart. You tell me how I know.*

Isha kicked him, not seriously. He pushed her shoe aside, still chuckling.

Once the lightborn had settled on the ground, her attention focused on Tatters. She stared, ignoring her master, the shouts and applause, the people pleading for her blessing. She only had eyes for him. Isha looked down at Tatters – several people around her did the same. He didn't react to them any more than to the lightborn. He held her gaze, but didn't smile or wave or call out for a favour.

'You've met her already,' said Isha. She couldn't help herself. It was the only explanation that held.

Shaking his head, Tatters smiled indulgently. His eyes never left the lightborn. 'Never seen her before.'

Sir Daegan put a hand on the lightborn's shoulder. She didn't acknowledge him; her back barely tensed. She stood where he wanted her to stand as he started talking about Lady Siobhan's poor health and how, during her convalescence, a trusted circle of high mages ruled the Nest. Isha wasn't listening.

'Why's she staring like that?' she asked.

Tatters shrugged, but he seemed reluctant to break eye-contact with the lightborn.

'She's staring at the collar,' he said. 'We owe each other something, being two collarbounds.'

A mage behind them intruded on their conversation.

'That's not how collarbounds greet each other.'

Tatters tore himself away from the lightborn for the first time, to glance at the man behind him. 'Really? You should go and tell her. She doesn't seem to know.' It was rare for Tatters to drop his cheerful demeanour; the tone he used with the mage was anything but friendly.

He got up and dusted his cloak. 'The ground is freezing,' he mumbled.

Sir Daegan was still speaking. His lightborn was docile beside him, hands held in front of her, face angled towards an empty patch of sky. It wasn't clear whether she could understand him.

'Well, this was fun,' said Tatters. 'See you.'

'You're leaving?' Isha spoke and mindlinked together, which sometimes helped hide the messages being sent. *Ignore this soulworm. He's a fool.* Although he was right, of course, to say that wasn't how collarbounds greeted each other.

Tatters shook his head. 'You can tell me later if anything interesting happens.'

He's running away, Isha decided. *Before someone works it out.* There wasn't anything she could do about it. She watched Tatters disappear, ducking between the mages, never turning back. From behind, with his lanky hair over his neck, he was nothing more than another beggar in a poor city. He was naturally pushed to the back of the crowd.

Sir Daegan's speech continued. He talked about the next supreme mage, and who would inherit the Nest. He talked about how inefficient a group of high mages were in making quick decisions, especially in times of crisis.

'You need someone who can face up to the Renegades,' he said. 'Have you seen what happened to the Sunriser convents, how people have been forced to leave their homes behind? Do you want to be on the road too, with no-one to turn to for help? You need a supreme mage who will not only defend the Nest, but who will protect the people! Other mages say they'll guard the city, but will they hold that promise when war is at our door? Will they have what it takes to shield everyone?'

Isha was only half-attentive, but she sensed emotion crackling through the gathered mages. They didn't cheer, but the ungifted behind them did. A shopkeeper rattled his window shutter with his fists, and a few others copied him, or stamped the ground with their feet. The rumble rolled across the square.

'We need something the Renegades can't fight against,' Sir Daegan went on. And, in case it wasn't clear enough, he squeezed his slave's shoulder, guiding her in front of him. The clapping was deafening, as were the calls from the people she had blessed. Her face didn't show a glimmer of emotion.

'You don't want to send your children, your siblings, your parents to fight the Renegades. But that is who the Nest will send, if there is a war. Oh, they will drill the soldiers with mindlink. It will be the most efficient, most deadly of armies. But the blood that will spill will be your kin's.'

As she studied him, Isha could tell his outrage was crafted. The red flush of his cheeks and his bellowing accusations didn't match his pleasure at having secured a collared lightborn for himself. Yet his false anger resonated with the real resentment of the crowd. She could perceive the dominant thought on everyone's mind, the image of Lady Siobhan controlling ungifted to fight off Mezyan. Now that word of the Renegades' visit had got around, people were upset with the callous control Lady Siobhan had displayed.

'I am Sir Daegan, a high mage of the Nest. If you want to talk to me, you may. But you have to come one by one.'

He gestured to his disciples, who helped shape a funnel around him, so people could come up to Sir Daegan and his lightborn, but wouldn't crush them.

At the beginning, there were mostly mages. They lauded Sir Daegan, failing to hide their amazement or their dread. They asked him what his plans were, cautious not to confront him. No-one asked the important question: 'Will you defy Lady Siobhan?'

They stank of fear.

After the mages were the ungifted. They weren't as interested in engaging with Sir Daegan, although they did so, out of politeness. They were captivated by the lightborn. When they stroked her hands, when they kissed her fingers, when they bowed to her, when they talked to her master, she didn't react. She never spoke a word.

When the ungifted asked if the lightborn would bless them, Sir Daegan answered that he, with her help, could bless the whole city. He mentioned how the town would be a better place if it had a strong man to run it – if it had a father to tend for it.

Isha observed and listened. Kilian stood very straight beside her, his lips closed into a thin line. The disciples didn't catch each other's eyes, scared of what they might see.

Drawn in by Sir Daegan, people started mentioning politics, complaining about the high taxes, the refugees flooding the streets, the khers encroaching outside the borders of the Pit. He nodded and smiled and didn't reveal what he believed, but gave out a warmth that people thanked him for. They took off their hats to him.

All the while, Sir Daegan kept his knobbly grip on his collar-bound's shoulder.

Isha wondered if those were her only choices: following the Renegades and being part of the army that sowed refugees and death, or following the Nest and helping the man who crafted slaves out of light. Both were powerful. Both would battle. But it felt like she would always be on the wrong side of the war.

Chapter Fifteen

When at last it was time to return to the Nest, the weary disciples placed themselves in formation around Sir Daegan's horse, where his collarbound sat with her wimple folded on her lap. Kilian stayed quiet and thoughtful. Caitlin had adapted quickly and, after failing to spark up a conversation with the collarbound, settled with praising Sir Daegan. He was too euphoric to worry about his other disciples' ambivalent silence.

Isha spotted the lonely figure on the bridge from a distance. At first she didn't pay it much attention, until it became obvious that the person wasn't moving. She squinted. A man in black robes was standing in the centre of the bridge. As they came closer, two things became clear.

It was Passerine. And he was waiting for them.

She knew before they reached him that there would be trouble. The collarbound was poised on the horse like an elegant weapon. If Sir Daegan noticed Passerine, he hid it. He didn't acknowledge him until they were at shouting distance, and it became difficult to ignore the man barring the only passageway.

Your behaviour is disgraceful.

Passerine mindlinked loudly, broadly. The only movement came from the wind whipping his robes. The only sound was the sharp crack of fabric, like a flag in the breeze.

Sir Daegan stopped. His fingers tightened around the reins. *Are you jealous?* he asked. *You were not chosen by the gods.*

Their group had stopped before the bridge, where the bank of the river turned to stone. Passerine loomed above them, black on white marble, like a crow perched on a shrine. Up close, Isha could see his features were severe; clenched jaw, a frown, hard eyes.

You were not chosen. You are a thief, and you tricked her. You should be ashamed. Drops of water like pearls were caught in Passerine's hair. From this angle, at this distance from the Nest, he could have been as tall as the building, as tall as the old gates, a giant himself.

Set her free.

Sir Daegan laughed. He threw the reins across the horse's neck. The woman didn't so much as shiver. She was absorbed by the birds flying above them, by the white and black lines they drew across the clouds. The scene taking place before her, if she understood it, was of no interest to her.

Glowing with strength and confidence, Sir Daegan took a few steps forwards. He placed his ringed fingers on his hips, and each precious stone shone against his black robes.

They were close enough that the two high mages could hear each other, if they raised their voices.

'What will you do?' asked Sir Daegan. 'What can you do against me?'

'You will not go any further,' said Passerine.

Isha had known it would come to this. It had to. Sir Daegan waved her over. Slowly, she went to his side. It was like wading through water; she felt heavier with each step. The disciples watched her, some worriedly, like Kilian – and some with a downturned smirk, like Caitlin. Passerine also watched her, but his face said nothing of his thoughts.

Sir Daegan took her by the forearm, like he would a child, to place her before him.

'Do your duty,' he said.

Isha was numb. Her feet carried her from the beginning of the bridge up to Passerine. Underneath her leather soles, the ground changed from soft, muddy grass to rough, irregular cobblestones. His eyes weren't unkind. If anything, his expression was concerned for her. For the first time, she saw flecks of grey in the black of his hair.

And then they were both face-to-face, with only a few flagstones between them, and the spray of the river around them, and the rush of water as loud as the rush of blood in her temples.

Passerine didn't offer to fight her. His mind was guarded, but he didn't reach out to her. She wondered how it had happened, why she had followed him to safety, only to find herself pitted against him.

'This man has taught you everything he could,' said Passerine. He didn't shout; his words, though loud, didn't carry beyond the bridge. 'It is high time you cast him aside like the rubble he is.'

The wind filled and thinned his robes, shapeshifting his frame from moment to moment, his figure moulded by the gale.

'I will be your teacher,' he said.

She didn't know what to say. Why hadn't he offered this when she'd arrived, when she had needed him? Now she had a community, of sorts. Despite the frictions with the disciples, at least she wasn't alone, outcast. She had started to belong, if not completely – never completely.

Still, she could only give one answer. Sir Daegan hadn't come to her when the Renegades attacked her farm. Her life would not be devoted to building his cages.

She undid her golden belt, lifted it in one hand, for all to see, and let go. The belt was caught by a gust of air, snatched away. In seconds, it had been swallowed by the swirling water below. Without a belt to hold them, the robes were shapeless, like a sack thrown over her.

As she took her place beside him, Passerine put a protective hand on her shoulder.

'We will make enemies today,' he warned her.

They faced Sir Daegan. When she saw Kilian's expression, Isha worried she had made a mistake. The mage and his followers seemed small, standing in the damp track, amongst weeds and rust-coloured heather, channels of mud framing them like a dirty painting. Behind them, a queue – of merchants, servants, apprentices, kher guards – were waiting for the mages to finish so they could cross the bridge. Beyond and further behind, there was the city; a brown, flat, smoky thing, like a smouldering piece of manure.

'Isha denies her allegiance to you,' Passerine announced, 'and vows it to me instead.'

Kilian was white. He begged Isha with his eyes, shaking his head, as if Passerine couldn't see him, as if the decision hadn't already been made.

What do you want me to do? she wondered. *What else can I do?*

Sir Daegan was pale too, but the emotion draining the blood from his face was fury.

'Are you going to send another child to fight in your place?' asked Passerine.

Sir Daegan snarled. His fingers tightened around his sides. He pounced.

Isha had never seen fights outside of controlled duels, with no settler, no neutral space where both mages could stand, no safe ground. Sir Daegan projected himself into Passerine's mind, and Isha sensed the mush of thoughts and impressions that comprised him as it crashed against Passerine. She perceived, too, like bile rising inside her mouth, the taste of Passerine's mind as it flung Sir Daegan aside.

From the edges of the battle, Isha could only access the aftermath of the high mages' mindlink. Images flashed before her eyes; sensations crawled down her forearms, making her hairs rise. She saw Sir Daegan amongst statues of salt, and the statues melted away as rain poured over them, and he was alone. She saw Passerine clawing at a gold collar throttling him, foam at the corners of his mouth.

The lacunants around the gates started moaning at the violence of the mindlink taking place. Even though they were at a fair distance from the bridge, they yowled like wolves. Human mouths filled the air with inhuman sounds.

As the images pressed against each other, struggling for dominance, they became more and more erratic. *Teeth breaking like glass inside your mouth. A heavy wooden yoke weighing against your neck. Flash of red, a flying lightborn, leaving a trail of gore across your skin. The tip of your fingers peeling off like chunks of rotting fruit, showing bone.*

To Isha, they were two lions fighting. Suddenly there were claws as long as hands and fangs that could snap a neck, and they were tearing chunks out of each other's sleek fur, spilling blood as thick as sap.

But for an ungifted, there was little to see. Sir Daegan was standing at one end of the bridge, his eyes bloodshot, his mouth set in a determined scowl. Passerine was just as still, except for a muscle twitching on the back of his hand.

Until there was something to see.

Sir Daegan lifted one hand. The lightborn reacted like a puppet tugged by its string. She shifted into light while she was still seated on the horse, making her mount shy sideways.

The ray of gold raced through the air above Sir Daegan, a shooting star headed for Passerine. Isha only had time to gasp. She threw up her arms, uselessly, as if that would stop the movement from unfolding.

The light crashed into Passerine. He crumpled. It was even more impressive because he was so tall, and had always seemed solid, unmovable. Seeing a grown man – a man bigger than her, built of muscle and thick bones – collapse to the ground was terrifying. She rushed to his side, but he was too heavy, and she could only cushion his fall, not prevent it. He folded over as if punched; his mind shut down as if wiped. He dropped like a stone, and for a moment she feared he was dead.

The lightborn drew a circle in the air before returning to her master. Isha cradled Passerine's head where it had hit the bridge. When he opened his eyes, relief nearly choked her.

Sir Daegan will kill him. It was all she could think of. Passerine struggled to his feet, but he moved with a lurch, as if drunk. He could do nothing about this kind of power. *He will get himself killed.*

Isha only noticed the lawmage when she pushed past them, shoving against Isha's shoulder, thrusting her mind like a wedge before Sir Daegan.

Shame on both of you! What is this? The lawmage was wearing a thick lilac cloak, a slash of colour in the grey and brown landscape, amongst the grey and black robes. Her cheeks were flushed, her breath came in gasps. *Break apart now, by word of law!*

She repeated it out loud, maybe for the onlookers' sake: 'Break apart now, by word of law!'

Sir Daegan pulled back. When his mind stilled, the lacunants' screams calmed down somewhat. A few of them still let out sharp yelps, as if in pain.

'Sir Daegan!' The lawmage was a tall woman, with a matron's

fleshy figure, a mage's wrinkled forehead. 'I did not expect you, of all people, to behave like a back-alley mindbrawler.' She was just as sharp with Passerine. 'And you should know that this is poor behaviour for a guest, living at the Nest thanks to Lady Siobhan's gracious leave.'

'Sir Passerine was forbidding me access to the Nest,' said Sir Daegan reasonably. 'I did not wish to cause trouble, but I cannot let a foreigner bar the door of my home.'

'Sir Daegan has spent his morning in town spreading slander on Lady Siobhan's health,' said Passerine, his tone not quite as controlled as usual, still stunned from the lightborn's attack. 'It is poor behaviour indeed, if foreigners are more loyal to the Nest's ruler than her own people.'

The lawmage looked from one to the other, frowning. A few kher guards and more lawmages were pouring out of the Nest's gates. Soon their audience would grow enough for this to become an outdoor trial, where violence would easily escalate, and only the crowd could judge. Already the lacunants were agitated, servants were gasping at Passerine's accusations, and others were pointing at the collarbound on Sir Daegan's horse.

'Silence!' The lawmage spread out her arms in a gesture which indicated that no nonsense would be tolerated. 'I will consider these allegations. In the meantime, Sir Daegan is free to come to the Nest. Sir Passerine, step aside. Sir Daegan, I request that you stay inside your chambers for the time being. We will talk about your new ...' She hesitated at the sight of the collarbound, before catching herself. 'Your new acquisition.'

Sir Daegan was so tense, it seemed he wouldn't obey the lawmage. But, at last, he bowed to her. Isha and Passerine moved to the side to let his procession through.

The lawmage stayed beside them while Sir Daegan retrieved his horse's reins. After its initial surprise and short, nervous jump, the animal had wandered off to graze on the lush grass. The collarbound had done nothing to stop it.

When Sir Daegan crossed them, he turned towards Isha. She shrank under the fire of his glare. As he opened his mouth to speak, she braced herself for a word of abuse. But before Sir Daegan could say anything, Passerine interrupted:

'You have escaped fighting me twice so far.' Sir Daegan's eyes flickered from Isha's face to Passerine's. Passerine had bunched his hands into fists and, although they were partly hidden by his sleeves, Isha could see them shaking. 'You won't be lucky three times.'

Sir Daegan lowered his voice so the lawmage wouldn't hear him and hissed:

'All that proves is that you backed down twice.'

Then he was gone, and they were left staring at the swish of the horse's tail, the pale blue of the collarbound's dress. Isha didn't get a chance to speak to Kilian. She couldn't help but gaze after them as the group left the bridge and disappeared into the Nest.

***

Tatters had watched the whole showdown in horror. Even from the margins of the fight, even at the back of the group of curious onlookers who had trailed after the lightborn, even with his cloak pulled over his hair to hide its tell-tale colour, he didn't feel safe with Passerine so close. It was bad enough to see him stand against a high mage and nearly win. It was worse to see him fight a lightborn, which awakened dark memories, monsters that had lain in wait and were now shaking their fur and rising to their feet.

The worst, however, was Isha.

He couldn't have described the feeling that squeezed his heart when she had left her master, discarded her signs of allegiance, and joined Passerine on the bridge.

Lal could have described her feeling, though. It was anger. He hadn't felt his sister this upset in a long time; she was raw with the sense of betrayal. *We have to deal with her*, she fumed.

Tatters could have laughed, but not because what Lal said was funny.

It's Isha we're talking about. You know? Feisty kid, sort of intro-verted. You might have seen her around. Sometimes she buys me a beer.

Ha ha. Lal was not amused. But then, neither was Tatters.

She's not my enemy, he said firmly. He remembered his younger self, pledging himself to Hawk, ready to take over the world with her, believing he would be safe from mages that way. Isha was making a mistake; he knew it was a mistake, because it was one he had made before.

He lurked at the back of the crowd as the mages and mer-chants started crossing. Sir Daegan went first, with his lightborn straight in her saddle. Guards, peddlers, servants followed. A couple of stragglers, Tatters amongst them, hung around to see if anything else might happen.

From where he was, Tatters could glimpse Isha's profile, nerv-ously scanning the people as they passed her on the bridge. The wind pushed her hair back, showing her tattoo in full – the sharp triangles along her cheek, the strange slender shape at the top, the knotted, rope-like tangle at the bottom. As he stared at it, even blurred from the distance, Tatters wondered again if he had seen it before, or something like it, and recently too – a stylised animal of the same sort, if one imagined this patch was an eye, this line the curve of the head...

Actually, maybe she is our enemy, said Lal. She was excited, jittery, like she had just worked out something. As she spoke, the shape of Isha's tattoo settled in Tatters' mind. Yes, he had seen it recently – on Mezyan's banner. The same line of the wing. The same beak. The same talons as the hawk dived towards its prey.

Do you know why you had that uncanny feeling you'd seen her before? Lal insisted, despite the turmoil Tatters was already in. *Why the collar always seems stronger when she's around?* Lal pictured Isha and Hawk side-by-side. She chose one of their earliest memories of Hawk, when she was younger. She removed the tattoo from Isha's features, trying to visualise her without it. Its absence made her face more striking, showed the lines of her forehead, nose and chin.

And it revealed the similarities. Between that and the tattoo, there could be no doubt.

Isha was Hawk's daughter.

He felt slow-witted, stupid. It should have been the first thing he'd guessed when he'd seen her. It should have struck him immediately. He found himself backing away from the bridge, as if that could help, as if he wasn't too late. The Renegades' banner on her face, and he didn't run when he saw her? He should never have had anything to do with Isha.

Ducking his head between his shoulders, he strode away, not sure of his destination, back to the city, for now; away from Isha and Passerine, for sure.

Lal was already setting up a plan. *Wear some kher horn. No-one can mindlink you and you won't slip. Leave the Nest. Find work in a field in the Meddyns. Lie low for a while.*

Tatters tried to imagine it. Kher horn – which meant no Lal – for weeks, maybe months. He would have to leave Arushi behind, too, all to go break his back over meagre crops meant for mages, with the sun and wind wrinkling his skin. He wasn't cut out to be a farmer.

Because you're better cut out to be dead, are you?

Give me a break, he snarled. He regretted it as soon as he lost his temper. But he was tired too. He was frightened too. He couldn't walk fast enough on the muddy, slippery road.

We're not sure Isha is on Hawk's side, thought Tatters. *Maybe she's like us. Maybe she ran away. That's what she said, after all.*

Why would she run from the army her mother commands? Lal scoffed. *No. Forget Isha. We need to get out of here while we can.*

There is a problem with leaving, said Tatters.

If they bolted now, they would be safe. Maybe. For a time. But the Nest would stay in the clutches of Passerine, with Hawk on her way, Mezyan to lead her army, her own daughter to spy on their foes. Despite Passerine and Mezyan both behaving as if Passerine had betrayed the Renegades, Tatters doubted it. It could be part of a complicated scheme. Hawk wasn't beyond complicated schemes.

Then what? If Tatters abandoned the Nest, Hawk would win. She would get what she wanted.

He probably couldn't stop her. But he wasn't sure he could turn away and let her do it, either.

We can't save the city, said Lal. *We'll be lucky if we can save ourselves.*

And yet, when Tatters threw one last look at the bridge, when he remembered Passerine brazenly defying the mages, when he envisioned Hawk laying siege to the rusted gates and tearing down the spires, he knew he wouldn't be able to leave.

Maybe we can't save it, he admitted. *But we'll have to try.*

***

It only took a few minutes for the Nest to return to its usual state. The lacunants begged and mumbled and slept. The river roared. The wind pushed Isha's hair inside her mouth.

Passerine rested his forearms on the bridge's railings.

He rubbed his hand where the muscle still jerked with contained tension.

'I am sorry it happened this way,' he said. She had forgotten how rich his voice could be, like something buried deep within the earth. 'It was too soon. He forced my hand.'

But you were the one who challenged him. Before she answered, Isha considered what she had witnessed today. The other mages had gone to the city square and listened to speeches denigrating Lady Siobhan and said nothing. No-one had stood up to Sir Daegan. No-one had blocked his path to say that binding lightborns to his purpose was wrong.

She remembered the soldiers who had come to take her back to Hawk. At the time, there was only one person to face them, to say that binding her child to her purpose was wrong.

So instead of telling Passerine that he could have avoided this fight, Isha asked: 'You knew something like this would happen?'

'I knew I would have to defend my place at the Nest – and yours. And I knew I would be your teacher one day. I didn't want it to happen before we were strong enough, but it has happened, and we will deal with it.'

He breathed in the spray from the river, pressing his hands flat against the stone banister. A flock of white flew overhead, in formation, like apprentices around their master.

'Your other teacher,' Passerine added. 'He might be able to help.'

Isha was surprised; she had nearly forgotten their conversation at the Temple, during the festival. She didn't remember that she had let away Tatters' gender. Uneasy, she muttered, 'He doesn't get involved with Nest politics.'

Passerine was contemplating the horizon beyond the Edge, where earth and sky and water met.

'No,' he whispered. 'I'm sure he doesn't.'

Not for the first time, Isha worried who Tatters would support, whether Passerine could persuade him to ally with them. She thought of friends and foes, of long-buried dreams. Of a woman in armour speaking inside a tent of red cloth. Her mother, giving her advice. *What does his bind look like?*

From what she had seen today, the lightborn's collar was as bright as molten gold. Whereas Tatters' was dull.

His bind wasn't active. Isha couldn't believe she had taken so long to reach that conclusion. Obviously, Tatters didn't have a master. He must have had one and found a way to free himself. Or partly free himself, at least. That was what his bind looked like: it looked like it was broken.

I belonged to the Renegades and I escaped. Tatters belonged to someone, and he escaped as well. They were more similar than she'd realised. But she wasn't sure whether, when the time came, they would be on the same side or not.

Passerine sighed. His face hardened.

'If we are to win this war, we will need all the help we can get.'

And they would have to join the struggle, whatever the outcome. She let her gaze trail from the Nest, the tall black husk the giants had left behind, to the foot of the bridge, where Mezyan had planted his banner, long since taken down and burnt by the mages.

Isha and Passerine were neither Renegades nor members of the Nest – they stood somewhere in the middle, somewhere on the bridge between worlds.

If this was where she belonged, in the space in between, then this was where she would hold her ground.

This was where she would fight.

TO BE CONTINUED IN VOLUME 2:
THE EYAS

Acknowledgements

I am always awed at how many people are involved in the creation of a book, and this one is no different. First of all, none of this would be possible without my fantastic agent Alice Speilburg, who was the first person from the publishing industry to get excited about this novel and to offer thoughtful, constructive feedback. Thank you so much for your ongoing support.

I would like to thank the Gollancz team for their hard work. Thank you to Marcus Gipps and Rachel Winterbottom for giving this book a chance to meet its readers, and to the Future Bookshelf Scheme for giving me a such a great boost. I also want to thank my tutors on the Creative Writing team of the University of Manchester, particularly Jeanette Winterson and Geoff Ryman. Jeanette, your help was invaluable, and I hope one day I can give an aspiring writer as much as you gave me.

This journey was only possible thanks to my fellow writers' feedback and support – Sui Annukka, Sam Case, Orla Cronin, Tom Patterson and Sarah Wenig. You saw this story through its every iteration, and I am forever grateful for your advice. Ciaran Grace, a special shout-out for your help with all the language nitty-gritty worldbuilding stuff, and of course you get credit for the Coop's name.

Finally, I'd like to thank my family, close and distant, who read my work when it was printed on the home computer and lovingly packed into cardboard folders, when it was a messy pile of loose pages annotated by hand. Mum, Dad, thank you for your trust. Rose, you are the best little sister ever, and your fanart of Passerine is a sight for sore eyes.

Last but not least, to the person who supported me, listened to me ranting about writing, offered helpful advice or simply kept believing – thank you, Nicolas, for everything.

Credits

Rebecca Zahabi and Gollancz would like to thank everyone at Orion who worked on the publication of *The Collarbound*.

Editorial
Marcus Gipps
Rachel Winterbottom
Claire Ormsby-Potter

Copy-editor
Abigail Nathan

Editorial Management
Jane Hughes
Charlie Panayiotou
Tamara Morriss
Claire Boyle

Inventory
Jo Jacobs
Dan Stevens

Marketing
Lucy Cameron

Audio
Paul Stark
Jake Alderson
Georgina Cutler

Contracts
Anne Goddard
Ellie Bowker
Humayra Ahmed

Design
Nick Shah
Rachael Lancaster
Joanna Ridley
Helen Ewing

Production
Paul Hussey
Fiona McIntosh

Sales
Jen Wilson
Victoria Laws
Esther Waters
Frances Doyle
Ben Goddard
Jack Hallam
Anna Egelstaff
Inês Figueira
Barbara Ronan
Andrew Hally
Dominic Smith
Deborah Deyong
Lauren Buck
Maggy Park
Linda McGregor
Sinead White
Jemimah James
Rachael Jones
Jack Dennison
Nigel Andrews
Ian Williamson
Julia Benson
Declan Kyle
Robert Mackenzie
Megan Smith
Charlotte Clay
Rebecca Cobbold

Finance
Nick Gibson
Jasdip Nandra
Elizabeth Beaumont
Ibukun Ademefun
Afeera Ahmed
Sue Baker
Tom Costello

Publicity
Will O'Mullane

Operations
Sharon Willis

Rights
Susan Howe
Krystyna Kujawinska
Jessica Purdue
Ayesha Kinley
Louise Henderson